TIME BEFORE

TIME

VOL

03

WRITERS **RORY McCONVILLE** (#13-#14),

RORY McCONVILLE / **DECLAN SHALVEY** (#15-#17)

ARTISTS **RON SALAS** (#13-#14), **ERIC ZAWADZKI** (#15-#17)

COLORIST **CHRIS O'HALLORAN**

LETTERER **HASSAN OTSMANE-ELHAOU**

———

EDITOR **HEATHER ANTOS**

DESIGNER **SASHA E HEAD**

COVER **DECLAN SHALVEY**

BEFORE

TIME

TIME BEFORE TIME, VOL. 3. First printing. November 2022. Published by Image Comics,
Inc. Office of publication. PO BOX 14457, Portland, OR 97293. Copyright © 2022
Declan Shalvey, Rory McConville & Joe Palmer. All rights reserved. Contains material
originally published in single magazine form as TIME BEFORE TIME #13-17. "TIME BEFORE
TIME," its logos, and the likenesses of all characters herein are trademarks of
Declan Shalvey, Rory McConville & Joe Palmer, unless otherwise noted. "Image" and the
Image Comics logos are registered trademarks of Image Comics, Inc. No part of this
publication may be reproduced or transmitted, in any form or by any means (except
for short excerpts for journalistic or review purposes), without the express written
permission of Declan Shalvey, Rory McConville & Joe Palmer, or Image Comics, Inc. All
names, characters, events, and locales in this publication are entirely fictional.
Any resemblance to actual persons (living or dead), events, or places, without
satirical intent, is coincidental. Printed in Canada. For international rights,
contact: foreignlicensing@imagecomics.com. ISBN: 978-1-5343-2387-2

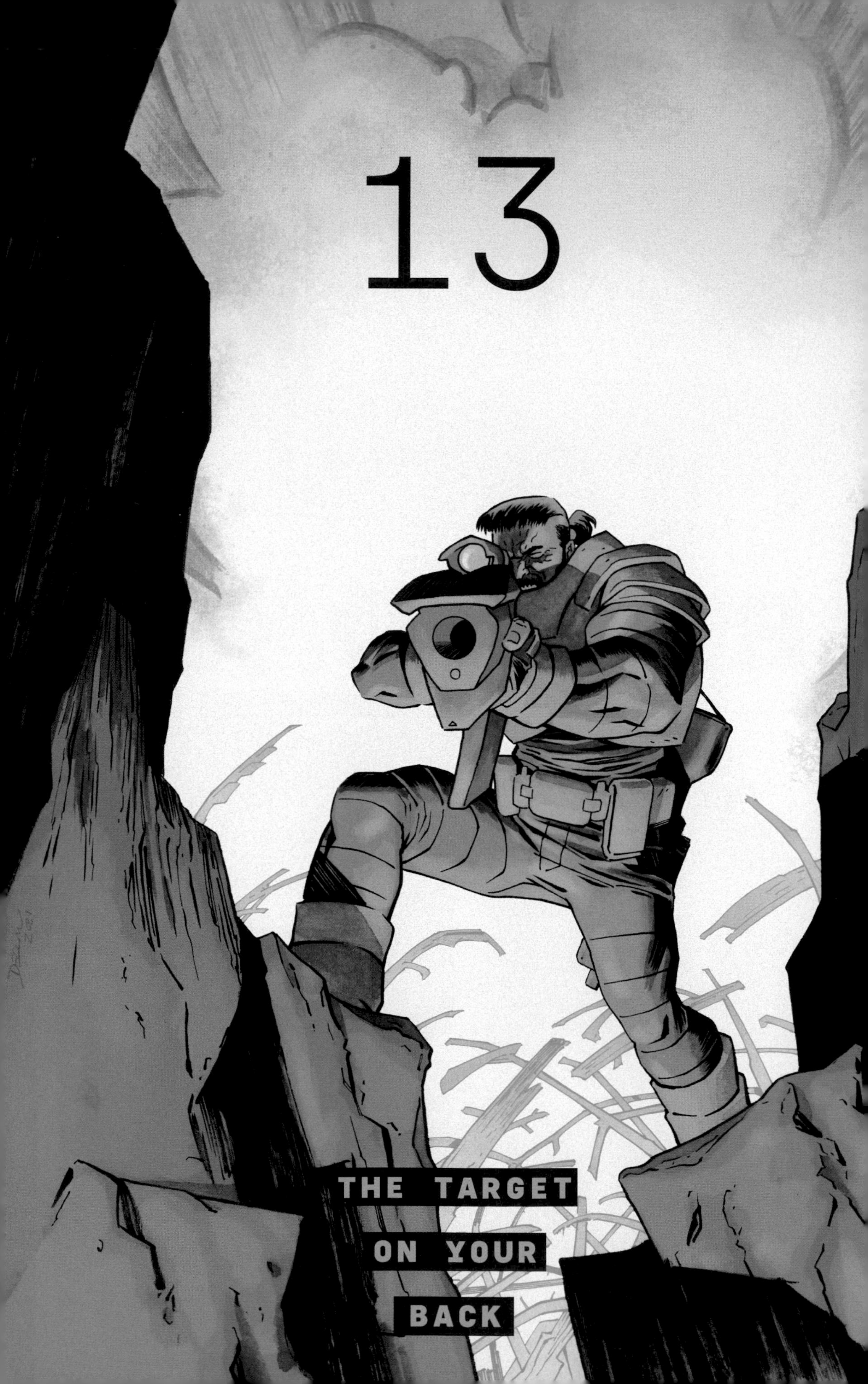
13
THE TARGET
ON YOUR
BACK

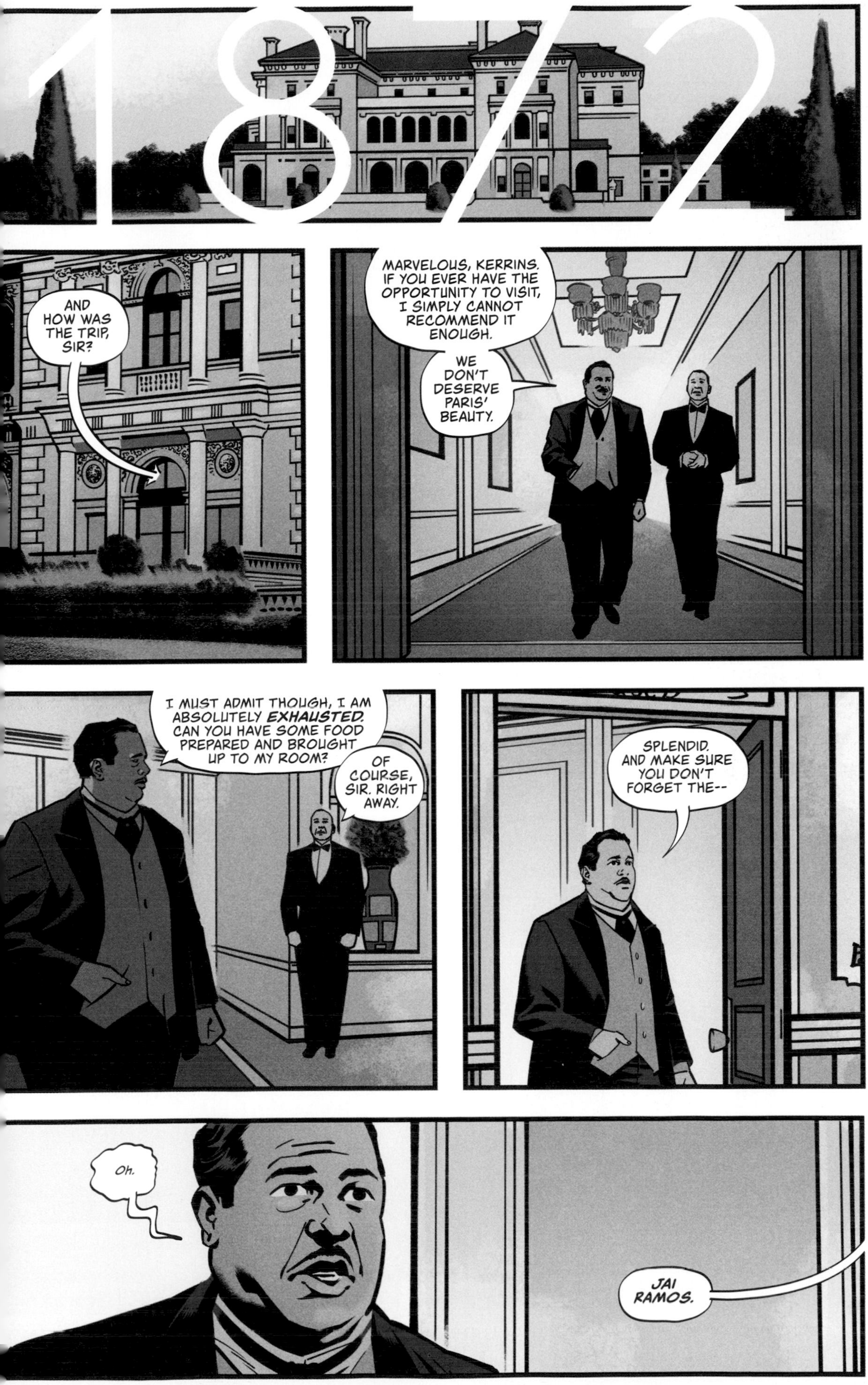
1872
AND HOW WAS THE TRIP, SIR?
MARVELOUS, KERRINS. IF YOU EVER HAVE THE OPPORTUNITY TO VISIT, I SIMPLY CANNOT RECOMMEND IT ENOUGH.
WE DON'T DESERVE PARIS' BEAUTY.
I MUST ADMIT THOUGH, I AM ABSOLUTELY **EXHAUSTED.** CAN YOU HAVE SOME FOOD PREPARED AND BROUGHT UP TO MY ROOM?
OF COURSE, SIR. RIGHT AWAY.
SPLENDID. AND MAKE SURE YOU DON'T FORGET THE--
Oh.
JAI RAMOS.

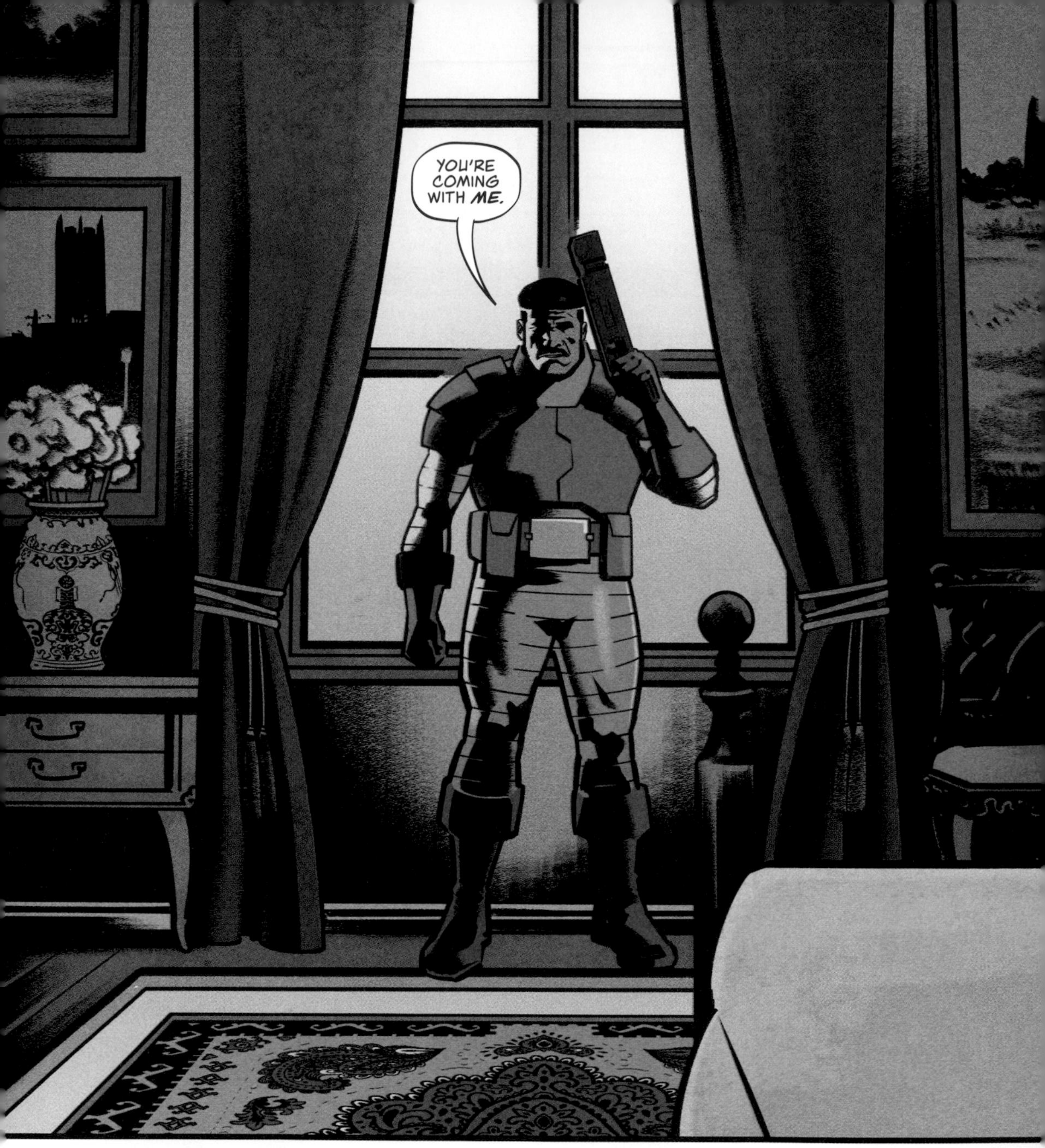
YOU'RE COMING WITH ME.
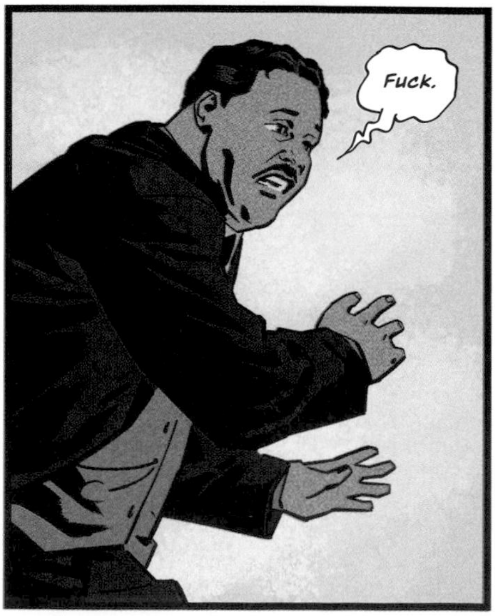
Fuck.
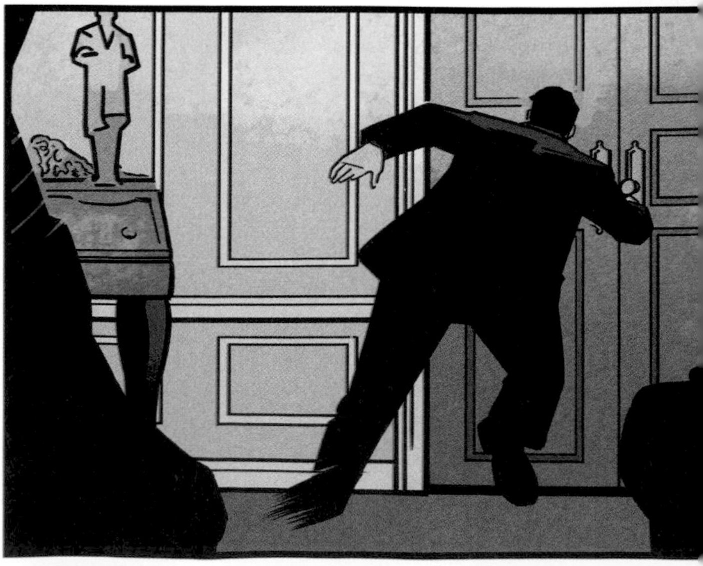

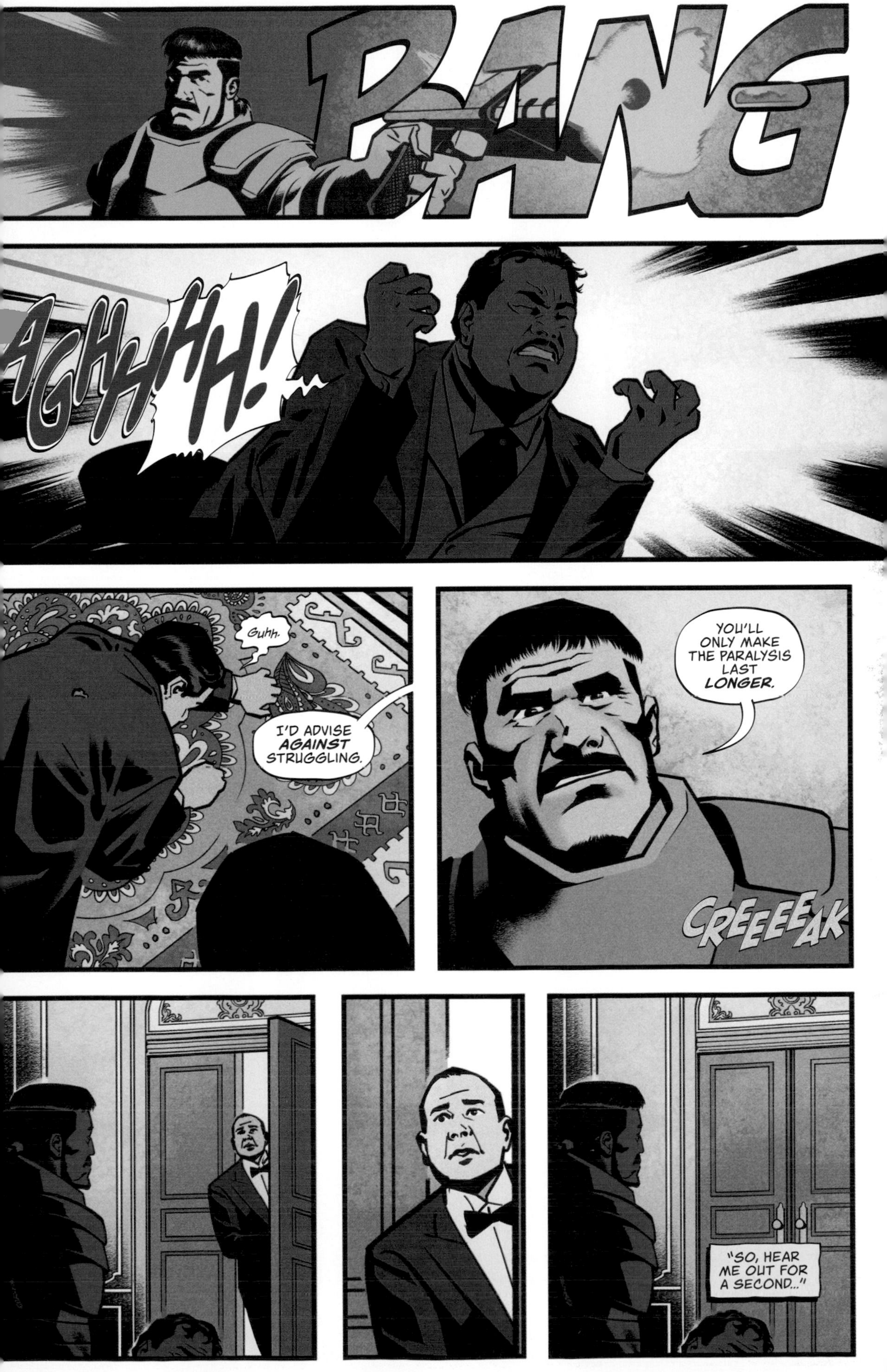
BANG
AGHHHH!
Guhh.
I'D ADVISE AGAINST STRUGGLING.
YOU'LL ONLY MAKE THE PARALYSIS LAST LONGER.
CREEEEAK
"SO, HEAR ME OUT FOR A SECOND..."

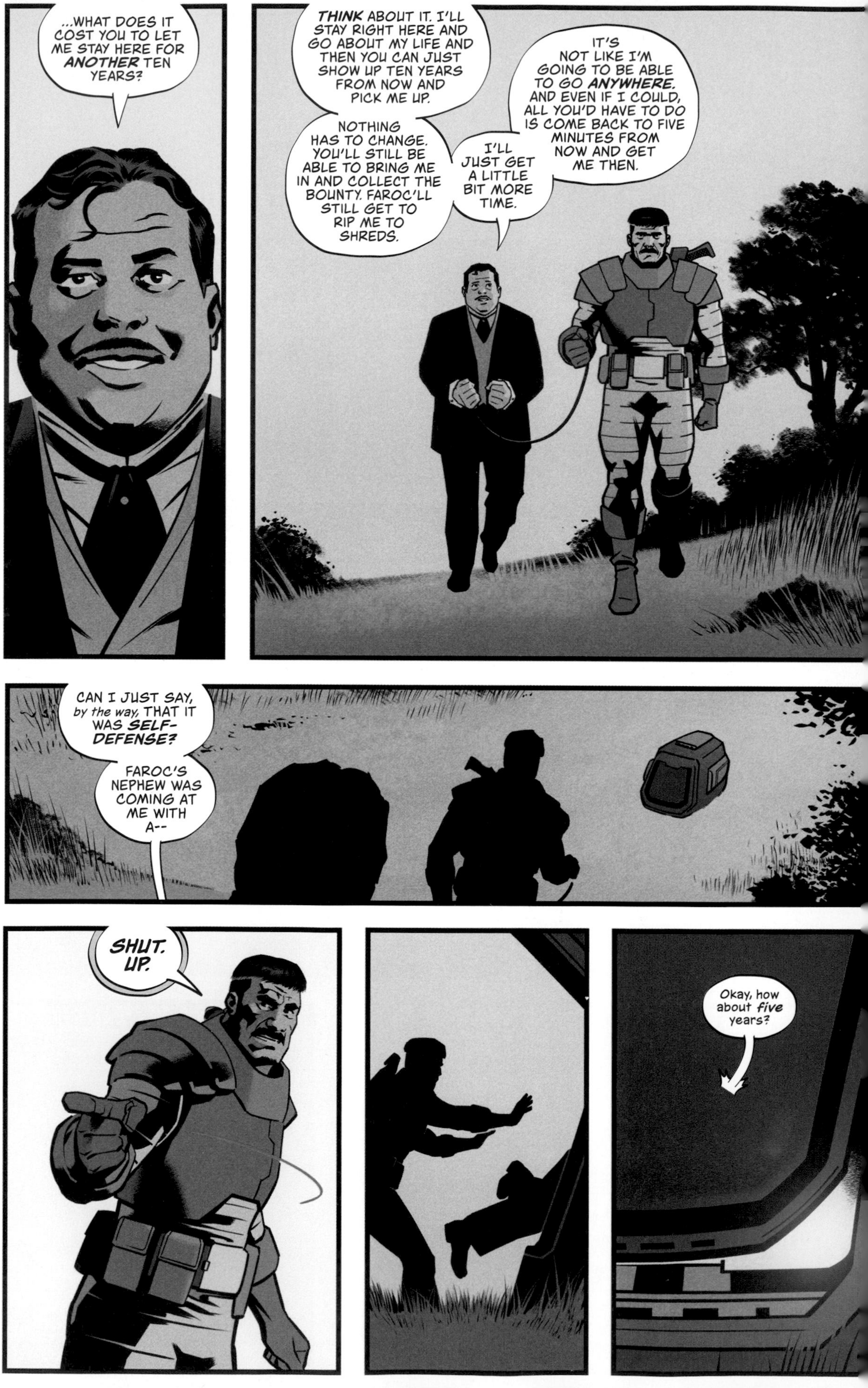
...WHAT DOES IT COST YOU TO LET ME STAY HERE FOR *ANOTHER* TEN YEARS?
THINK ABOUT IT. I'LL STAY RIGHT HERE AND GO ABOUT MY LIFE AND THEN YOU CAN JUST SHOW UP TEN YEARS FROM NOW AND PICK ME UP.
NOTHING HAS TO CHANGE. YOU'LL STILL BE ABLE TO BRING ME IN AND COLLECT THE BOUNTY. FAROC'LL STILL GET TO RIP ME TO SHREDS.
I'LL JUST GET A LITTLE BIT MORE TIME.
IT'S NOT LIKE I'M GOING TO BE ABLE TO GO *ANYWHERE.* AND EVEN IF I COULD, ALL YOU'D HAVE TO DO IS COME BACK TO FIVE MINUTES FROM NOW AND GET ME THEN.
CAN I JUST SAY, *by the way,* THAT IT WAS *SELF-DEFENSE?*
FAROC'S NEPHEW WAS COMING AT ME WITH A--
SHUT. UP.
Okay, how about *five* years?

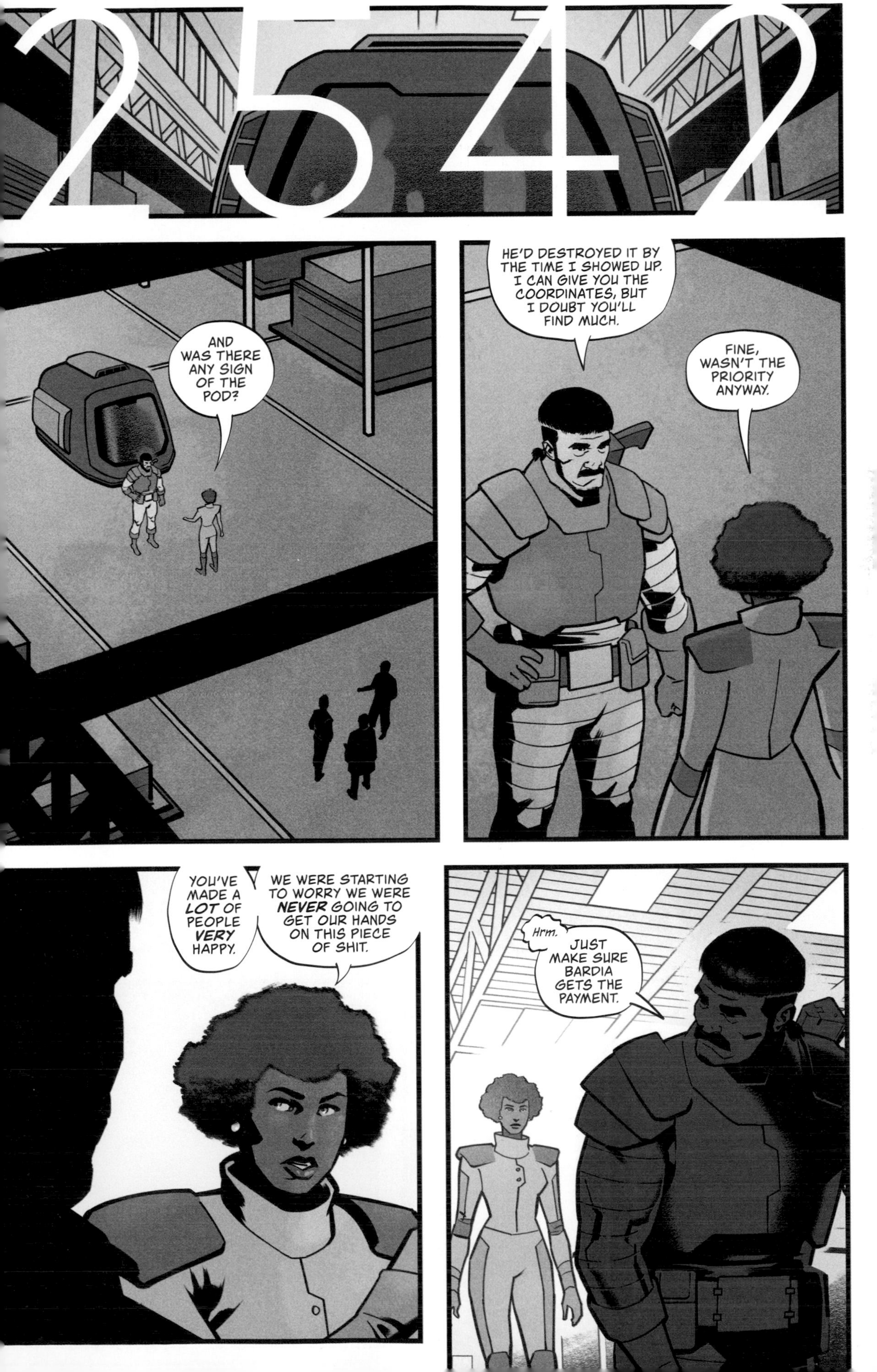
2542
AND WAS THERE ANY SIGN OF THE POD?
HE'D DESTROYED IT BY THE TIME I SHOWED UP. I CAN GIVE YOU THE COORDINATES, BUT I DOUBT YOU'LL FIND MUCH.
FINE, WASN'T THE PRIORITY ANYWAY.
YOU'VE MADE A LOT OF PEOPLE VERY HAPPY.
WE WERE STARTING TO WORRY WE WERE NEVER GOING TO GET OUR HANDS ON THIS PIECE OF SHIT.
Hrm.
JUST MAKE SURE BARDIA GETS THE PAYMENT.

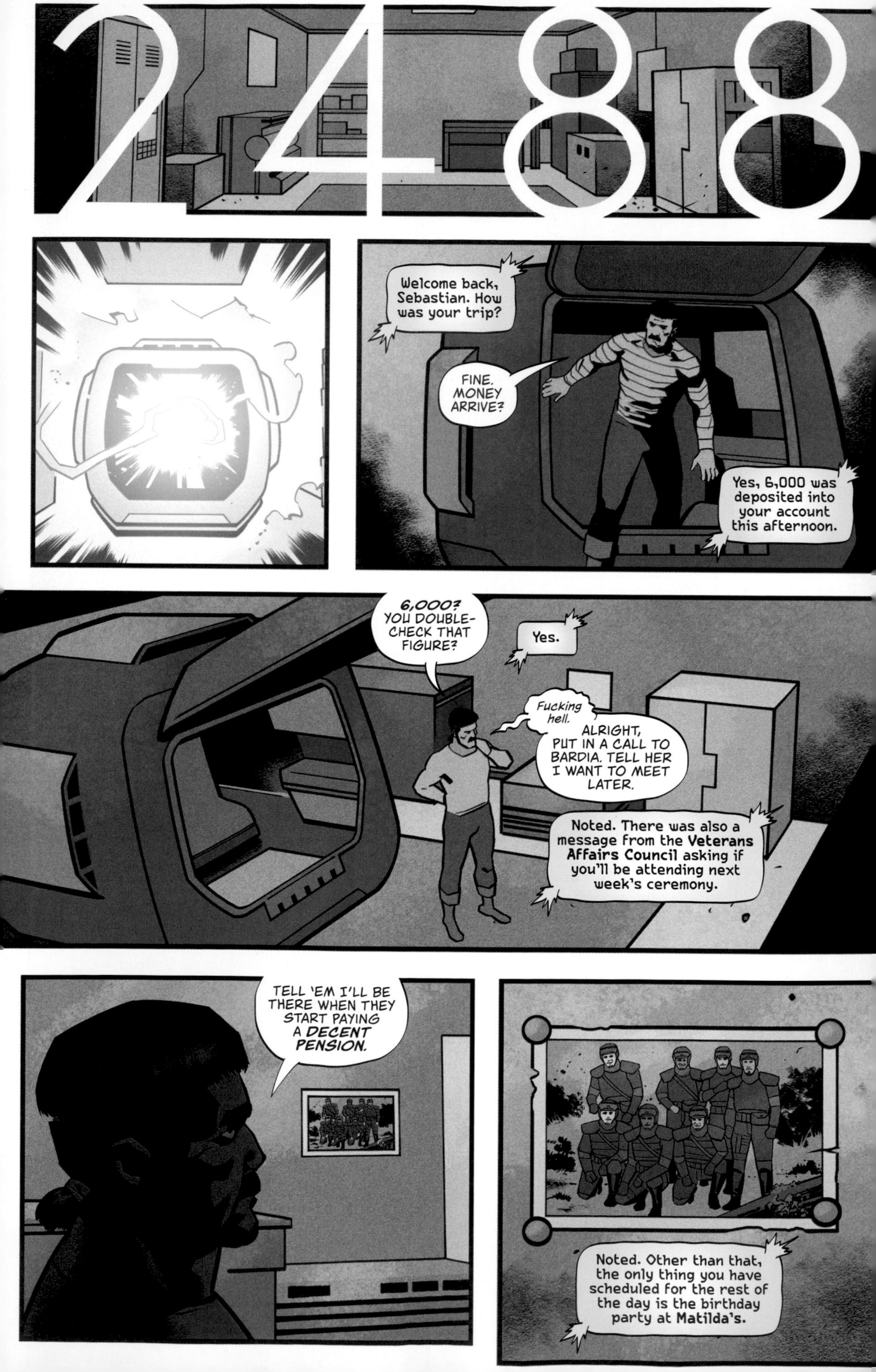
2488
Welcome back, Sebastian. How was your trip?
FINE. MONEY ARRIVE?
Yes, 6,000 was deposited into your account this afternoon.
6,000? YOU DOUBLE-CHECK THAT FIGURE?
Yes.
Fucking hell.
ALRIGHT, PUT IN A CALL TO BARDIA. TELL HER I WANT TO MEET LATER.
Noted. There was also a message from the Veterans Affairs Council asking if you'll be attending next week's ceremony.
TELL 'EM I'LL BE THERE WHEN THEY START PAYING A DECENT PENSION.
Noted. Other than that, the only thing you have scheduled for the rest of the day is the birthday party at Matilda's.

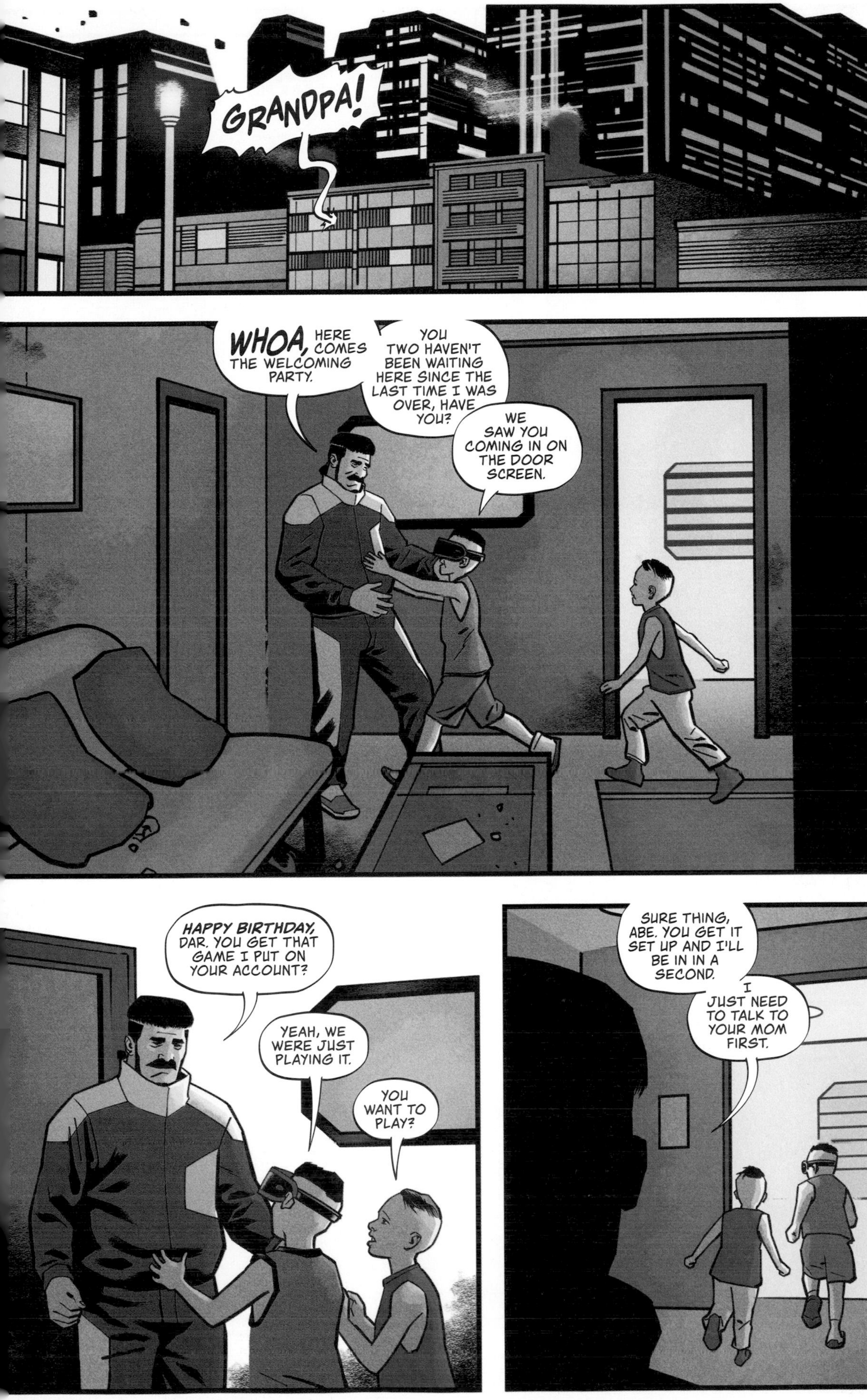
GRANDPA!
WHOA, HERE COMES THE WELCOMING PARTY.
YOU TWO HAVEN'T BEEN WAITING HERE SINCE THE LAST TIME I WAS OVER, HAVE YOU?
WE SAW YOU COMING IN ON THE DOOR SCREEN.
HAPPY BIRTHDAY, DAR. YOU GET THAT GAME I PUT ON YOUR ACCOUNT?
YEAH, WE WERE JUST PLAYING IT.
YOU WANT TO PLAY?
SURE THING, ABE. YOU GET IT SET UP AND I'LL BE IN IN A SECOND.
I JUST NEED TO TALK TO YOUR MOM FIRST.

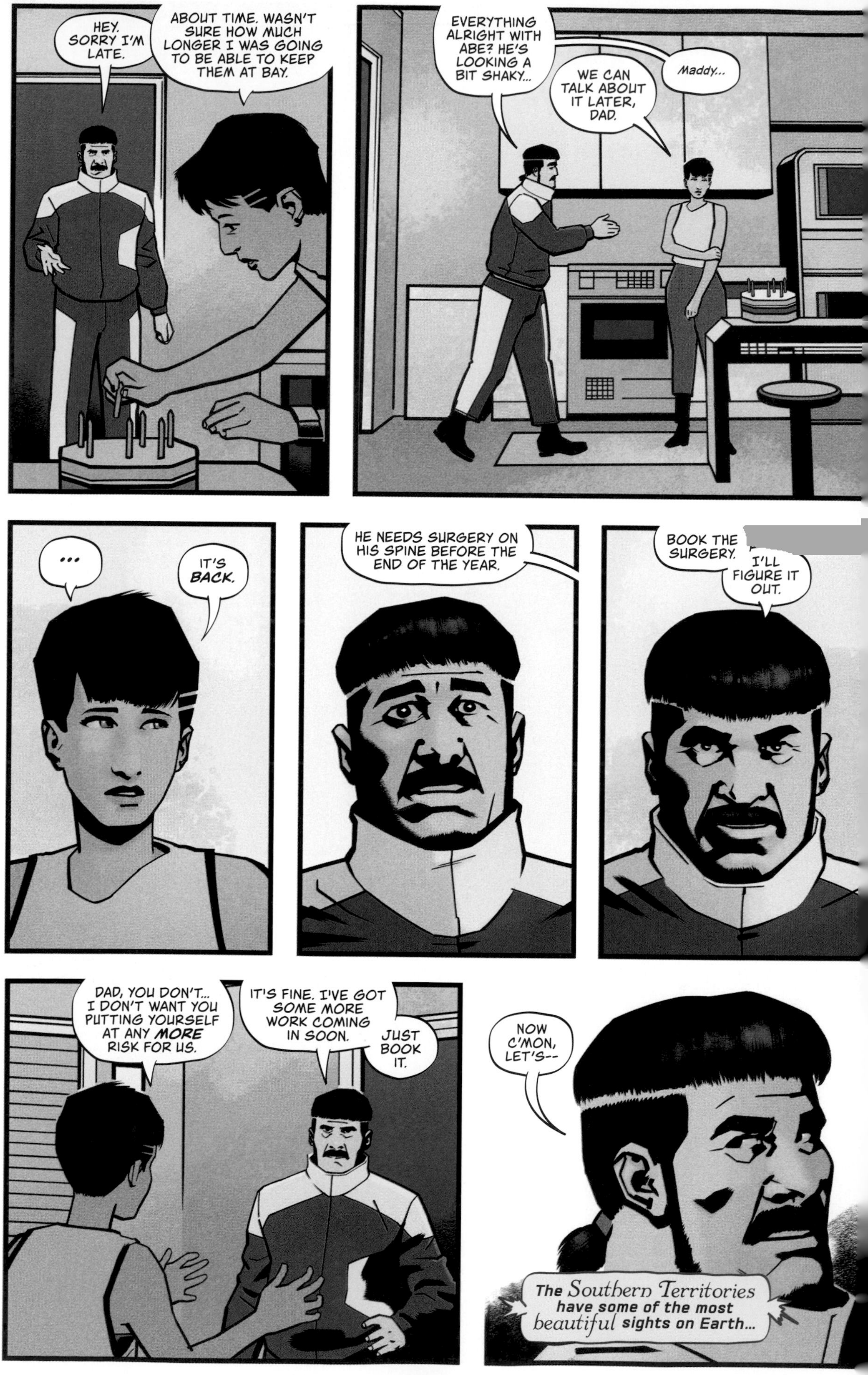
HEY. SORRY I'M LATE.
ABOUT TIME. WASN'T SURE HOW MUCH LONGER I WAS GOING TO BE ABLE TO KEEP THEM AT BAY.
EVERYTHING ALRIGHT WITH ABE? HE'S LOOKING A BIT SHAKY...
WE CAN TALK ABOUT IT LATER, DAD.
Maddy...
...
IT'S BACK.
HE NEEDS SURGERY ON HIS SPINE BEFORE THE END OF THE YEAR.
BOOK THE SURGERY.
I'LL FIGURE IT OUT.
DAD, YOU DON'T... I DON'T WANT YOU PUTTING YOURSELF AT ANY MORE RISK FOR US.
IT'S FINE. I'VE GOT SOME MORE WORK COMING IN SOON.
JUST BOOK IT.
NOW C'MON, LET'S--
The Southern Territories have some of the most beautiful sights on Earth...

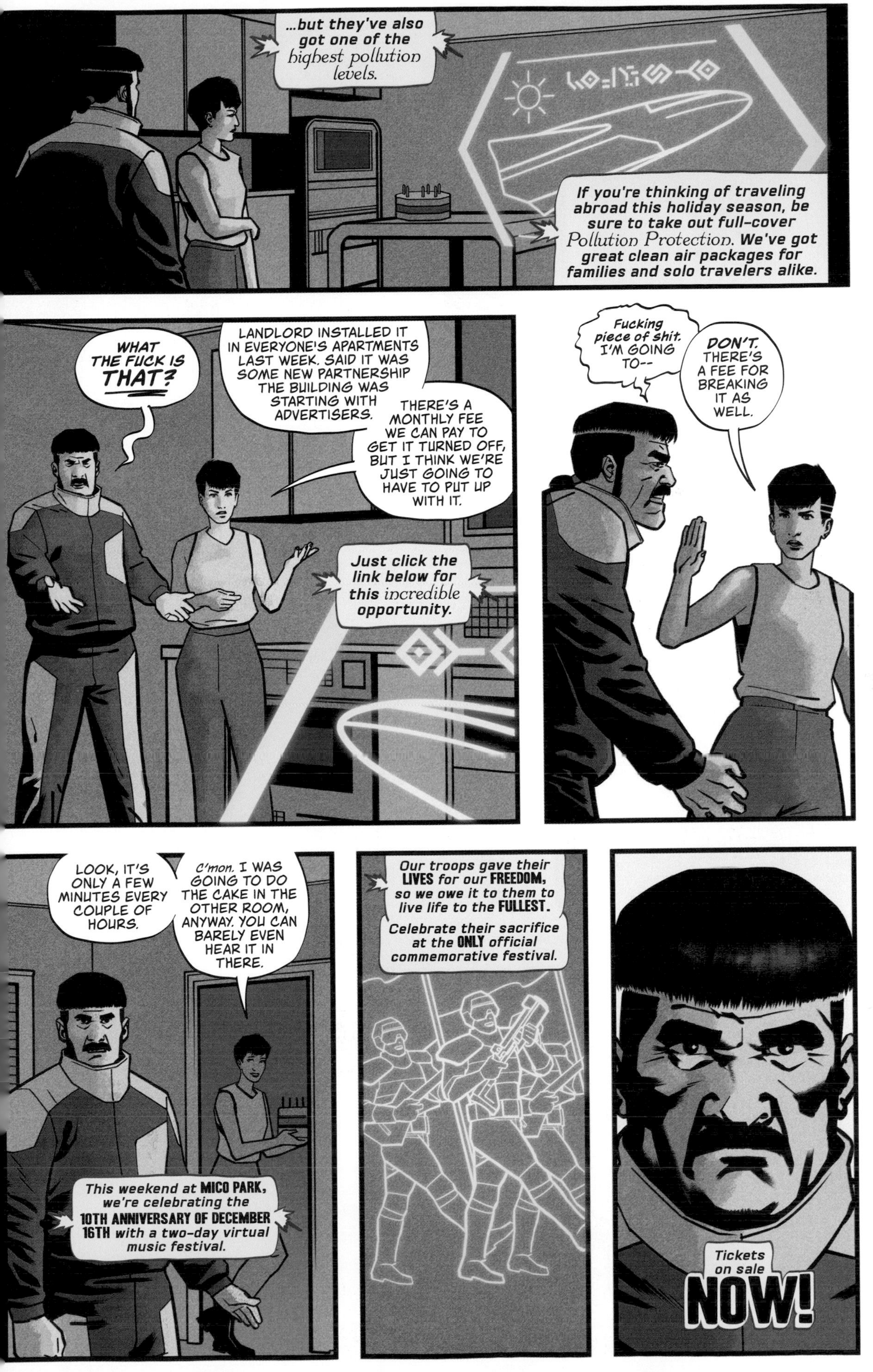

...but they've also got one of the highest pollution levels.
If you're thinking of traveling abroad this holiday season, be sure to take out full-cover Pollution Protection. We've got great clean air packages for families and solo travelers alike.
WHAT THE FUCK IS THAT?
LANDLORD INSTALLED IT IN EVERYONE'S APARTMENTS LAST WEEK. SAID IT WAS SOME NEW PARTNERSHIP THE BUILDING WAS STARTING WITH ADVERTISERS.
THERE'S A MONTHLY FEE WE CAN PAY TO GET IT TURNED OFF, BUT I THINK WE'RE JUST GOING TO HAVE TO PUT UP WITH IT.
Just click the link below for this incredible opportunity.
Fucking piece of shit. I'M GOING TO--
DON'T. THERE'S A FEE FOR BREAKING IT AS WELL.
LOOK, IT'S ONLY A FEW MINUTES EVERY COUPLE OF HOURS.
C'mon. I WAS GOING TO DO THE CAKE IN THE OTHER ROOM, ANYWAY. YOU CAN BARELY EVEN HEAR IT IN THERE.
This weekend at MICO PARK, we're celebrating the 10TH ANNIVERSARY OF DECEMBER 16TH with a two-day virtual music festival.
Our troops gave their LIVES for our FREEDOM, so we owe it to them to live life to the FULLEST.
Celebrate their sacrifice at the ONLY official commemorative festival.
Tickets on sale NOW!

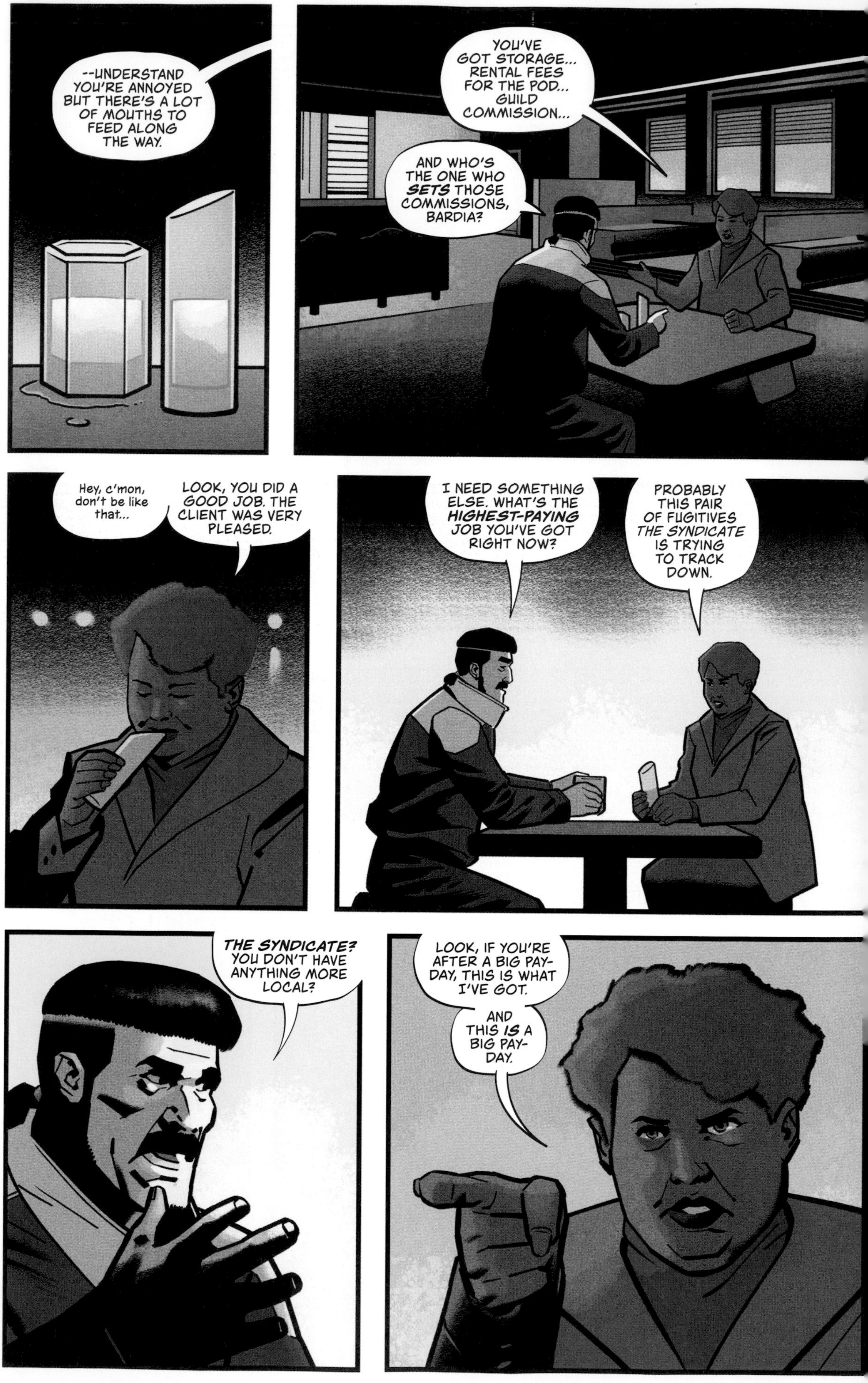
--UNDERSTAND YOU'RE ANNOYED BUT THERE'S A LOT OF MOUTHS TO FEED ALONG THE WAY.
YOU'VE GOT STORAGE... RENTAL FEES FOR THE POD... GUILD COMMISSION...
AND WHO'S THE ONE WHO SETS THOSE COMMISSIONS, BARDIA?
Hey, c'mon, don't be like that...
LOOK, YOU DID A GOOD JOB. THE CLIENT WAS VERY PLEASED.
I NEED SOMETHING ELSE. WHAT'S THE HIGHEST-PAYING JOB YOU'VE GOT RIGHT NOW?
PROBABLY THIS PAIR OF FUGITIVES THE SYNDICATE IS TRYING TO TRACK DOWN.
THE SYNDICATE? YOU DON'T HAVE ANYTHING MORE LOCAL?
LOOK, IF YOU'RE AFTER A BIG PAY-DAY, THIS IS WHAT I'VE GOT.
AND THIS IS A BIG PAY-DAY.

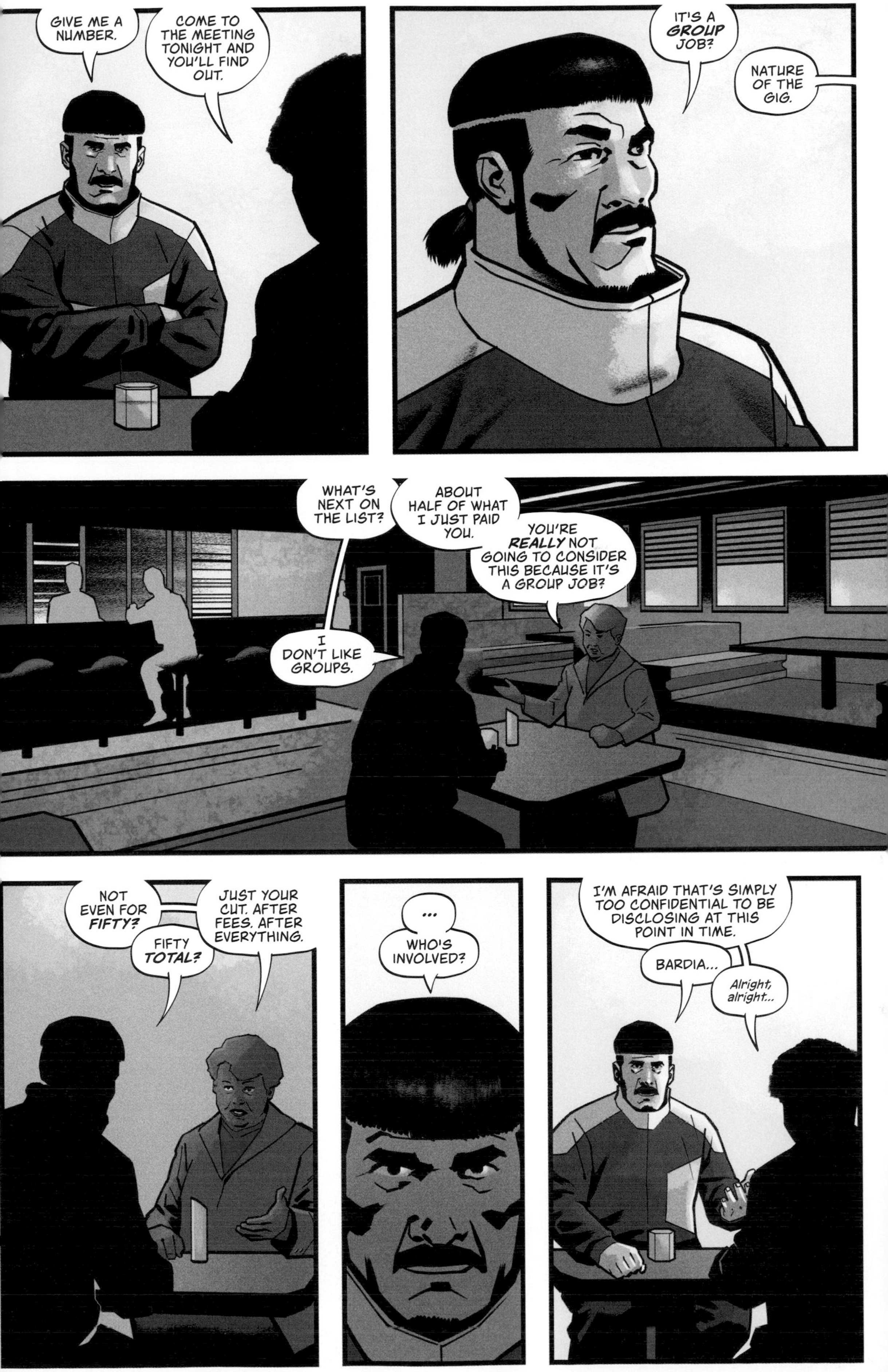
GIVE ME A NUMBER.
COME TO THE MEETING TONIGHT AND YOU'LL FIND OUT.
IT'S A *GROUP* JOB?
NATURE OF THE GIG.
WHAT'S NEXT ON THE LIST?
ABOUT HALF OF WHAT I JUST PAID YOU.
YOU'RE *REALLY* NOT GOING TO CONSIDER THIS BECAUSE IT'S A GROUP JOB?
I DON'T LIKE GROUPS.
NOT EVEN FOR *FIFTY?*
FIFTY *TOTAL?*
JUST YOUR CUT. AFTER FEES. AFTER EVERYTHING.
...
WHO'S INVOLVED?
I'M AFRAID THAT'S SIMPLY TOO CONFIDENTIAL TO BE DISCLOSING AT THIS POINT IN TIME.
BARDIA...
Alright, alright...

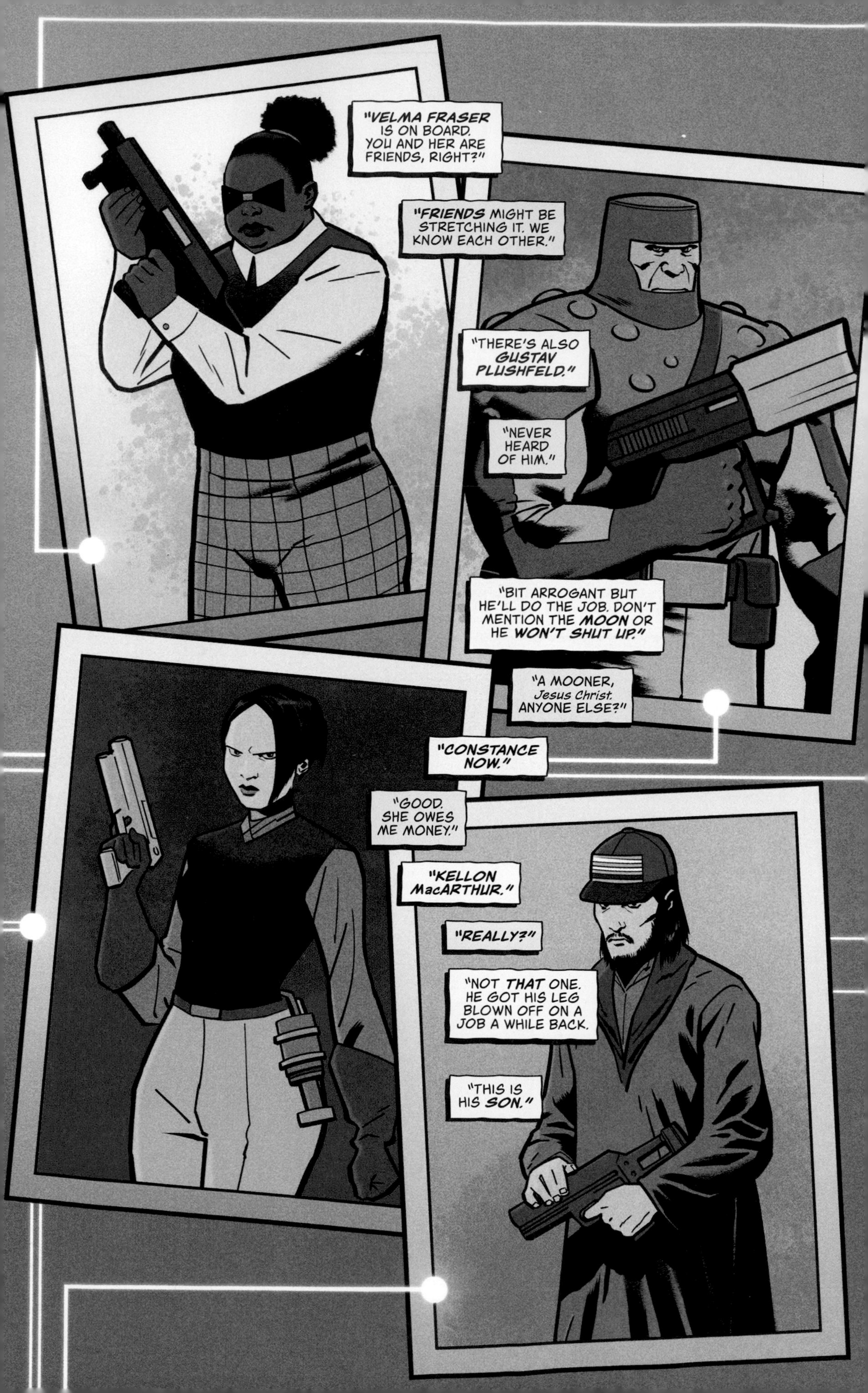
"VELMA FRASER IS ON BOARD. YOU AND HER ARE FRIENDS, RIGHT?"
"FRIENDS MIGHT BE STRETCHING IT. WE KNOW EACH OTHER."
"THERE'S ALSO GUSTAV PLUSHFELD."
"NEVER HEARD OF HIM."
"BIT ARROGANT BUT HE'LL DO THE JOB. DON'T MENTION THE MOON OR HE WON'T SHUT UP."
"A MOONER, Jesus Christ. ANYONE ELSE?"
"CONSTANCE NOW."
"GOOD. SHE OWES ME MONEY."
"KELLON MacARTHUR."
"REALLY?"
"NOT THAT ONE. HE GOT HIS LEG BLOWN OFF ON A JOB A WHILE BACK.
"THIS IS HIS SON."

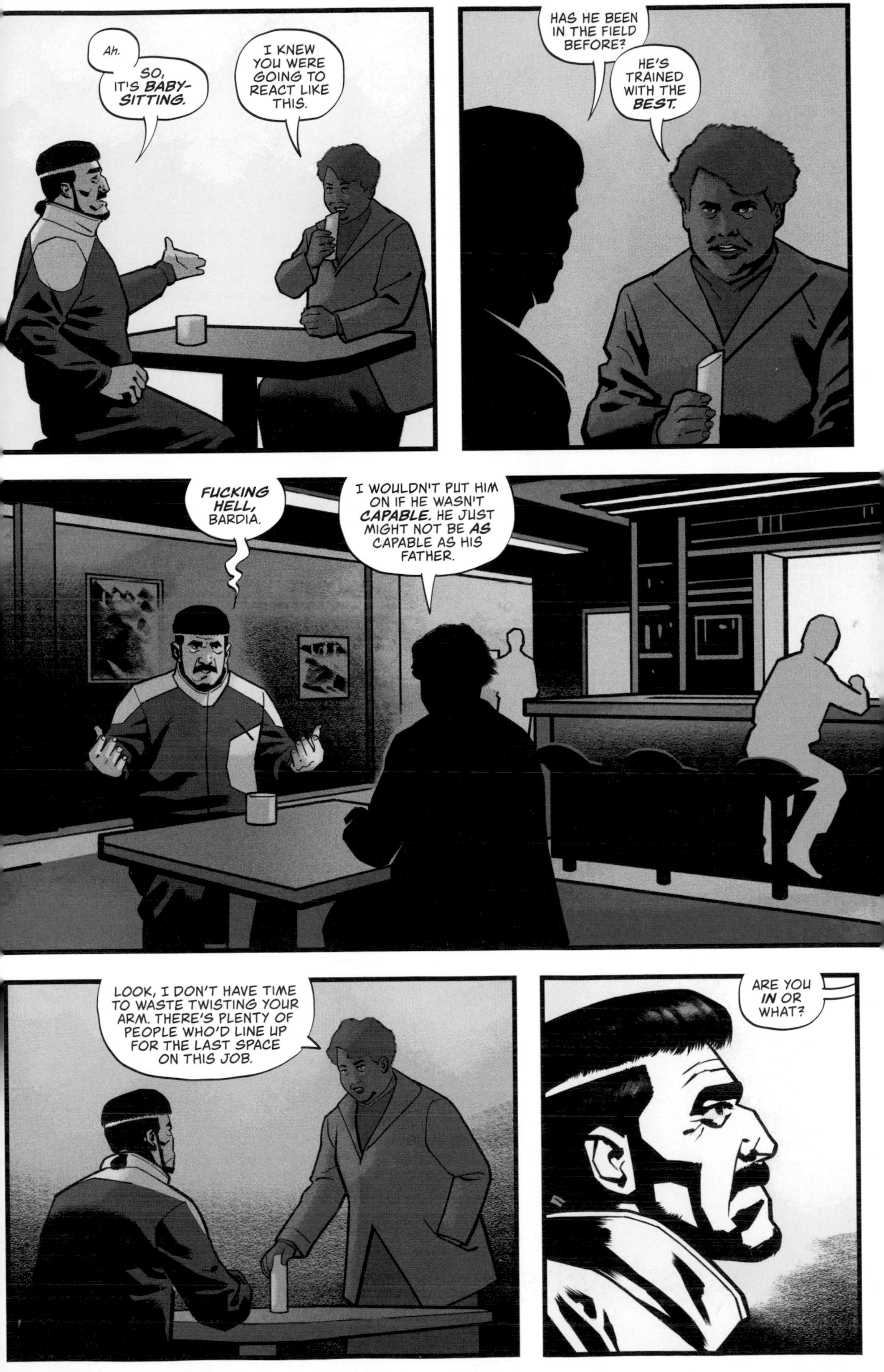
Ah.
SO, IT'S BABY-SITTING.
I KNEW YOU WERE GOING TO REACT LIKE THIS.
HAS HE BEEN IN THE FIELD BEFORE?
HE'S TRAINED WITH THE BEST.
FUCKING HELL, BARDIA.
I WOULDN'T PUT HIM ON IF HE WASN'T CAPABLE. HE JUST MIGHT NOT BE AS CAPABLE AS HIS FATHER.
LOOK, I DON'T HAVE TIME TO WASTE TWISTING YOUR ARM. THERE'S PLENTY OF PEOPLE WHO'D LINE UP FOR THE LAST SPACE ON THIS JOB.
ARE YOU IN OR WHAT?

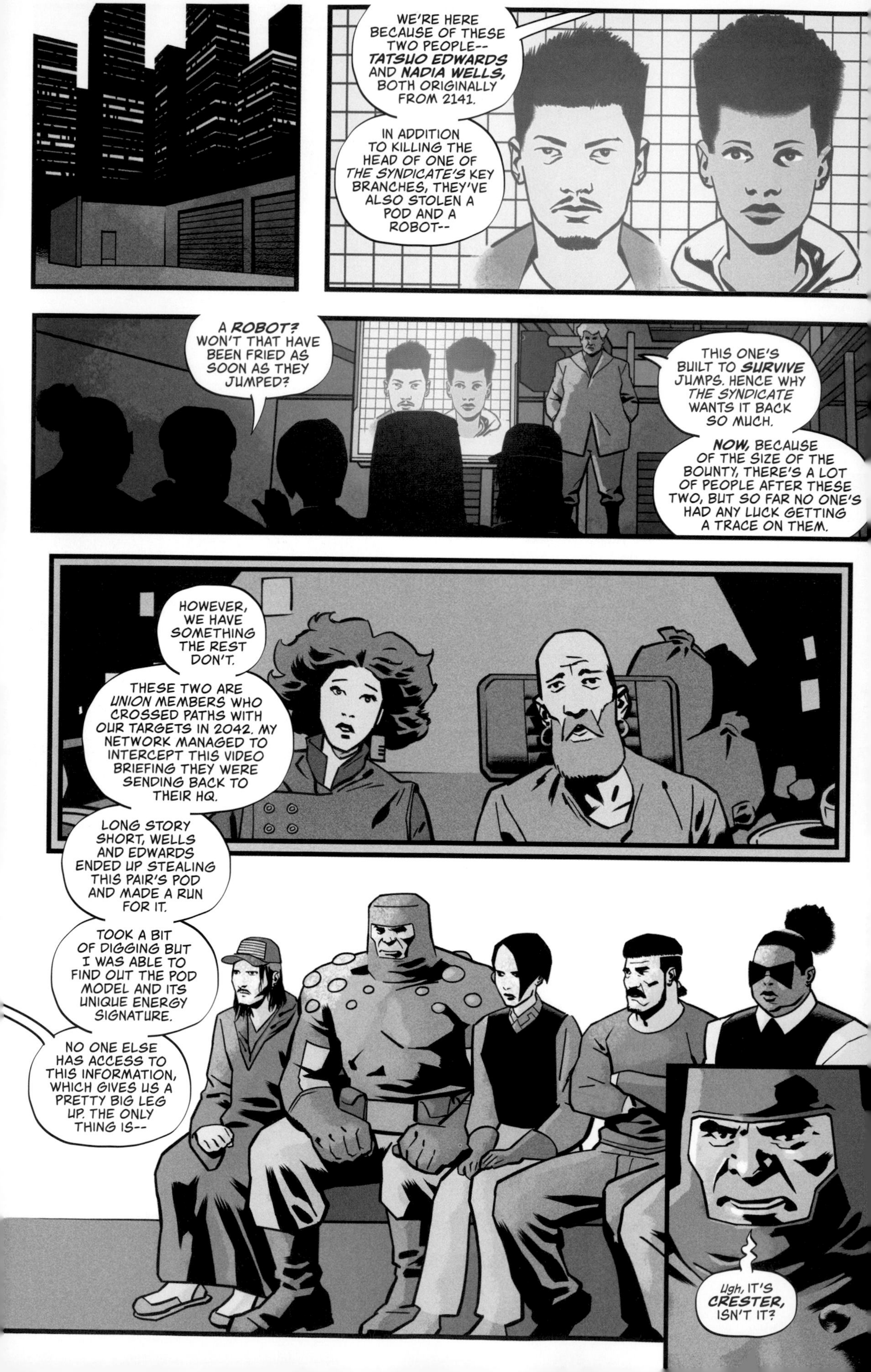
WE'RE HERE BECAUSE OF THESE TWO PEOPLE-- **TATSUO EDWARDS** AND **NADIA WELLS,** BOTH ORIGINALLY FROM 2141.
IN ADDITION TO KILLING THE HEAD OF ONE OF *THE SYNDICATE'S* KEY BRANCHES, THEY'VE ALSO STOLEN A POD AND A ROBOT--
A *ROBOT?* WON'T THAT HAVE BEEN FRIED AS SOON AS THEY JUMPED?
THIS ONE'S BUILT TO **SURVIVE** JUMPS. HENCE WHY *THE SYNDICATE* WANTS IT BACK SO MUCH.
NOW, BECAUSE OF THE SIZE OF THE BOUNTY, THERE'S A LOT OF PEOPLE AFTER THESE TWO, BUT SO FAR NO ONE'S HAD ANY LUCK GETTING A TRACE ON THEM.
HOWEVER, WE HAVE SOMETHING THE REST DON'T.
THESE TWO ARE *UNION* MEMBERS WHO CROSSED PATHS WITH OUR TARGETS IN 2042. MY NETWORK MANAGED TO INTERCEPT THIS VIDEO BRIEFING THEY WERE SENDING BACK TO THEIR HQ.
LONG STORY SHORT, WELLS AND EDWARDS ENDED UP STEALING THIS PAIR'S POD AND MADE A RUN FOR IT.
TOOK A BIT OF DIGGING BUT I WAS ABLE TO FIND OUT THE POD MODEL AND ITS UNIQUE ENERGY SIGNATURE.
NO ONE ELSE HAS ACCESS TO THIS INFORMATION, WHICH GIVES US A PRETTY BIG LEG UP. THE ONLY THING IS--
Ugh, IT'S **CRESTER,** ISN'T IT?

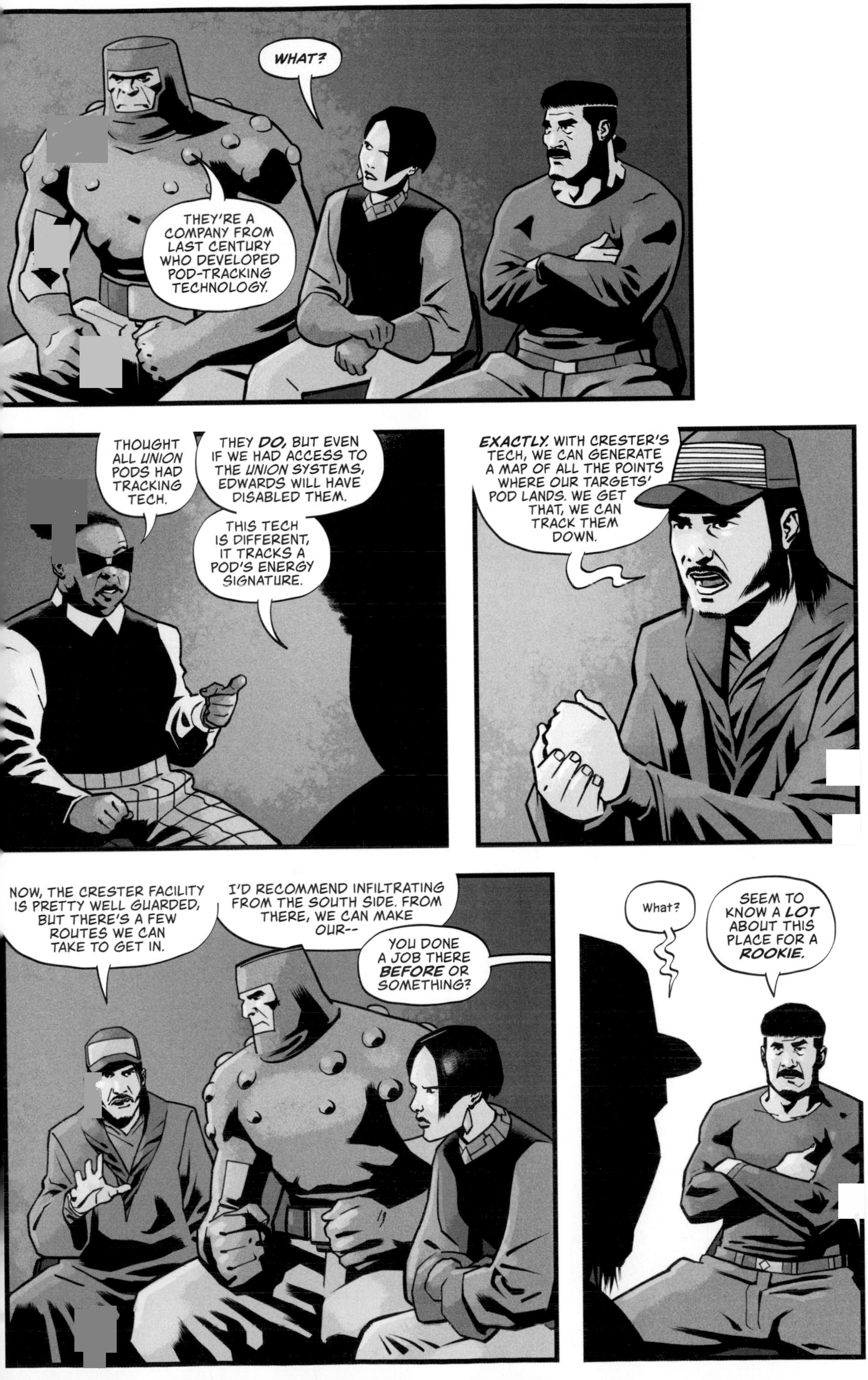
WHAT?
THEY'RE A COMPANY FROM LAST CENTURY WHO DEVELOPED POD-TRACKING TECHNOLOGY.
THOUGHT ALL *UNION* PODS HAD TRACKING TECH.
THEY *DO,* BUT EVEN IF WE HAD ACCESS TO THE *UNION* SYSTEMS, EDWARDS WILL HAVE DISABLED THEM.
THIS TECH IS DIFFERENT, IT TRACKS A POD'S ENERGY SIGNATURE.
EXACTLY. WITH CRESTER'S TECH, WE CAN GENERATE A MAP OF ALL THE POINTS WHERE OUR TARGETS' POD LANDS. WE GET THAT, WE CAN TRACK THEM DOWN.
NOW, THE CRESTER FACILITY IS PRETTY WELL GUARDED, BUT THERE'S A FEW ROUTES WE CAN TAKE TO GET IN.
I'D RECOMMEND INFILTRATING FROM THE SOUTH SIDE. FROM THERE, WE CAN MAKE OUR--
YOU DONE A JOB THERE *BEFORE* OR SOMETHING?
What?
SEEM TO KNOW A *LOT* ABOUT THIS PLACE FOR A *ROOKIE.*

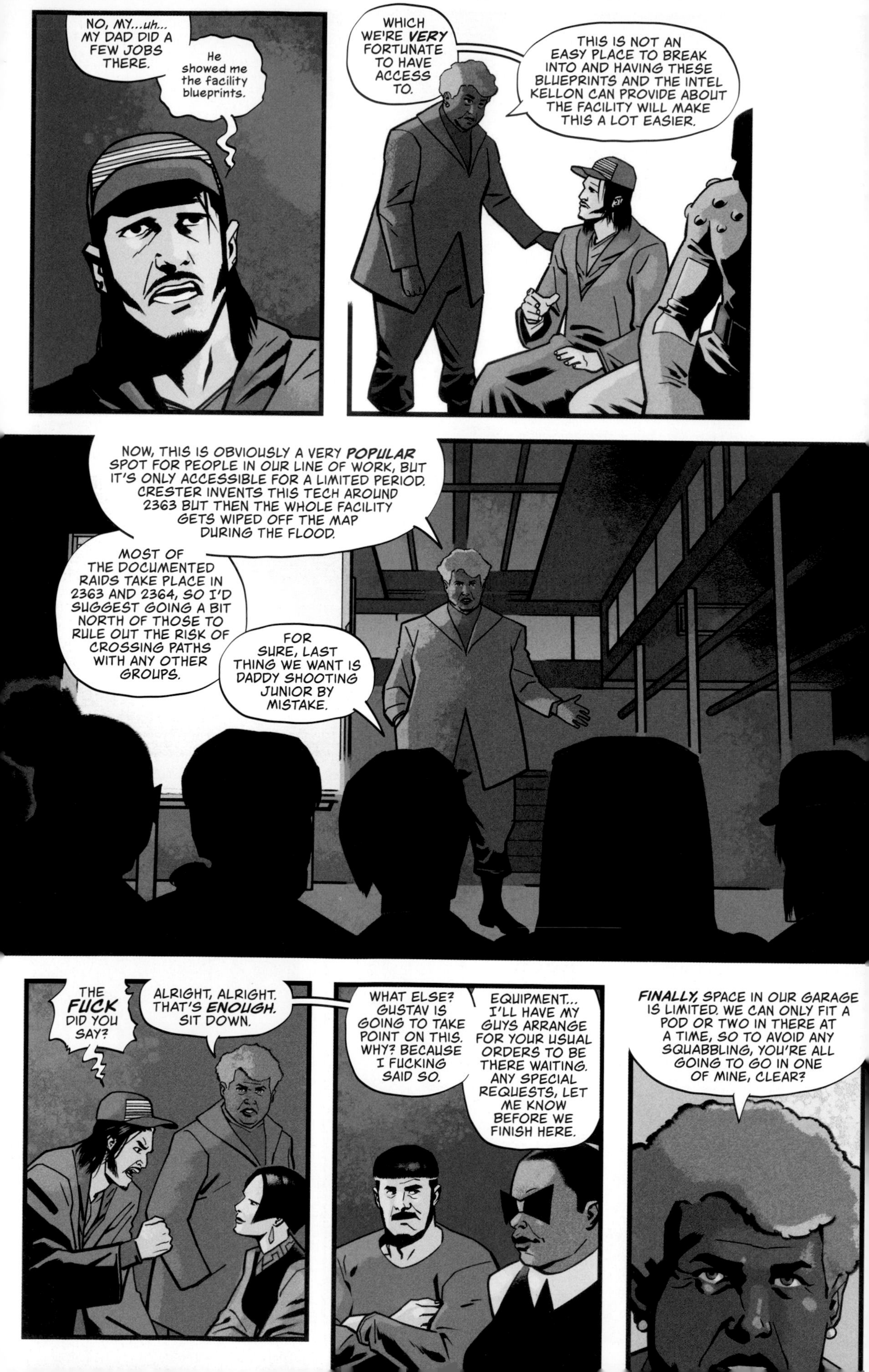
NO, MY...uh... MY DAD DID A FEW JOBS THERE.
He showed me the facility blueprints.
WHICH WE'RE VERY FORTUNATE TO HAVE ACCESS TO.
THIS IS NOT AN EASY PLACE TO BREAK INTO AND HAVING THESE BLUEPRINTS AND THE INTEL KELLON CAN PROVIDE ABOUT THE FACILITY WILL MAKE THIS A LOT EASIER.
NOW, THIS IS OBVIOUSLY A VERY POPULAR SPOT FOR PEOPLE IN OUR LINE OF WORK, BUT IT'S ONLY ACCESSIBLE FOR A LIMITED PERIOD. CRESTER INVENTS THIS TECH AROUND 2363 BUT THEN THE WHOLE FACILITY GETS WIPED OFF THE MAP DURING THE FLOOD.
MOST OF THE DOCUMENTED RAIDS TAKE PLACE IN 2363 AND 2364, SO I'D SUGGEST GOING A BIT NORTH OF THOSE TO RULE OUT THE RISK OF CROSSING PATHS WITH ANY OTHER GROUPS.
FOR SURE, LAST THING WE WANT IS DADDY SHOOTING JUNIOR BY MISTAKE.
THE FUCK DID YOU SAY?
ALRIGHT, ALRIGHT. THAT'S ENOUGH. SIT DOWN.
WHAT ELSE? GUSTAV IS GOING TO TAKE POINT ON THIS. WHY? BECAUSE I FUCKING SAID SO.
EQUIPMENT... I'LL HAVE MY GUYS ARRANGE FOR YOUR USUAL ORDERS TO BE THERE WAITING. ANY SPECIAL REQUESTS, LET ME KNOW BEFORE WE FINISH HERE.
FINALLY, SPACE IN OUR GARAGE IS LIMITED. WE CAN ONLY FIT A POD OR TWO IN THERE AT A TIME, SO TO AVOID ANY SQUABBLING, YOU'RE ALL GOING TO GO IN ONE OF MINE, CLEAR?

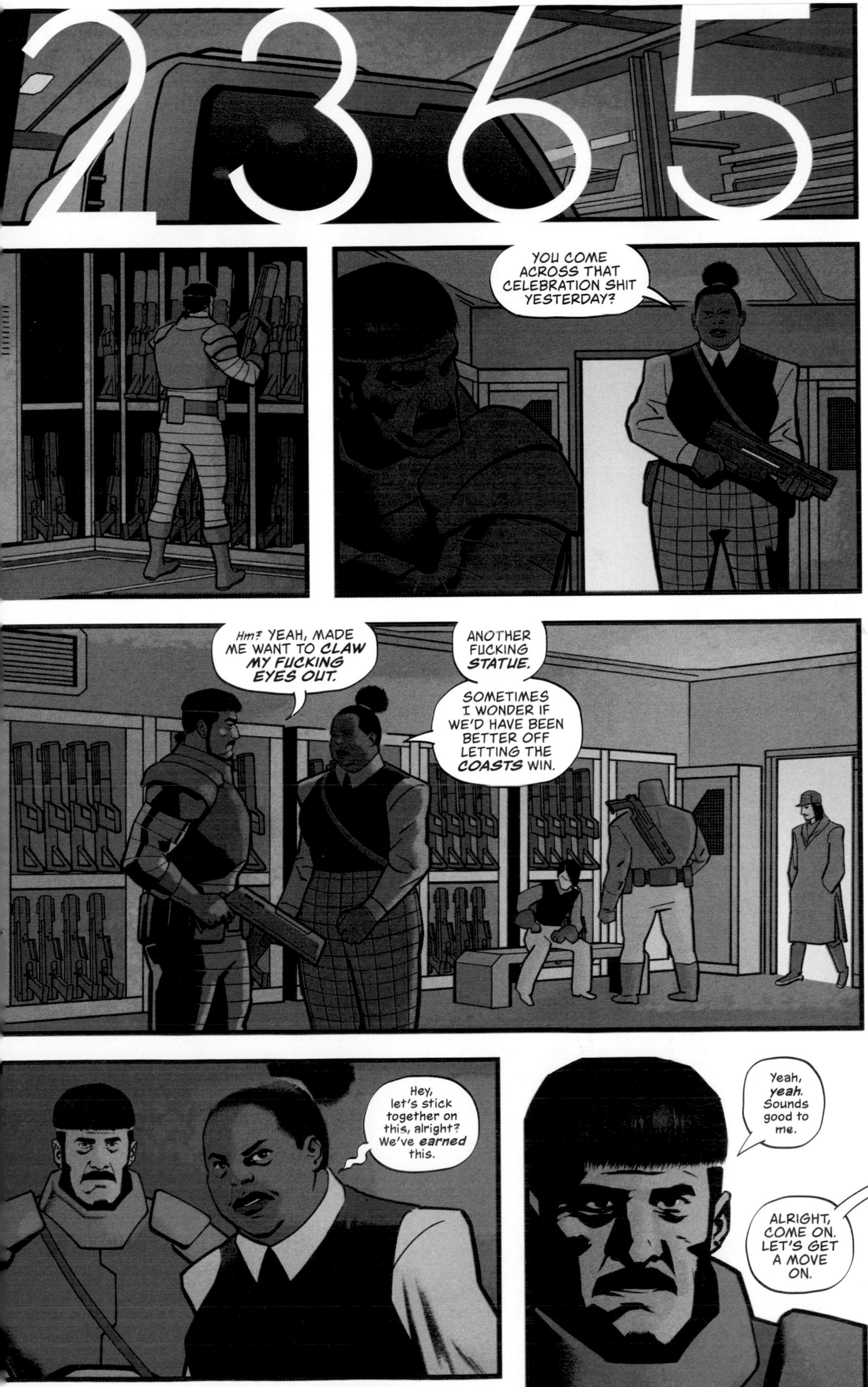
2365
YOU COME ACROSS THAT CELEBRATION SHIT YESTERDAY?
Hm? YEAH, MADE ME WANT TO CLAW MY FUCKING EYES OUT.
ANOTHER FUCKING STATUE.
SOMETIMES I WONDER IF WE'D HAVE BEEN BETTER OFF LETTING THE COASTS WIN.
Hey, let's stick together on this, alright? We've earned this.
Yeah, yeah. Sounds good to me.
ALRIGHT, COME ON. LET'S GET A MOVE ON.

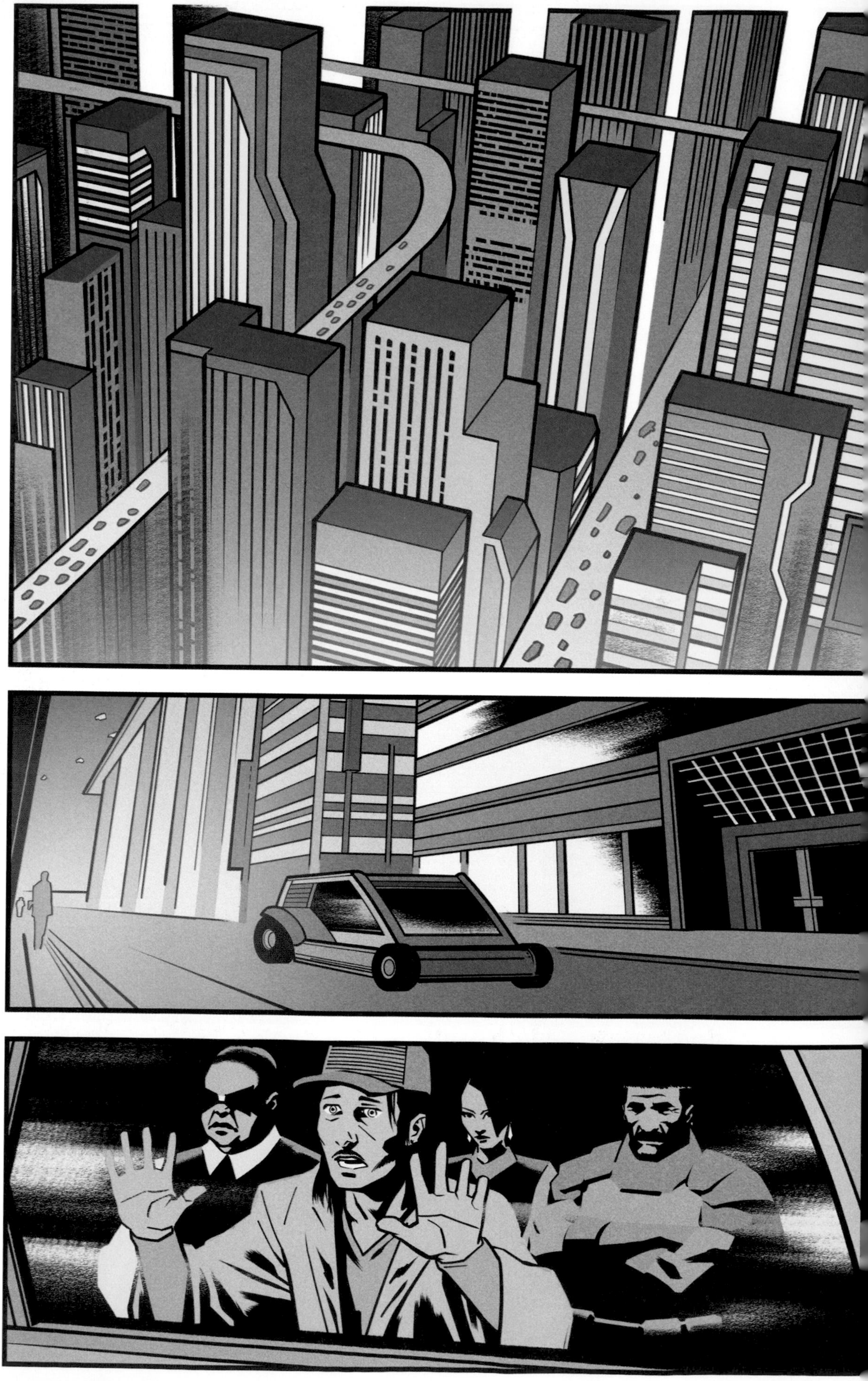

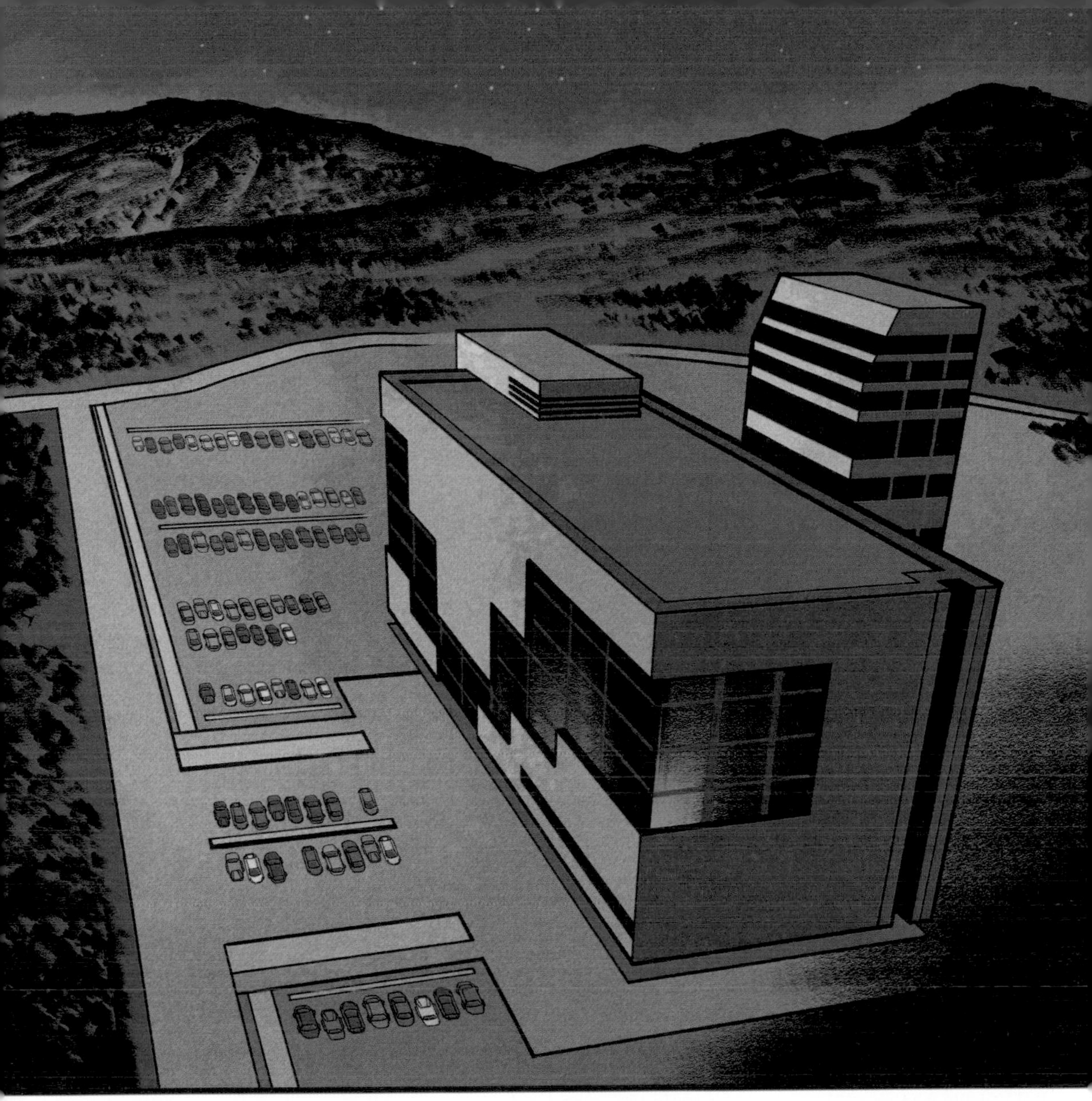

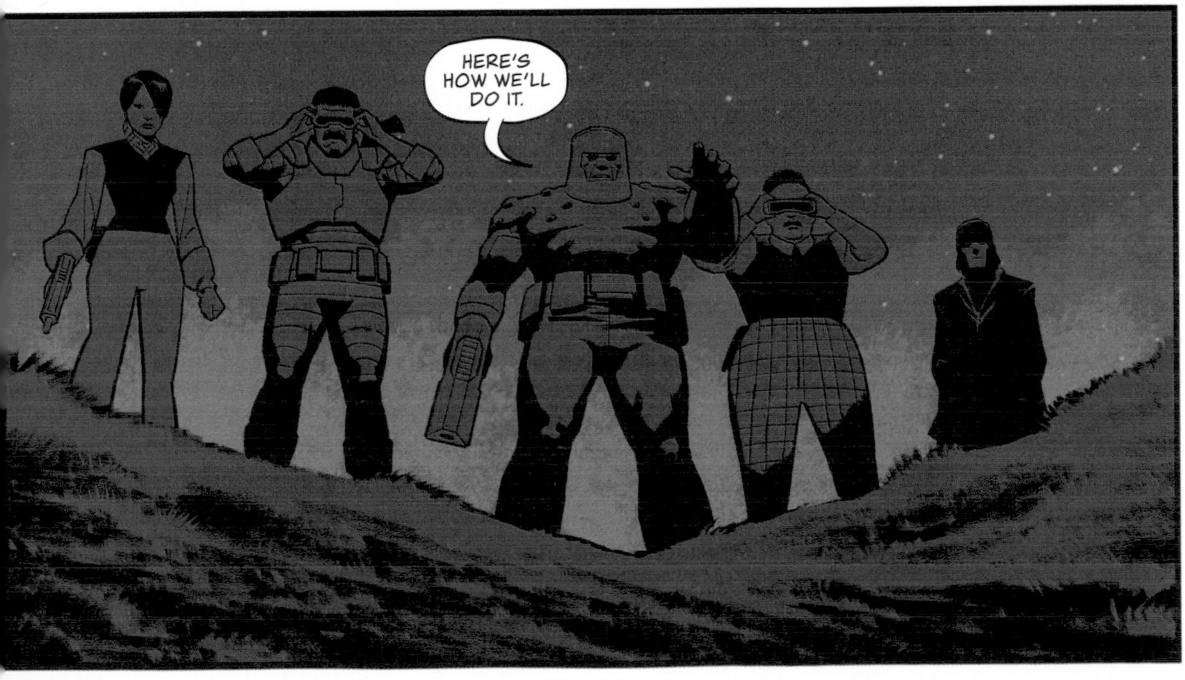
HERE'S HOW WE'LL DO IT.

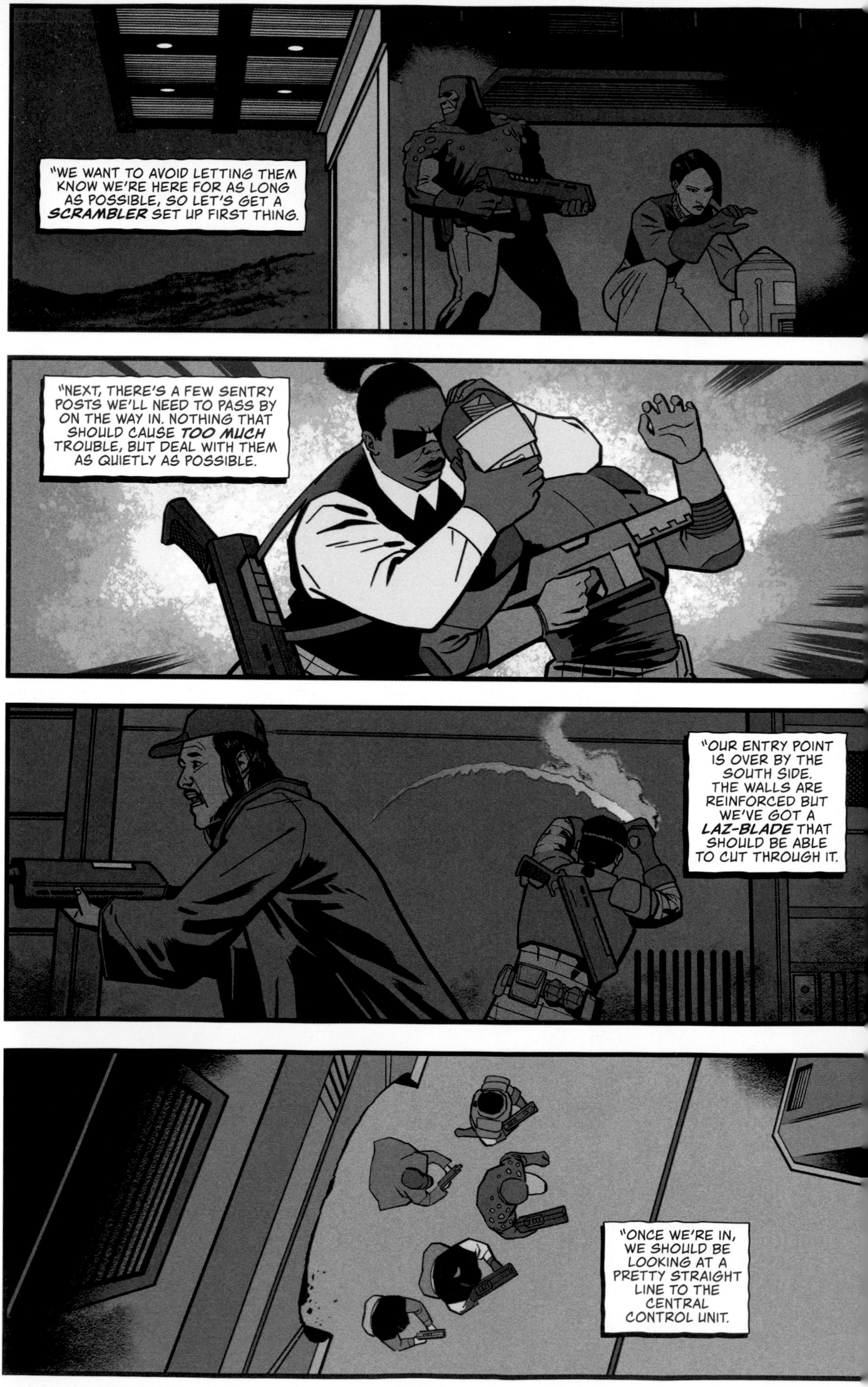
"WE WANT TO AVOID LETTING THEM KNOW WE'RE HERE FOR AS LONG AS POSSIBLE, SO LET'S GET A SCRAMBLER SET UP FIRST THING.
"NEXT, THERE'S A FEW SENTRY POSTS WE'LL NEED TO PASS BY ON THE WAY IN. NOTHING THAT SHOULD CAUSE TOO MUCH TROUBLE, BUT DEAL WITH THEM AS QUIETLY AS POSSIBLE.
"OUR ENTRY POINT IS OVER BY THE SOUTH SIDE. THE WALLS ARE REINFORCED BUT WE'VE GOT A LAZ-BLADE THAT SHOULD BE ABLE TO CUT THROUGH IT.
"ONCE WE'RE IN, WE SHOULD BE LOOKING AT A PRETTY STRAIGHT LINE TO THE CENTRAL CONTROL UNIT.

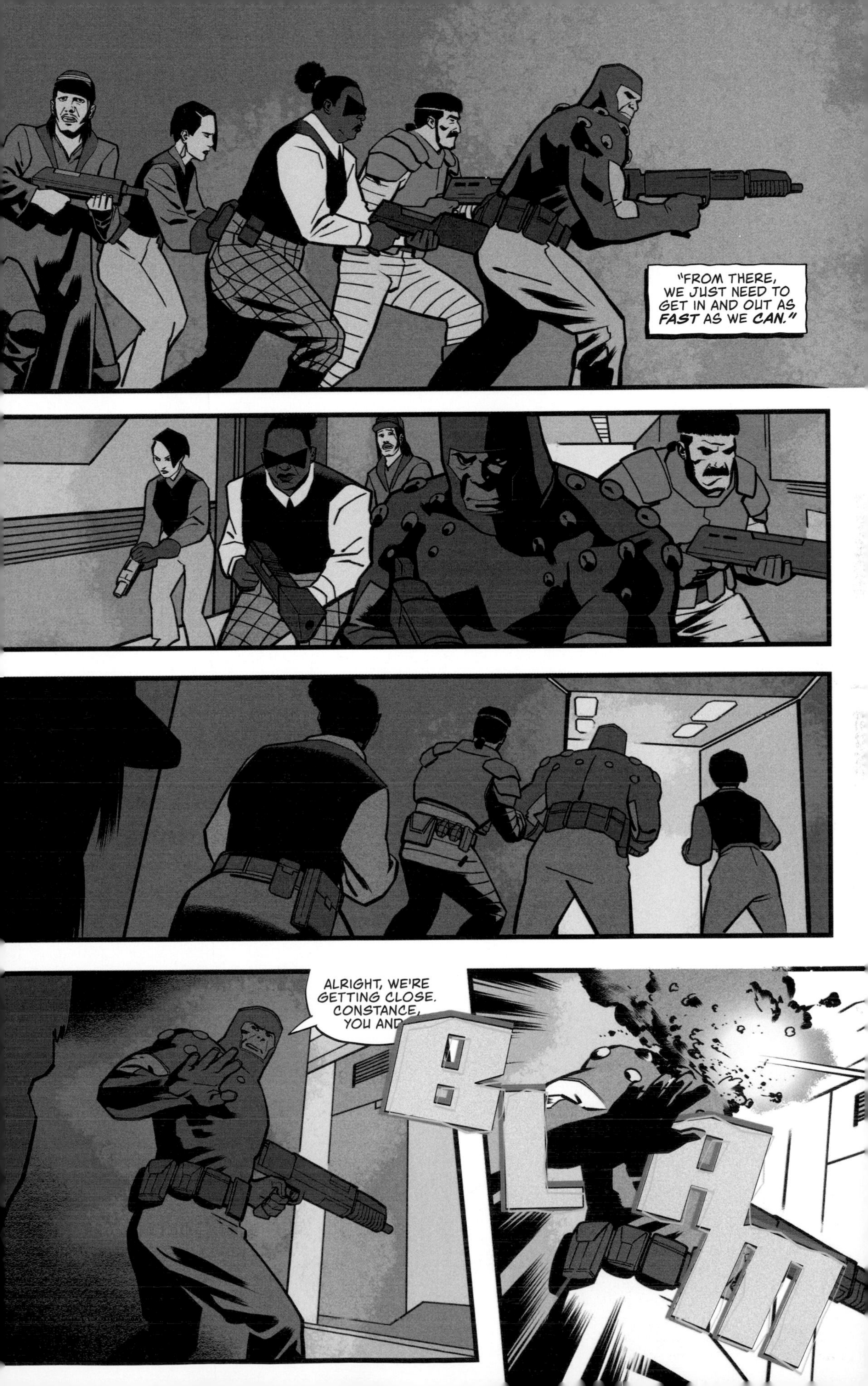
"FROM THERE, WE JUST NEED TO GET IN AND OUT AS FAST AS WE CAN."
ALRIGHT, WE'RE GETTING CLOSE. CONSTANCE, YOU AND
BLAM

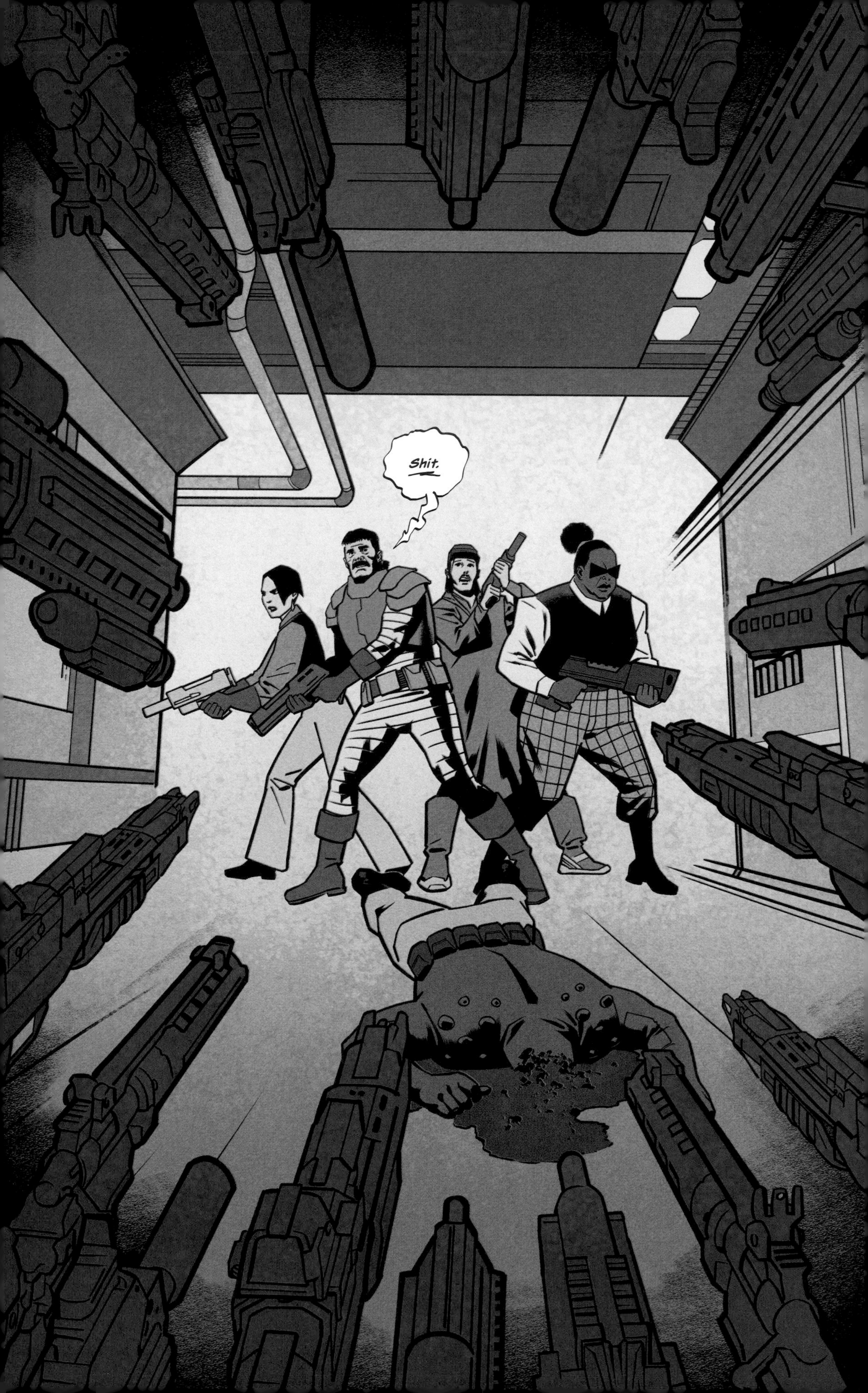
Shit.

久

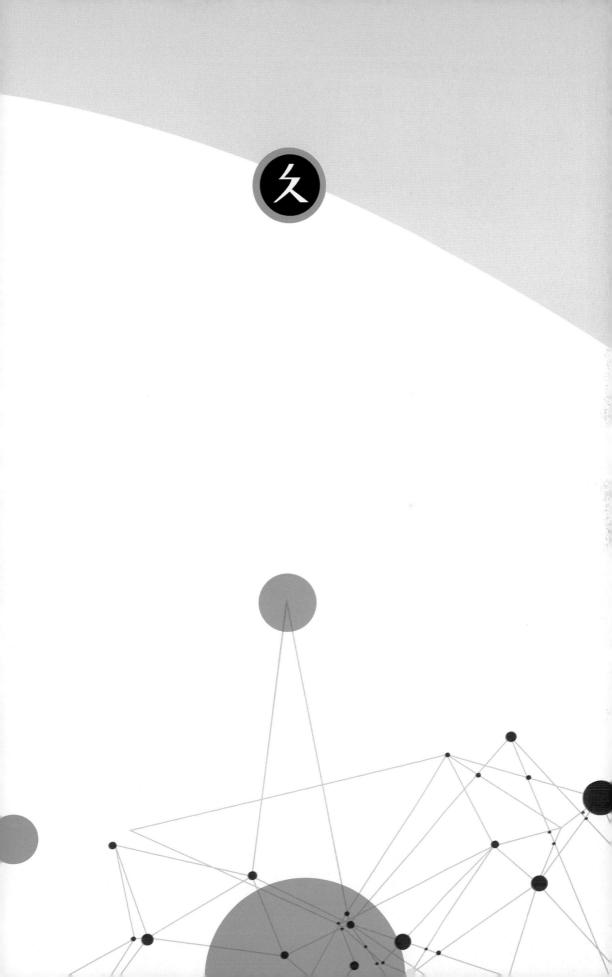

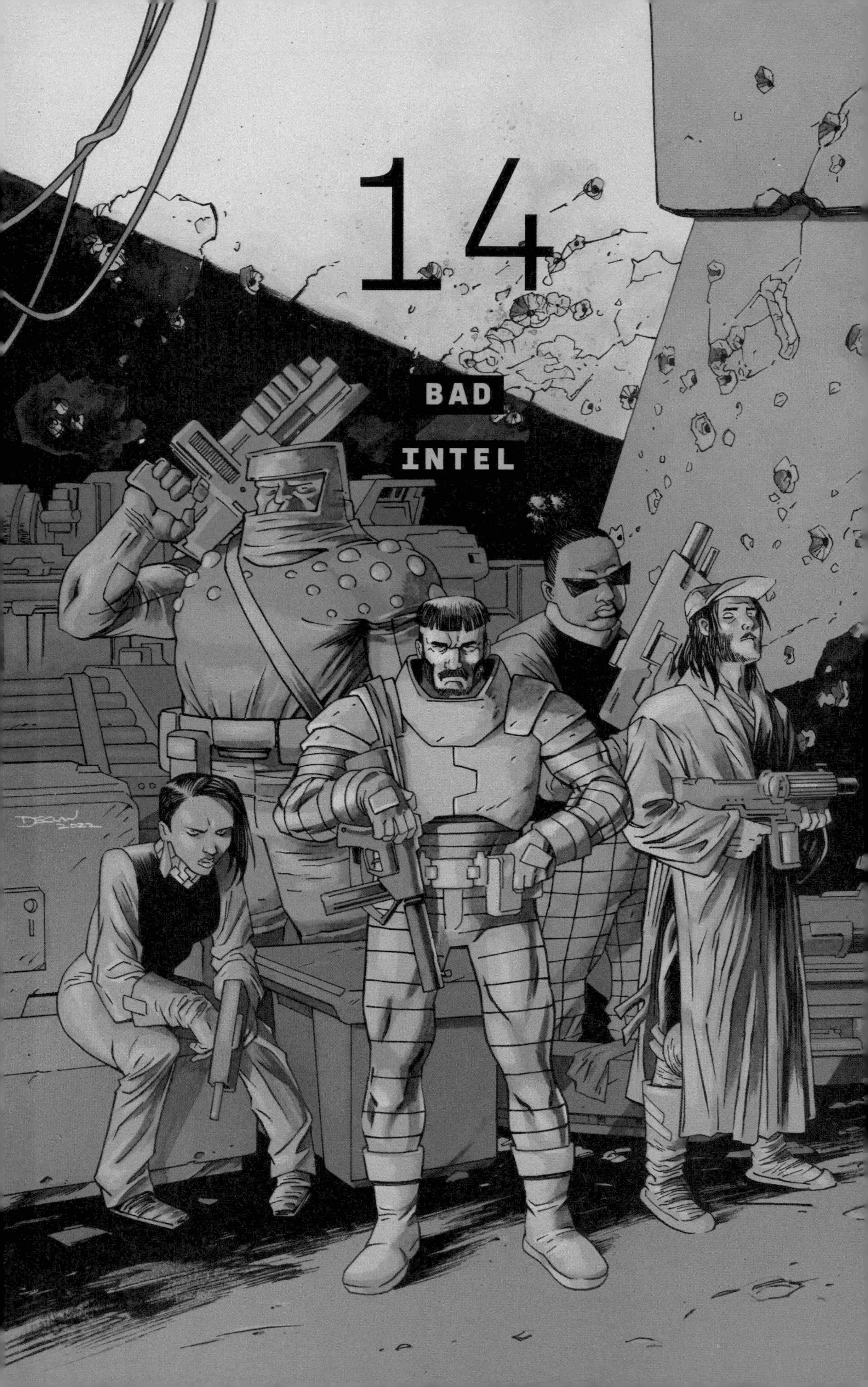
14
BAD
INTEL

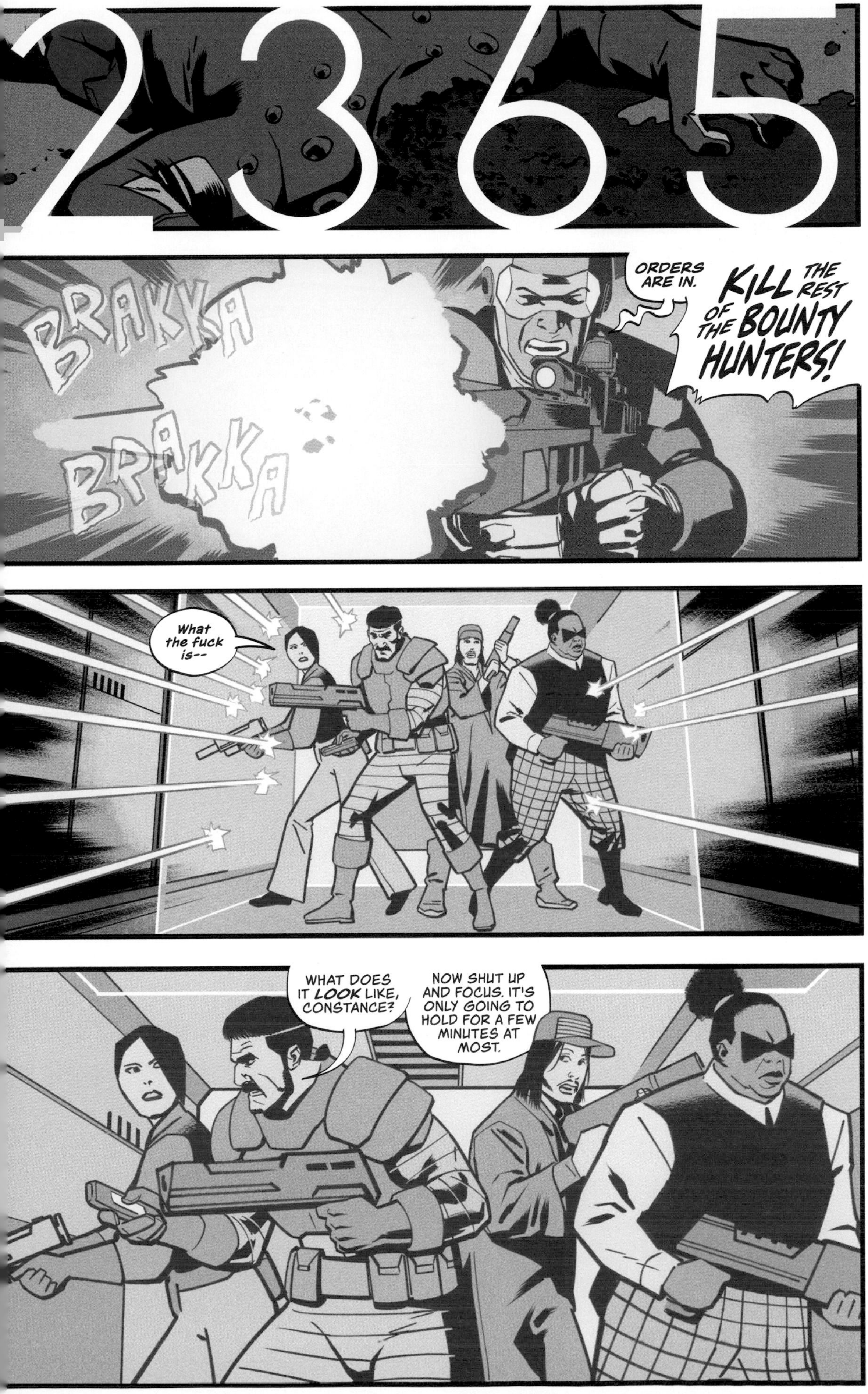
2365
BRAKKA
BRAKKA
ORDERS ARE IN.
KILL THE REST OF THE BOUNTY HUNTERS!
What the fuck is--
WHAT DOES IT LOOK LIKE, CONSTANCE?
NOW SHUT UP AND FOCUS. IT'S ONLY GOING TO HOLD FOR A FEW MINUTES AT MOST.

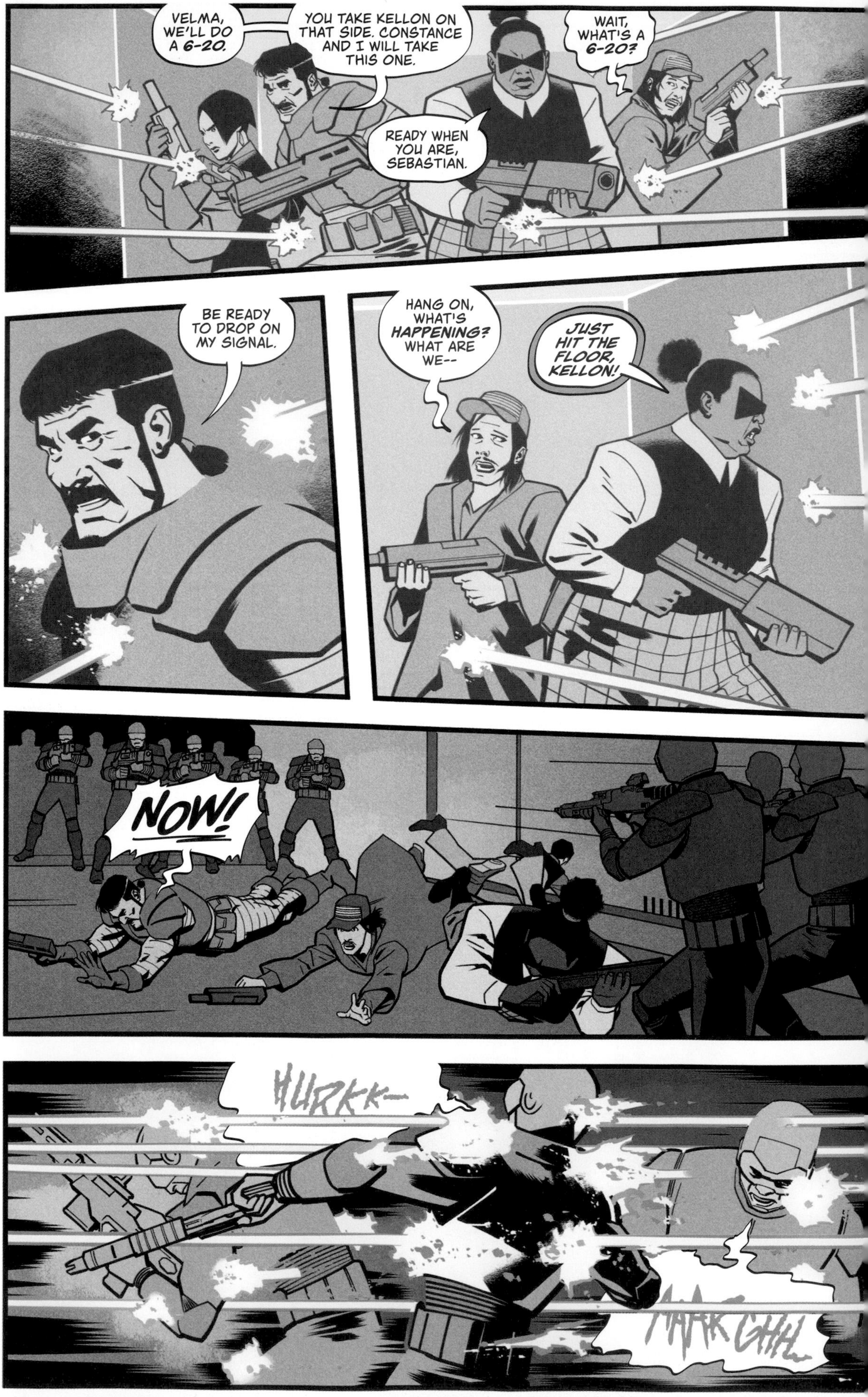
VELMA, WE'LL DO A 6-20.
YOU TAKE KELLON ON THAT SIDE. CONSTANCE AND I WILL TAKE THIS ONE.
READY WHEN YOU ARE, SEBASTIAN.
WAIT, WHAT'S A 6-20?
BE READY TO DROP ON MY SIGNAL.
HANG ON, WHAT'S HAPPENING? WHAT ARE WE--
JUST HIT THE FLOOR, KELLON!
NOW!
HURKK--
AAARKGHH

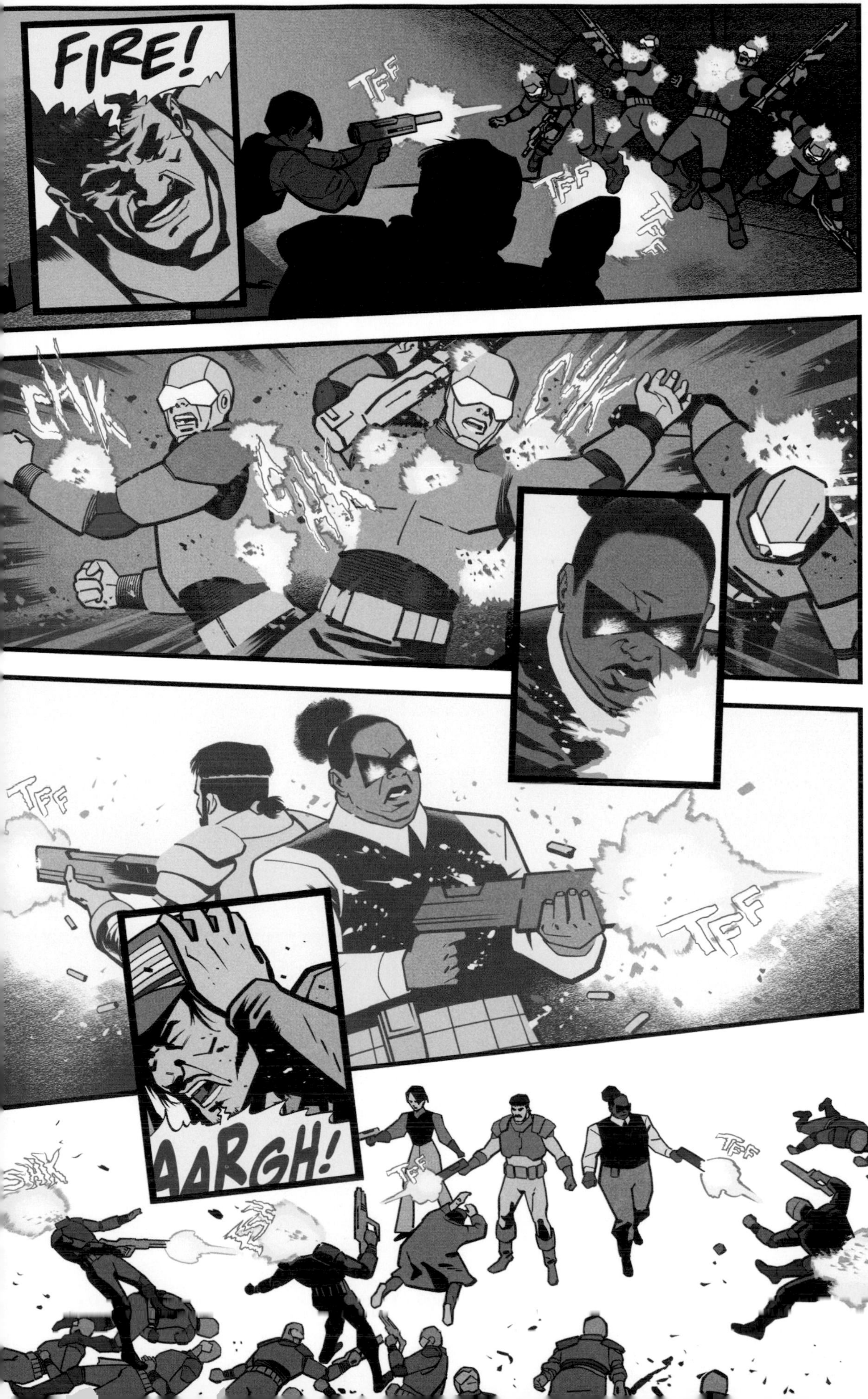

FIRE!
TFF
TFF
TFF
CHK
CHK
CHK
TFF
TFF
AARGH!
TFF
TFF

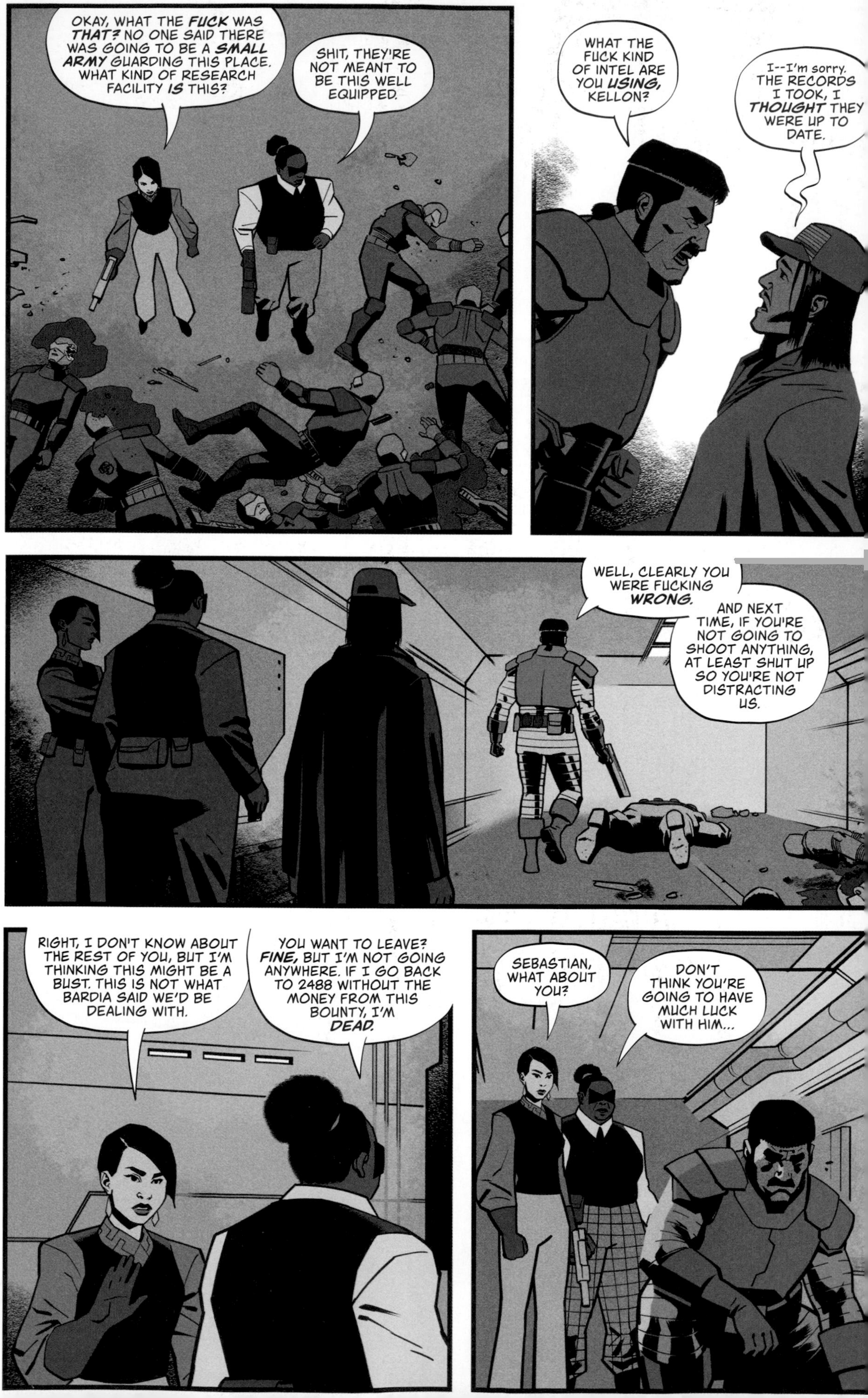
OKAY, WHAT THE FUCK WAS THAT? NO ONE SAID THERE WAS GOING TO BE A SMALL ARMY GUARDING THIS PLACE. WHAT KIND OF RESEARCH FACILITY IS THIS?
SHIT, THEY'RE NOT MEANT TO BE THIS WELL EQUIPPED.
WHAT THE FUCK KIND OF INTEL ARE YOU USING, KELLON?
I--I'm sorry. THE RECORDS I TOOK, I THOUGHT THEY WERE UP TO DATE.
WELL, CLEARLY YOU WERE FUCKING WRONG.
AND NEXT TIME, IF YOU'RE NOT GOING TO SHOOT ANYTHING, AT LEAST SHUT UP SO YOU'RE NOT DISTRACTING US.
RIGHT, I DON'T KNOW ABOUT THE REST OF YOU, BUT I'M THINKING THIS MIGHT BE A BUST. THIS IS NOT WHAT BARDIA SAID WE'D BE DEALING WITH.
YOU WANT TO LEAVE? FINE, BUT I'M NOT GOING ANYWHERE. IF I GO BACK TO 2488 WITHOUT THE MONEY FROM THIS BOUNTY, I'M DEAD.
SEBASTIAN, WHAT ABOUT YOU?
DON'T THINK YOU'RE GOING TO HAVE MUCH LUCK WITH HIM...

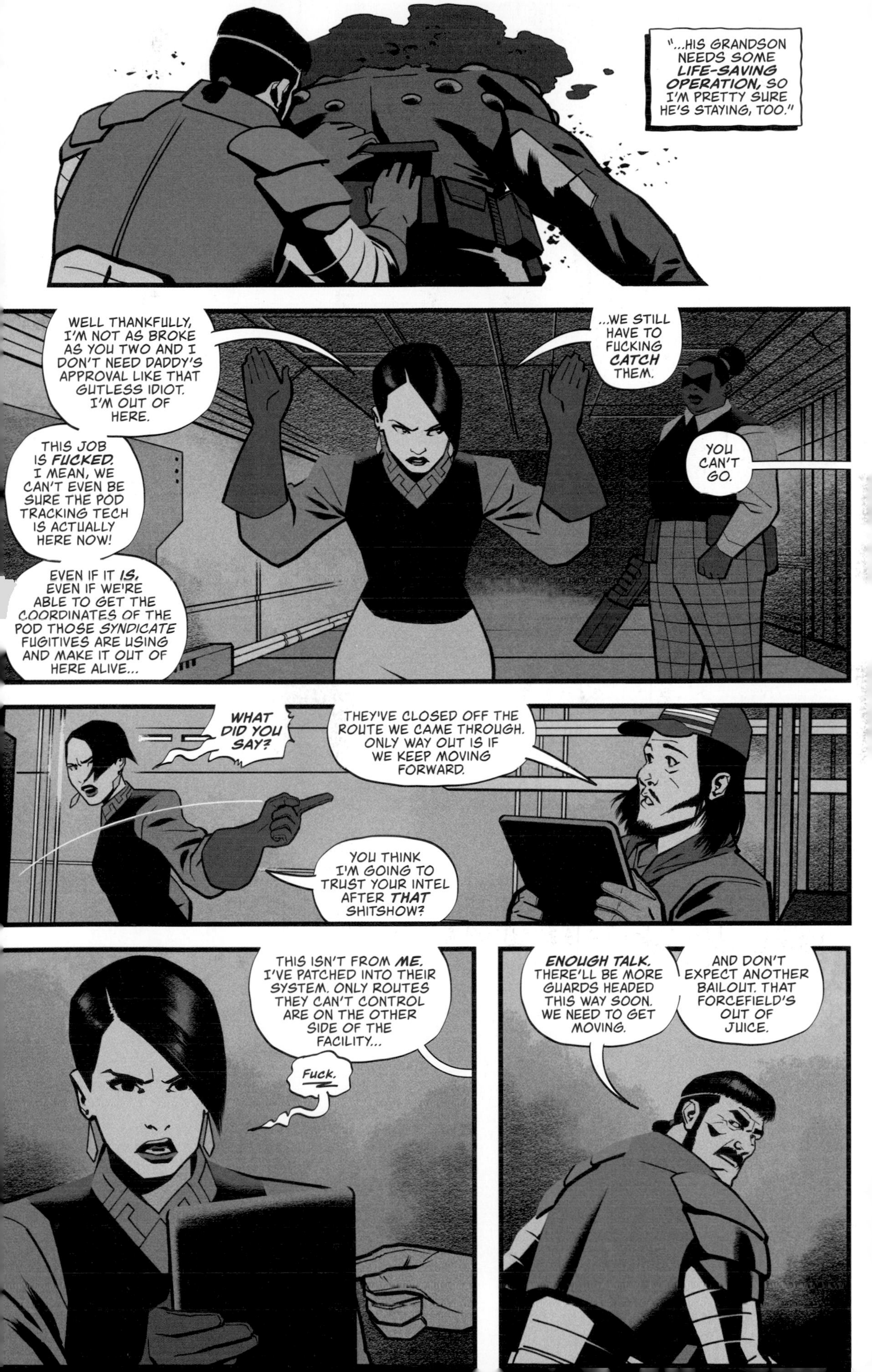
"...HIS GRANDSON NEEDS SOME LIFE-SAVING OPERATION, SO I'M PRETTY SURE HE'S STAYING, TOO."
WELL THANKFULLY, I'M NOT AS BROKE AS YOU TWO AND I DON'T NEED DADDY'S APPROVAL LIKE THAT GUTLESS IDIOT. I'M OUT OF HERE.
THIS JOB IS FUCKED. I MEAN, WE CAN'T EVEN BE SURE THE POD TRACKING TECH IS ACTUALLY HERE NOW!
EVEN IF IT IS, EVEN IF WE'RE ABLE TO GET THE COORDINATES OF THE POD THOSE SYNDICATE FUGITIVES ARE USING AND MAKE IT OUT OF HERE ALIVE...
...WE STILL HAVE TO FUCKING CATCH THEM.
YOU CAN'T GO.
WHAT DID YOU SAY?
THEY'VE CLOSED OFF THE ROUTE WE CAME THROUGH. ONLY WAY OUT IS IF WE KEEP MOVING FORWARD.
YOU THINK I'M GOING TO TRUST YOUR INTEL AFTER THAT SHITSHOW?
THIS ISN'T FROM ME. I'VE PATCHED INTO THEIR SYSTEM. ONLY ROUTES THEY CAN'T CONTROL ARE ON THE OTHER SIDE OF THE FACILITY...
Fuck.
ENOUGH TALK. THERE'LL BE MORE GUARDS HEADED THIS WAY SOON. WE NEED TO GET MOVING.
AND DON'T EXPECT ANOTHER BAILOUT. THAT FORCEFIELD'S OUT OF JUICE.

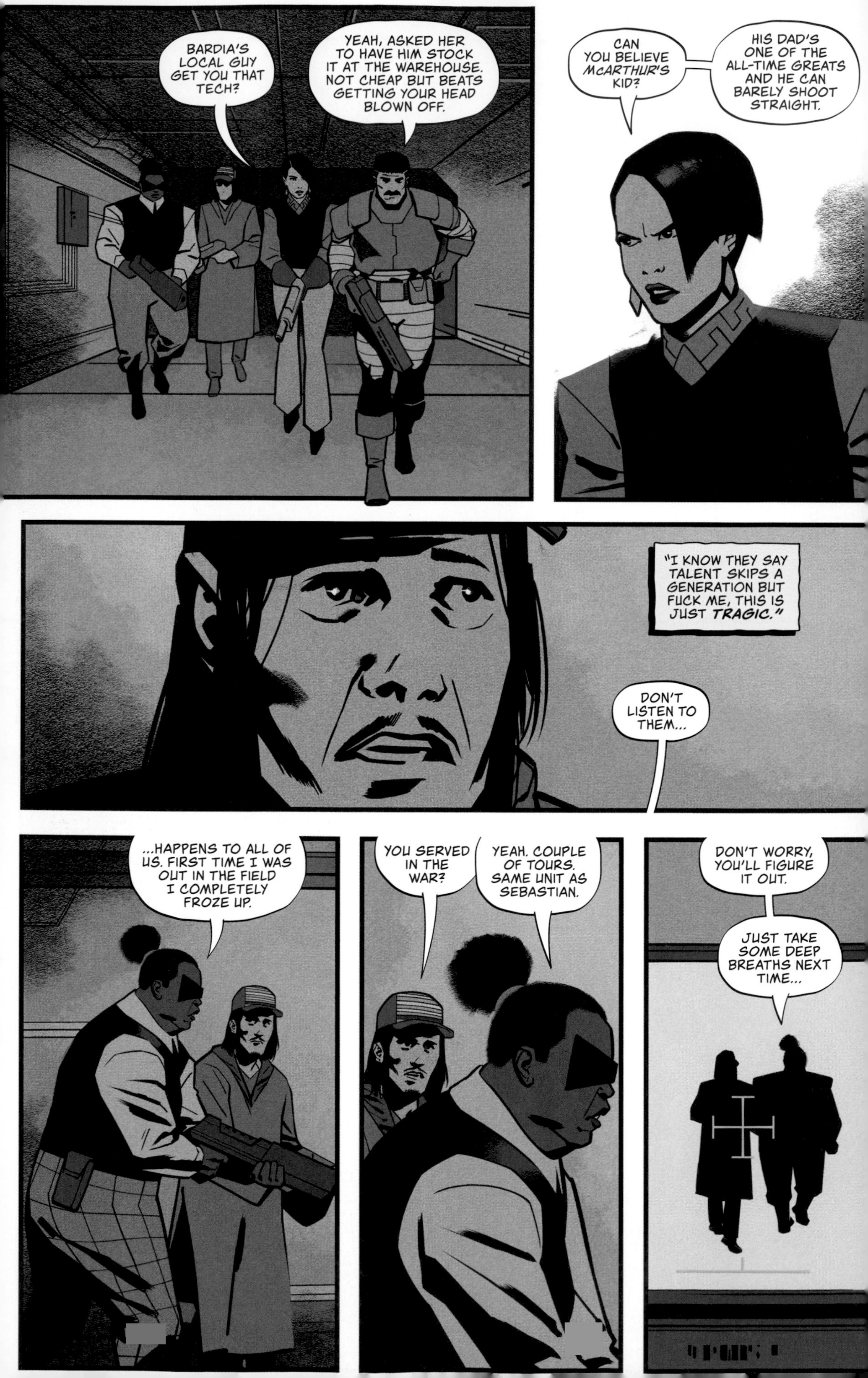
BARDIA'S LOCAL GUY GET YOU THAT TECH?
YEAH, ASKED HER TO HAVE HIM STOCK IT AT THE WAREHOUSE. NOT CHEAP BUT BEATS GETTING YOUR HEAD BLOWN OFF.
CAN YOU BELIEVE McARTHUR'S KID?
HIS DAD'S ONE OF THE ALL-TIME GREATS AND HE CAN BARELY SHOOT STRAIGHT.
"I KNOW THEY SAY TALENT SKIPS A GENERATION BUT FUCK ME, THIS IS JUST *TRAGIC.*"
DON'T LISTEN TO THEM...
...HAPPENS TO ALL OF US. FIRST TIME I WAS OUT IN THE FIELD I COMPLETELY FROZE UP.
YOU SERVED IN THE WAR?
YEAH. COUPLE OF TOURS. SAME UNIT AS SEBASTIAN.
DON'T WORRY, YOU'LL FIGURE IT OUT.
JUST TAKE SOME DEEP BREATHS NEXT TIME...

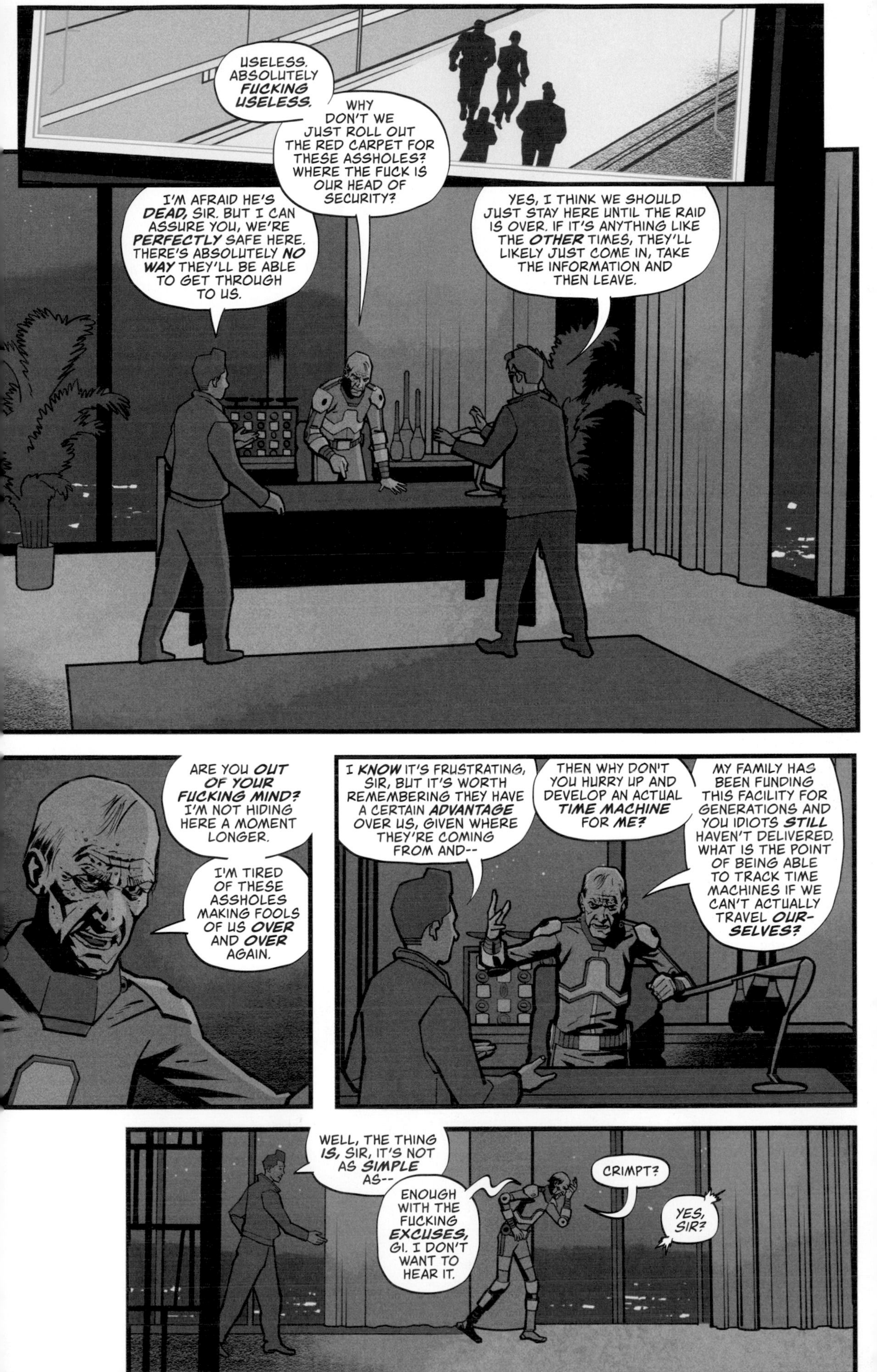
USELESS. ABSOLUTELY FUCKING USELESS.
WHY DON'T WE JUST ROLL OUT THE RED CARPET FOR THESE ASSHOLES? WHERE THE FUCK IS OUR HEAD OF SECURITY?
I'M AFRAID HE'S DEAD, SIR. BUT I CAN ASSURE YOU, WE'RE PERFECTLY SAFE HERE. THERE'S ABSOLUTELY NO WAY THEY'LL BE ABLE TO GET THROUGH TO US.
YES, I THINK WE SHOULD JUST STAY HERE UNTIL THE RAID IS OVER. IF IT'S ANYTHING LIKE THE OTHER TIMES, THEY'LL LIKELY JUST COME IN, TAKE THE INFORMATION AND THEN LEAVE.
ARE YOU OUT OF YOUR FUCKING MIND? I'M NOT HIDING HERE A MOMENT LONGER.
I'M TIRED OF THESE ASSHOLES MAKING FOOLS OF US OVER AND OVER AGAIN.
I KNOW IT'S FRUSTRATING, SIR, BUT IT'S WORTH REMEMBERING THEY HAVE A CERTAIN ADVANTAGE OVER US, GIVEN WHERE THEY'RE COMING FROM AND--
THEN WHY DON'T YOU HURRY UP AND DEVELOP AN ACTUAL TIME MACHINE FOR ME?
MY FAMILY HAS BEEN FUNDING THIS FACILITY FOR GENERATIONS AND YOU IDIOTS STILL HAVEN'T DELIVERED. WHAT IS THE POINT OF BEING ABLE TO TRACK TIME MACHINES IF WE CAN'T ACTUALLY TRAVEL OURSELVES?
WELL, THE THING IS, SIR, IT'S NOT AS SIMPLE AS--
ENOUGH WITH THE FUCKING EXCUSES, GI. I DON'T WANT TO HEAR IT.
CRIMPT?
YES, SIR?

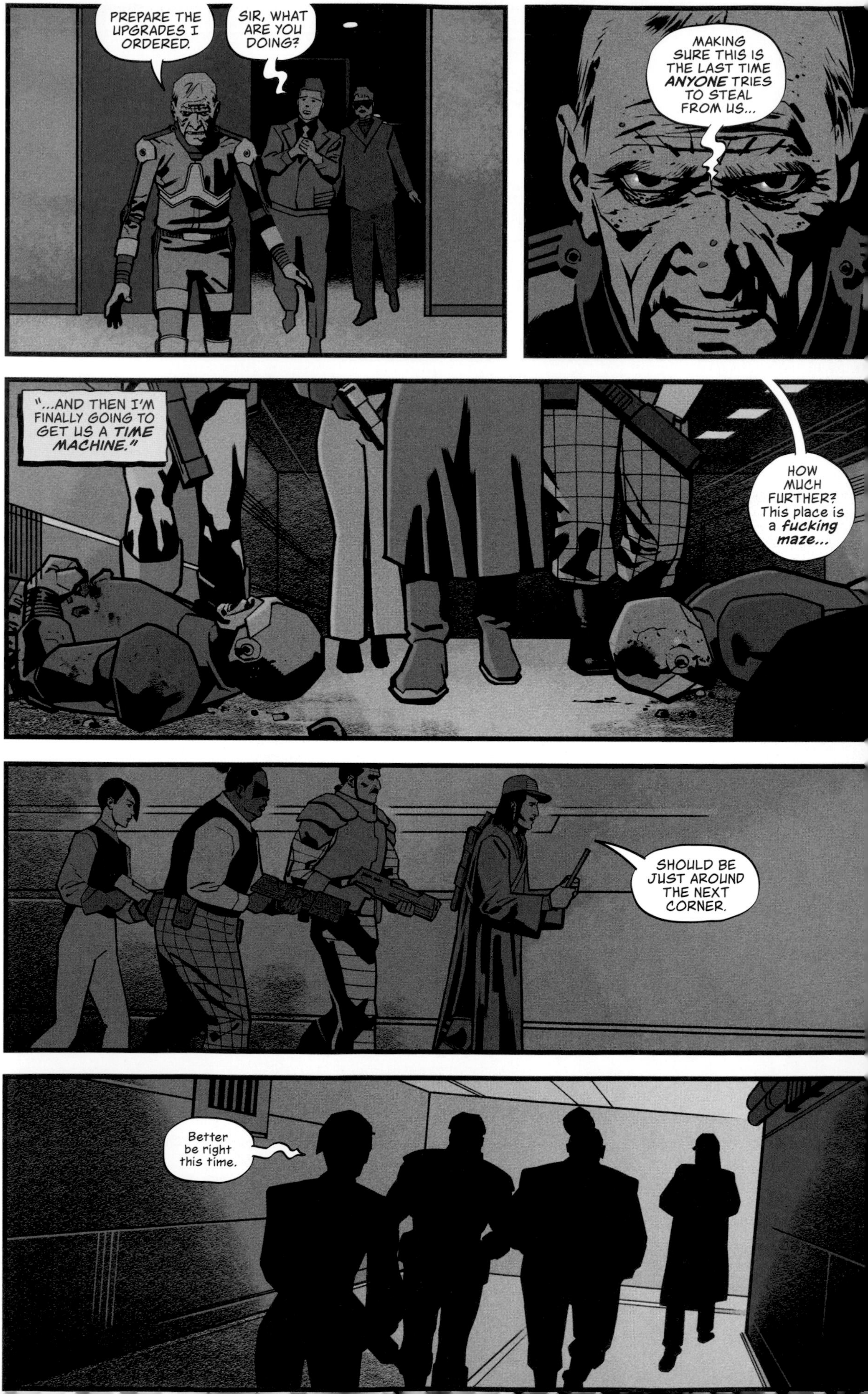
PREPARE THE UPGRADES I ORDERED.
SIR, WHAT ARE YOU DOING?
MAKING SURE THIS IS THE LAST TIME ANYONE TRIES TO STEAL FROM US...
"...AND THEN I'M FINALLY GOING TO GET US A TIME MACHINE."
HOW MUCH FURTHER? This place is a fucking maze...
SHOULD BE JUST AROUND THE NEXT CORNER.
Better be right this time.

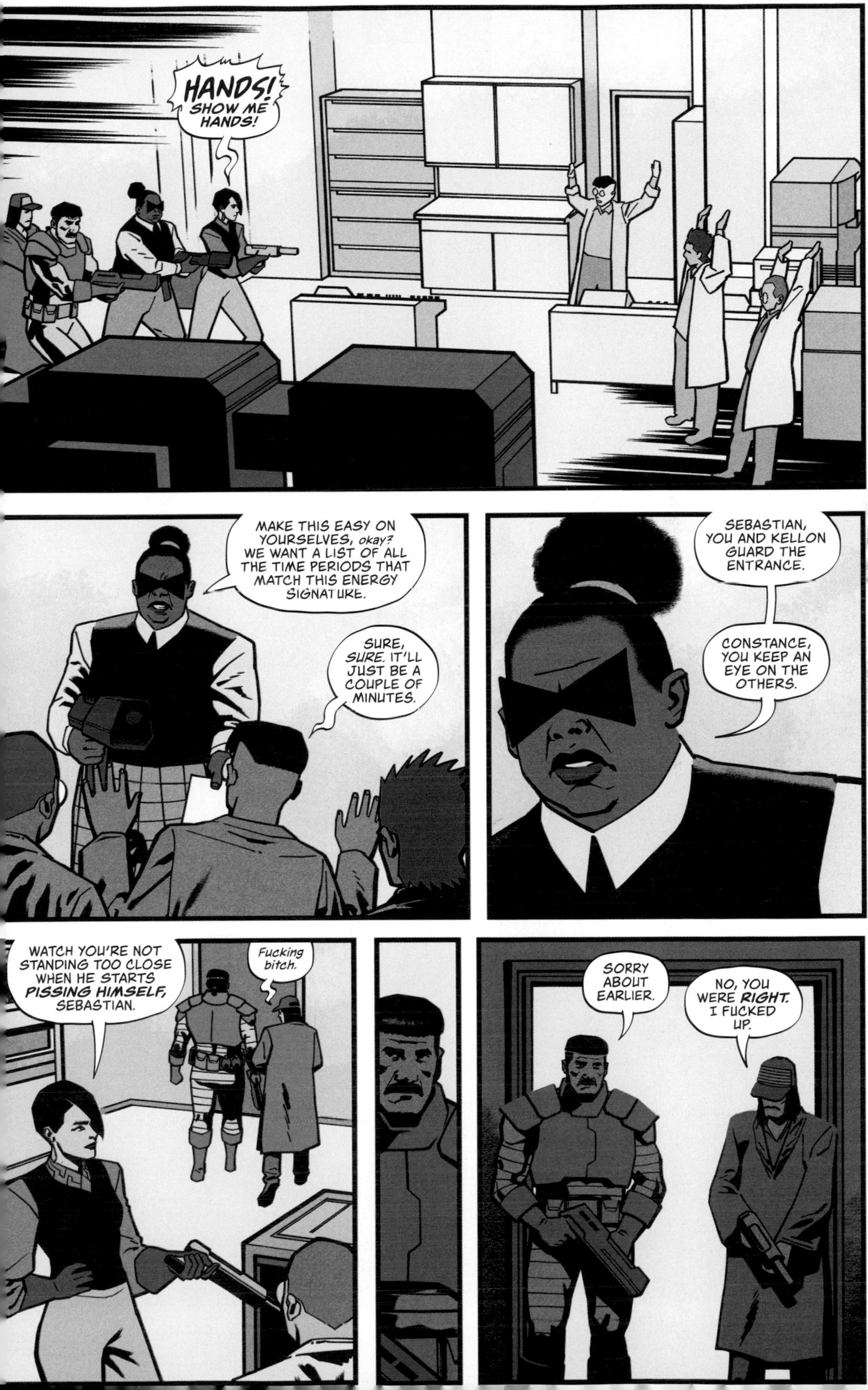
HANDS! SHOW ME HANDS!
MAKE THIS EASY ON YOURSELVES, *okay?* WE WANT A LIST OF ALL THE TIME PERIODS THAT MATCH THIS ENERGY SIGNATURE.
SURE, *SURE.* IT'LL JUST BE A COUPLE OF MINUTES.
SEBASTIAN, YOU AND KELLON GUARD THE ENTRANCE.
CONSTANCE, YOU KEEP AN EYE ON THE OTHERS.
WATCH YOU'RE NOT STANDING TOO CLOSE WHEN HE STARTS ***PISSING HIMSELF,*** SEBASTIAN.
Fucking bitch.
SORRY ABOUT EARLIER.
NO, YOU WERE ***RIGHT.*** I FUCKED UP.

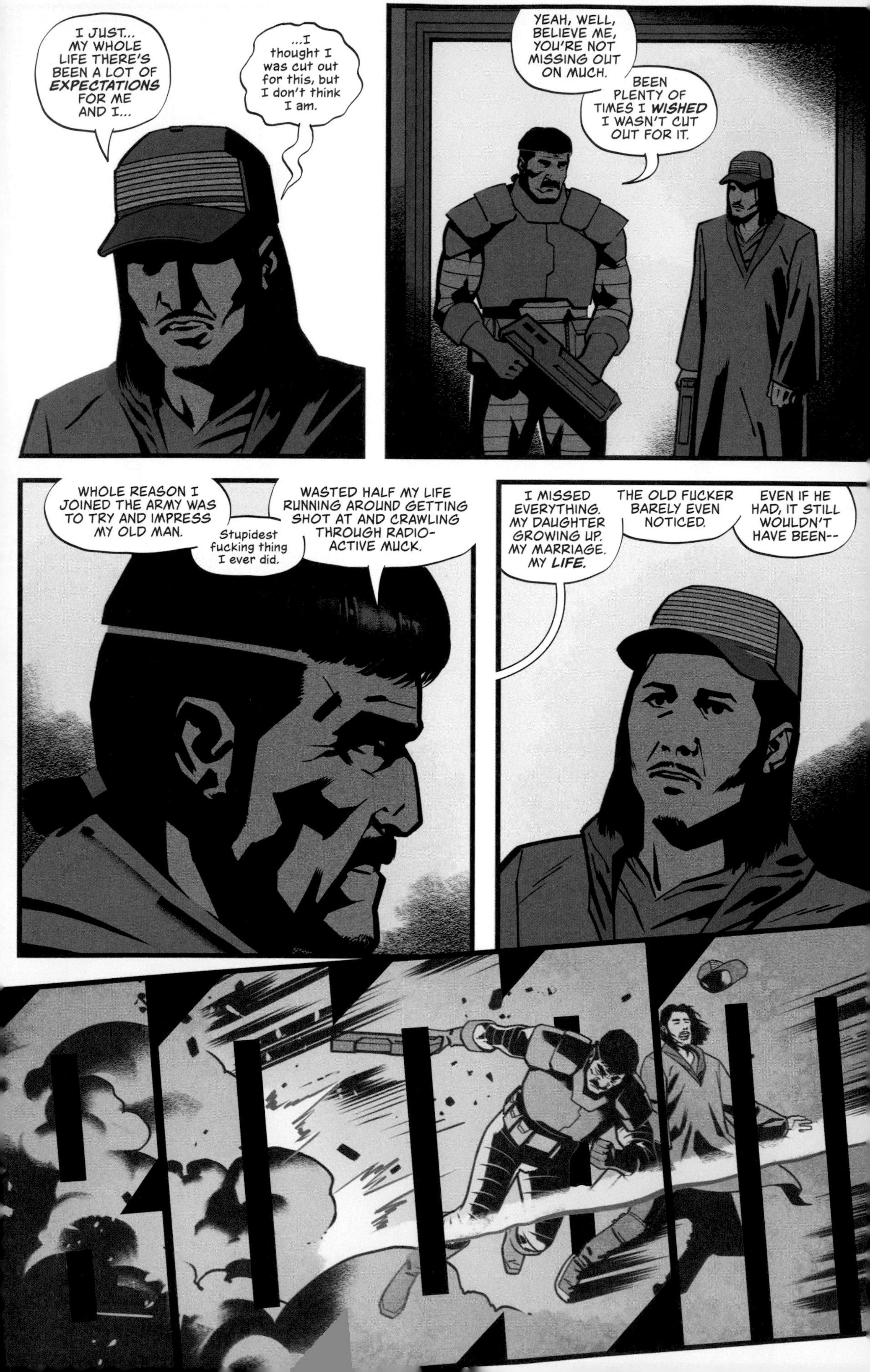
I JUST... MY WHOLE LIFE THERE'S BEEN A LOT OF EXPECTATIONS FOR ME AND I...
...I thought I was cut out for this, but I don't think I am.
YEAH, WELL, BELIEVE ME, YOU'RE NOT MISSING OUT ON MUCH.
BEEN PLENTY OF TIMES I WISHED I WASN'T CUT OUT FOR IT.
WHOLE REASON I JOINED THE ARMY WAS TO TRY AND IMPRESS MY OLD MAN.
Stupidest fucking thing I ever did.
WASTED HALF MY LIFE RUNNING AROUND GETTING SHOT AT AND CRAWLING THROUGH RADIO-ACTIVE MUCK.
I MISSED EVERYTHING. MY DAUGHTER GROWING UP. MY MARRIAGE. MY LIFE.
THE OLD FUCKER BARELY EVEN NOTICED.
EVEN IF HE HAD, IT STILL WOULDN'T HAVE BEEN--

THE FUCK'S TAKING SO LONG?

Sorry, sorry. THERE'S JUST A LOT MORE LOCATIONS THAN I WAS EXPECTING.

...BECAUSE I *REALLY* DON'T SEE HOW THE FUCK YOU COULD BE THE KELLON MCARTHUR'S SON.

Y'KNOW, I'VE BEEN TRYING TO MAKE SENSE OF THIS, KELLON, AND I THINK YOU'RE GOING TO HAVE TO GET A PATERNITY TEST WHEN WE GET BACK...

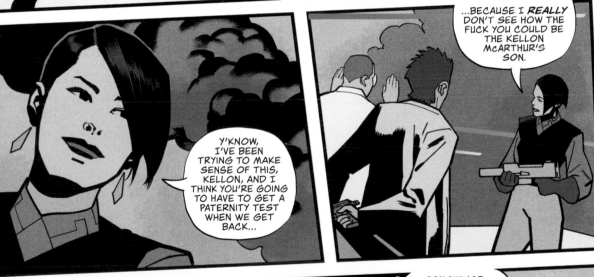

CONSTANCE, DO US ALL A FAVOR AND *SHUT UP* A SECOND.

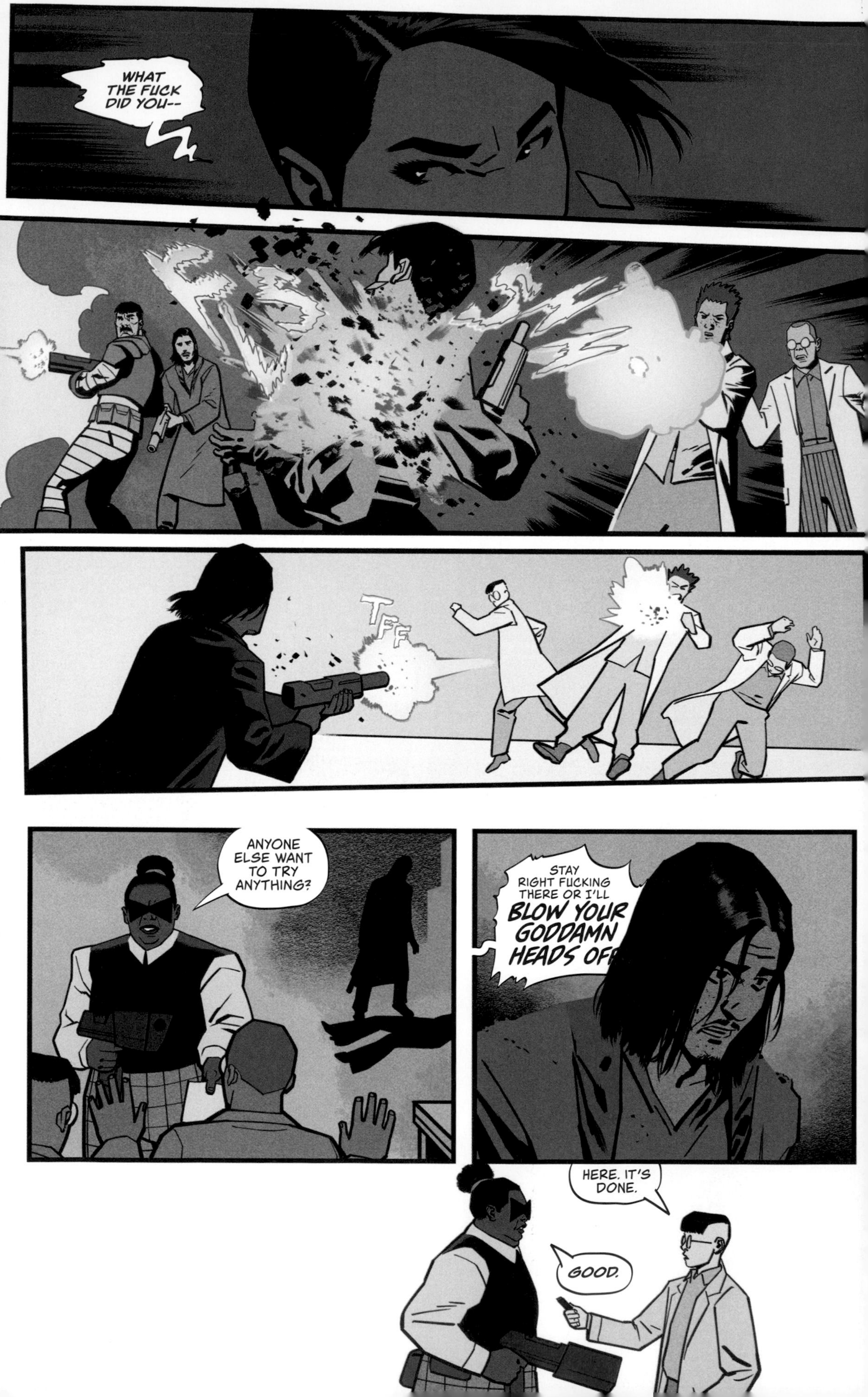
WHAT THE FUCK DID YOU--
TFF
ANYONE ELSE WANT TO TRY ANYTHING?
STAY RIGHT FUCKING THERE OR I'LL BLOW YOUR GODDAMN HEADS OFF
HERE. IT'S DONE.
GOOD.

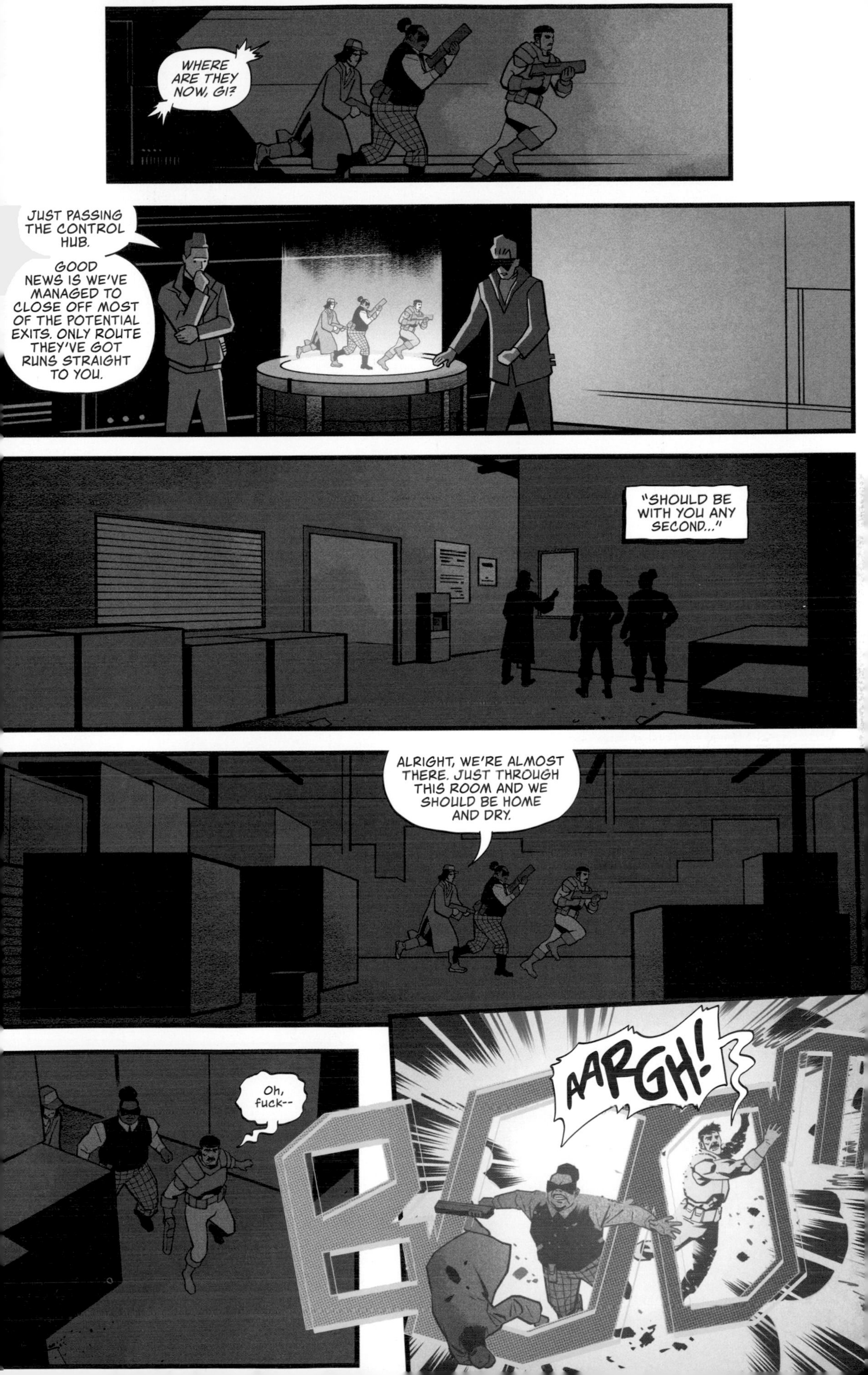
WHERE ARE THEY NOW, GI?
JUST PASSING THE CONTROL HUB.
GOOD NEWS IS WE'VE MANAGED TO CLOSE OFF MOST OF THE POTENTIAL EXITS. ONLY ROUTE THEY'VE GOT RUNS STRAIGHT TO YOU.
"SHOULD BE WITH YOU ANY SECOND..."
ALRIGHT, WE'RE ALMOST THERE. JUST THROUGH THIS ROOM AND WE SHOULD BE HOME AND DRY.
Oh, fuck--
AARGH!

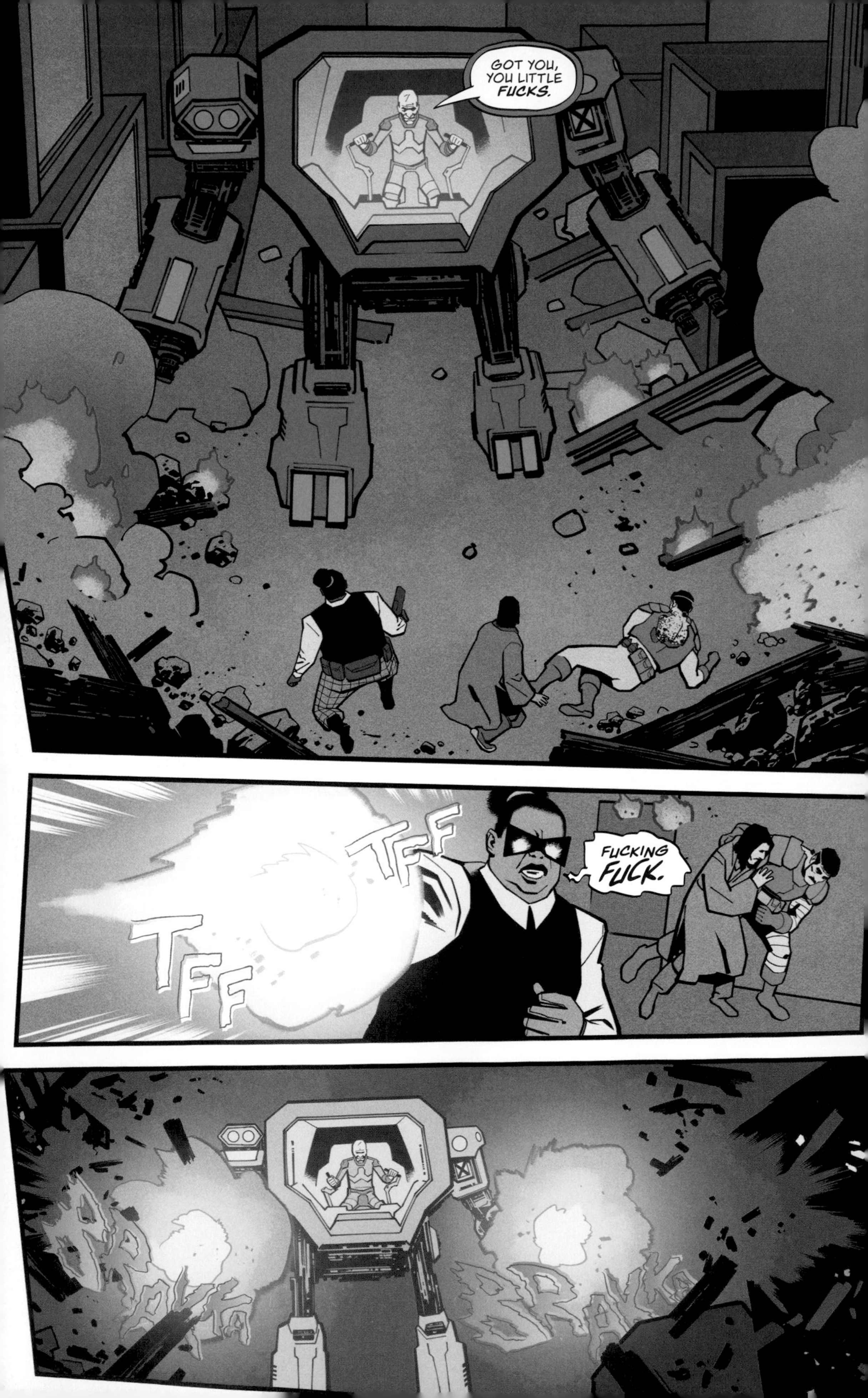
GOT YOU, YOU LITTLE FUCKS.
TFF
TFF
FUCKING FUCK.

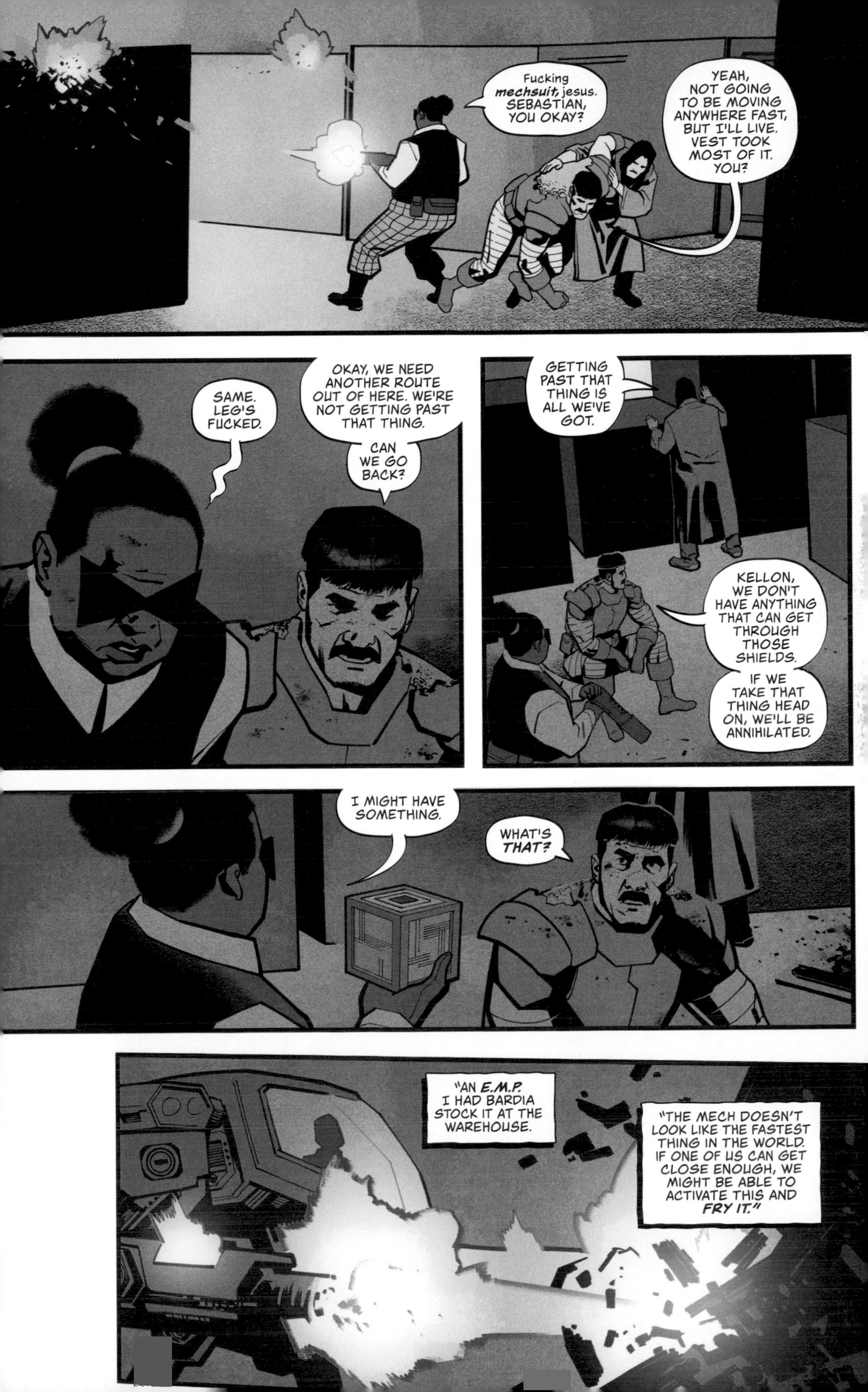

Fucking *mechsuit*, jesus. SEBASTIAN, YOU OKAY?
YEAH, NOT GOING TO BE MOVING ANYWHERE FAST, BUT I'LL LIVE. VEST TOOK MOST OF IT. YOU?
SAME. LEG'S FUCKED.
OKAY, WE NEED ANOTHER ROUTE OUT OF HERE. WE'RE NOT GETTING PAST THAT THING.
CAN WE GO BACK?
GETTING PAST THAT THING IS ALL WE'VE GOT.
KELLON, WE DON'T HAVE ANYTHING THAT CAN GET THROUGH THOSE SHIELDS.
IF WE TAKE THAT THING HEAD ON, WE'LL BE ANNIHILATED.
I MIGHT HAVE SOMETHING.
WHAT'S *THAT?*
"AN *E.M.P.* I HAD BARDIA STOCK IT AT THE WAREHOUSE.
"THE MECH DOESN'T LOOK LIKE THE FASTEST THING IN THE WORLD. IF ONE OF US CAN GET CLOSE ENOUGH, WE MIGHT BE ABLE TO ACTIVATE THIS AND *FRY IT.*"

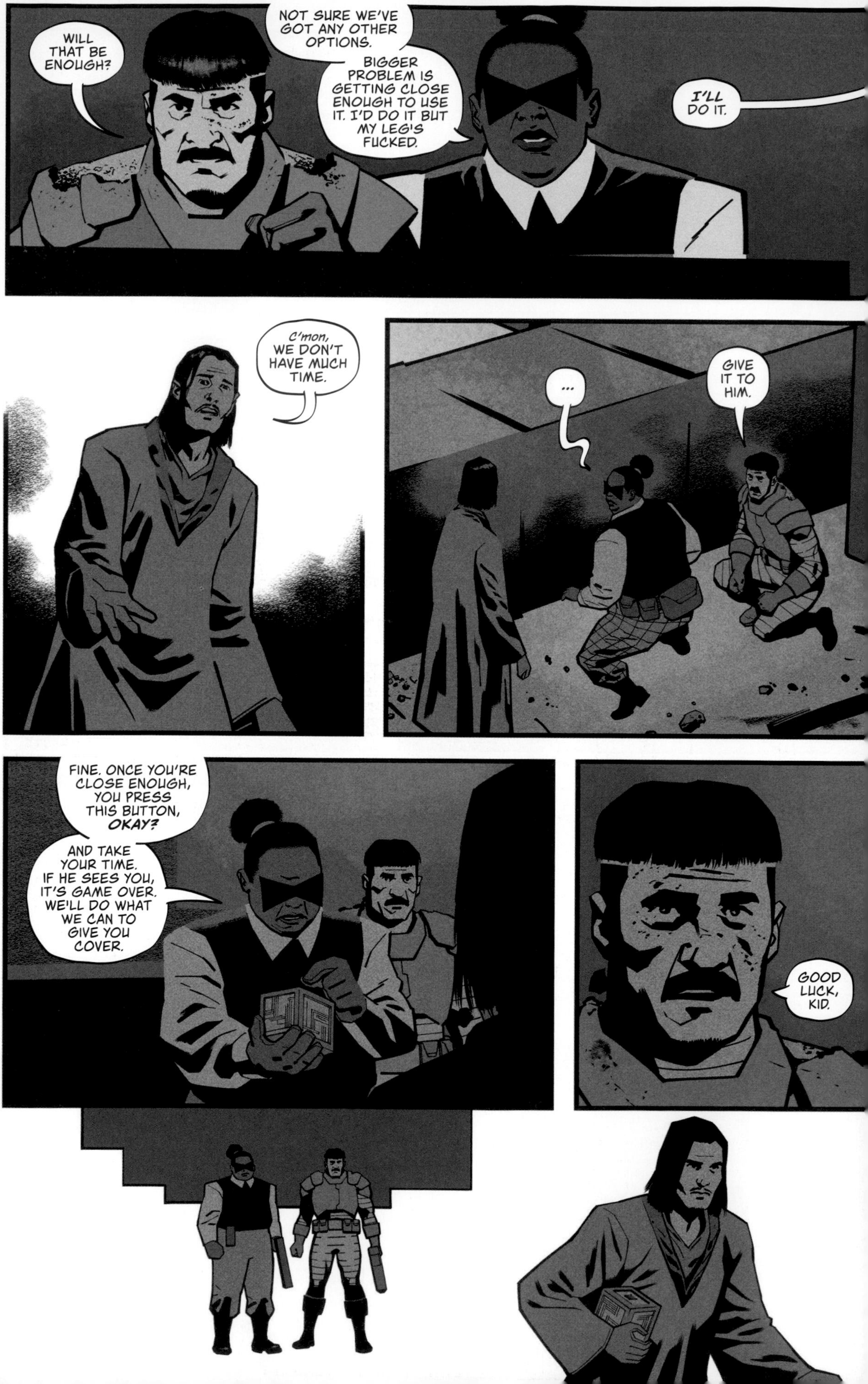
WILL THAT BE ENOUGH?
NOT SURE WE'VE GOT ANY OTHER OPTIONS.
BIGGER PROBLEM IS GETTING CLOSE ENOUGH TO USE IT. I'D DO IT BUT MY LEG'S FUCKED.
I'LL DO IT.
C'mon, WE DON'T HAVE MUCH TIME.
...
GIVE IT TO HIM.
FINE. ONCE YOU'RE CLOSE ENOUGH, YOU PRESS THIS BUTTON, OKAY?
AND TAKE YOUR TIME. IF HE SEES YOU, IT'S GAME OVER. WE'LL DO WHAT WE CAN TO GIVE YOU COVER.
GOOD LUCK, KID.

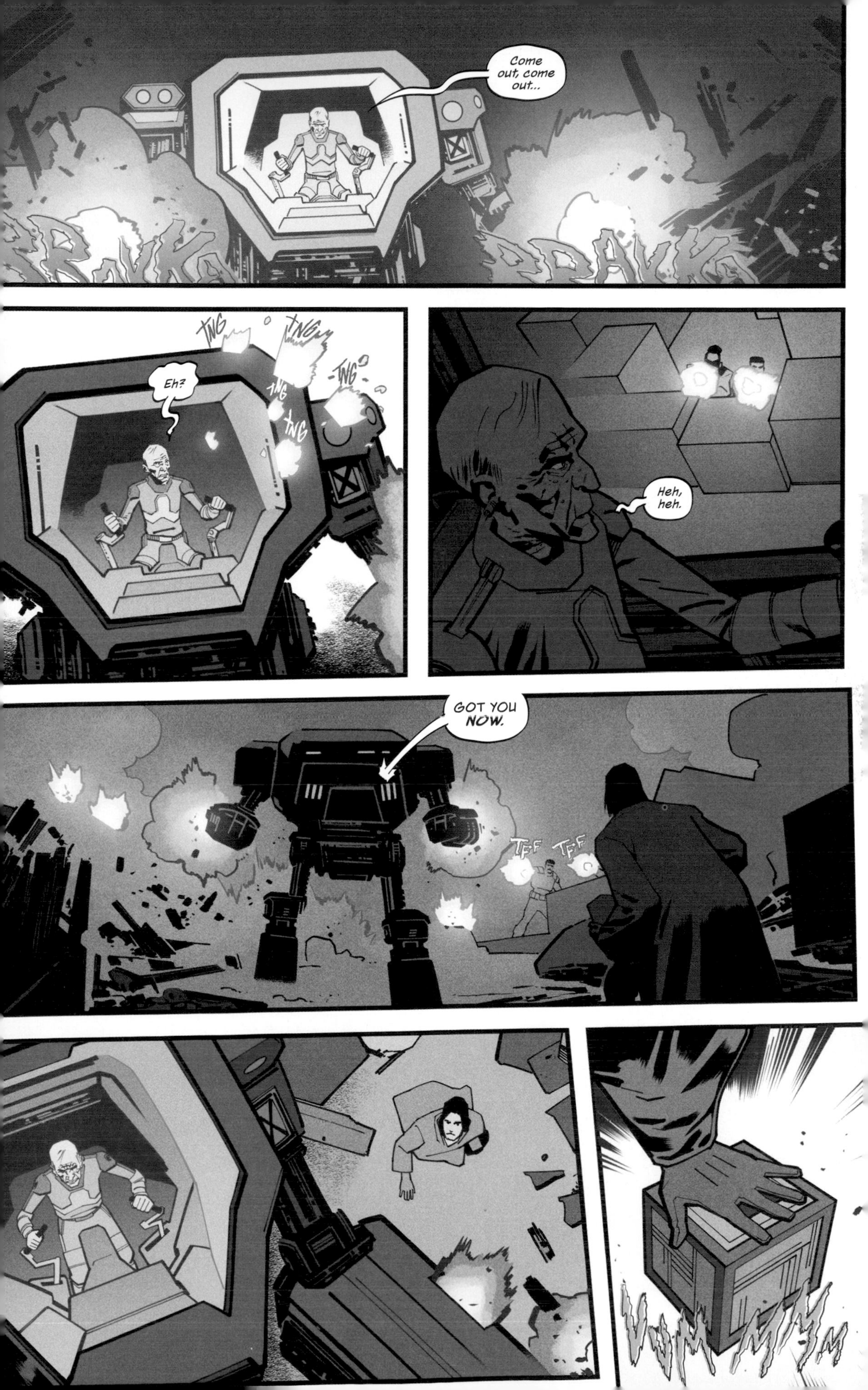
Come out, come out...
BRAKA
BRAKA
TNG
TNG
TNG
TNG
TNG
Eh?
Heh, heh.
GOT YOU NOW.
TFF
TFF
VOMMM

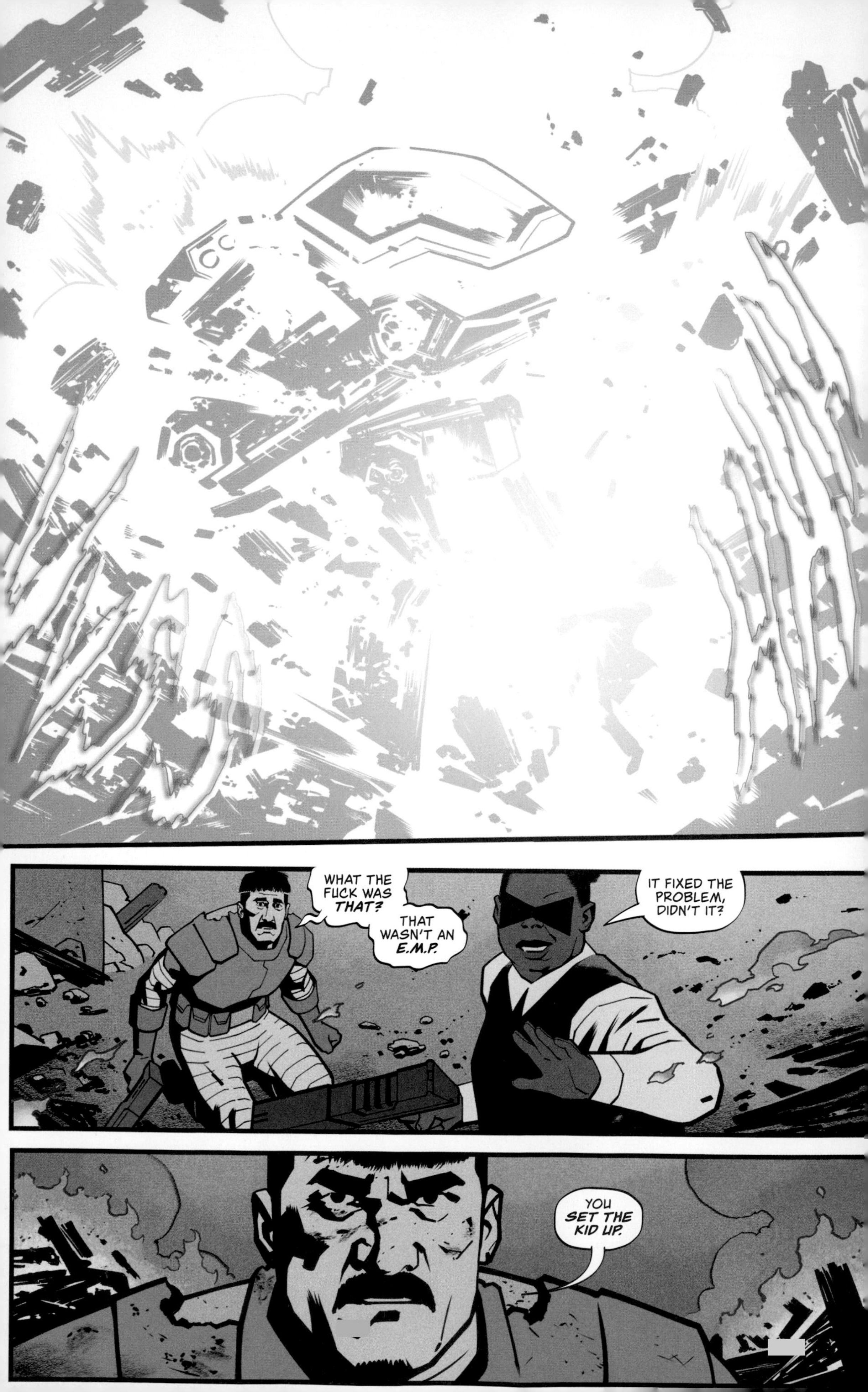
WHAT THE FUCK WAS THAT?
THAT WASN'T AN E.M.P.
IT FIXED THE PROBLEM, DIDN'T IT?
YOU SET THE KID UP.

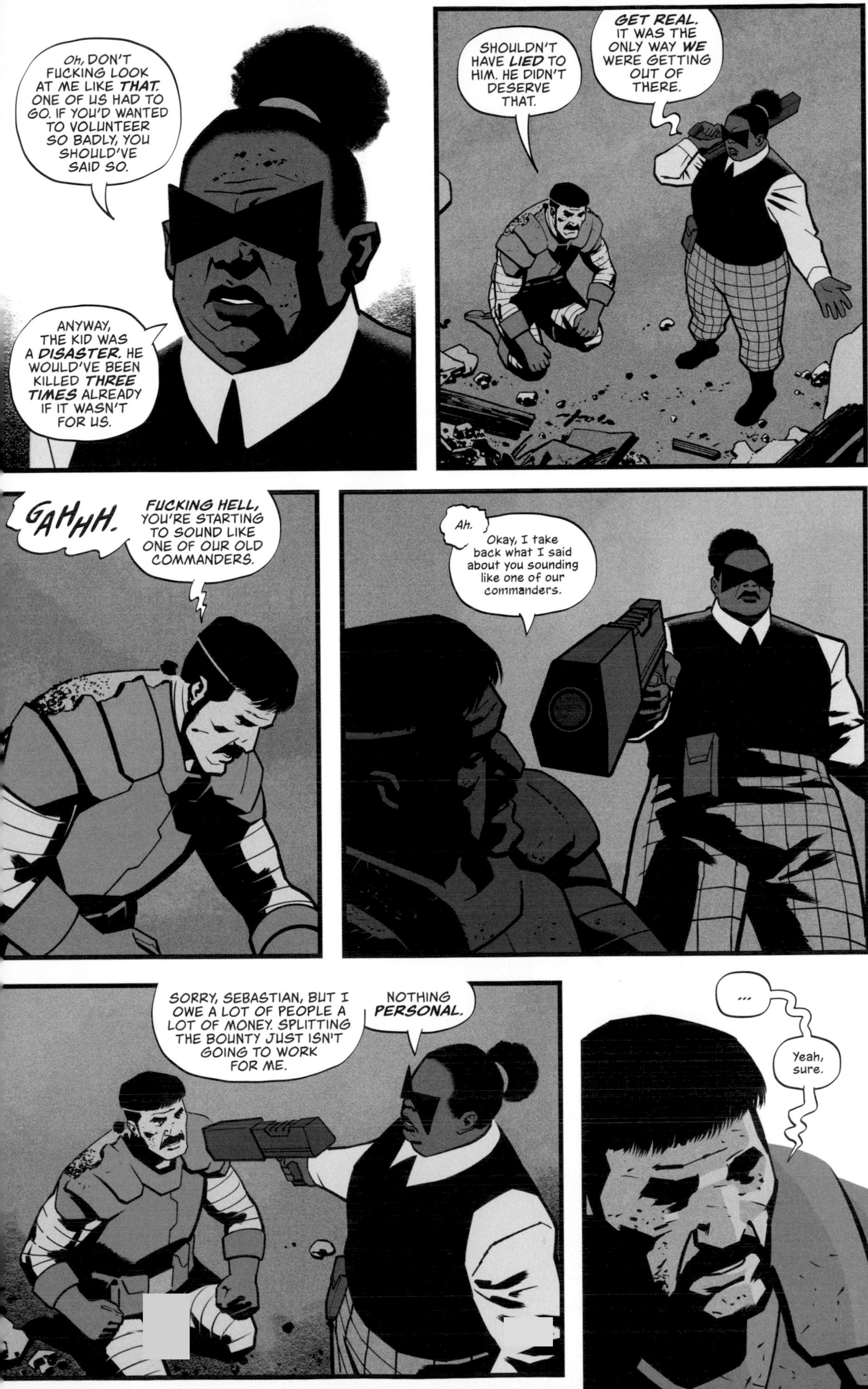
Oh, DON'T FUCKING LOOK AT ME LIKE THAT. ONE OF US HAD TO GO. IF YOU'D WANTED TO VOLUNTEER SO BADLY, YOU SHOULD'VE SAID SO.
ANYWAY, THE KID WAS A DISASTER. HE WOULD'VE BEEN KILLED THREE TIMES ALREADY IF IT WASN'T FOR US.
SHOULDN'T HAVE LIED TO HIM. HE DIDN'T DESERVE THAT.
GET REAL. IT WAS THE ONLY WAY WE WERE GETTING OUT OF THERE.
GAHHH.
FUCKING HELL, YOU'RE STARTING TO SOUND LIKE ONE OF OUR OLD COMMANDERS.
Ah.
Okay, I take back what I said about you sounding like one of our commanders.
SORRY, SEBASTIAN, BUT I OWE A LOT OF PEOPLE A LOT OF MONEY. SPLITTING THE BOUNTY JUST ISN'T GOING TO WORK FOR ME.
NOTHING PERSONAL.
...
Yeah, sure.

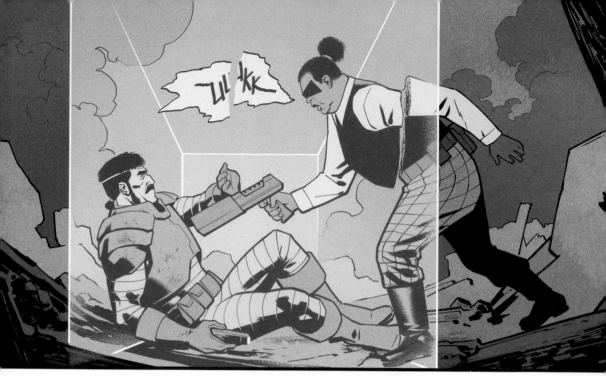

GUESS YOU'RE NOT THE *ONLY ONE* GOOD AT KEEPING SECRETS.

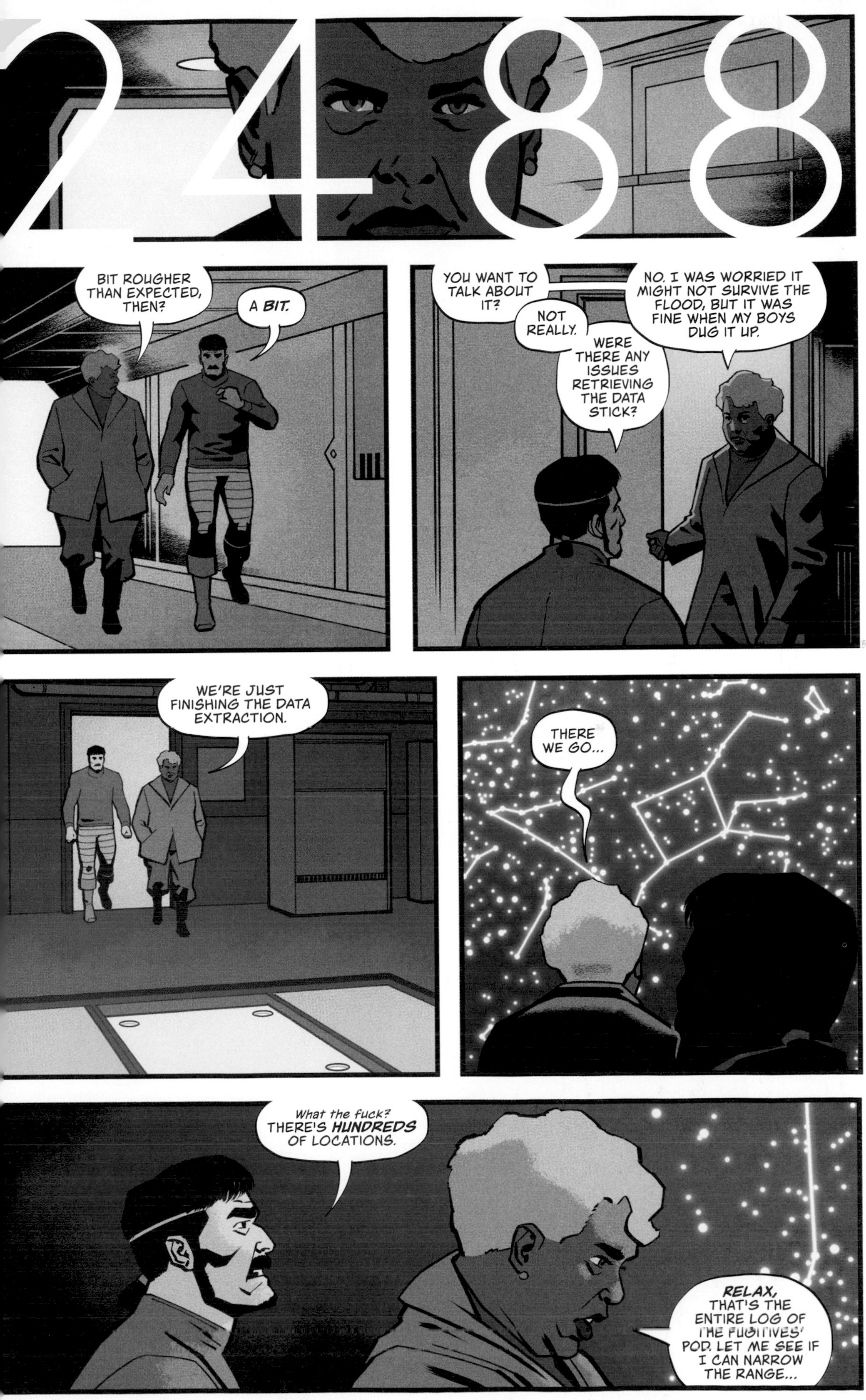
2488
BIT ROUGHER THAN EXPECTED, THEN?
A BIT.
YOU WANT TO TALK ABOUT IT?
NOT REALLY.
WERE THERE ANY ISSUES RETRIEVING THE DATA STICK?
NO. I WAS WORRIED IT MIGHT NOT SURVIVE THE FLOOD, BUT IT WAS FINE WHEN MY BOYS DUG IT UP.
WE'RE JUST FINISHING THE DATA EXTRACTION.
THERE WE GO...
What the fuck? THERE'S HUNDREDS OF LOCATIONS.
RELAX, THAT'S THE ENTIRE LOG OF THE FUGITIVES' POD. LET ME SEE IF I CAN NARROW THE RANGE...

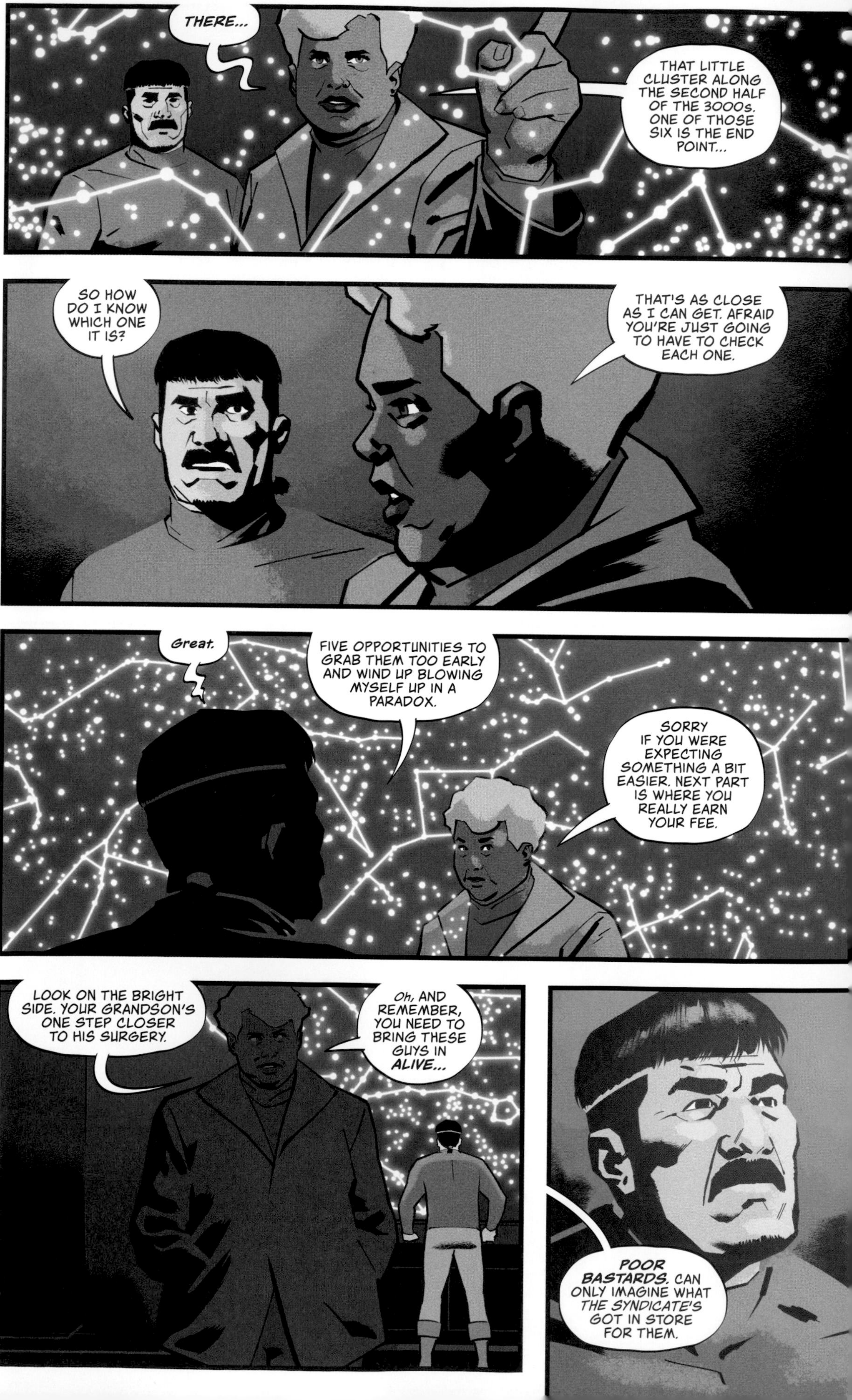
THERE...
THAT LITTLE CLUSTER ALONG THE SECOND HALF OF THE 3000s. ONE OF THOSE SIX IS THE END POINT...
SO HOW DO I KNOW WHICH ONE IT IS?
THAT'S AS CLOSE AS I CAN GET. AFRAID YOU'RE JUST GOING TO HAVE TO CHECK EACH ONE.
Great.
FIVE OPPORTUNITIES TO GRAB THEM TOO EARLY AND WIND UP BLOWING MYSELF UP IN A PARADOX.
SORRY IF YOU WERE EXPECTING SOMETHING A BIT EASIER. NEXT PART IS WHERE YOU REALLY EARN YOUR FEE.
LOOK ON THE BRIGHT SIDE. YOUR GRANDSON'S ONE STEP CLOSER TO HIS SURGERY.
Oh, AND REMEMBER, YOU NEED TO BRING THESE GUYS IN ALIVE...
POOR BASTARDS. CAN ONLY IMAGINE WHAT THE SYNDICATE'S GOT IN STORE FOR THEM.

久

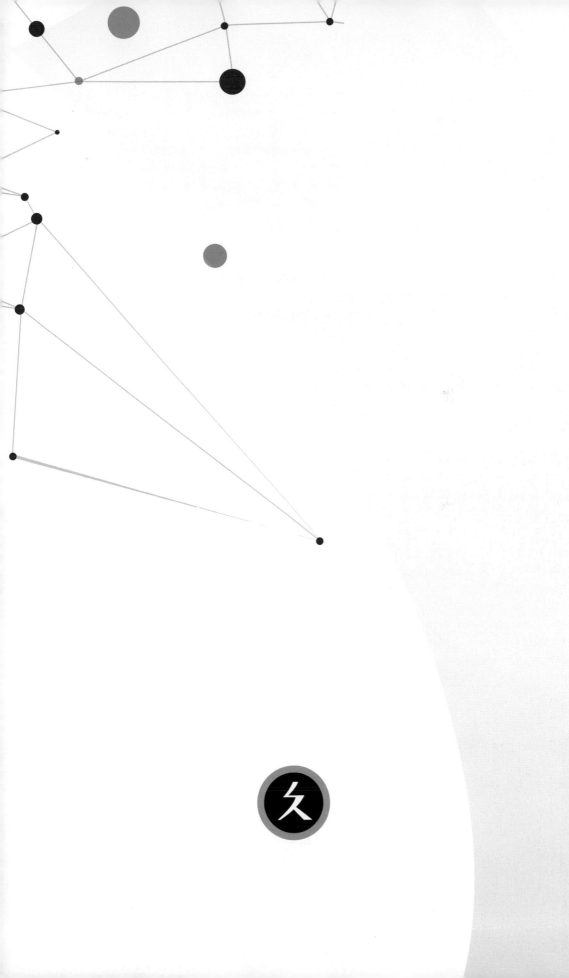

15

SECOND OPINION

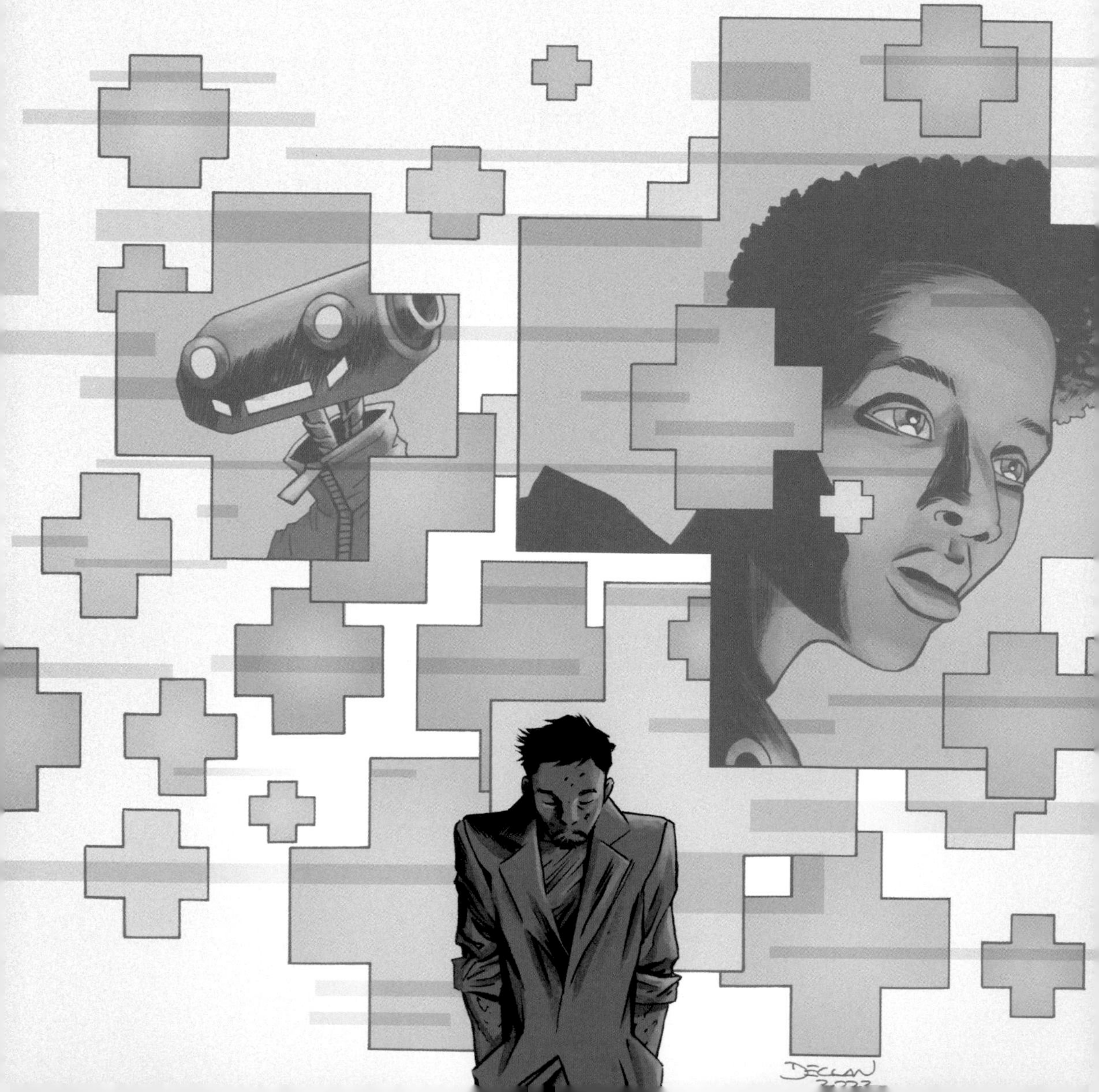

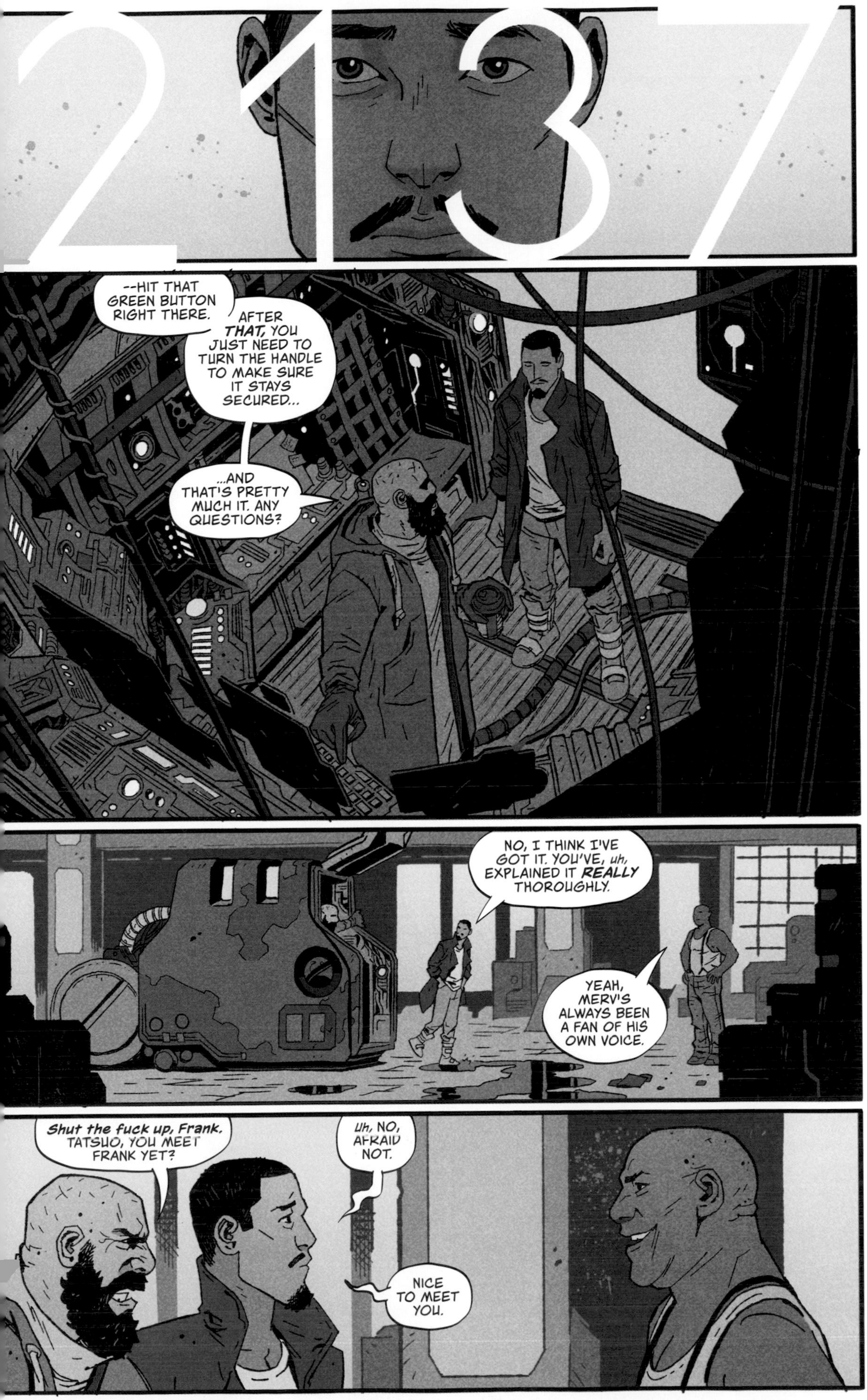
2137
--HIT THAT GREEN BUTTON RIGHT THERE.
AFTER THAT, YOU JUST NEED TO TURN THE HANDLE TO MAKE SURE IT STAYS SECURED...
...AND THAT'S PRETTY MUCH IT. ANY QUESTIONS?
NO, I THINK I'VE GOT IT. YOU'VE, uh, EXPLAINED IT REALLY THOROUGHLY.
YEAH, MERV'S ALWAYS BEEN A FAN OF HIS OWN VOICE.
Shut the fuck up, Frank. TATSUO, YOU MEET FRANK YET?
uh, NO, AFRAID NOT.
NICE TO MEET YOU.

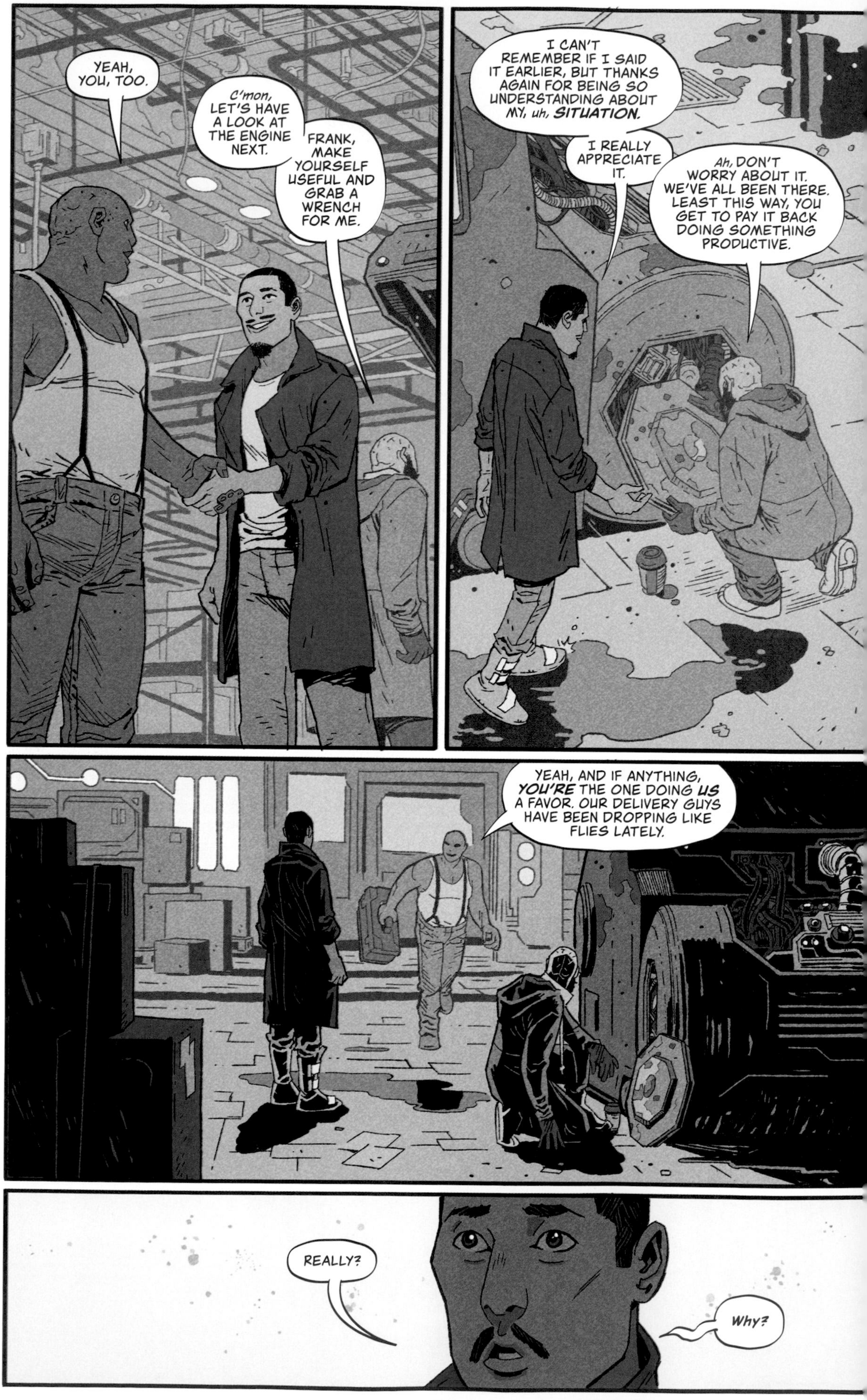
YEAH, YOU, TOO.
C'mon, LET'S HAVE A LOOK AT THE ENGINE NEXT.
FRANK, MAKE YOURSELF USEFUL AND GRAB A WRENCH FOR ME.
I CAN'T REMEMBER IF I SAID IT EARLIER, BUT THANKS AGAIN FOR BEING SO UNDERSTANDING ABOUT MY, uh, SITUATION.
I REALLY APPRECIATE IT.
Ah, DON'T WORRY ABOUT IT. WE'VE ALL BEEN THERE. LEAST THIS WAY, YOU GET TO PAY IT BACK DOING SOMETHING PRODUCTIVE.
YEAH, AND IF ANYTHING, YOU'RE THE ONE DOING US A FAVOR. OUR DELIVERY GUYS HAVE BEEN DROPPING LIKE FLIES LATELY.
REALLY?
Why?

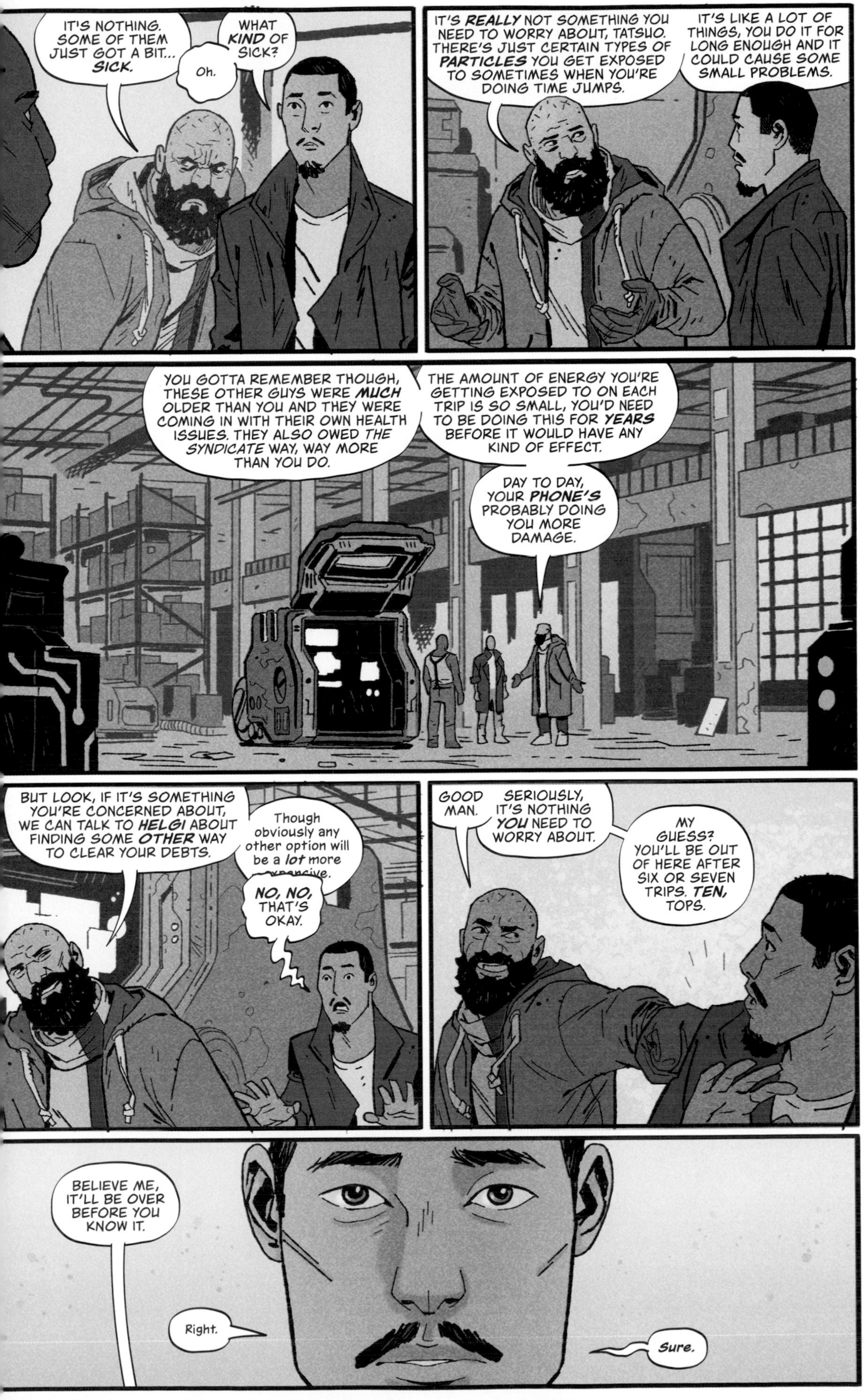
IT'S NOTHING. SOME OF THEM JUST GOT A BIT... SICK.
Oh.
WHAT KIND OF SICK?
IT'S REALLY NOT SOMETHING YOU NEED TO WORRY ABOUT, TATSUO. THERE'S JUST CERTAIN TYPES OF PARTICLES YOU GET EXPOSED TO SOMETIMES WHEN YOU'RE DOING TIME JUMPS.
IT'S LIKE A LOT OF THINGS, YOU DO IT FOR LONG ENOUGH AND IT COULD CAUSE SOME SMALL PROBLEMS.
YOU GOTTA REMEMBER THOUGH, THESE OTHER GUYS WERE MUCH OLDER THAN YOU AND THEY WERE COMING IN WITH THEIR OWN HEALTH ISSUES. THEY ALSO OWED THE SYNDICATE WAY, WAY MORE THAN YOU DO.
THE AMOUNT OF ENERGY YOU'RE GETTING EXPOSED TO ON EACH TRIP IS SO SMALL, YOU'D NEED TO BE DOING THIS FOR YEARS BEFORE IT WOULD HAVE ANY KIND OF EFFECT.
DAY TO DAY, YOUR PHONE'S PROBABLY DOING YOU MORE DAMAGE.
BUT LOOK, IF IT'S SOMETHING YOU'RE CONCERNED ABOUT, WE CAN TALK TO HELGI ABOUT FINDING SOME OTHER WAY TO CLEAR YOUR DEBTS.
Though obviously any other option will be a lot more
NO, NO, THAT'S OKAY.
GOOD MAN.
SERIOUSLY, IT'S NOTHING YOU NEED TO WORRY ABOUT.
MY GUESS? YOU'LL BE OUT OF HERE AFTER SIX OR SEVEN TRIPS. TEN, TOPS.
BELIEVE ME, IT'LL BE OVER BEFORE YOU KNOW IT.
Right.
Sure.

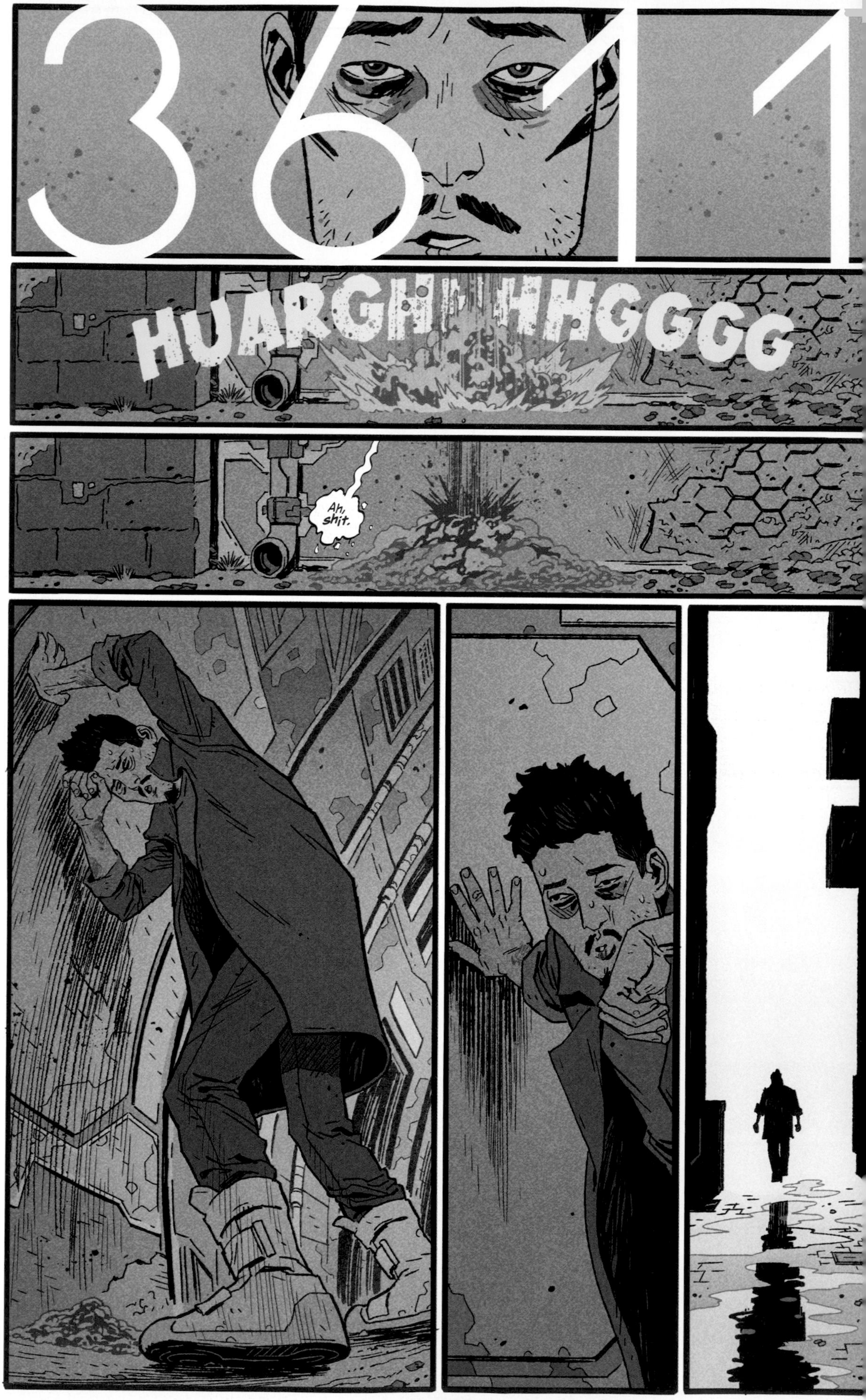

3611
HUARGHHHHGGGGG
Ah, shit.

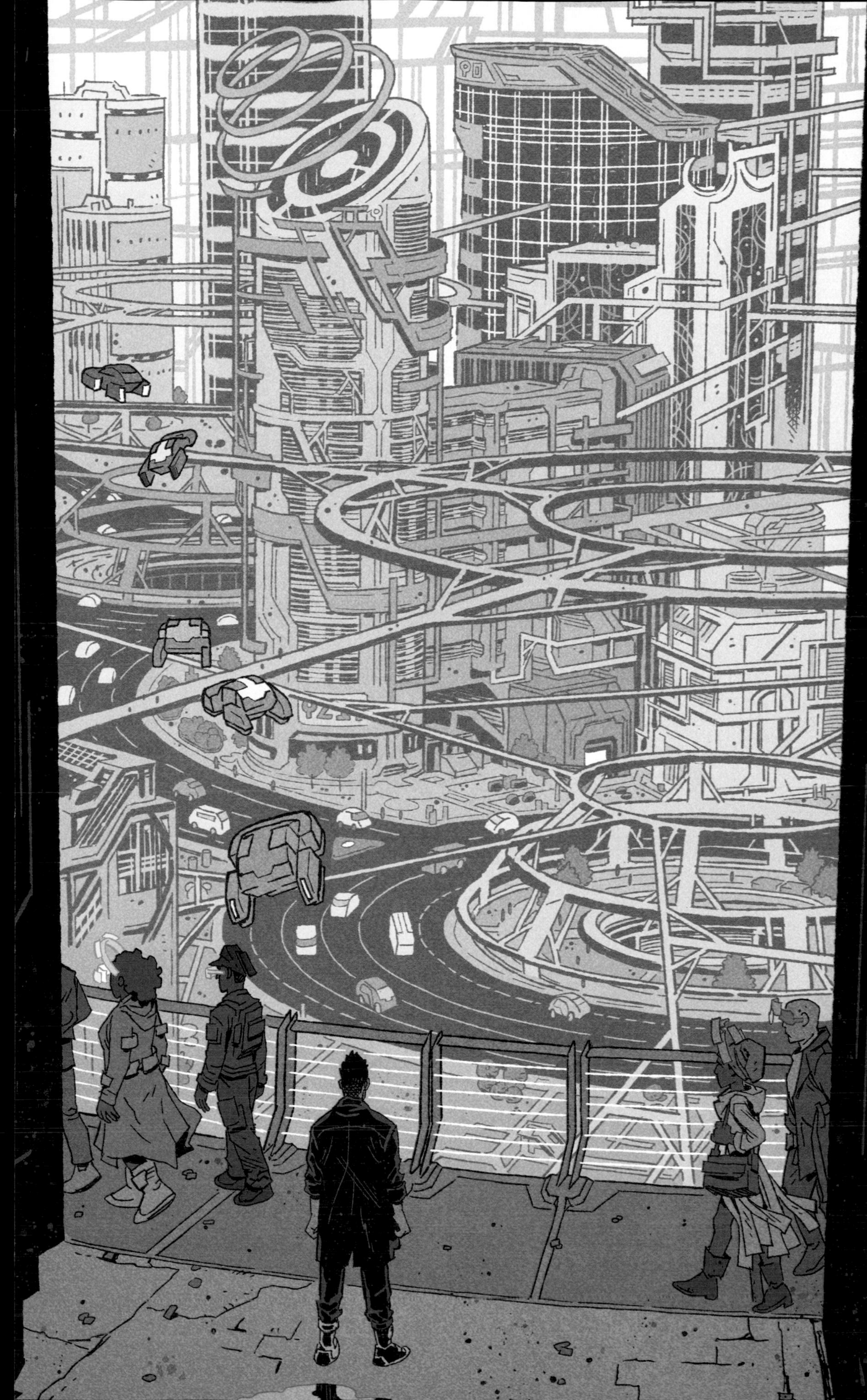

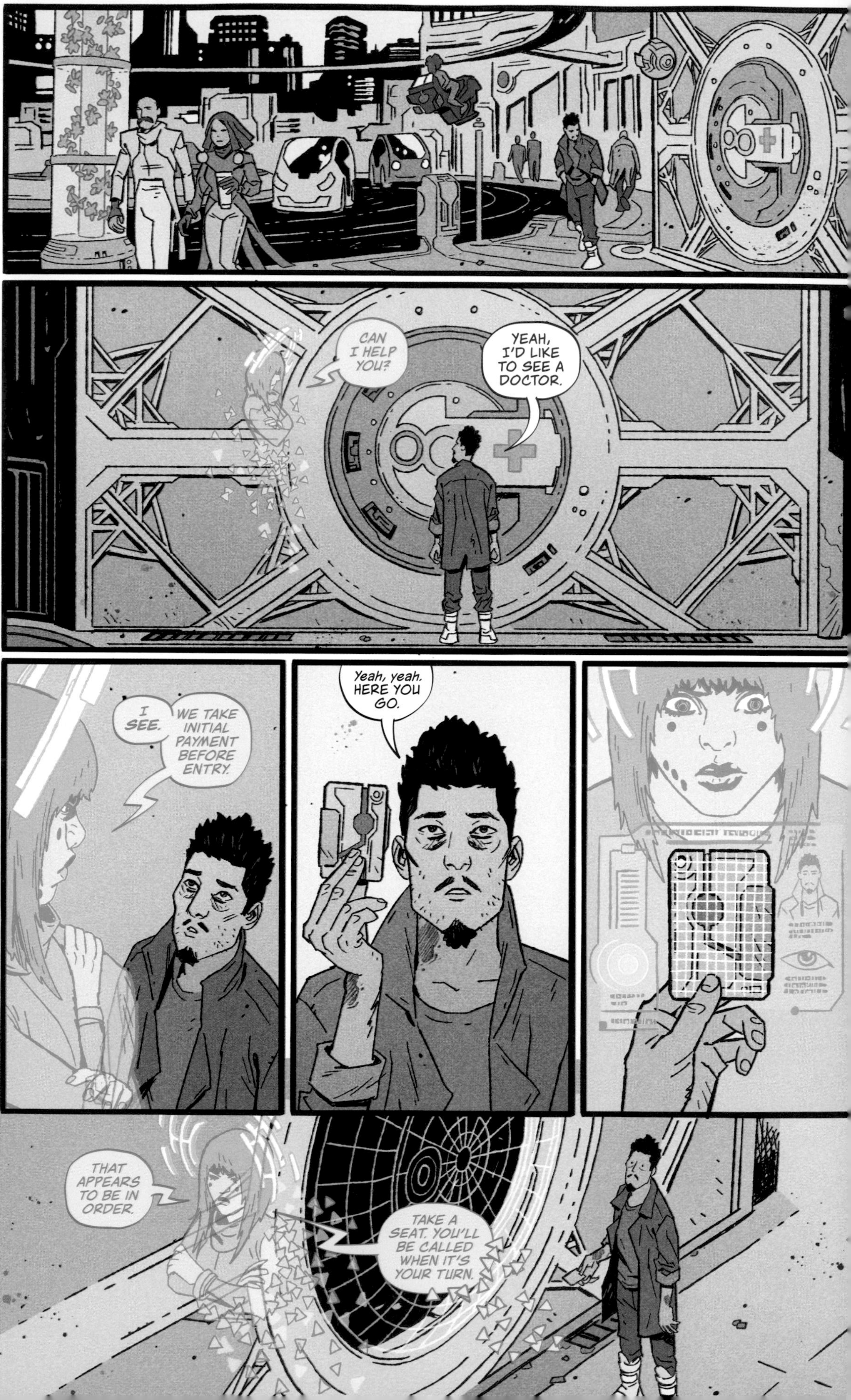
CAN I HELP YOU?
YEAH, I'D LIKE TO SEE A DOCTOR.
I SEE.
WE TAKE INITIAL PAYMENT BEFORE ENTRY.
Yeah, yeah. HERE YOU GO.
THAT APPEARS TO BE IN ORDER.
TAKE A SEAT. YOU'LL BE CALLED WHEN IT'S YOUR TURN.

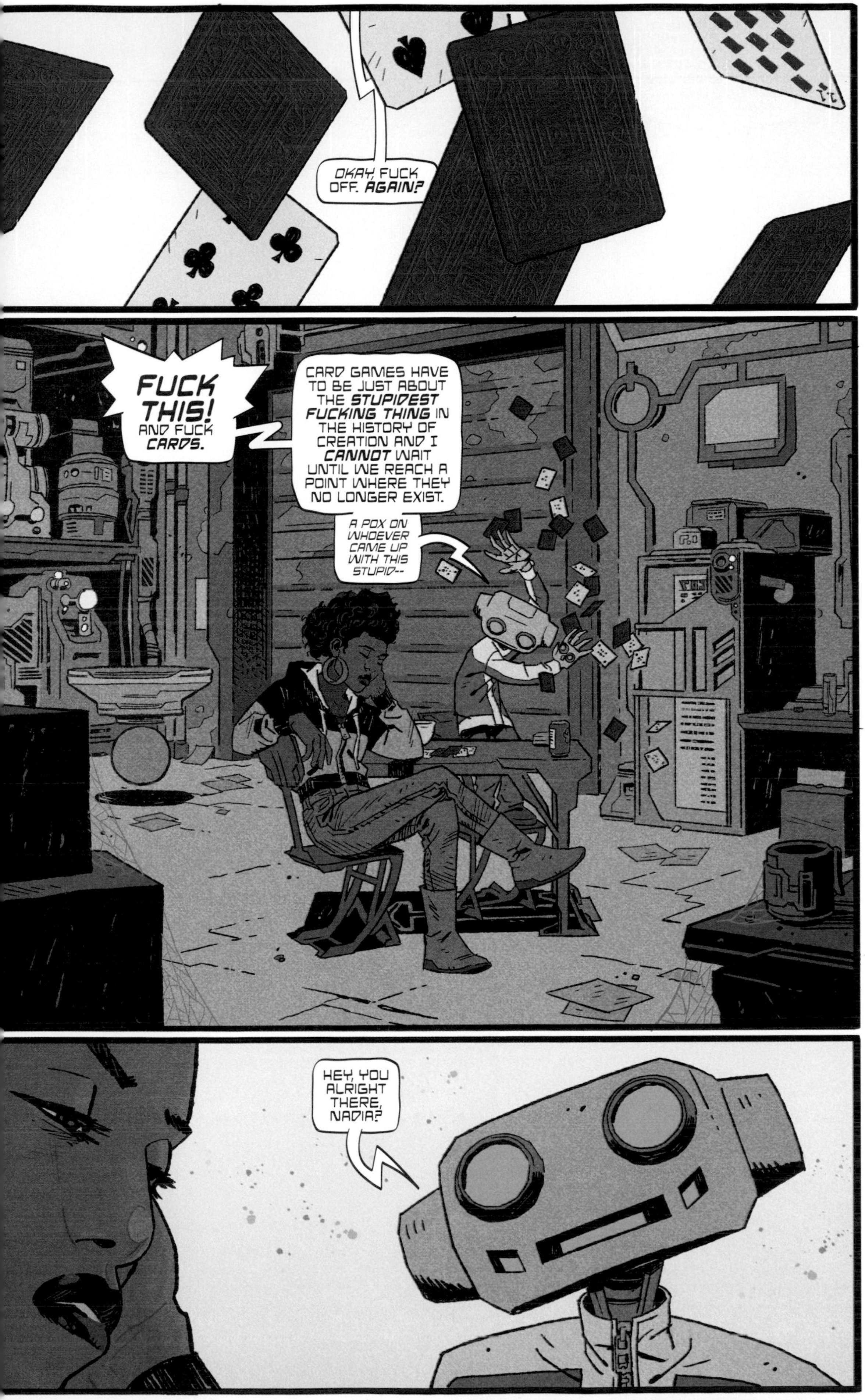
OKAY, FUCK OFF. AGAIN?
FUCK THIS! AND FUCK CARDS.
CARD GAMES HAVE TO BE JUST ABOUT THE STUPIDEST FUCKING THING IN THE HISTORY OF CREATION AND I CANNOT WAIT UNTIL WE REACH A POINT WHERE THEY NO LONGER EXIST.
A POX ON WHOEVER CAME UP WITH THIS STUPID--
HEY, YOU ALRIGHT THERE, NADIA?

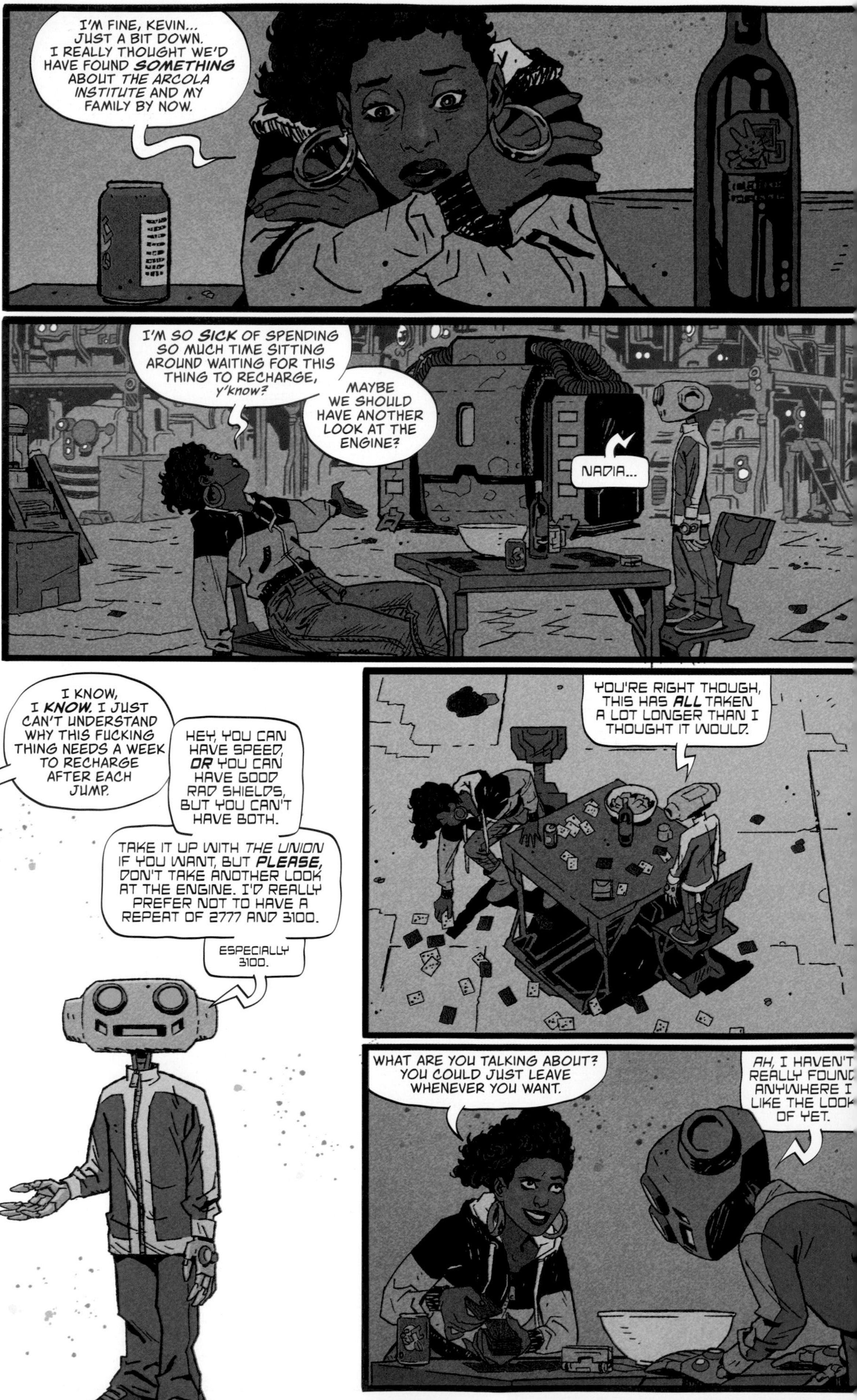
I'M FINE, KEVIN... JUST A BIT DOWN. I REALLY THOUGHT WE'D HAVE FOUND SOMETHING ABOUT THE ARCOLA INSTITUTE AND MY FAMILY BY NOW.
I'M SO SICK OF SPENDING SO MUCH TIME SITTING AROUND WAITING FOR THIS THING TO RECHARGE, y'know?
MAYBE WE SHOULD HAVE ANOTHER LOOK AT THE ENGINE?
NADIA...
I KNOW, I KNOW. I JUST CAN'T UNDERSTAND WHY THIS FUCKING THING NEEDS A WEEK TO RECHARGE AFTER EACH JUMP.
HEY, YOU CAN HAVE SPEED, OR YOU CAN HAVE GOOD RAD SHIELDS, BUT YOU CAN'T HAVE BOTH.
TAKE IT UP WITH THE UNION IF YOU WANT, BUT PLEASE, DON'T TAKE ANOTHER LOOK AT THE ENGINE. I'D REALLY PREFER NOT TO HAVE A REPEAT OF 2777 AND 3100.
ESPECIALLY 3100.
YOU'RE RIGHT THOUGH, THIS HAS ALL TAKEN A LOT LONGER THAN I THOUGHT IT WOULD.
WHAT ARE YOU TALKING ABOUT? YOU COULD JUST LEAVE WHENEVER YOU WANT.
AH, I HAVEN'T REALLY FOUND ANYWHERE I LIKE THE LOOK OF YET.

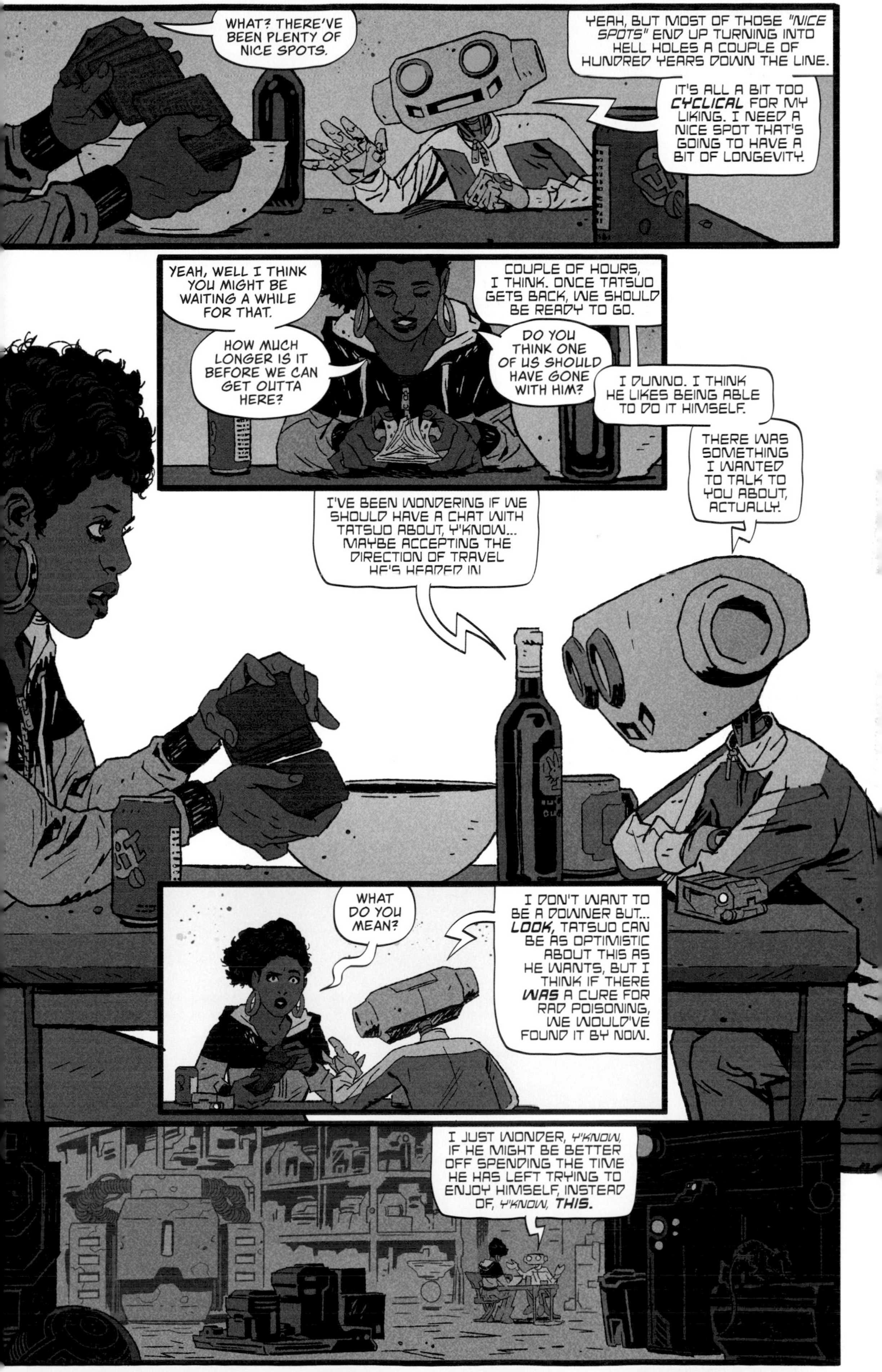
WHAT? THERE'VE BEEN PLENTY OF NICE SPOTS.
YEAH, BUT MOST OF THOSE "NICE SPOTS" END UP TURNING INTO HELL HOLES A COUPLE OF HUNDRED YEARS DOWN THE LINE.
IT'S ALL A BIT TOO CYCLICAL FOR MY LIKING. I NEED A NICE SPOT THAT'S GOING TO HAVE A BIT OF LONGEVITY.
YEAH, WELL I THINK YOU MIGHT BE WAITING A WHILE FOR THAT.
HOW MUCH LONGER IS IT BEFORE WE CAN GET OUTTA HERE?
COUPLE OF HOURS, I THINK. ONCE TATSUO GETS BACK, WE SHOULD BE READY TO GO.
DO YOU THINK ONE OF US SHOULD HAVE GONE WITH HIM?
I DUNNO. I THINK HE LIKES BEING ABLE TO DO IT HIMSELF.
THERE WAS SOMETHING I WANTED TO TALK TO YOU ABOUT, ACTUALLY.
I'VE BEEN WONDERING IF WE SHOULD HAVE A CHAT WITH TATSUO ABOUT, Y'KNOW... MAYBE ACCEPTING THE DIRECTION OF TRAVEL HE'S HEADED IN.
WHAT DO YOU MEAN?
I DON'T WANT TO BE A DOWNER BUT... LOOK, TATSUO CAN BE AS OPTIMISTIC ABOUT THIS AS HE WANTS, BUT I THINK IF THERE WAS A CURE FOR RAD POISONING, WE WOULD'VE FOUND IT BY NOW.
I JUST WONDER, Y'KNOW, IF HE MIGHT BE BETTER OFF SPENDING THE TIME HE HAS LEFT TRYING TO ENJOY HIMSELF, INSTEAD OF, Y'KNOW, THIS.

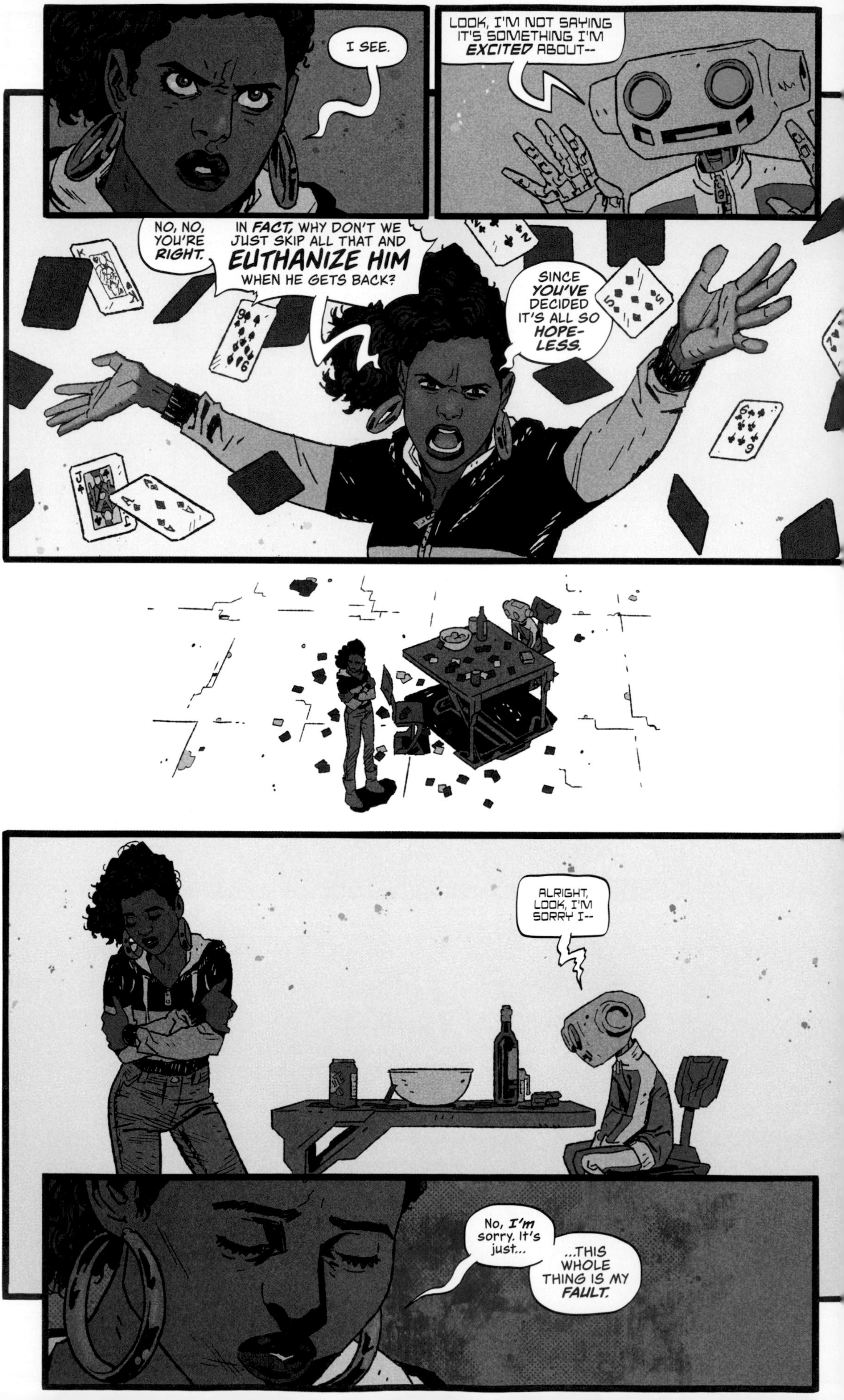

I SEE.
LOOK, I'M NOT SAYING IT'S SOMETHING I'M EXCITED ABOUT--
NO, NO, YOU'RE RIGHT.
IN FACT, WHY DON'T WE JUST SKIP ALL THAT AND EUTHANIZE HIM WHEN HE GETS BACK?
SINCE YOU'VE DECIDED IT'S ALL SO HOPELESS.
ALRIGHT, LOOK, I'M SORRY I--
No, I'm sorry. It's just...
...THIS WHOLE THING IS MY FAULT.

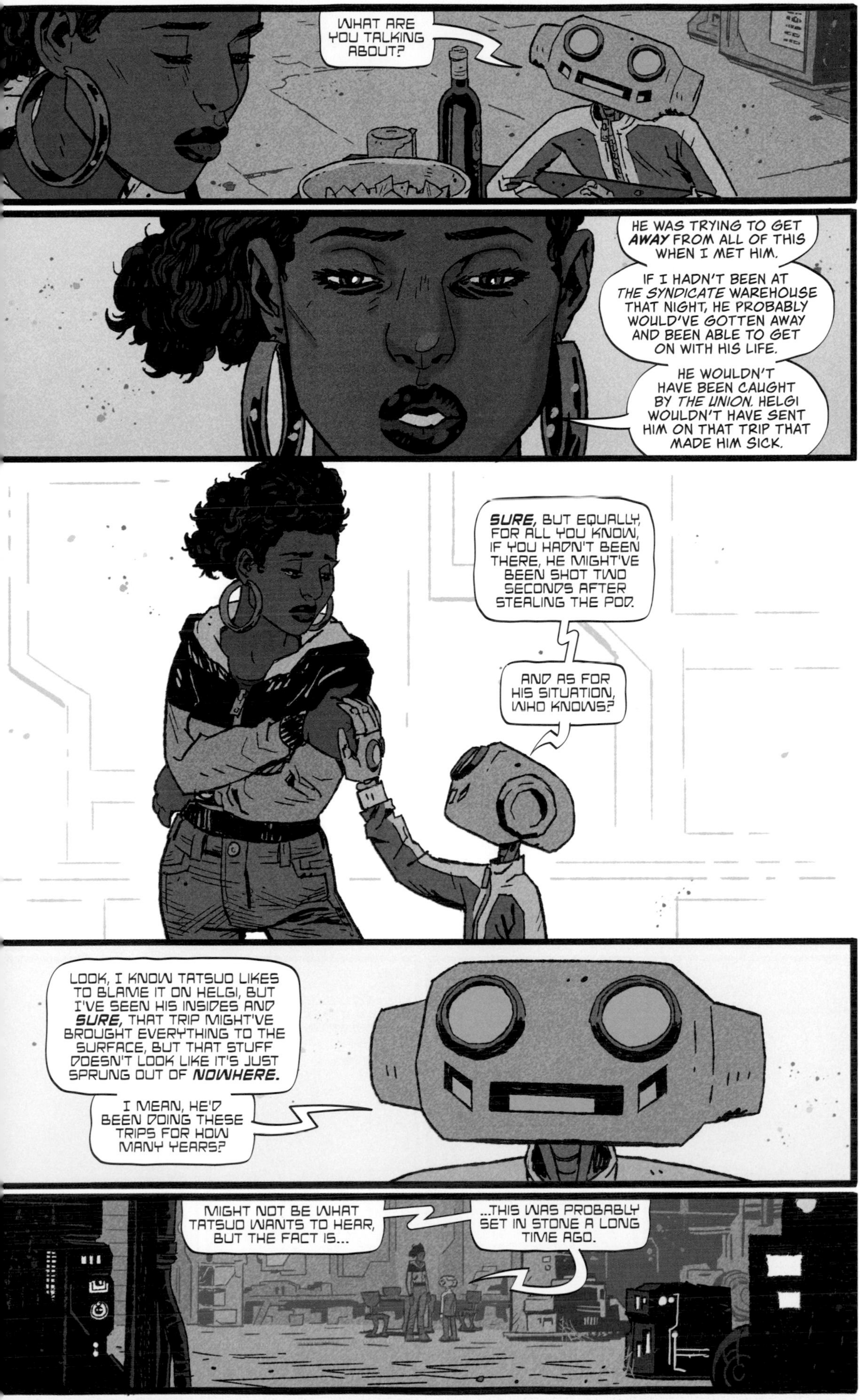
WHAT ARE YOU TALKING ABOUT?
HE WAS TRYING TO GET *AWAY* FROM ALL OF THIS WHEN I MET HIM.
IF I HADN'T BEEN AT *THE SYNDICATE* WAREHOUSE THAT NIGHT, HE PROBABLY WOULD'VE GOTTEN AWAY AND BEEN ABLE TO GET ON WITH HIS LIFE.
HE WOULDN'T HAVE BEEN CAUGHT BY *THE UNION*. HELGI WOULDN'T HAVE SENT HIM ON THAT TRIP THAT MADE HIM SICK.
SURE, BUT EQUALLY, FOR ALL YOU KNOW, IF YOU HADN'T BEEN THERE, HE MIGHT'VE BEEN SHOT TWO SECONDS AFTER STEALING THE POD.
AND AS FOR HIS SITUATION, WHO KNOWS?
LOOK, I KNOW TATSUO LIKES TO BLAME IT ON HELGI, BUT I'VE SEEN HIS INSIDES AND **SURE,** THAT TRIP MIGHT'VE BROUGHT EVERYTHING TO THE SURFACE, BUT THAT STUFF DOESN'T LOOK LIKE IT'S JUST SPRUNG OUT OF **NOWHERE.**
I MEAN, HE'D BEEN DOING THESE TRIPS FOR HOW MANY YEARS?
MIGHT NOT BE WHAT TATSUO WANTS TO HEAR, BUT THE FACT IS...
...THIS WAS PROBABLY SET IN STONE A LONG TIME AGO.

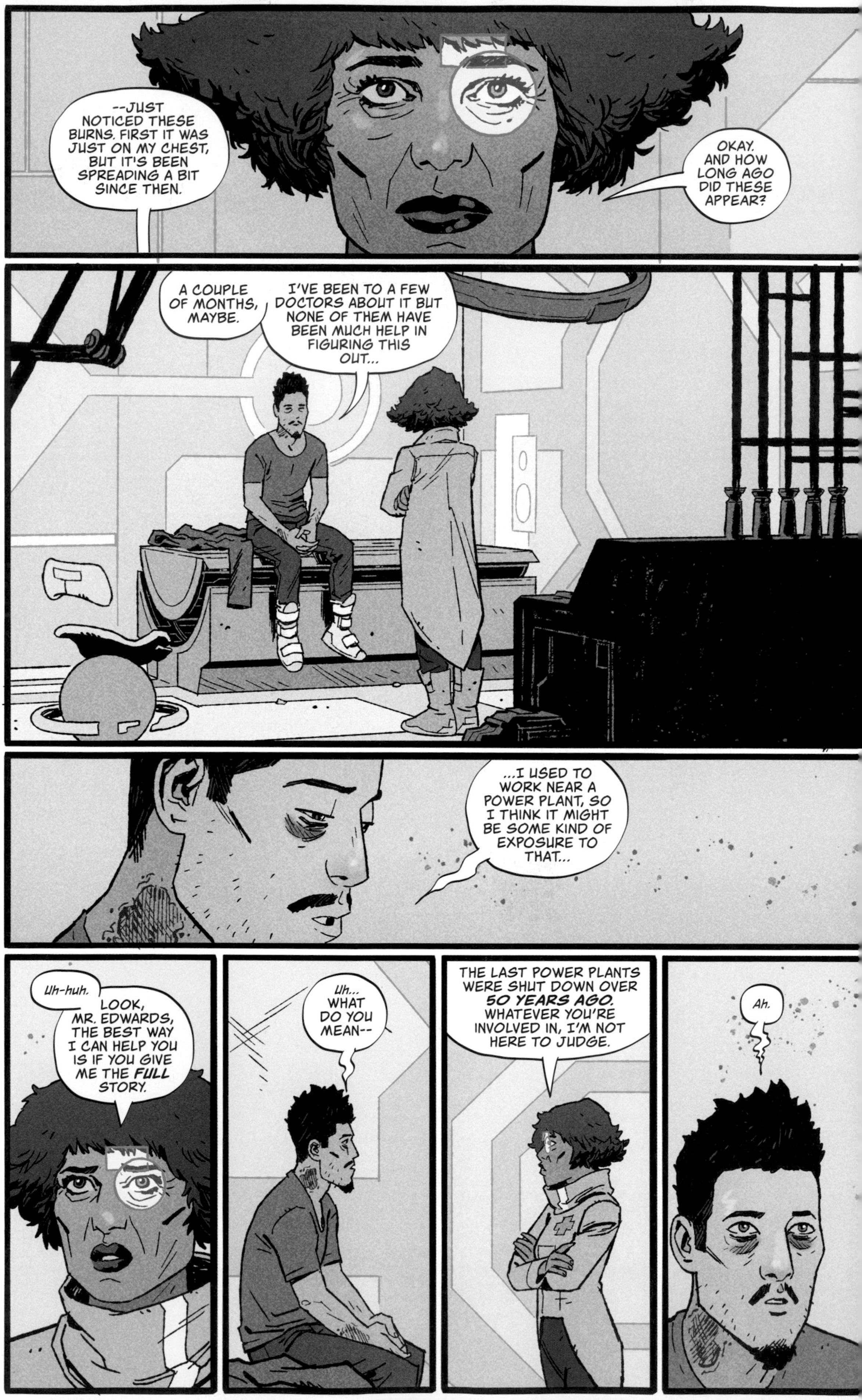
--JUST NOTICED THESE BURNS. FIRST IT WAS JUST ON MY CHEST, BUT IT'S BEEN SPREADING A BIT SINCE THEN.
OKAY. AND HOW LONG AGO DID THESE APPEAR?
A COUPLE OF MONTHS, MAYBE.
I'VE BEEN TO A FEW DOCTORS ABOUT IT BUT NONE OF THEM HAVE BEEN MUCH HELP IN FIGURING THIS OUT...
...I USED TO WORK NEAR A POWER PLANT, SO I THINK IT MIGHT BE SOME KIND OF EXPOSURE TO THAT...
Uh-huh.
LOOK, MR. EDWARDS, THE BEST WAY I CAN HELP YOU IS IF YOU GIVE ME THE ***FULL*** STORY.
Uh... WHAT DO YOU MEAN--
THE LAST POWER PLANTS WERE SHUT DOWN OVER ***50 YEARS AGO.*** WHATEVER YOU'RE INVOLVED IN, I'M NOT HERE TO JUDGE.
Ah.

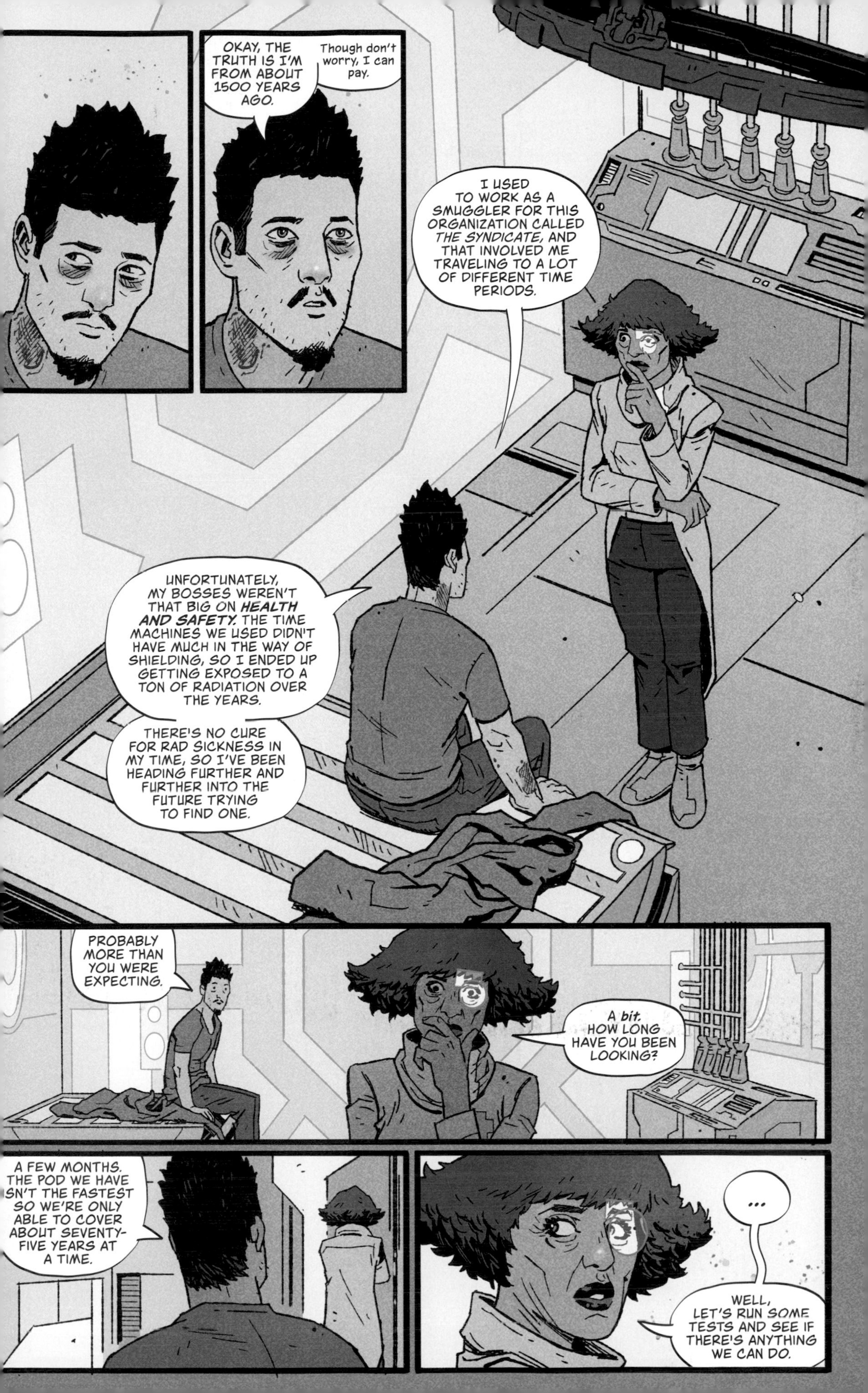
OKAY, THE TRUTH IS I'M FROM ABOUT 1500 YEARS AGO.
Though don't worry, I can pay.
I USED TO WORK AS A SMUGGLER FOR THIS ORGANIZATION CALLED *THE SYNDICATE*, AND THAT INVOLVED ME TRAVELING TO A LOT OF DIFFERENT TIME PERIODS.
UNFORTUNATELY, MY BOSSES WEREN'T THAT BIG ON ***HEALTH AND SAFETY.*** THE TIME MACHINES WE USED DIDN'T HAVE MUCH IN THE WAY OF SHIELDING, SO I ENDED UP GETTING EXPOSED TO A TON OF RADIATION OVER THE YEARS.
THERE'S NO CURE FOR RAD SICKNESS IN MY TIME, SO I'VE BEEN HEADING FURTHER AND FURTHER INTO THE FUTURE TRYING TO FIND ONE.
PROBABLY MORE THAN YOU WERE EXPECTING.
A *bit.* HOW LONG HAVE YOU BEEN LOOKING?
A FEW MONTHS. THE POD WE HAVE ISN'T THE FASTEST SO WE'RE ONLY ABLE TO COVER ABOUT SEVENTY-FIVE YEARS AT A TIME.
...
WELL, LET'S RUN SOME TESTS AND SEE IF THERE'S ANYTHING WE CAN DO.

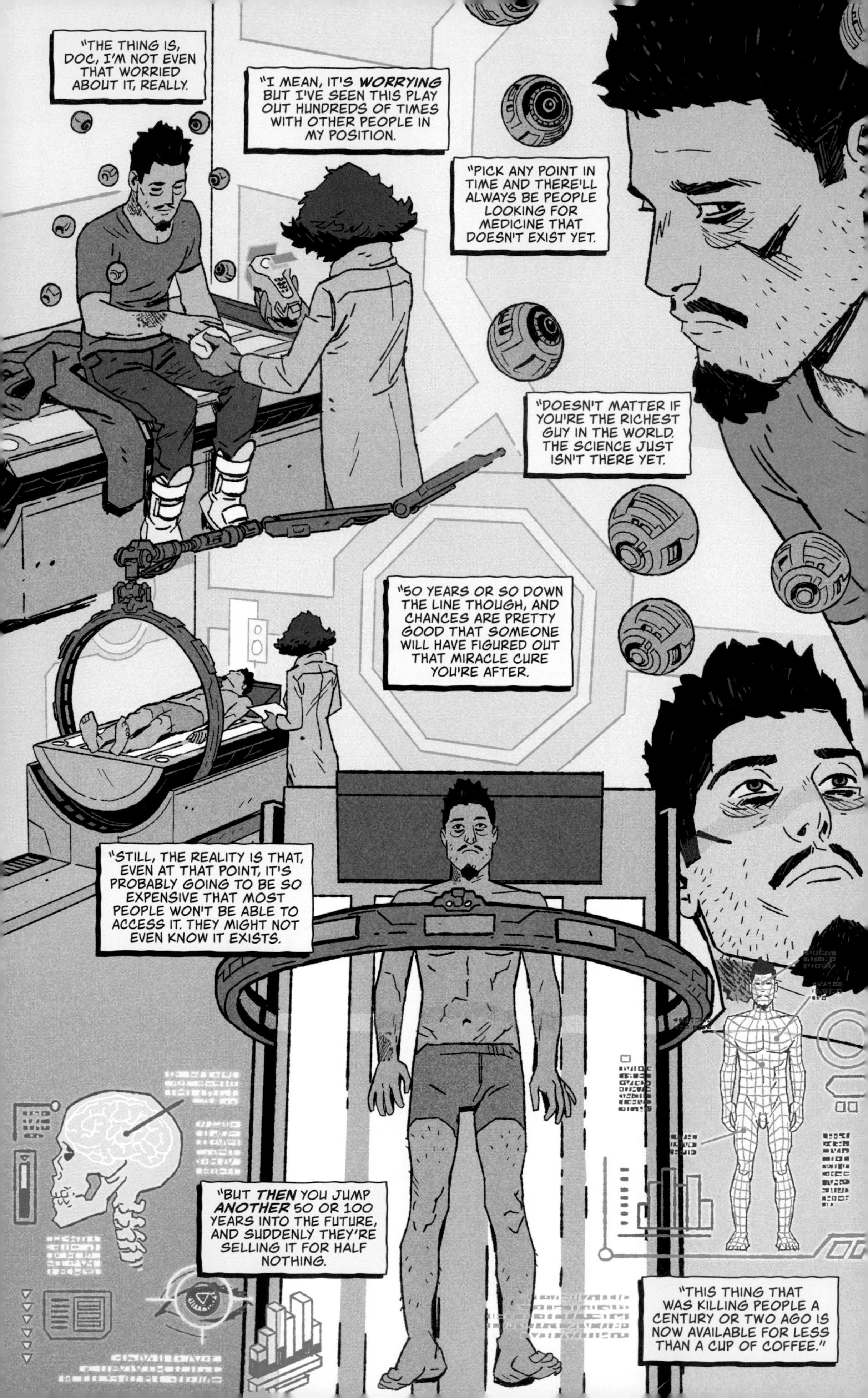
"THE THING IS, DOC, I'M NOT EVEN THAT WORRIED ABOUT IT, REALLY.
"I MEAN, IT'S WORRYING BUT I'VE SEEN THIS PLAY OUT HUNDREDS OF TIMES WITH OTHER PEOPLE IN MY POSITION.
"PICK ANY POINT IN TIME AND THERE'LL ALWAYS BE PEOPLE LOOKING FOR MEDICINE THAT DOESN'T EXIST YET.
"DOESN'T MATTER IF YOU'RE THE RICHEST GUY IN THE WORLD. THE SCIENCE JUST ISN'T THERE YET.
"50 YEARS OR SO DOWN THE LINE THOUGH, AND CHANCES ARE PRETTY GOOD THAT SOMEONE WILL HAVE FIGURED OUT THAT MIRACLE CURE YOU'RE AFTER.
"STILL, THE REALITY IS THAT, EVEN AT THAT POINT, IT'S PROBABLY GOING TO BE SO EXPENSIVE THAT MOST PEOPLE WON'T BE ABLE TO ACCESS IT. THEY MIGHT NOT EVEN KNOW IT EXISTS.
"BUT THEN YOU JUMP ANOTHER 50 OR 100 YEARS INTO THE FUTURE, AND SUDDENLY THEY'RE SELLING IT FOR HALF NOTHING.
"THIS THING THAT WAS KILLING PEOPLE A CENTURY OR TWO AGO IS NOW AVAILABLE FOR LESS THAN A CUP OF COFFEE."

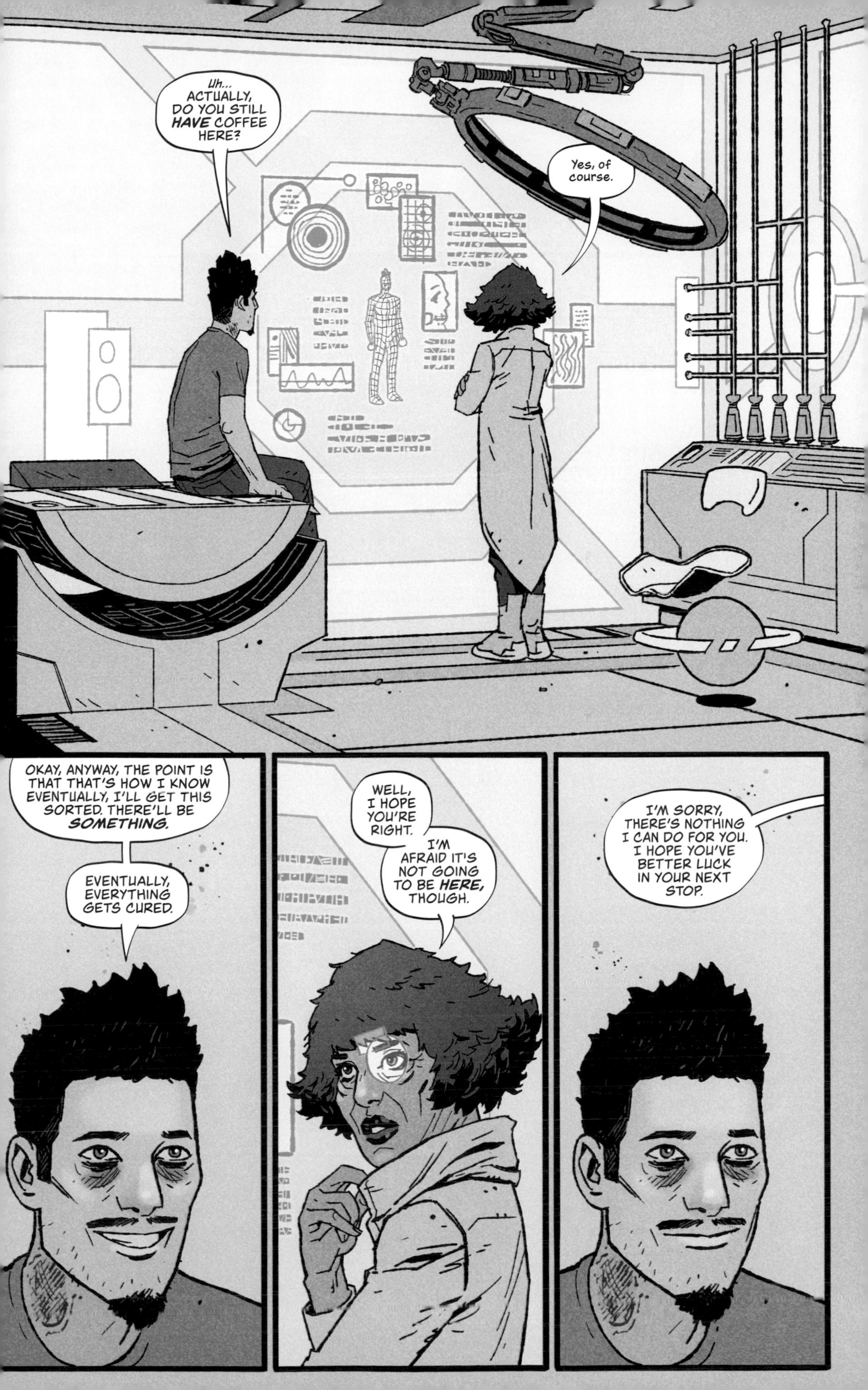
Uh... ACTUALLY, DO YOU STILL HAVE COFFEE HERE?
Yes, of course.
OKAY, ANYWAY, THE POINT IS THAT THAT'S HOW I KNOW EVENTUALLY, I'LL GET THIS SORTED. THERE'LL BE SOMETHING.
EVENTUALLY, EVERYTHING GETS CURED.
WELL, I HOPE YOU'RE RIGHT.
I'M AFRAID IT'S NOT GOING TO BE HERE, THOUGH.
I'M SORRY, THERE'S NOTHING I CAN DO FOR YOU. I HOPE YOU'VE BETTER LUCK IN YOUR NEXT STOP.

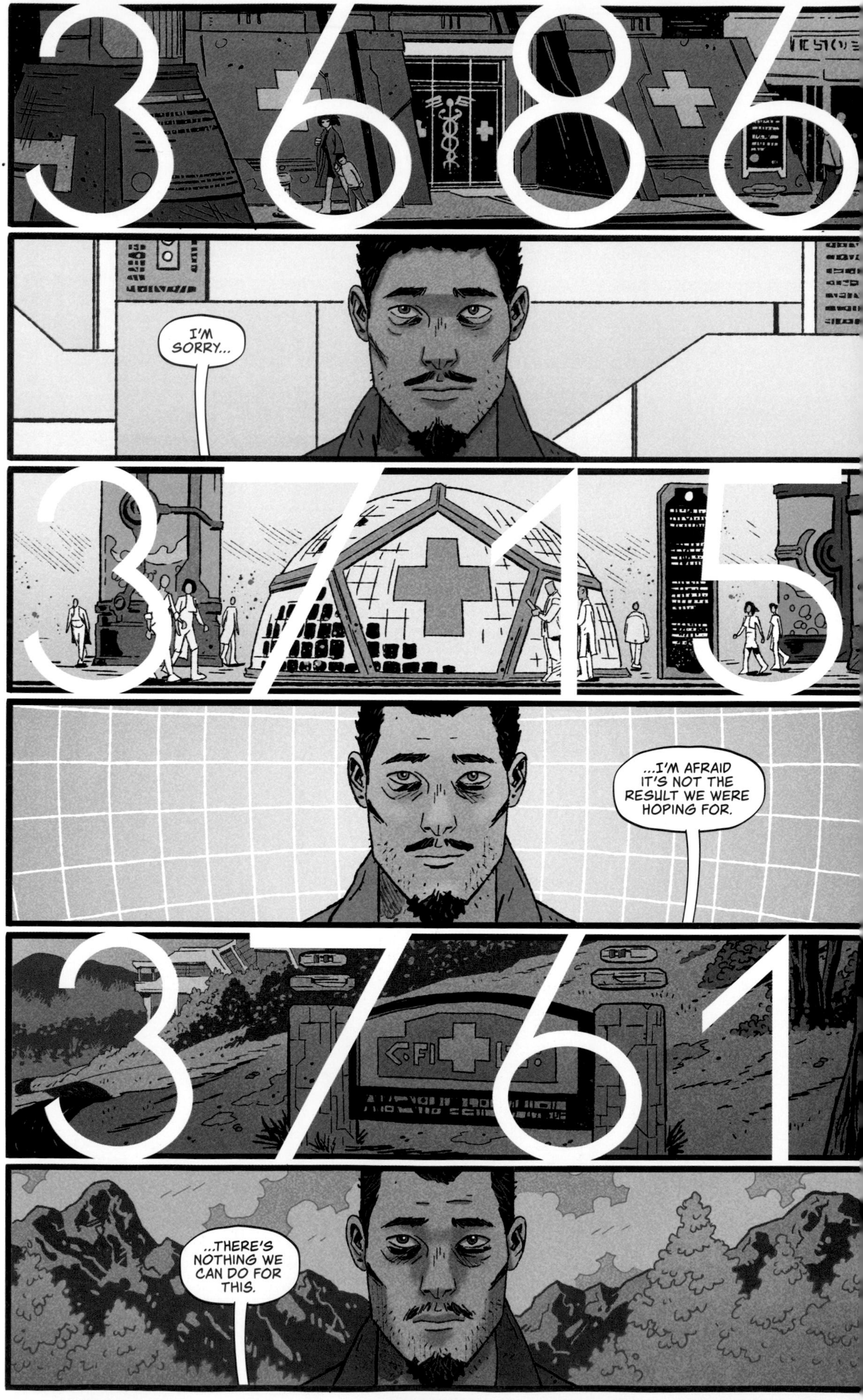
3686
I'M SORRY...
3715
...I'M AFRAID IT'S NOT THE RESULT WE WERE HOPING FOR.
3761
...THERE'S NOTHING WE CAN DO FOR THIS.

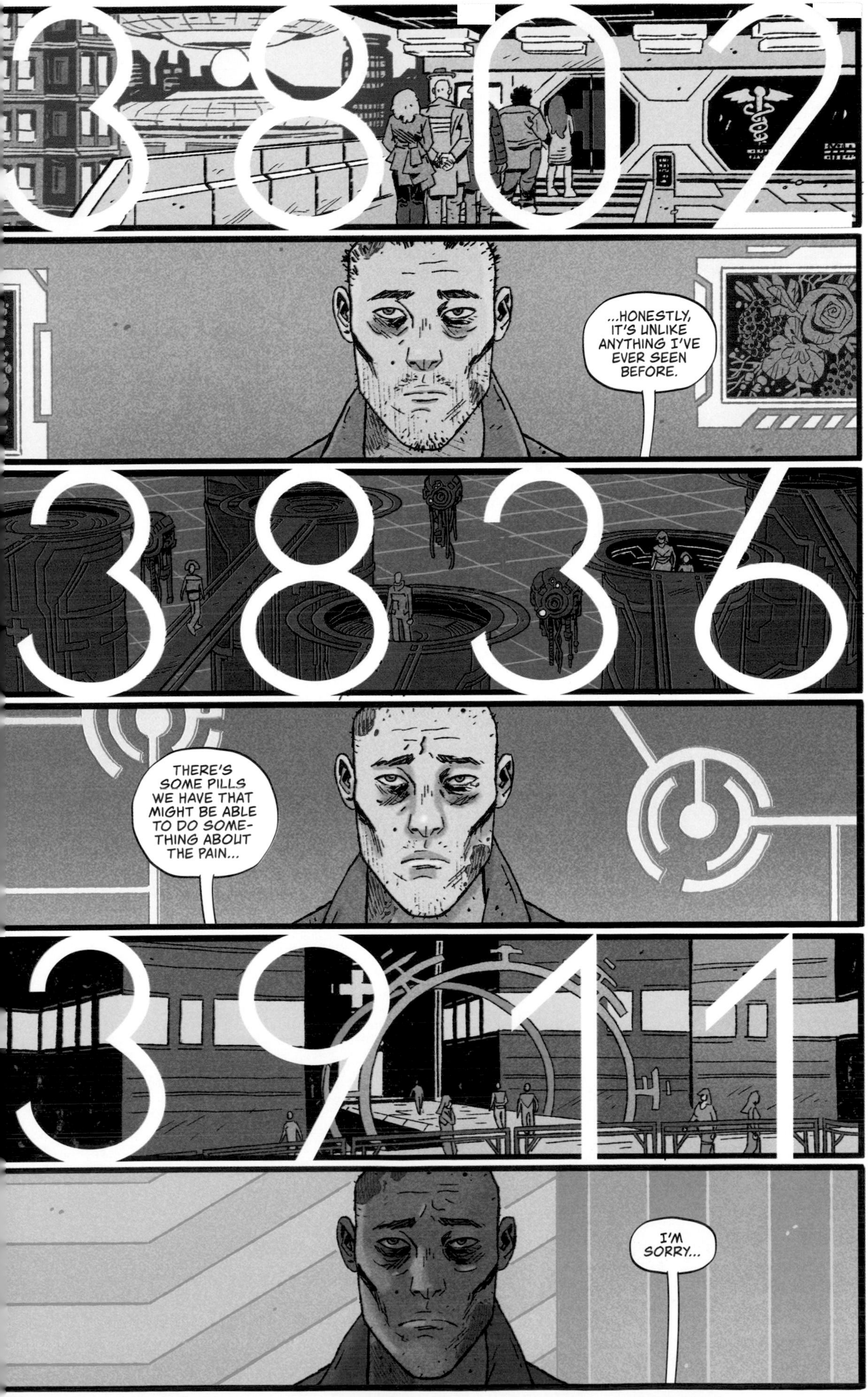
3802
...HONESTLY, IT'S UNLIKE ANYTHING I'VE EVER SEEN BEFORE.
3836
THERE'S SOME PILLS WE HAVE THAT MIGHT BE ABLE TO DO SOME-THING ABOUT THE PAIN...
3911
I'M SORRY...

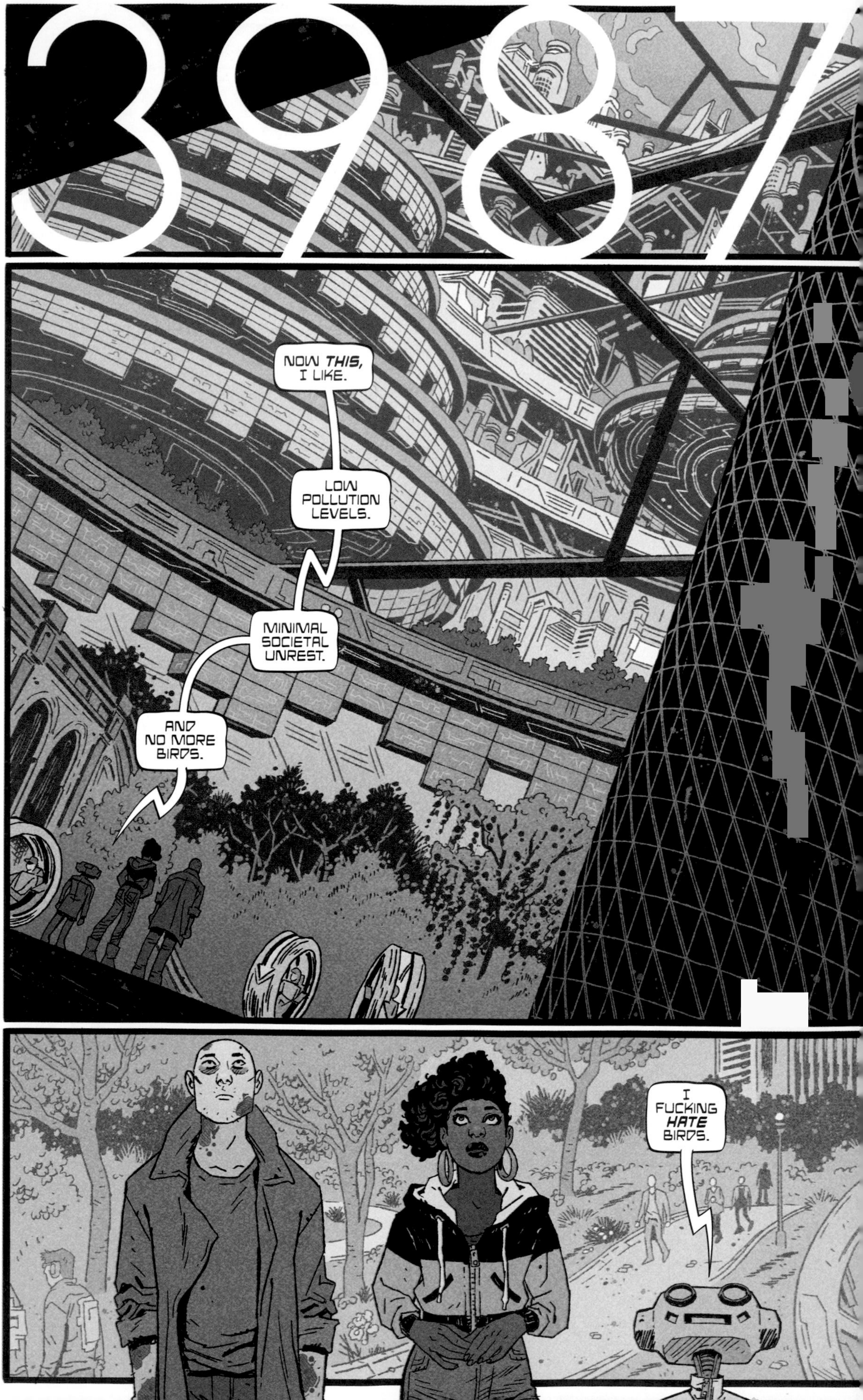
3987
NOW THIS, I LIKE.
LOW POLLUTION LEVELS.
MINIMAL SOCIETAL UNREST.
AND NO MORE BIRDS.
I FUCKING HATE BIRDS.

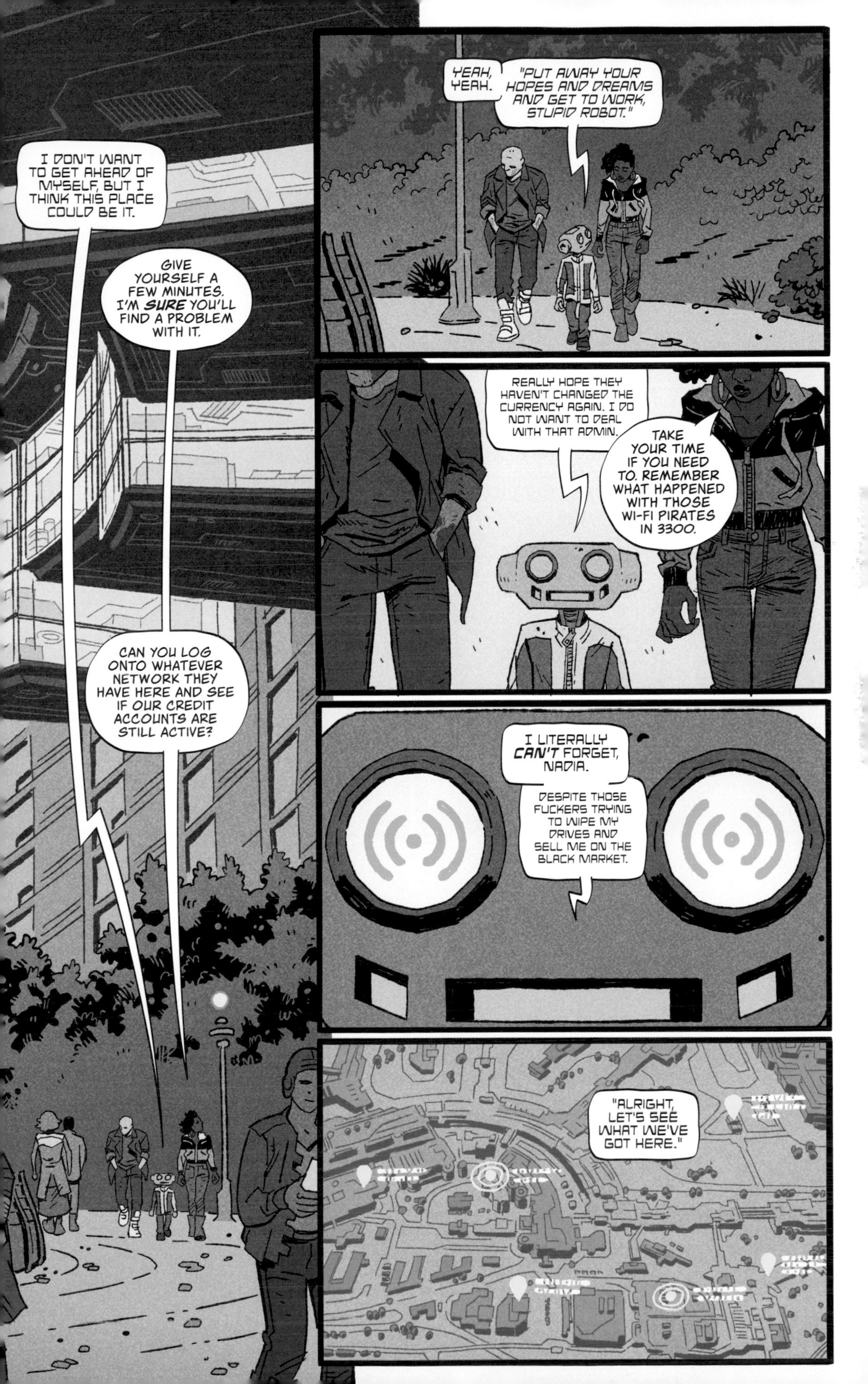
I DON'T WANT TO GET AHEAD OF MYSELF, BUT I THINK THIS PLACE COULD BE IT.
GIVE YOURSELF A FEW MINUTES. I'M SURE YOU'LL FIND A PROBLEM WITH IT.
CAN YOU LOG ONTO WHATEVER NETWORK THEY HAVE HERE AND SEE IF OUR CREDIT ACCOUNTS ARE STILL ACTIVE?
YEAH, YEAH.
"PUT AWAY YOUR HOPES AND DREAMS AND GET TO WORK, STUPID ROBOT."
REALLY HOPE THEY HAVEN'T CHANGED THE CURRENCY AGAIN. I DO NOT WANT TO DEAL WITH THAT ADMIN.
TAKE YOUR TIME IF YOU NEED TO. REMEMBER WHAT HAPPENED WITH THOSE WI-FI PIRATES IN 3300.
I LITERALLY CAN'T FORGET, NADIA.
DESPITE THOSE FUCKERS TRYING TO WIPE MY DRIVES AND SELL ME ON THE BLACK MARKET.
"ALRIGHT, LET'S SEE WHAT WE'VE GOT HERE."

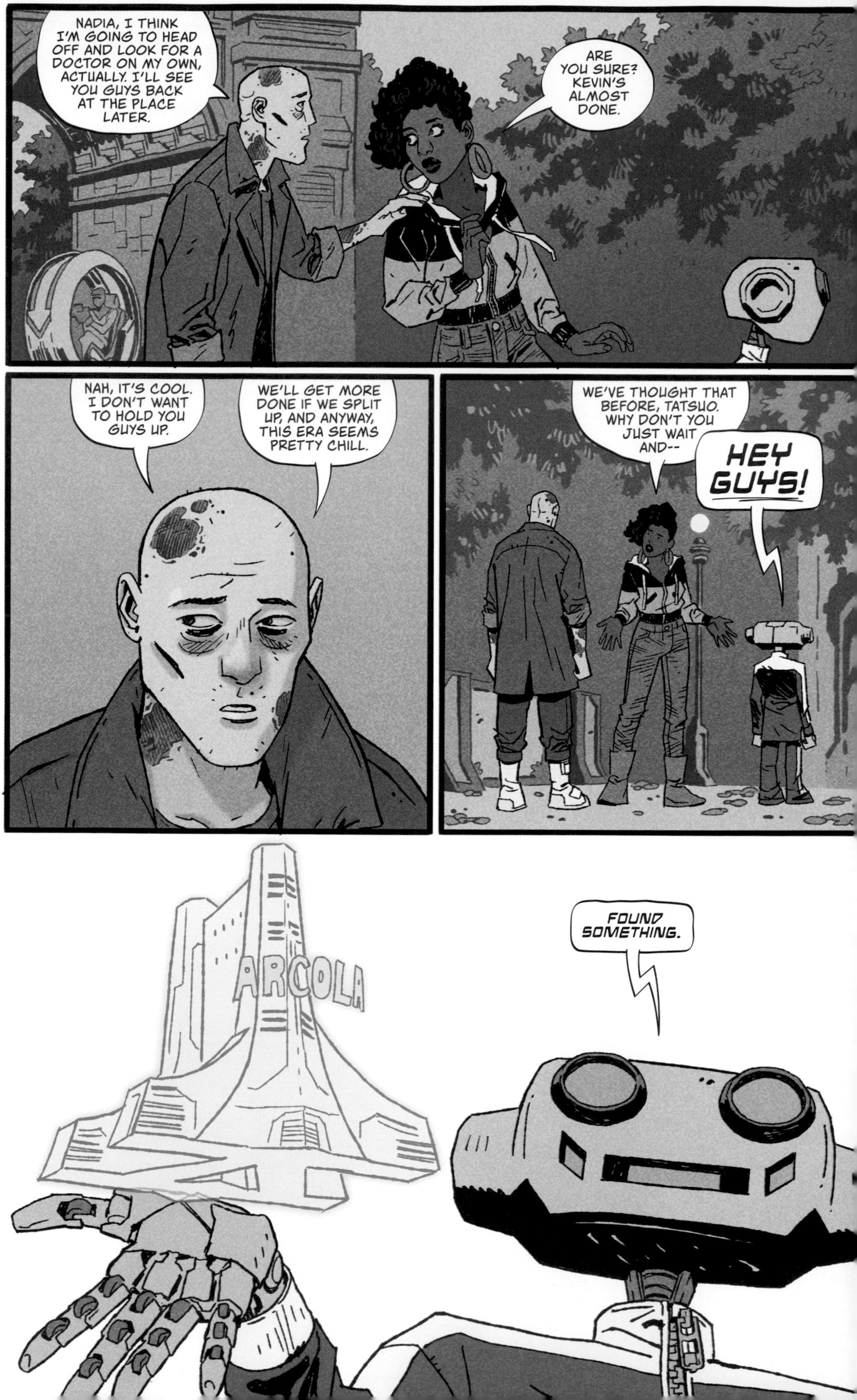
NADIA, I THINK I'M GOING TO HEAD OFF AND LOOK FOR A DOCTOR ON MY OWN, ACTUALLY. I'LL SEE YOU GUYS BACK AT THE PLACE LATER.
ARE YOU SURE? KEVIN'S ALMOST DONE.
NAH, IT'S COOL. I DON'T WANT TO HOLD YOU GUYS UP.
WE'LL GET MORE DONE IF WE SPLIT UP, AND ANYWAY, THIS ERA SEEMS PRETTY CHILL.
WE'VE THOUGHT THAT BEFORE, TATSUO. WHY DON'T YOU JUST WAIT AND--
HEY GUYS!
ARCOLA
FOUND SOMETHING.

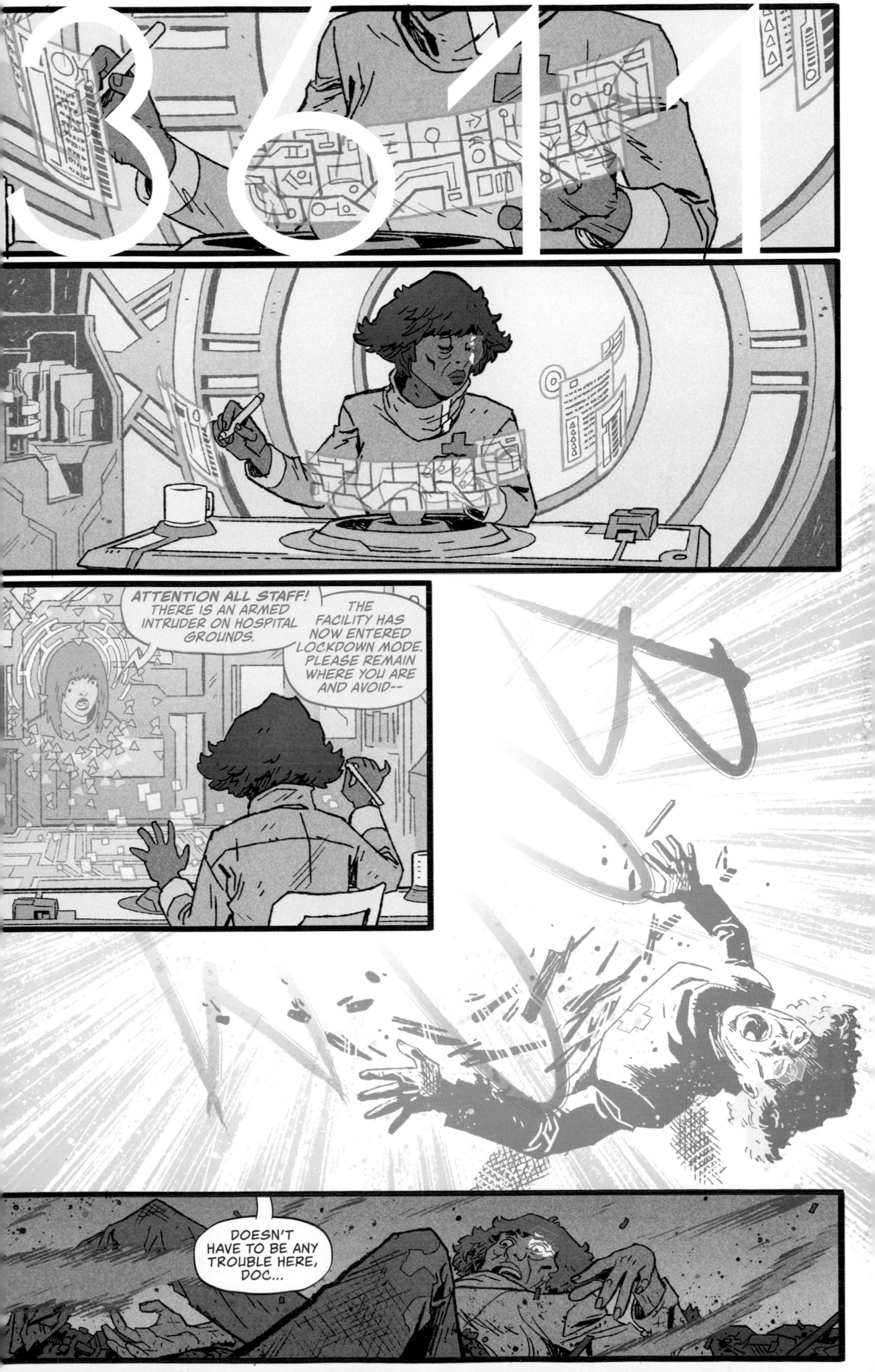
3611
ATTENTION ALL STAFF! THERE IS AN ARMED INTRUDER ON HOSPITAL GROUNDS.
THE FACILITY HAS NOW ENTERED LOCKDOWN MODE. PLEASE REMAIN WHERE YOU ARE AND AVOID--
DOESN'T HAVE TO BE ANY TROUBLE HERE, DOC...

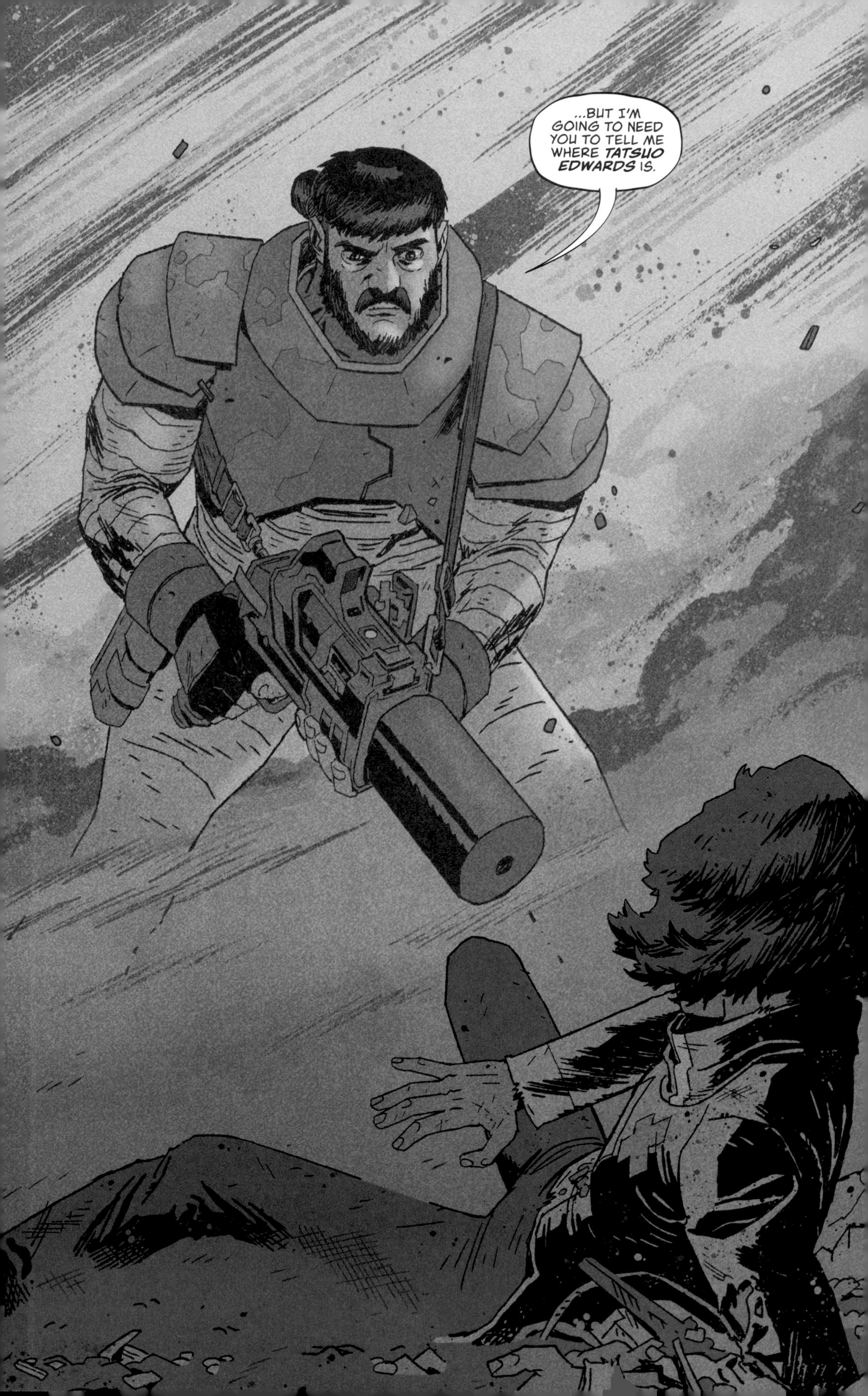
...BUT I'M GOING TO NEED YOU TO TELL ME WHERE TATSUO EDWARDS IS.

久

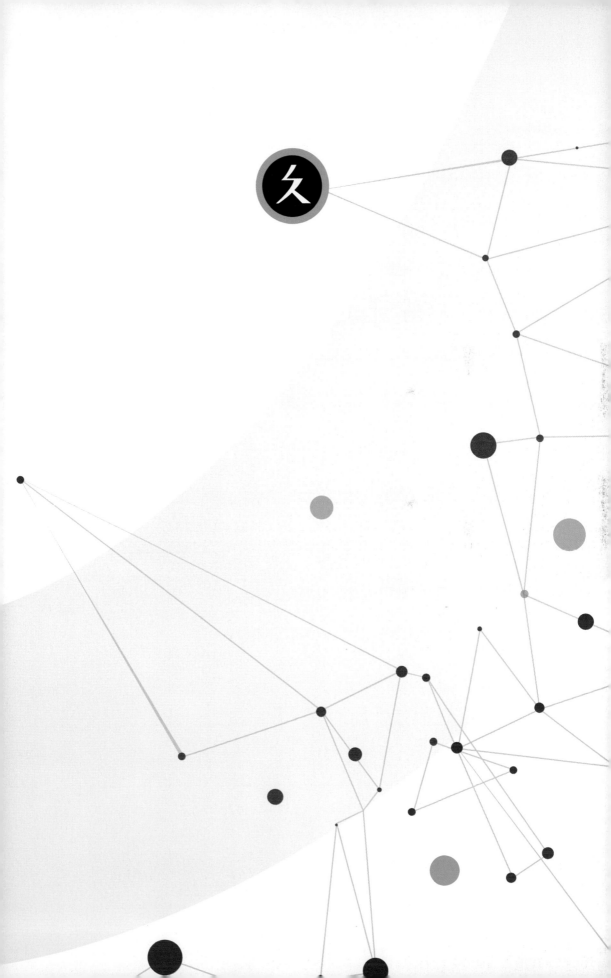

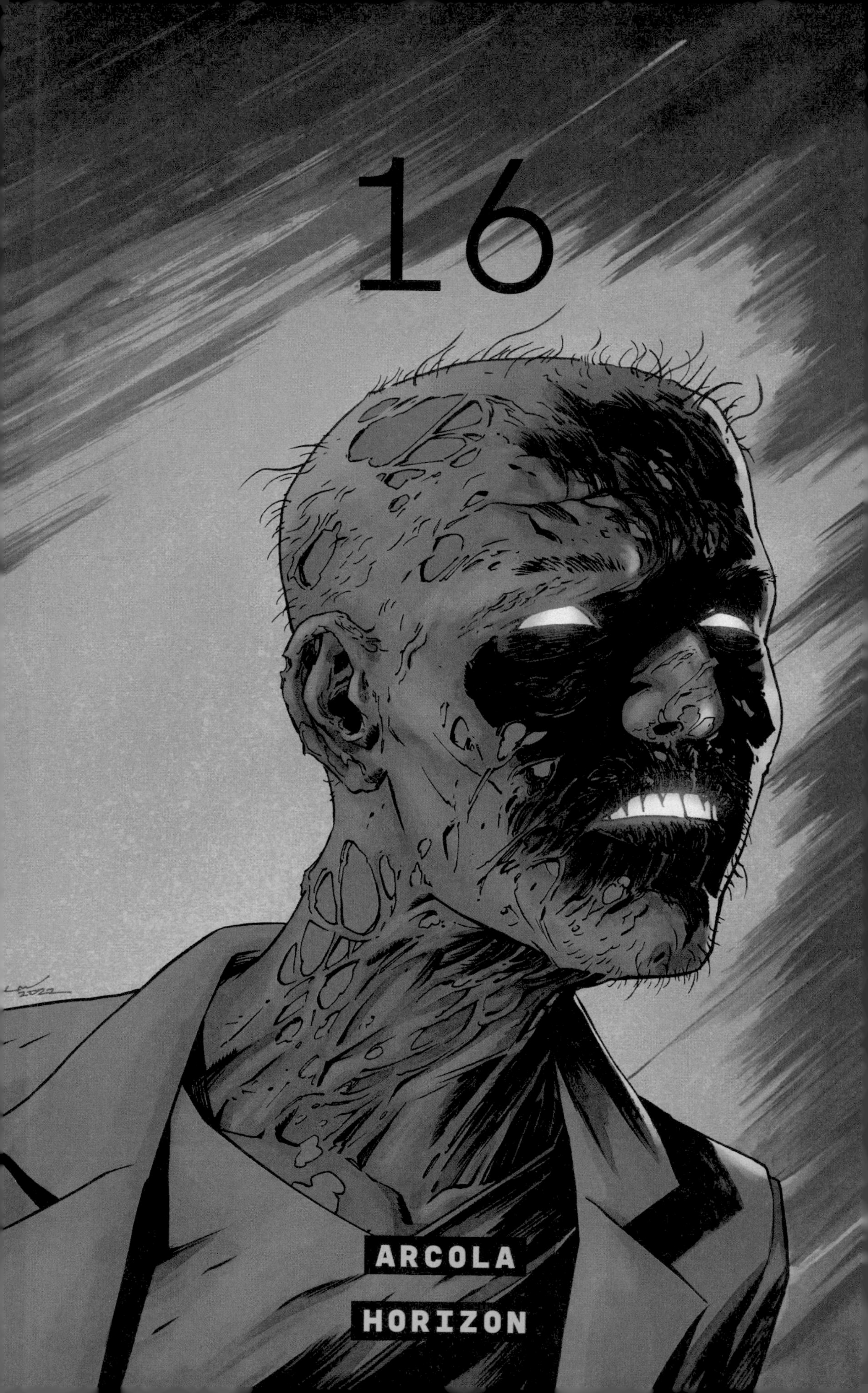
16
ARCOLA
HORIZON

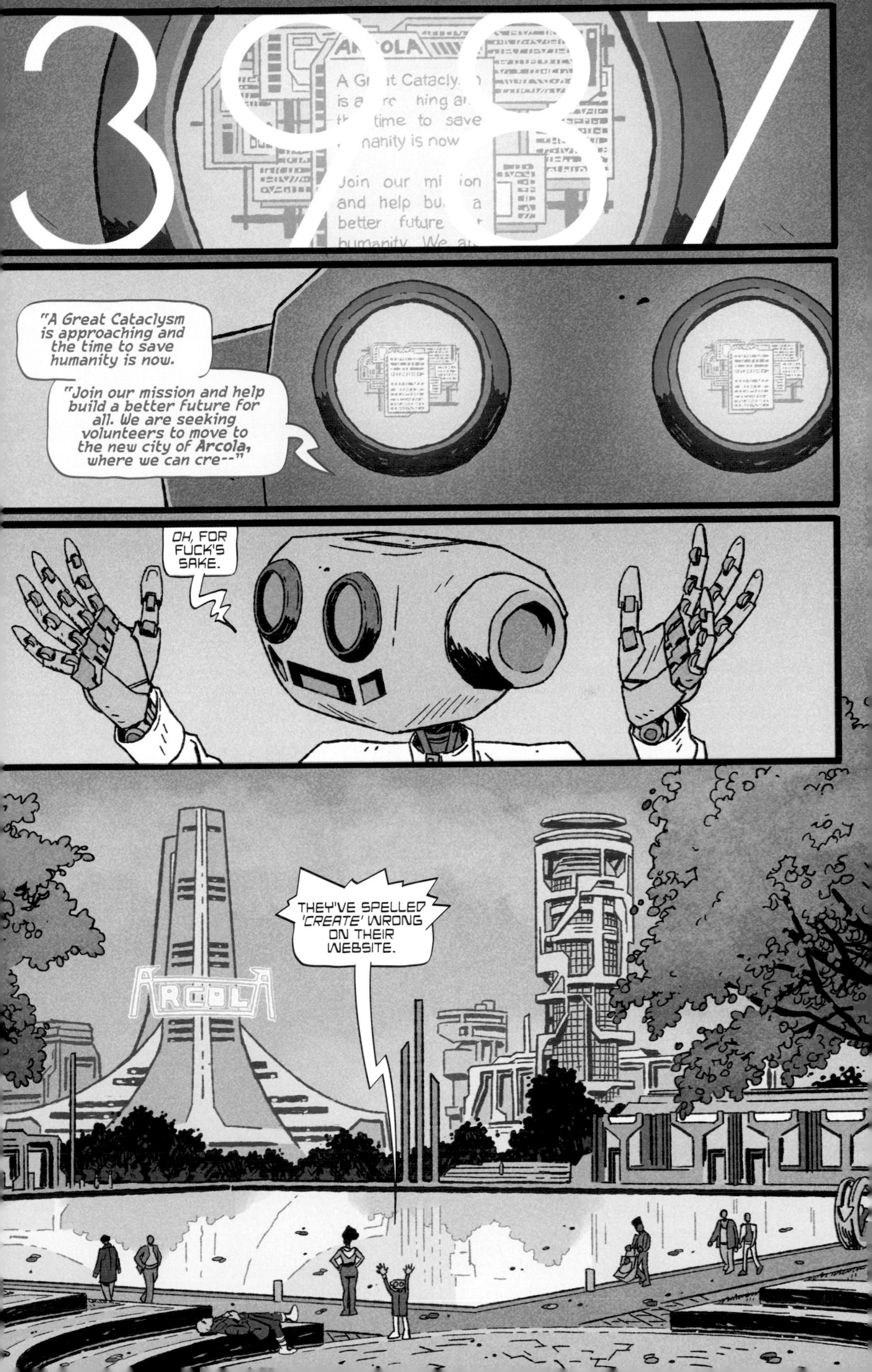
3987
"A Great Cataclysm is approaching and the time to save humanity is now.
"Join our mission and help build a better future for all. We are seeking volunteers to move to the new city of Arcola, where we can cre--"
OH, FOR FUCK'S SAKE.
THEY'VE SPELLED 'CREATE' WRONG ON THEIR WEBSITE.

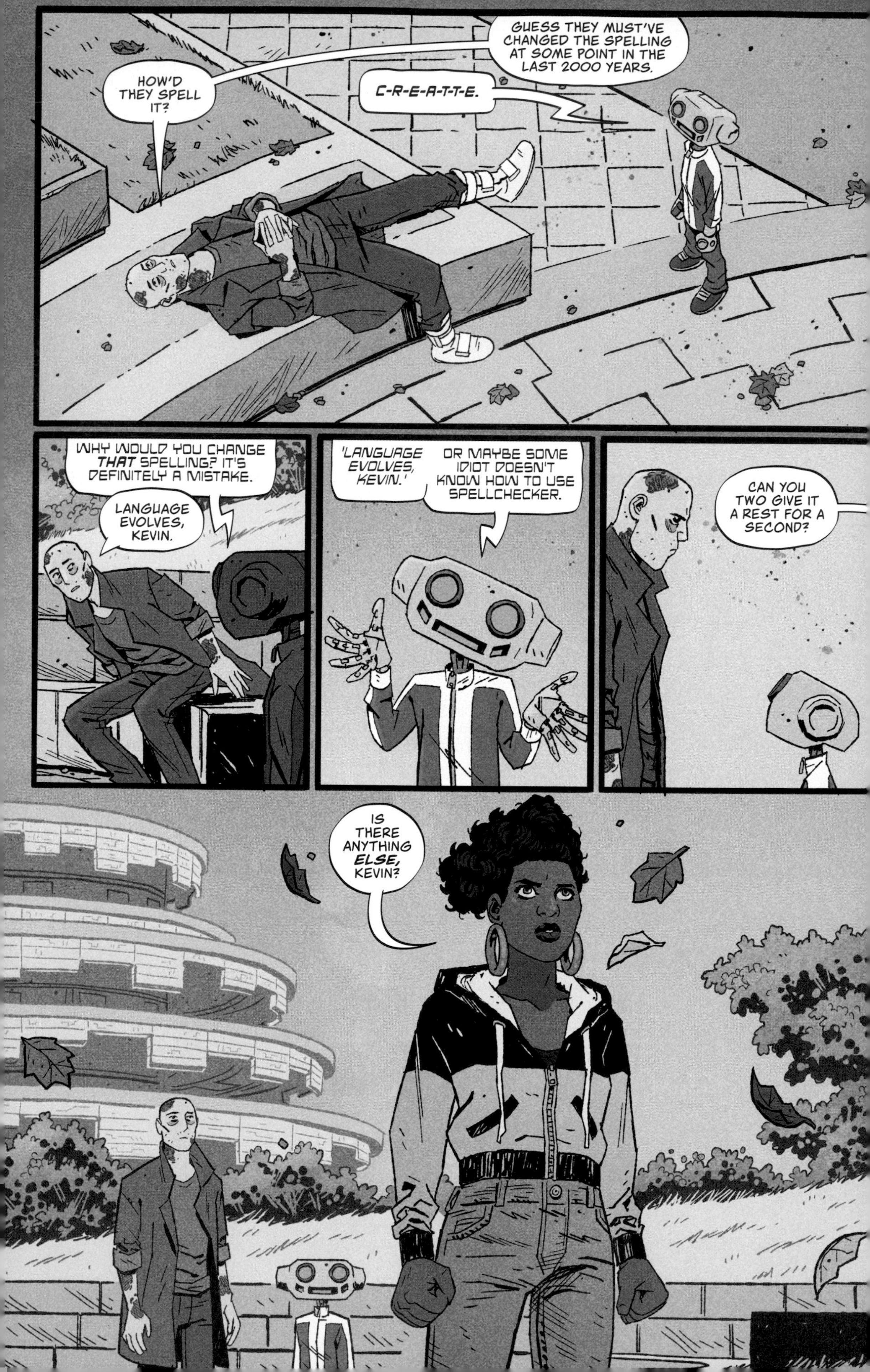
HOW'D THEY SPELL IT?
GUESS THEY MUST'VE CHANGED THE SPELLING AT SOME POINT IN THE LAST 2000 YEARS.
C-R-E-A-T-T-E.
WHY WOULD YOU CHANGE THAT SPELLING? IT'S DEFINITELY A MISTAKE.
LANGUAGE EVOLVES, KEVIN.
'LANGUAGE EVOLVES, KEVIN.'
OR MAYBE SOME IDIOT DOESN'T KNOW HOW TO USE SPELLCHECKER.
CAN YOU TWO GIVE IT A REST FOR A SECOND?
IS THERE ANYTHING ELSE, KEVIN?

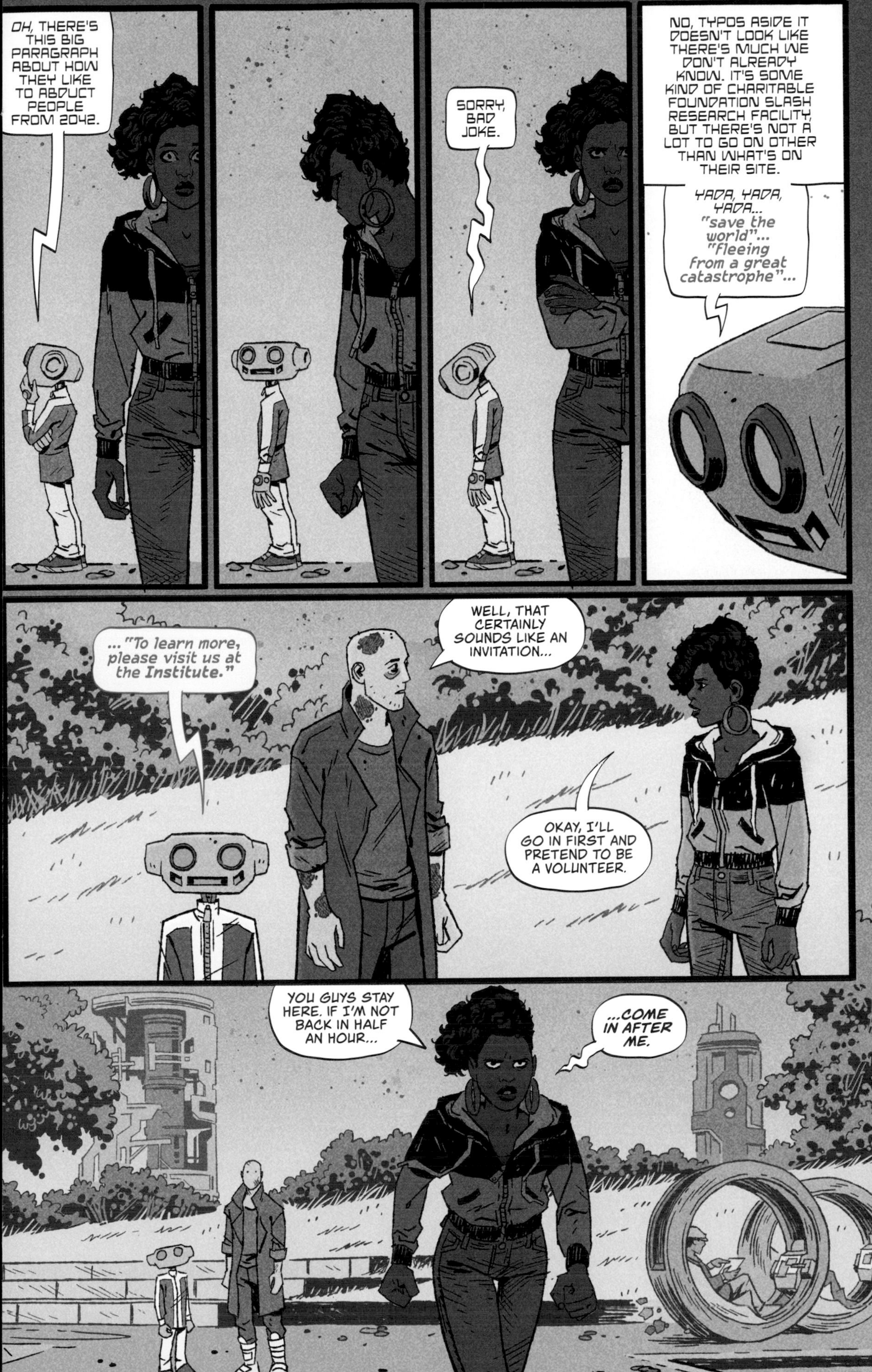
OH, THERE'S THIS BIG PARAGRAPH ABOUT HOW THEY LIKE TO ABDUCT PEOPLE FROM 2042.
SORRY, BAD JOKE.
NO, TYPOS ASIDE IT DOESN'T LOOK LIKE THERE'S MUCH WE DON'T ALREADY KNOW. IT'S SOME KIND OF CHARITABLE FOUNDATION SLASH RESEARCH FACILITY, BUT THERE'S NOT A LOT TO GO ON OTHER THAN WHAT'S ON THEIR SITE.
YADA, YADA, YADA... "save the world"... "Fleeing from a great catastrophe"...
..."To learn more, please visit us at the Institute."
WELL, THAT CERTAINLY SOUNDS LIKE AN INVITATION...
OKAY, I'LL GO IN FIRST AND PRETEND TO BE A VOLUNTEER.
YOU GUYS STAY HERE. IF I'M NOT BACK IN HALF AN HOUR...
...COME IN AFTER ME.

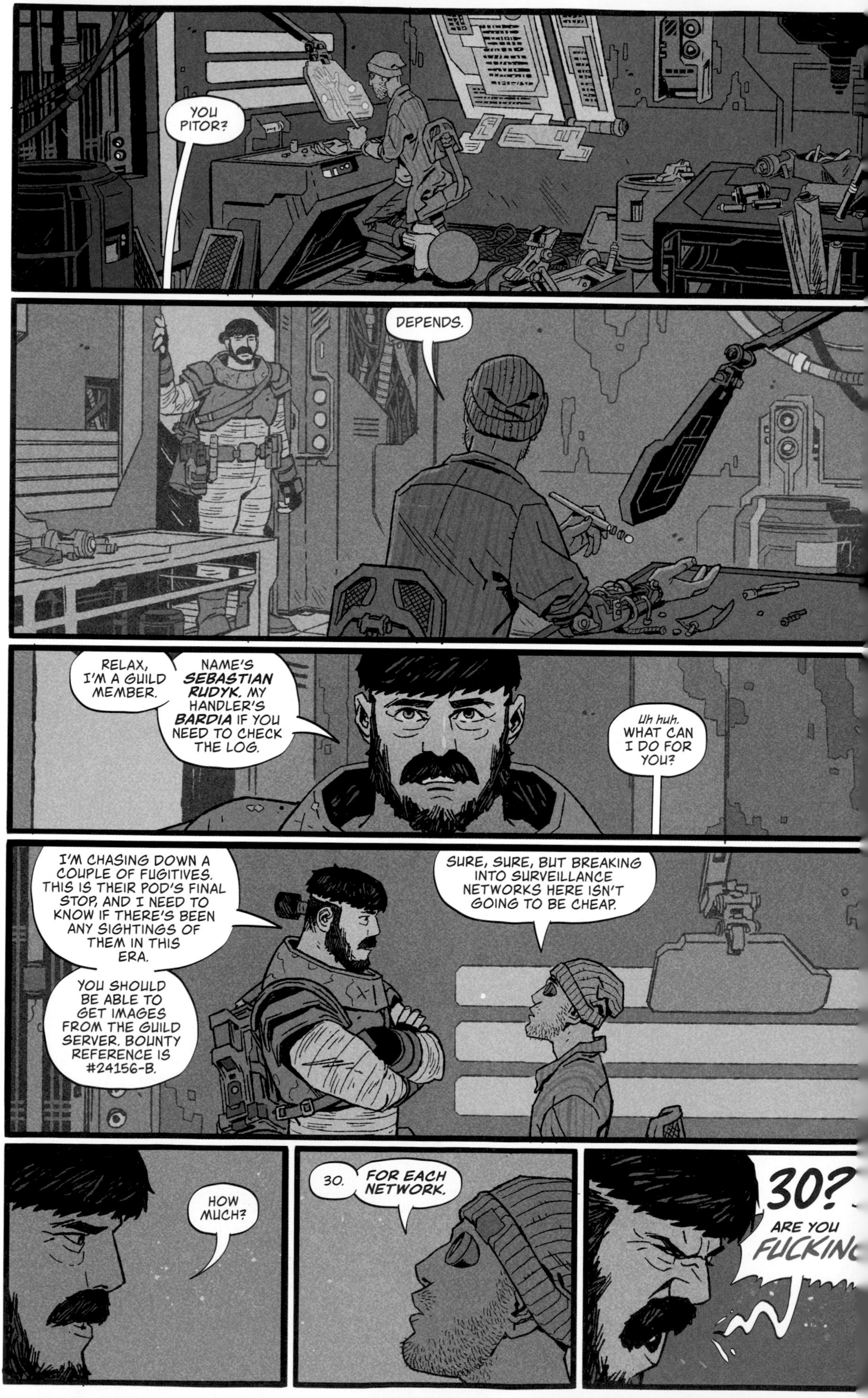

YOU PITOR?
DEPENDS.
RELAX, I'M A GUILD MEMBER.
NAME'S **SEBASTIAN RUDYK.** MY HANDLER'S **BARDIA** IF YOU NEED TO CHECK THE LOG.
Uh huh. WHAT CAN I DO FOR YOU?
I'M CHASING DOWN A COUPLE OF FUGITIVES. THIS IS THEIR POD'S FINAL STOP, AND I NEED TO KNOW IF THERE'S BEEN ANY SIGHTINGS OF THEM IN THIS ERA.
YOU SHOULD BE ABLE TO GET IMAGES FROM THE GUILD SERVER. BOUNTY REFERENCE IS #24156-B.
SURE, SURE, BUT BREAKING INTO SURVEILLANCE NETWORKS HERE ISN'T GOING TO BE CHEAP.
HOW MUCH?
30.
FOR EACH NETWORK.
30?
ARE YOU

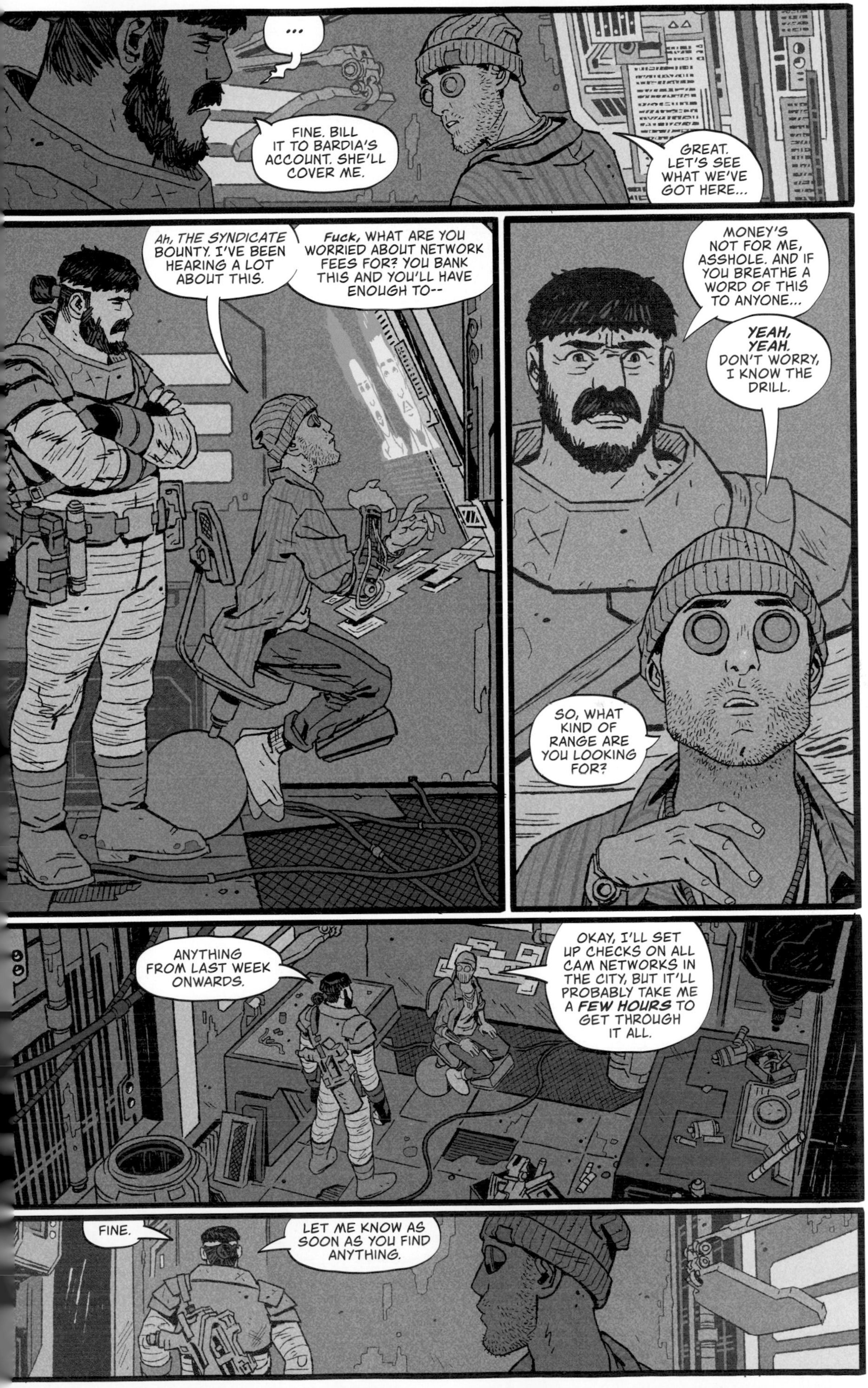
...
FINE. BILL IT TO BARDIA'S ACCOUNT. SHE'LL COVER ME.
GREAT. LET'S SEE WHAT WE'VE GOT HERE...
Ah, THE SYNDICATE BOUNTY. I'VE BEEN HEARING A LOT ABOUT THIS.
Fuck, WHAT ARE YOU WORRIED ABOUT NETWORK FEES FOR? YOU BANK THIS AND YOU'LL HAVE ENOUGH TO--
MONEY'S NOT FOR ME, ASSHOLE. AND IF YOU BREATHE A WORD OF THIS TO ANYONE...
YEAH, YEAH. DON'T WORRY, I KNOW THE DRILL.
SO, WHAT KIND OF RANGE ARE YOU LOOKING FOR?
ANYTHING FROM LAST WEEK ONWARDS.
OKAY, I'LL SET UP CHECKS ON ALL CAM NETWORKS IN THE CITY, BUT IT'LL PROBABLY TAKE ME A ***FEW HOURS*** TO GET THROUGH IT ALL.
FINE.
LET ME KNOW AS SOON AS YOU FIND ANYTHING.

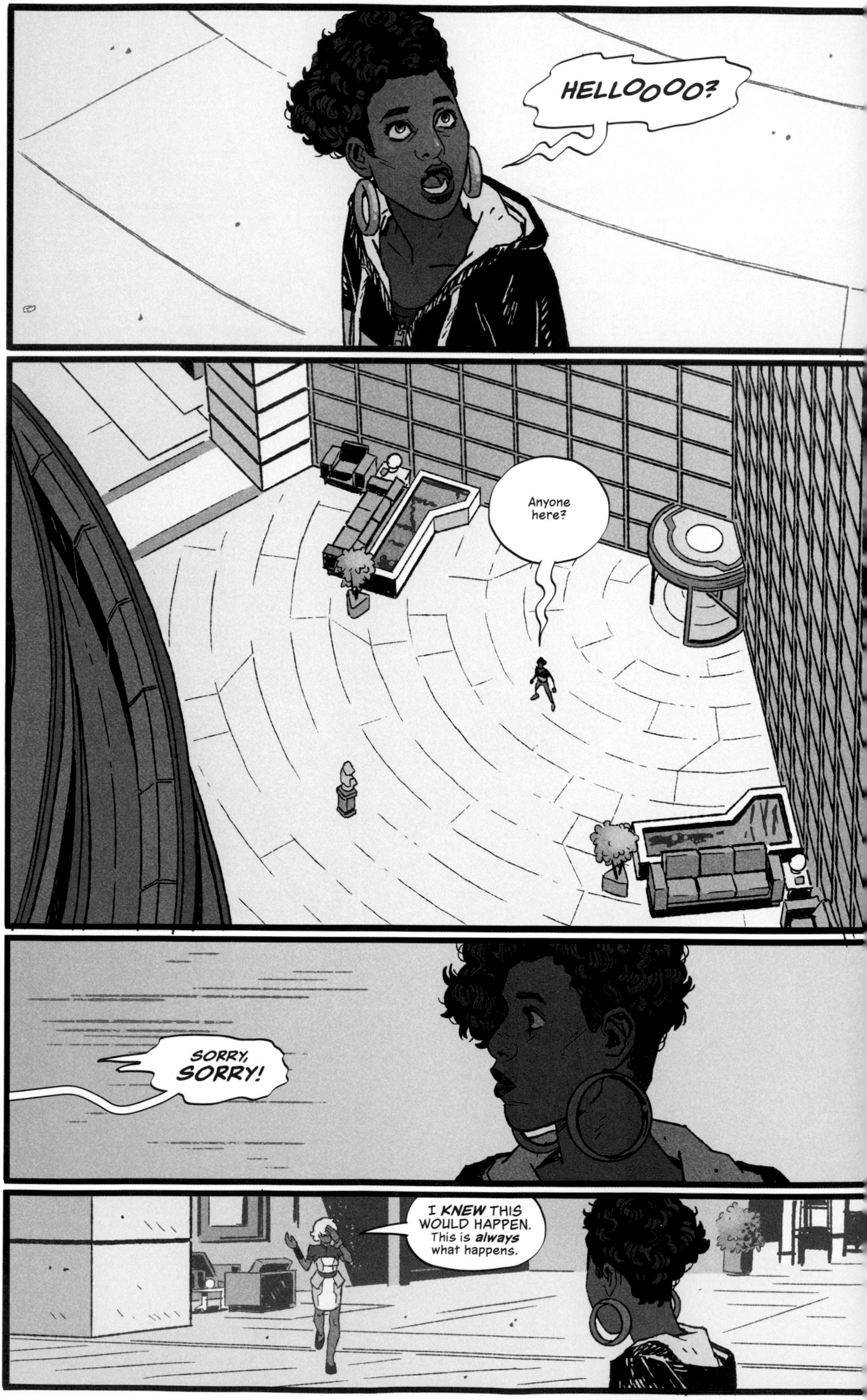
HELLOOOO?
Anyone here?
SORRY, SORRY!
I KNEW THIS WOULD HAPPEN. This is always what happens.

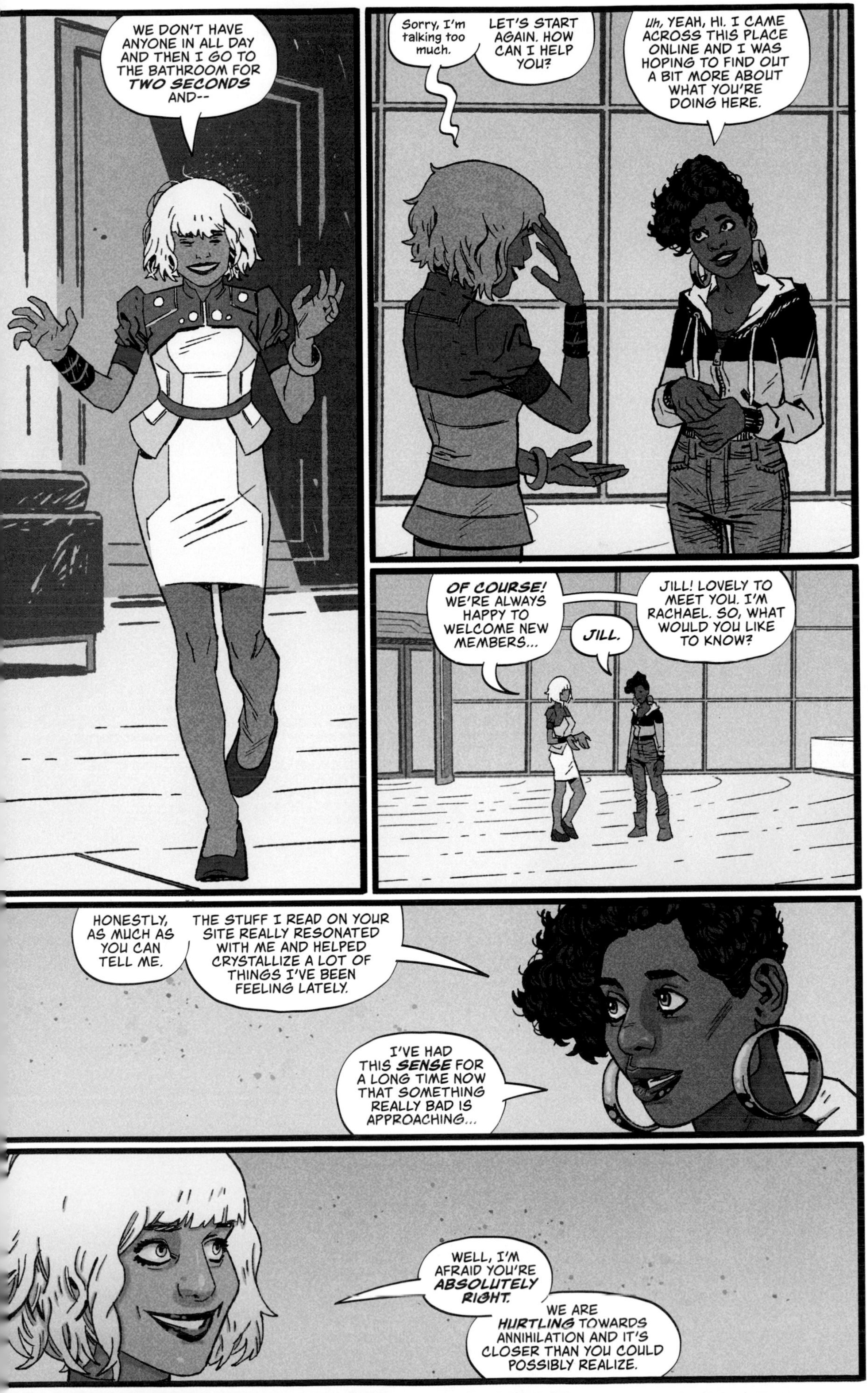
WE DON'T HAVE ANYONE IN ALL DAY AND THEN I GO TO THE BATHROOM FOR TWO SECONDS AND--
Sorry, I'm talking too much.
LET'S START AGAIN. HOW CAN I HELP YOU?
Uh, YEAH, HI. I CAME ACROSS THIS PLACE ONLINE AND I WAS HOPING TO FIND OUT A BIT MORE ABOUT WHAT YOU'RE DOING HERE.
OF COURSE! WE'RE ALWAYS HAPPY TO WELCOME NEW MEMBERS...
JILL.
JILL! LOVELY TO MEET YOU. I'M RACHAEL. SO, WHAT WOULD YOU LIKE TO KNOW?
HONESTLY, AS MUCH AS YOU CAN TELL ME.
THE STUFF I READ ON YOUR SITE REALLY RESONATED WITH ME AND HELPED CRYSTALLIZE A LOT OF THINGS I'VE BEEN FEELING LATELY.
I'VE HAD THIS SENSE FOR A LONG TIME NOW THAT SOMETHING REALLY BAD IS APPROACHING...
WELL, I'M AFRAID YOU'RE ABSOLUTELY RIGHT.
WE ARE HURTLING TOWARDS ANNIHILATION AND IT'S CLOSER THAN YOU COULD POSSIBLY REALIZE.

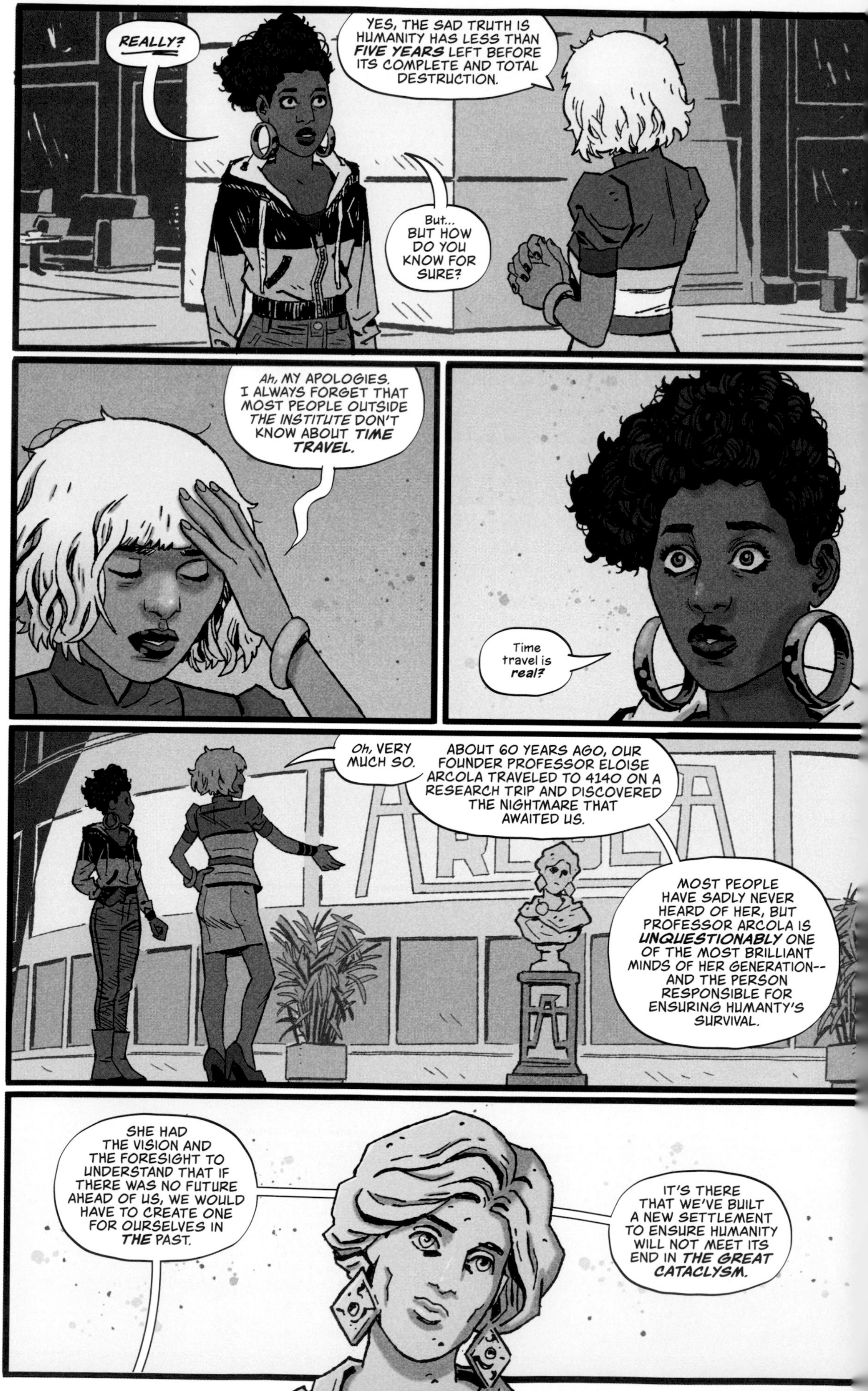
REALLY?
YES, THE SAD TRUTH IS HUMANITY HAS LESS THAN FIVE YEARS LEFT BEFORE ITS COMPLETE AND TOTAL DESTRUCTION.
But... BUT HOW DO YOU KNOW FOR SURE?
Ah, MY APOLOGIES. I ALWAYS FORGET THAT MOST PEOPLE OUTSIDE THE INSTITUTE DON'T KNOW ABOUT TIME TRAVEL.
Time travel is real?
Oh, VERY MUCH SO.
ABOUT 60 YEARS AGO, OUR FOUNDER PROFESSOR ELOISE ARCOLA TRAVELED TO 4140 ON A RESEARCH TRIP AND DISCOVERED THE NIGHTMARE THAT AWAITED US.
MOST PEOPLE HAVE SADLY NEVER HEARD OF HER, BUT PROFESSOR ARCOLA IS UNQUESTIONABLY ONE OF THE MOST BRILLIANT MINDS OF HER GENERATION-- AND THE PERSON RESPONSIBLE FOR ENSURING HUMANTY'S SURVIVAL.
SHE HAD THE VISION AND THE FORESIGHT TO UNDERSTAND THAT IF THERE WAS NO FUTURE AHEAD OF US, WE WOULD HAVE TO CREATE ONE FOR OURSELVES IN THE PAST.
IT'S THERE THAT WE'VE BUILT A NEW SETTLEMENT TO ENSURE HUMANITY WILL NOT MEET ITS END IN THE GREAT CATACLYSM.

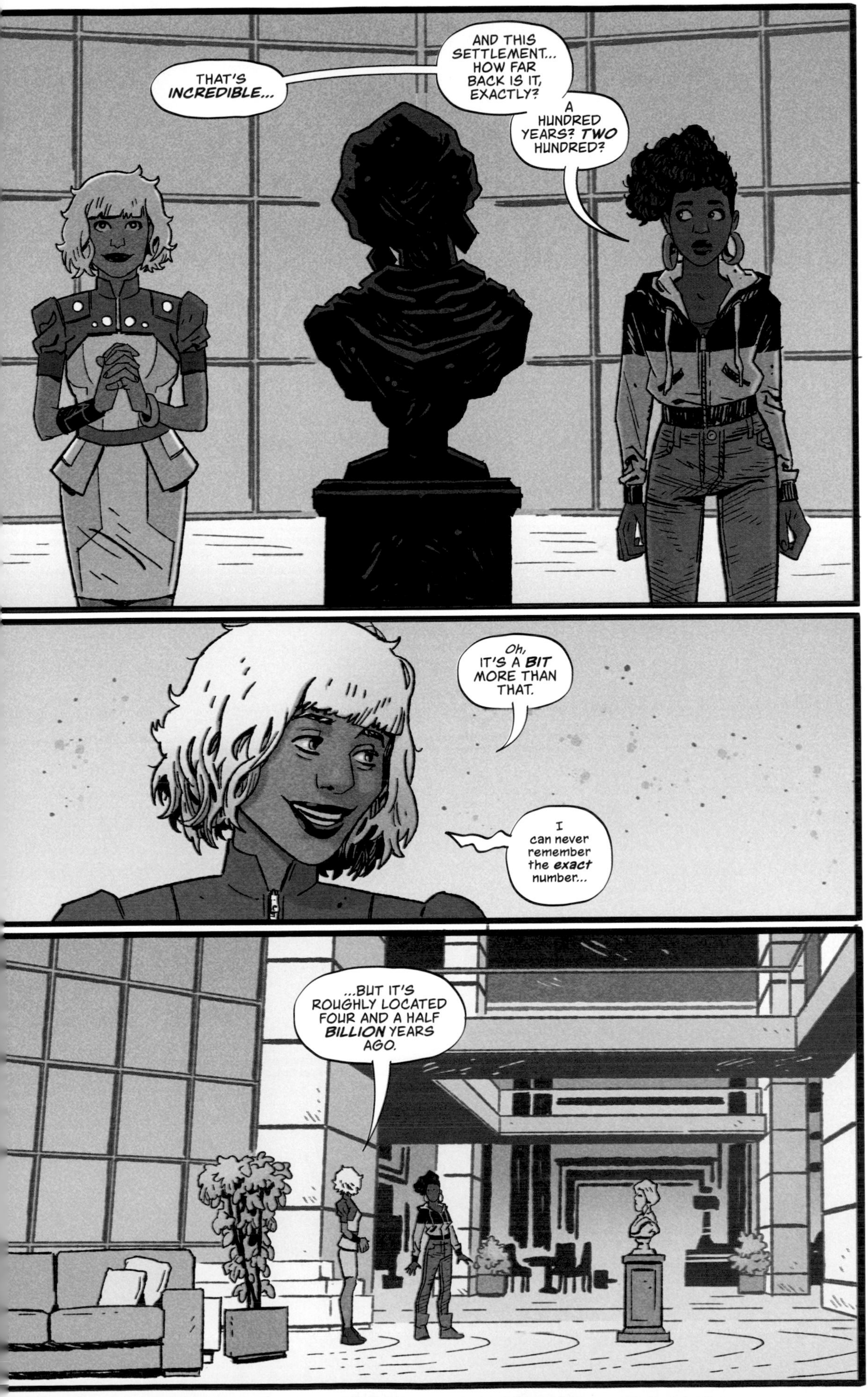
THAT'S INCREDIBLE...
AND THIS SETTLEMENT... HOW FAR BACK IS IT, EXACTLY?
A HUNDRED YEARS? TWO HUNDRED?
Oh, IT'S A BIT MORE THAN THAT.
I can never remember the exact number...
...BUT IT'S ROUGHLY LOCATED FOUR AND A HALF BILLION YEARS AGO.

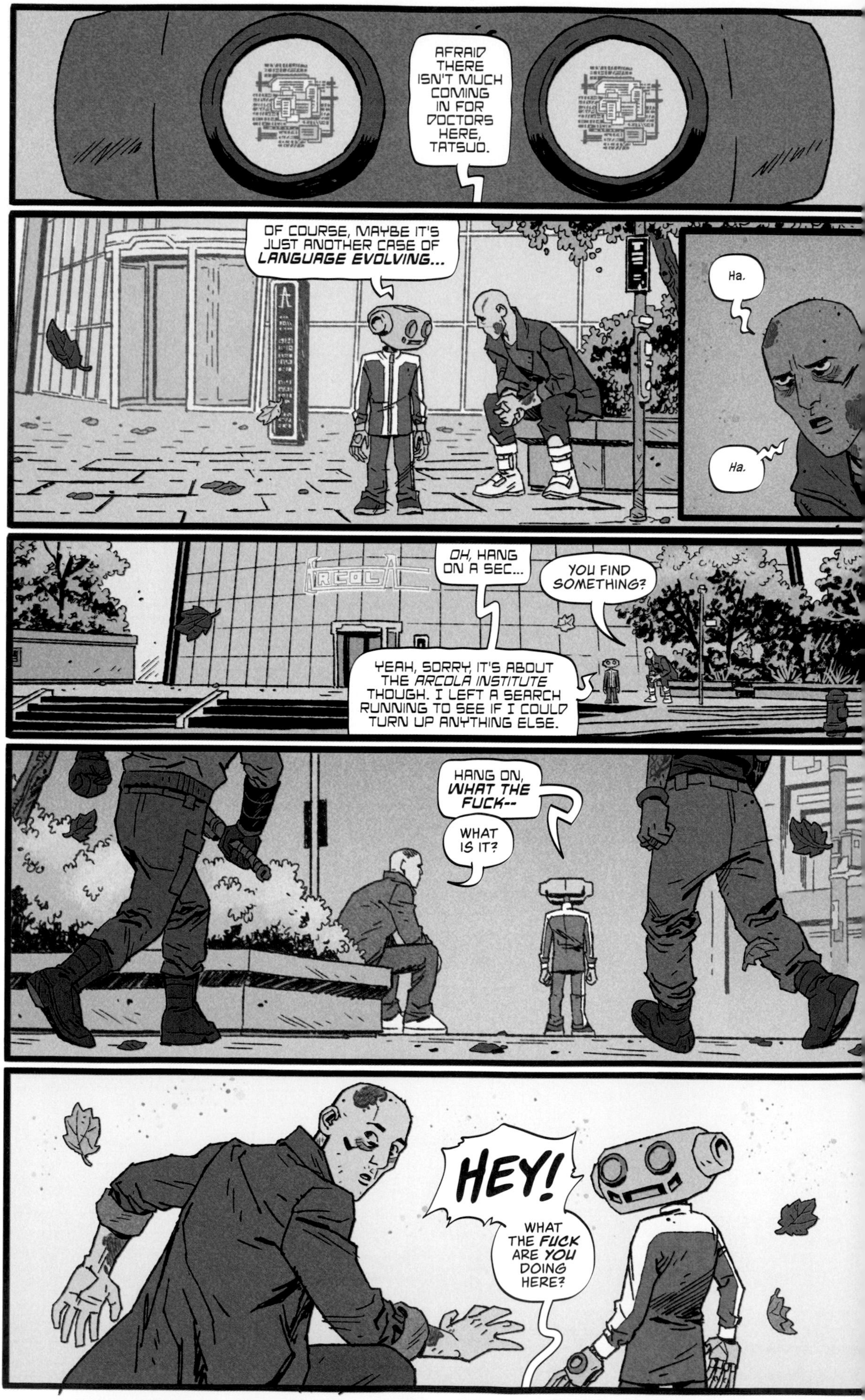
AFRAID THERE ISN'T MUCH COMING IN FOR DOCTORS HERE, TATSUO.
OF COURSE, MAYBE IT'S JUST ANOTHER CASE OF LANGUAGE EVOLVING...
Ha.
Ha.
OH, HANG ON A SEC...
YOU FIND SOMETHING?
YEAH, SORRY, IT'S ABOUT THE ARCOLA INSTITUTE THOUGH. I LEFT A SEARCH RUNNING TO SEE IF I COULD TURN UP ANYTHING ELSE.
HANG ON, WHAT THE FUCK--
WHAT IS IT?
HEY!
WHAT THE FUCK ARE YOU DOING HERE?

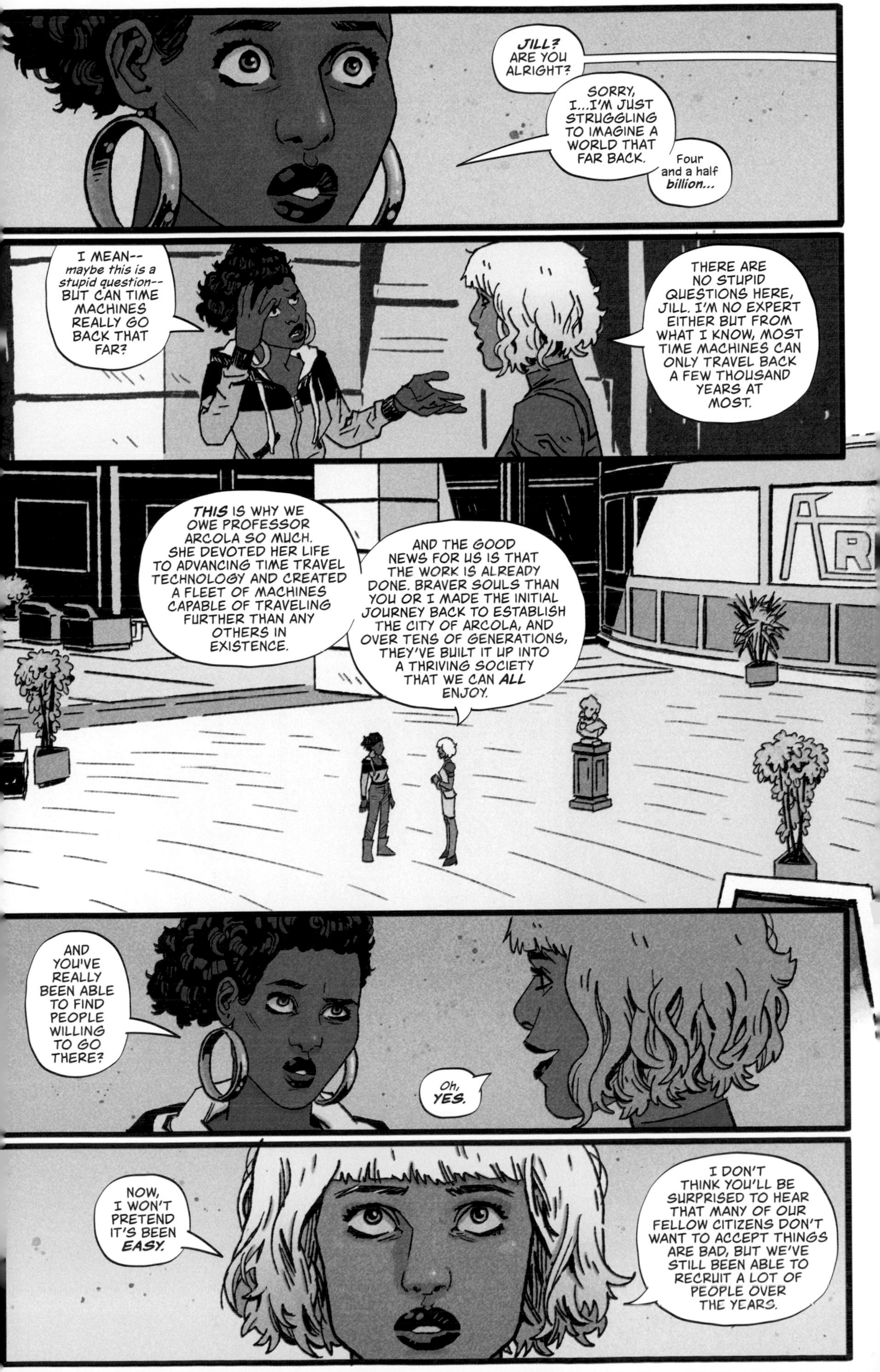
JILL? ARE YOU ALRIGHT?
SORRY, I...I'M JUST STRUGGLING TO IMAGINE A WORLD THAT FAR BACK.
Four and a half billion...
I MEAN--maybe this is a stupid question--BUT CAN TIME MACHINES REALLY GO BACK THAT FAR?
THERE ARE NO STUPID QUESTIONS HERE, JILL. I'M NO EXPERT EITHER BUT FROM WHAT I KNOW, MOST TIME MACHINES CAN ONLY TRAVEL BACK A FEW THOUSAND YEARS AT MOST.
THIS IS WHY WE OWE PROFESSOR ARCOLA SO MUCH. SHE DEVOTED HER LIFE TO ADVANCING TIME TRAVEL TECHNOLOGY AND CREATED A FLEET OF MACHINES CAPABLE OF TRAVELING FURTHER THAN ANY OTHERS IN EXISTENCE.
AND THE GOOD NEWS FOR US IS THAT THE WORK IS ALREADY DONE. BRAVER SOULS THAN YOU OR I MADE THE INITIAL JOURNEY BACK TO ESTABLISH THE CITY OF ARCOLA, AND OVER TENS OF GENERATIONS, THEY'VE BUILT IT UP INTO A THRIVING SOCIETY THAT WE CAN ALL ENJOY.
AND YOU'VE REALLY BEEN ABLE TO FIND PEOPLE WILLING TO GO THERE?
Oh, YES.
NOW, I WON'T PRETEND IT'S BEEN EASY.
I DON'T THINK YOU'LL BE SURPRISED TO HEAR THAT MANY OF OUR FELLOW CITIZENS DON'T WANT TO ACCEPT THINGS ARE BAD, BUT WE'VE STILL BEEN ABLE TO RECRUIT A LOT OF PEOPLE OVER THE YEARS.

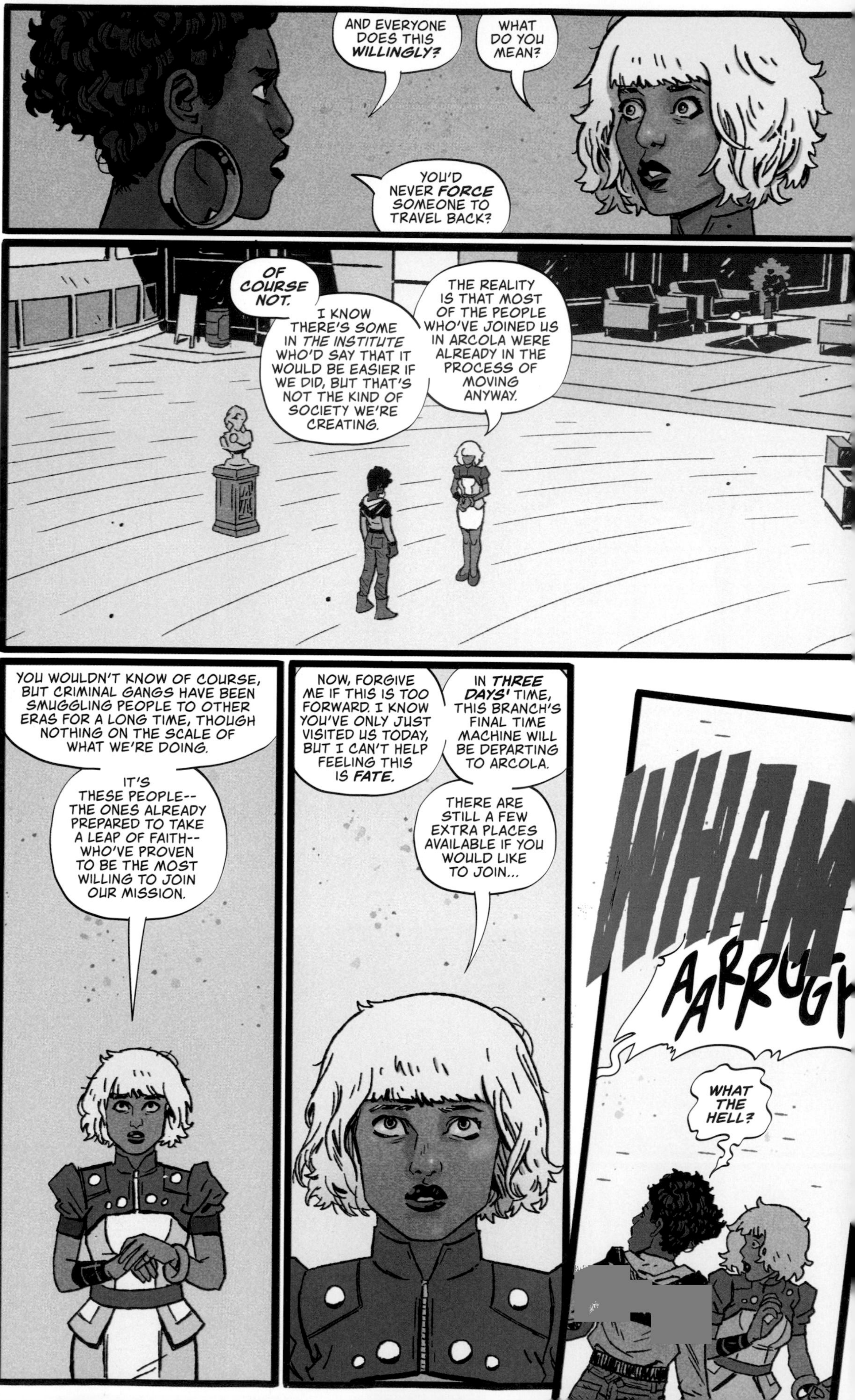
AND EVERYONE DOES THIS WILLINGLY?
WHAT DO YOU MEAN?
YOU'D NEVER FORCE SOMEONE TO TRAVEL BACK?
OF COURSE NOT.
I KNOW THERE'S SOME IN THE INSTITUTE WHO'D SAY THAT IT WOULD BE EASIER IF WE DID, BUT THAT'S NOT THE KIND OF SOCIETY WE'RE CREATING.
THE REALITY IS THAT MOST OF THE PEOPLE WHO'VE JOINED US IN ARCOLA WERE ALREADY IN THE PROCESS OF MOVING ANYWAY.
YOU WOULDN'T KNOW OF COURSE, BUT CRIMINAL GANGS HAVE BEEN SMUGGLING PEOPLE TO OTHER ERAS FOR A LONG TIME, THOUGH NOTHING ON THE SCALE OF WHAT WE'RE DOING.
IT'S THESE PEOPLE-- THE ONES ALREADY PREPARED TO TAKE A LEAP OF FAITH-- WHO'VE PROVEN TO BE THE MOST WILLING TO JOIN OUR MISSION.
NOW, FORGIVE ME IF THIS IS TOO FORWARD. I KNOW YOU'VE ONLY JUST VISITED US TODAY, BUT I CAN'T HELP FEELING THIS IS FATE.
IN THREE DAYS' TIME, THIS BRANCH'S FINAL TIME MACHINE WILL BE DEPARTING TO ARCOLA.
THERE ARE STILL A FEW EXTRA PLACES AVAILABLE IF YOU WOULD LIKE TO JOIN...
AARRUG
WHAT THE HELL?

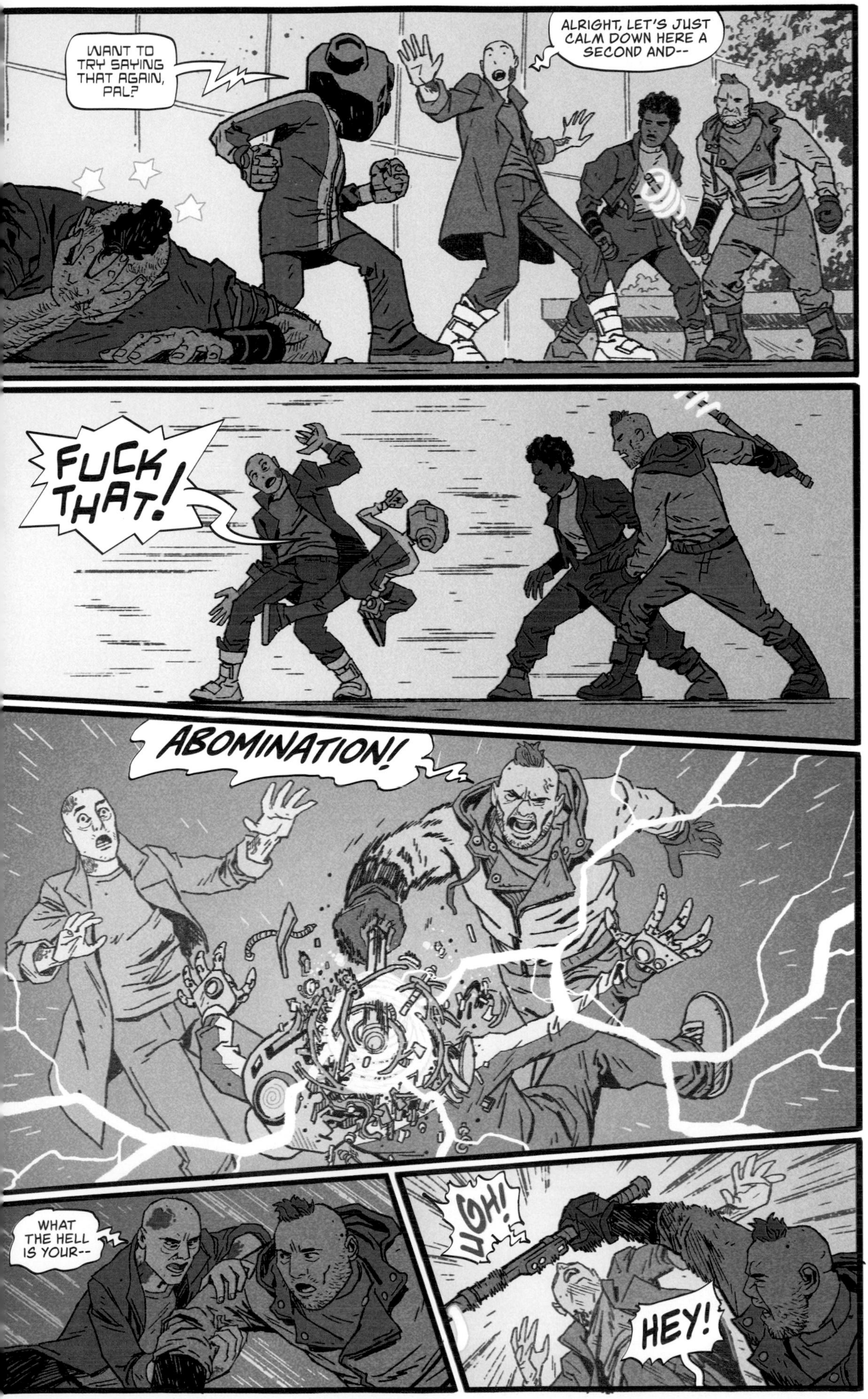
WANT TO TRY SAYING THAT AGAIN, PAL?
ALRIGHT, LET'S JUST CALM DOWN HERE A SECOND AND--
FUCK THAT!
ABOMINATION!
WHAT THE HELL IS YOUR--
UGH!
HEY!

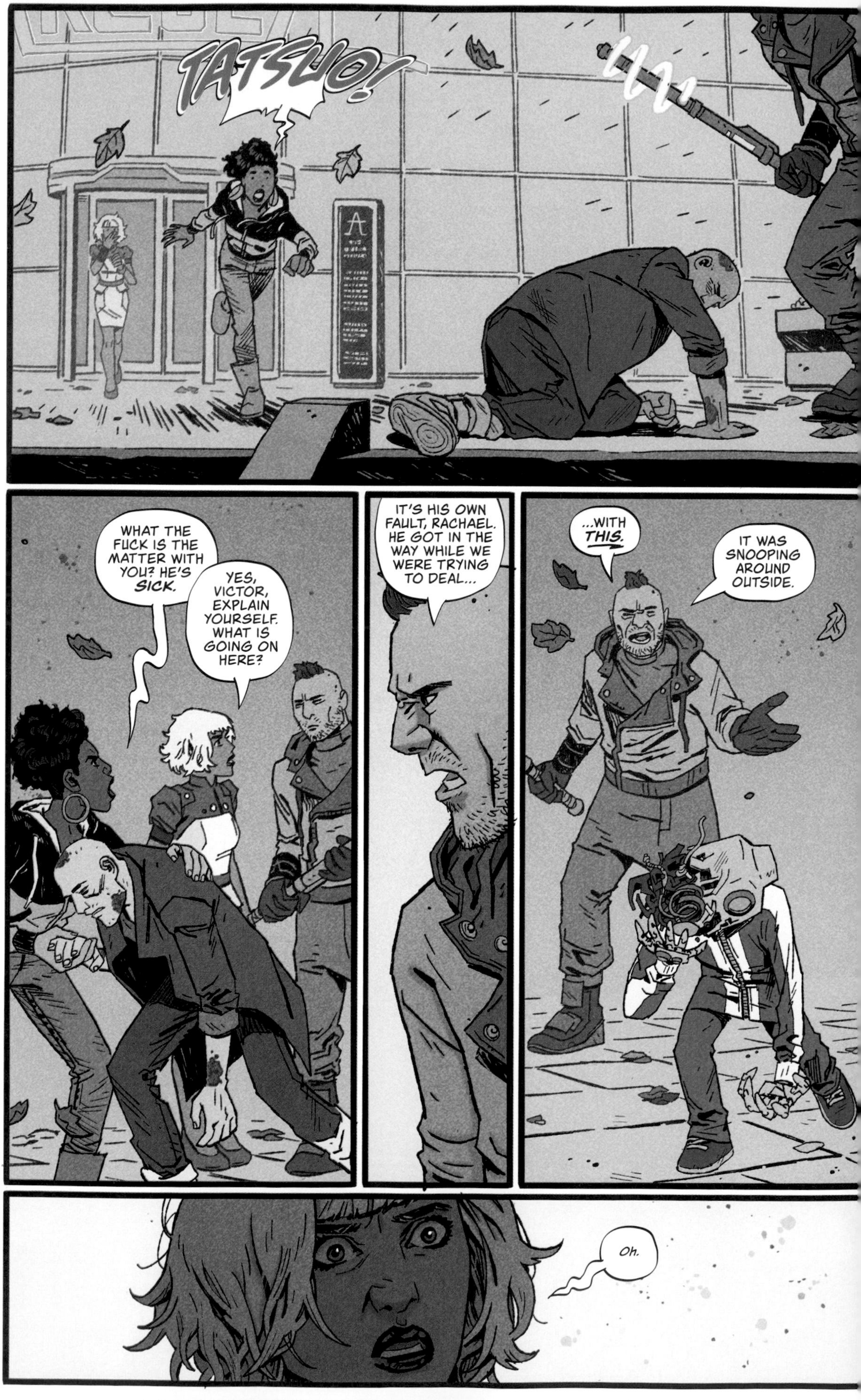
TATSUO!
WHAT THE FUCK IS THE MATTER WITH YOU? HE'S SICK.
YES, VICTOR, EXPLAIN YOURSELF. WHAT IS GOING ON HERE?
IT'S HIS OWN FAULT, RACHAEL. HE GOT IN THE WAY WHILE WE WERE TRYING TO DEAL...
...WITH THIS.
IT WAS SNOOPING AROUND OUTSIDE.
Oh.

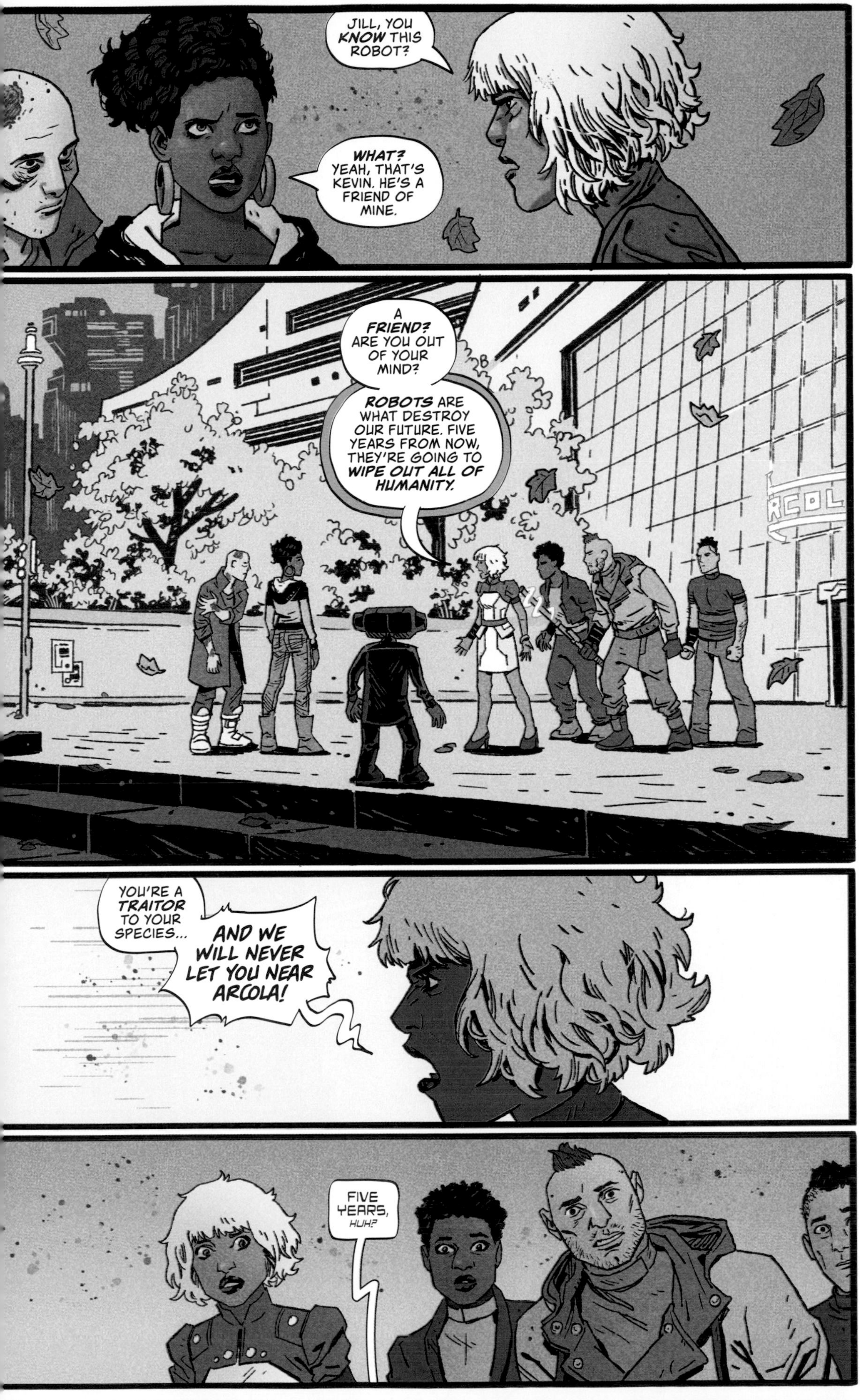
JILL, YOU KNOW THIS ROBOT?
WHAT? YEAH, THAT'S KEVIN. HE'S A FRIEND OF MINE.
A FRIEND? ARE YOU OUT OF YOUR MIND?
ROBOTS ARE WHAT DESTROY OUR FUTURE. FIVE YEARS FROM NOW, THEY'RE GOING TO WIPE OUT ALL OF HUMANITY.
ARCOL
YOU'RE A TRAITOR TO YOUR SPECIES...
AND WE WILL NEVER LET YOU NEAR ARCOLA!
FIVE YEARS, HUH?

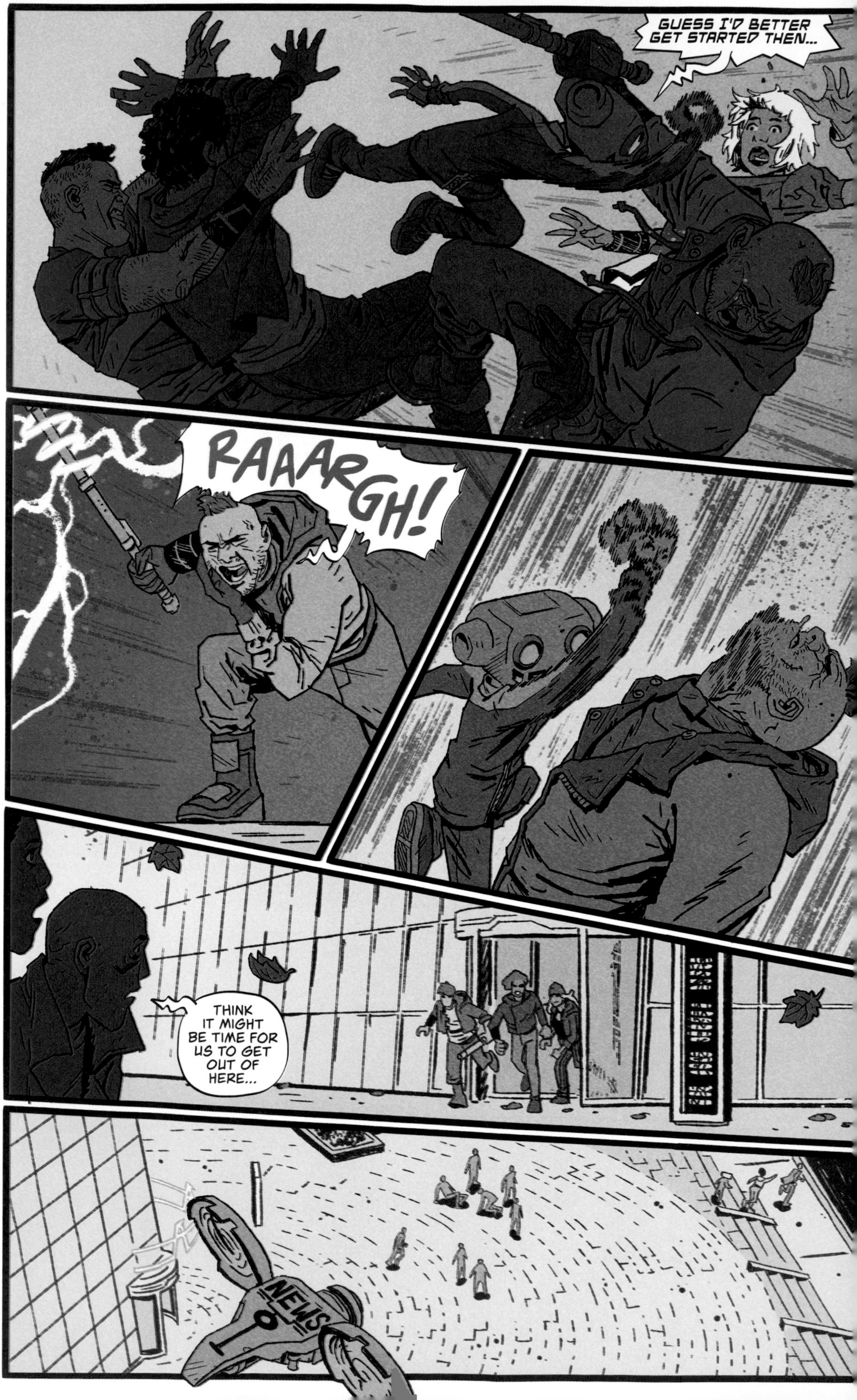
GUESS I'D BETTER GET STARTED THEN...
RAAARGH!
THINK IT MIGHT BE TIME FOR US TO GET OUT OF HERE...
NEWS

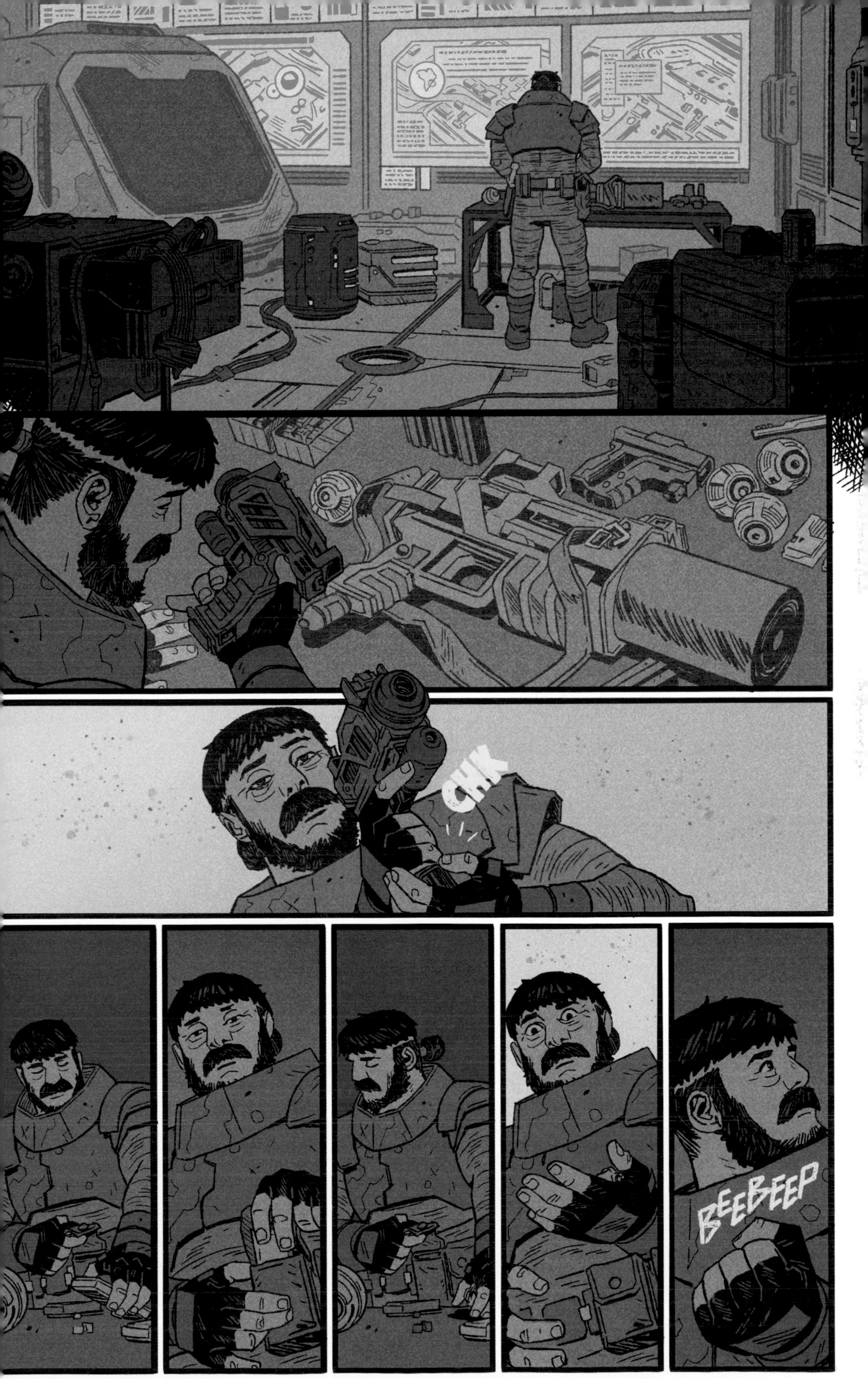
CHK
BEEBEEP

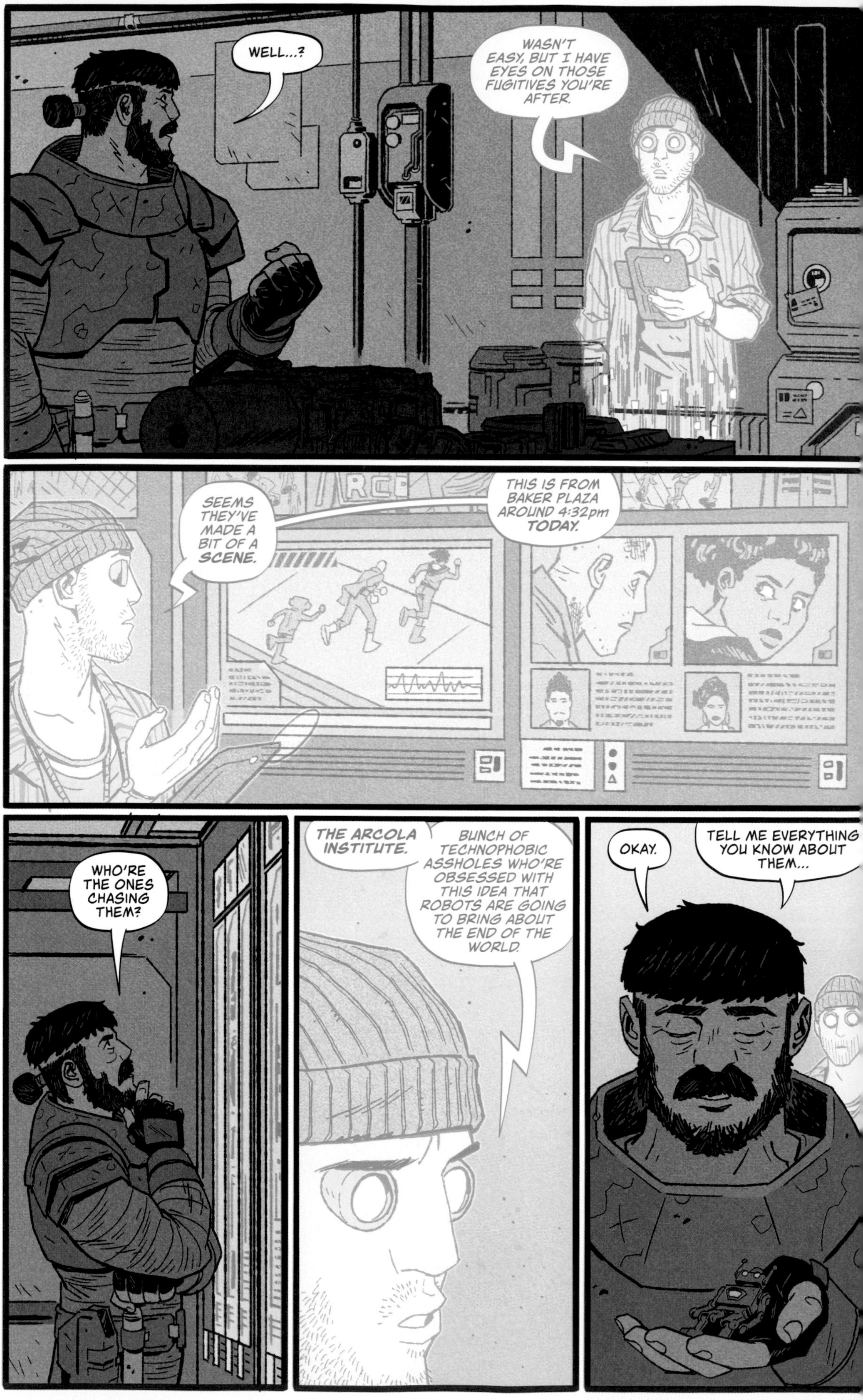
WELL...?
WASN'T EASY, BUT I HAVE EYES ON THOSE FUGITIVES YOU'RE AFTER.
SEEMS THEY'VE MADE A BIT OF A SCENE.
THIS IS FROM BAKER PLAZA AROUND 4:32pm TODAY.
WHO'RE THE ONES CHASING THEM?
THE ARCOLA INSTITUTE.
BUNCH OF TECHNOPHOBIC ASSHOLES WHO'RE OBSESSED WITH THIS IDEA THAT ROBOTS ARE GOING TO BRING ABOUT THE END OF THE WORLD.
OKAY.
TELL ME EVERYTHING YOU KNOW ABOUT THEM...

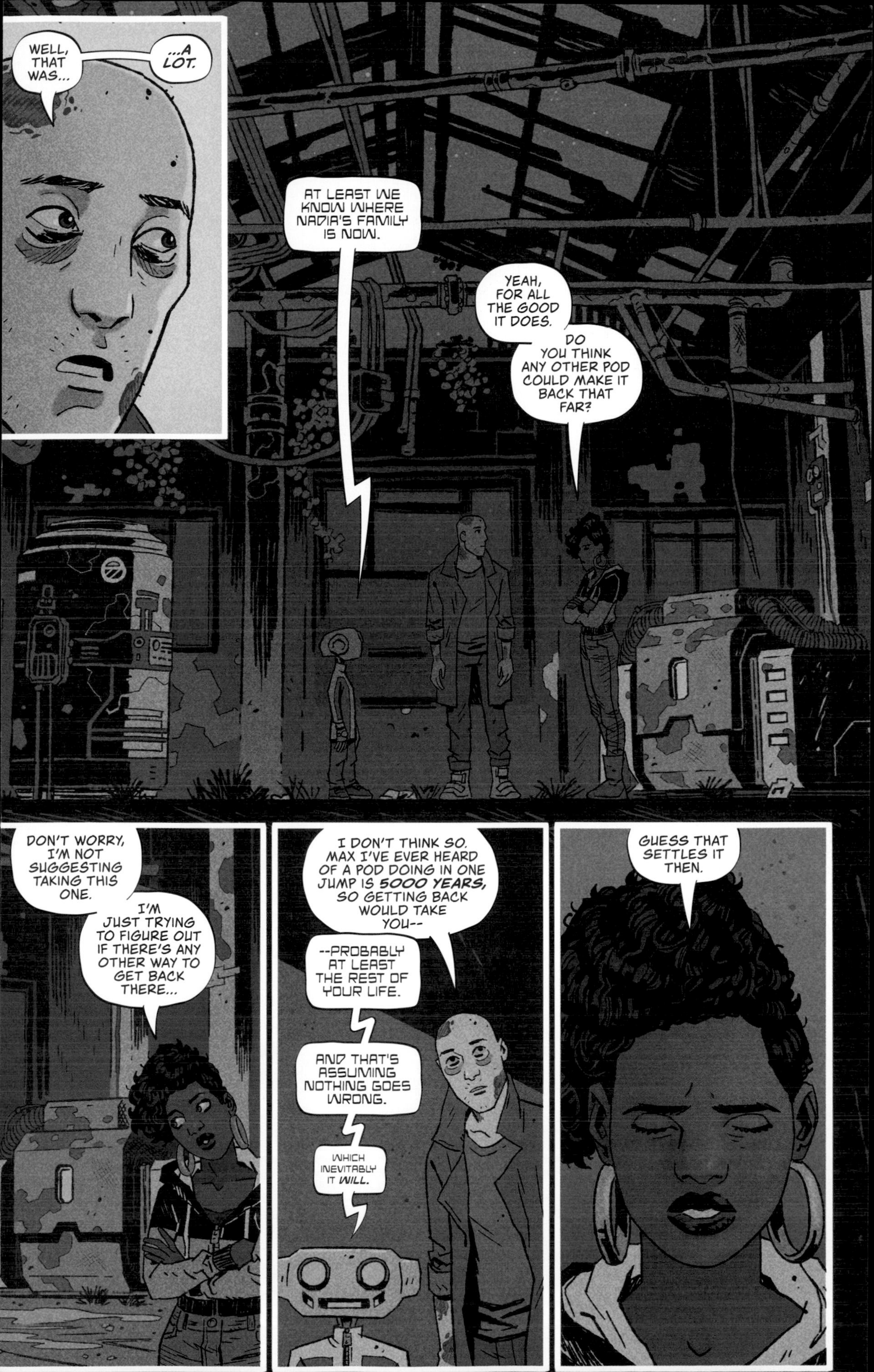
WELL, THAT WAS...
...A LOT.
AT LEAST WE KNOW WHERE NADIA'S FAMILY IS NOW.
YEAH, FOR ALL THE GOOD IT DOES.
DO YOU THINK ANY OTHER POD COULD MAKE IT BACK THAT FAR?
DON'T WORRY, I'M NOT SUGGESTING TAKING THIS ONE.
I'M JUST TRYING TO FIGURE OUT IF THERE'S ANY OTHER WAY TO GET BACK THERE...
I DON'T THINK SO. MAX I'VE EVER HEARD OF A POD DOING IN ONE JUMP IS 5000 YEARS, SO GETTING BACK WOULD TAKE YOU--
--PROBABLY AT LEAST THE REST OF YOUR LIFE.
AND THAT'S ASSUMING NOTHING GOES WRONG.
WHICH INEVITABLY IT WILL.
GUESS THAT SETTLES IT THEN.

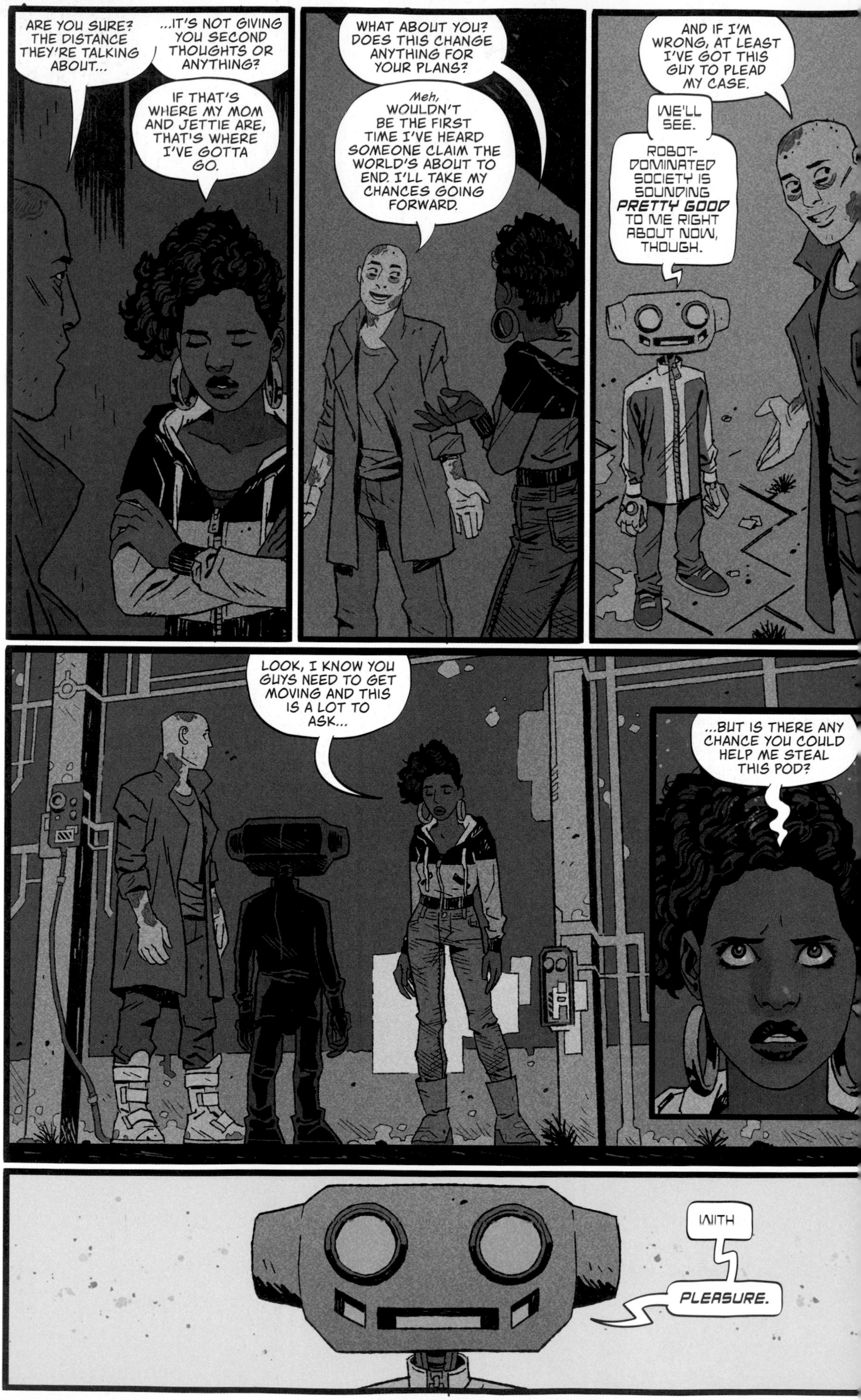
ARE YOU SURE? THE DISTANCE THEY'RE TALKING ABOUT...
...IT'S NOT GIVING YOU SECOND THOUGHTS OR ANYTHING?
IF THAT'S WHERE MY MOM AND JETTIE ARE, THAT'S WHERE I'VE GOTTA GO.
WHAT ABOUT YOU? DOES THIS CHANGE ANYTHING FOR YOUR PLANS?
Meh, WOULDN'T BE THE FIRST TIME I'VE HEARD SOMEONE CLAIM THE WORLD'S ABOUT TO END. I'LL TAKE MY CHANCES GOING FORWARD.
AND IF I'M WRONG, AT LEAST I'VE GOT THIS GUY TO PLEAD MY CASE.
WE'LL SEE.
ROBOT-DOMINATED SOCIETY IS SOUNDING PRETTY GOOD TO ME RIGHT ABOUT NOW, THOUGH.
LOOK, I KNOW YOU GUYS NEED TO GET MOVING AND THIS IS A LOT TO ASK...
...BUT IS THERE ANY CHANCE YOU COULD HELP ME STEAL THIS POD?
WITH
PLEASURE.

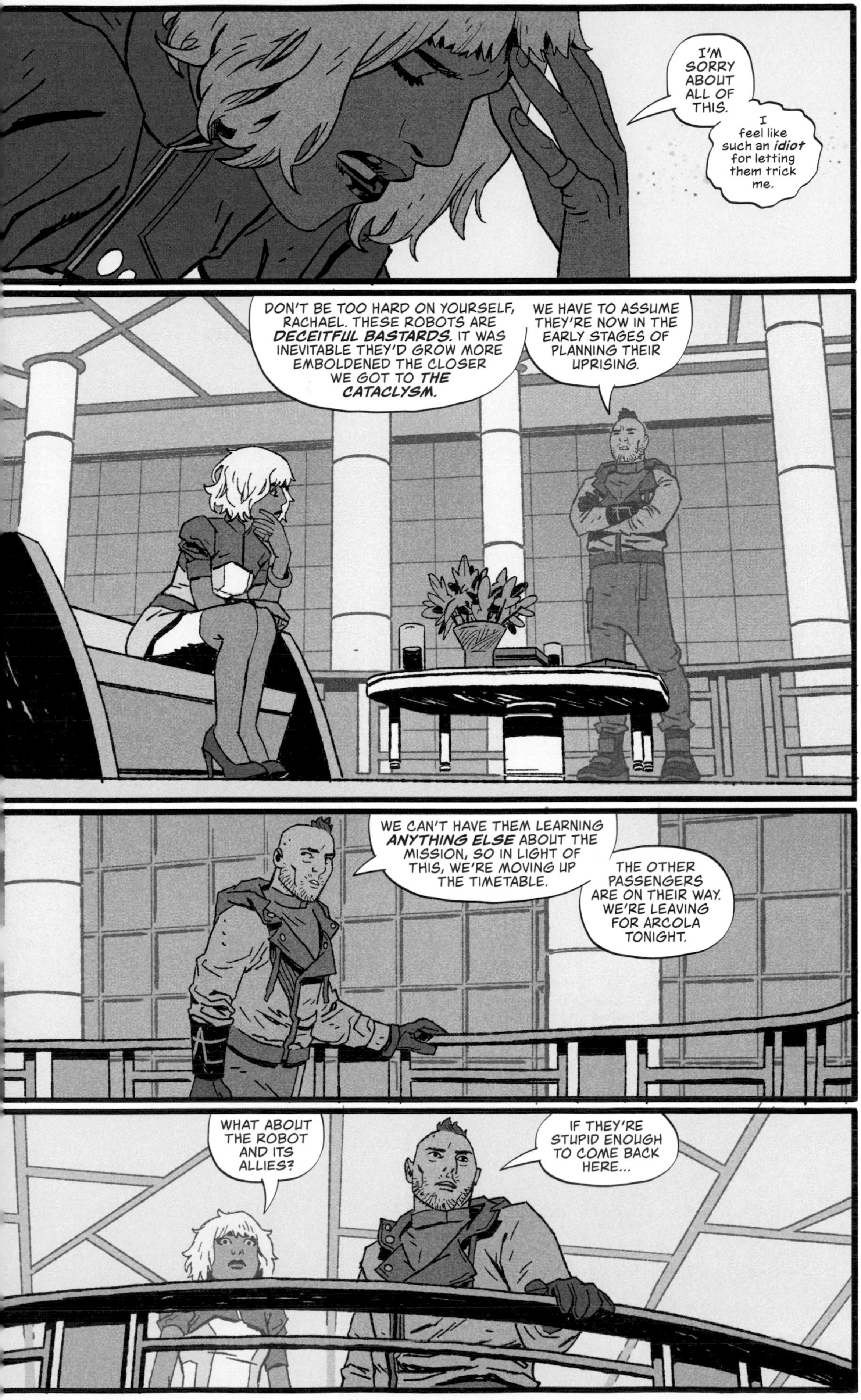

I'M SORRY ABOUT ALL OF THIS.
I feel like such an *idiot* for letting them trick me.
DON'T BE TOO HARD ON YOURSELF, RACHAEL. THESE ROBOTS ARE ***DECEITFUL BASTARDS.*** IT WAS INEVITABLE THEY'D GROW MORE EMBOLDENED THE CLOSER WE GOT TO ***THE CATACLYSM.***
WE HAVE TO ASSUME THEY'RE NOW IN THE EARLY STAGES OF PLANNING THEIR UPRISING.
WE CAN'T HAVE THEM LEARNING ***ANYTHING ELSE*** ABOUT THE MISSION, SO IN LIGHT OF THIS, WE'RE MOVING UP THE TIMETABLE.
THE OTHER PASSENGERS ARE ON THEIR WAY. WE'RE LEAVING FOR ARCOLA TONIGHT.
WHAT ABOUT THE ROBOT AND ITS ALLIES?
IF THEY'RE STUPID ENOUGH TO COME BACK HERE...

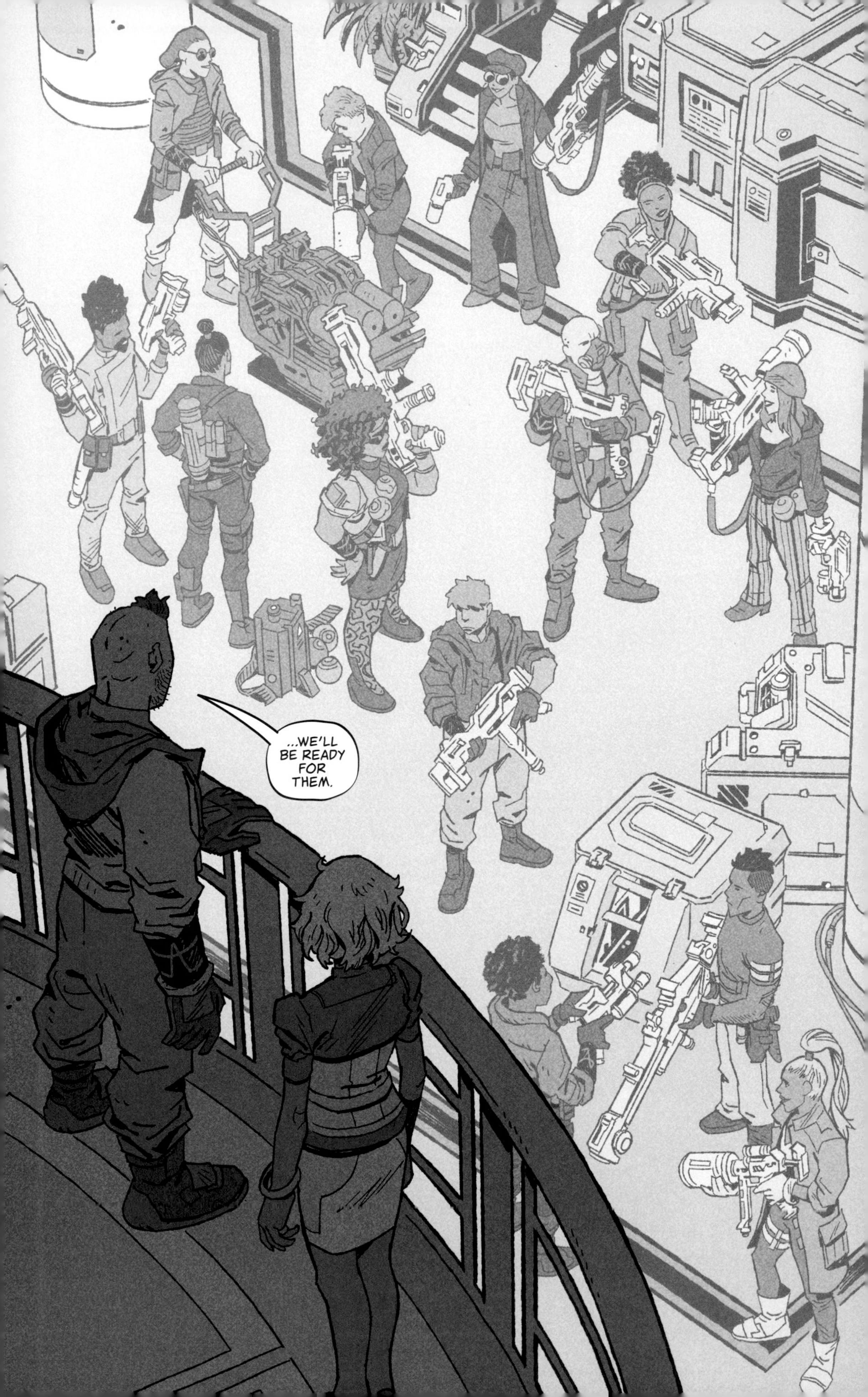
...WE'LL BE READY FOR THEM.

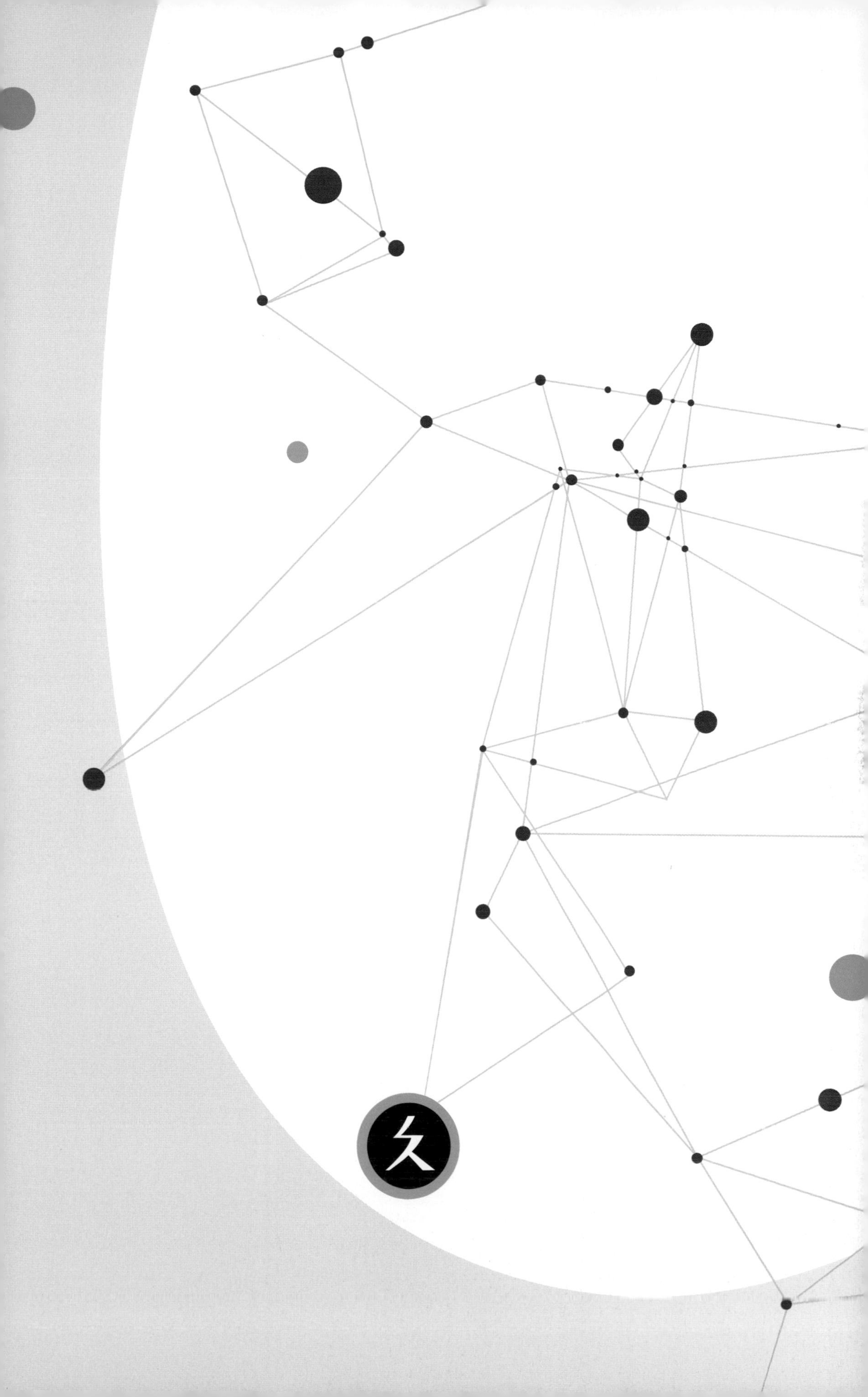
久

17

BREAKING
AND
ENTERING

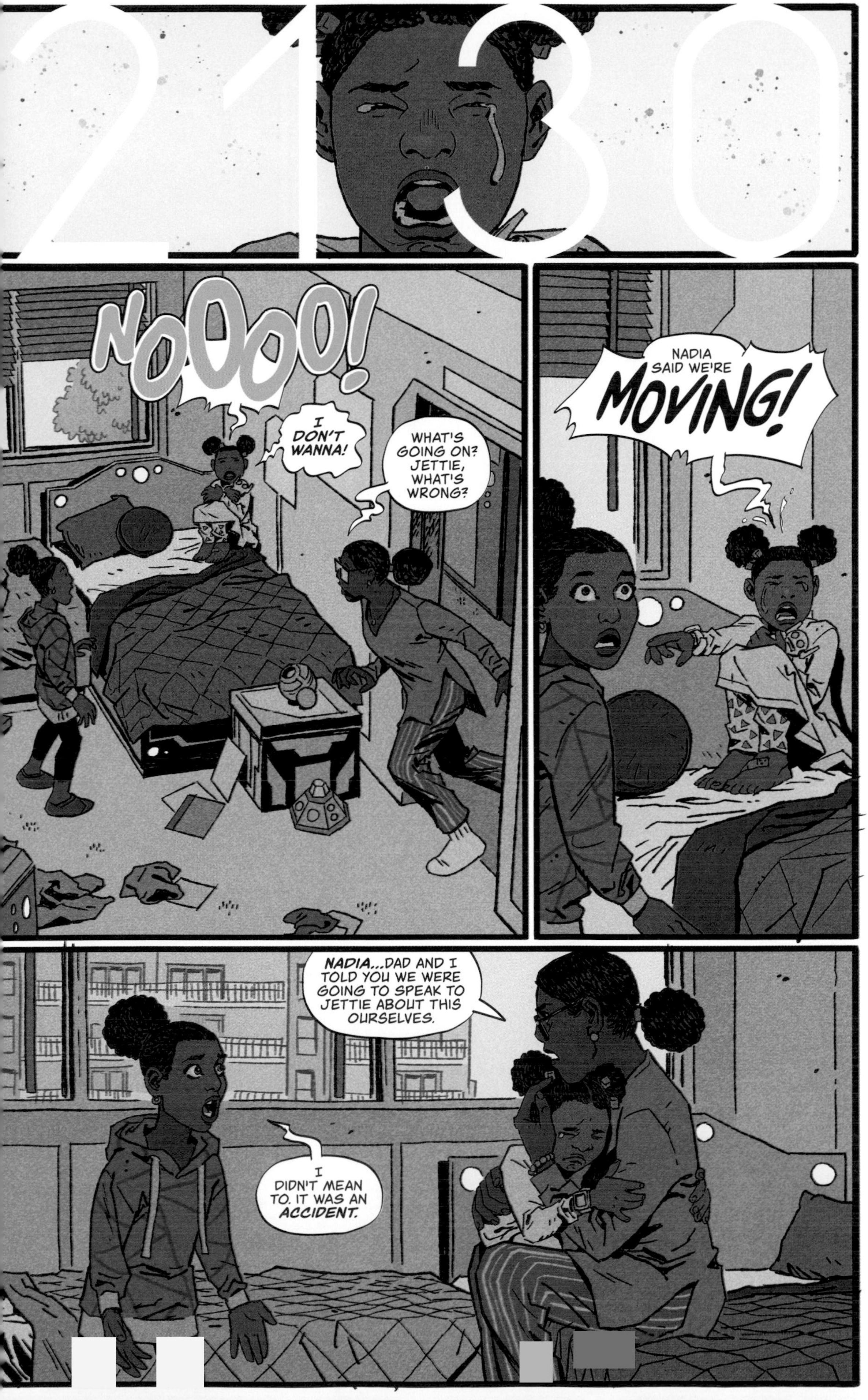
NOOOO!
I DON'T WANNA!
WHAT'S GOING ON? JETTIE, WHAT'S WRONG?
NADIA SAID WE'RE MOVING!
NADIA...DAD AND I TOLD YOU WE WERE GOING TO SPEAK TO JETTIE ABOUT THIS OURSELVES.
I DIDN'T MEAN TO. IT WAS AN ACCIDENT.

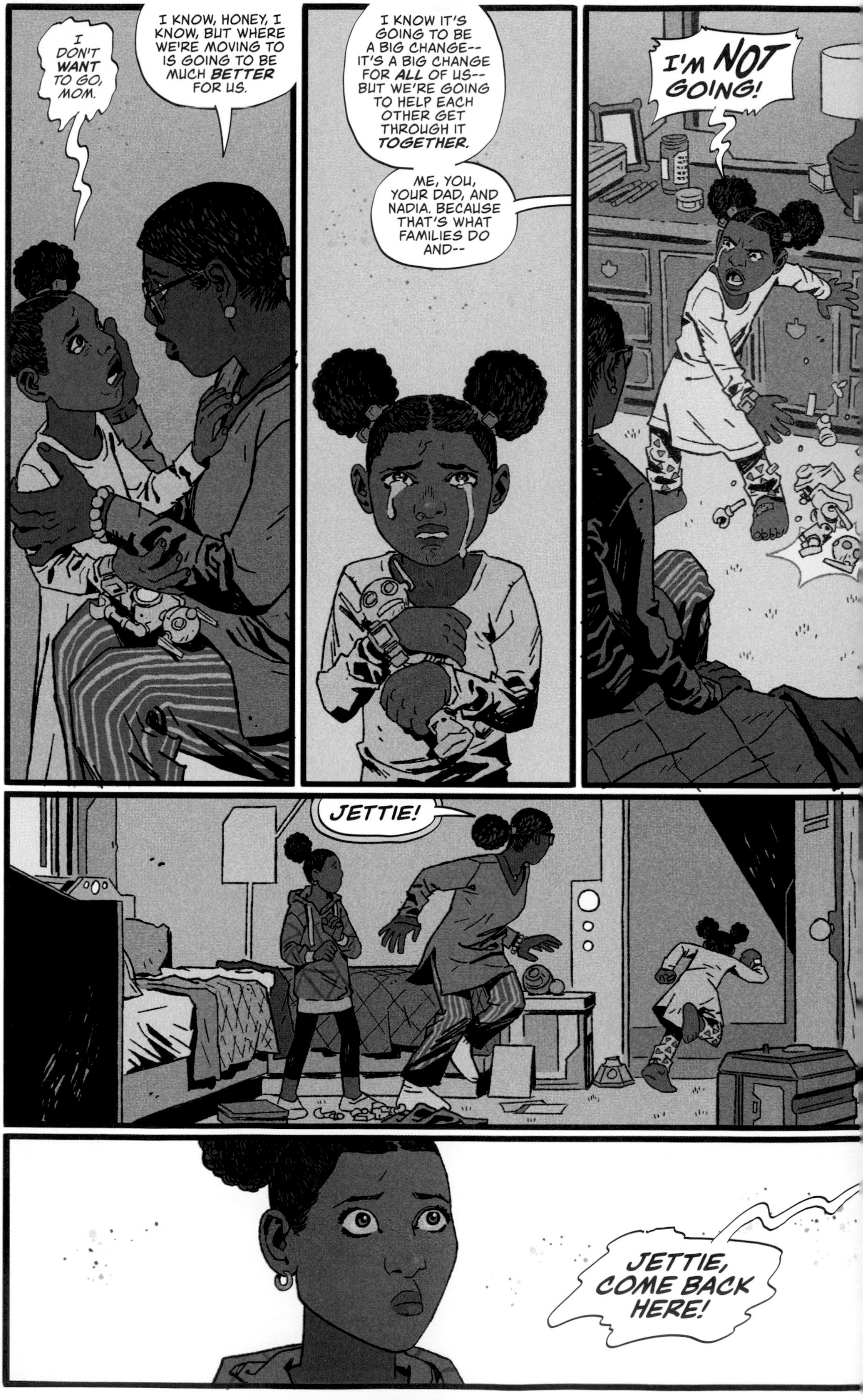
I DON'T WANT TO GO, MOM.
I KNOW, HONEY, I KNOW, BUT WHERE WE'RE MOVING TO IS GOING TO BE MUCH BETTER FOR US.
I KNOW IT'S GOING TO BE A BIG CHANGE-- IT'S A BIG CHANGE FOR ALL OF US-- BUT WE'RE GOING TO HELP EACH OTHER GET THROUGH IT TOGETHER.
ME, YOU, YOUR DAD, AND NADIA. BECAUSE THAT'S WHAT FAMILIES DO AND--
I'M NOT GOING!
JETTIE!
JETTIE, COME BACK HERE!

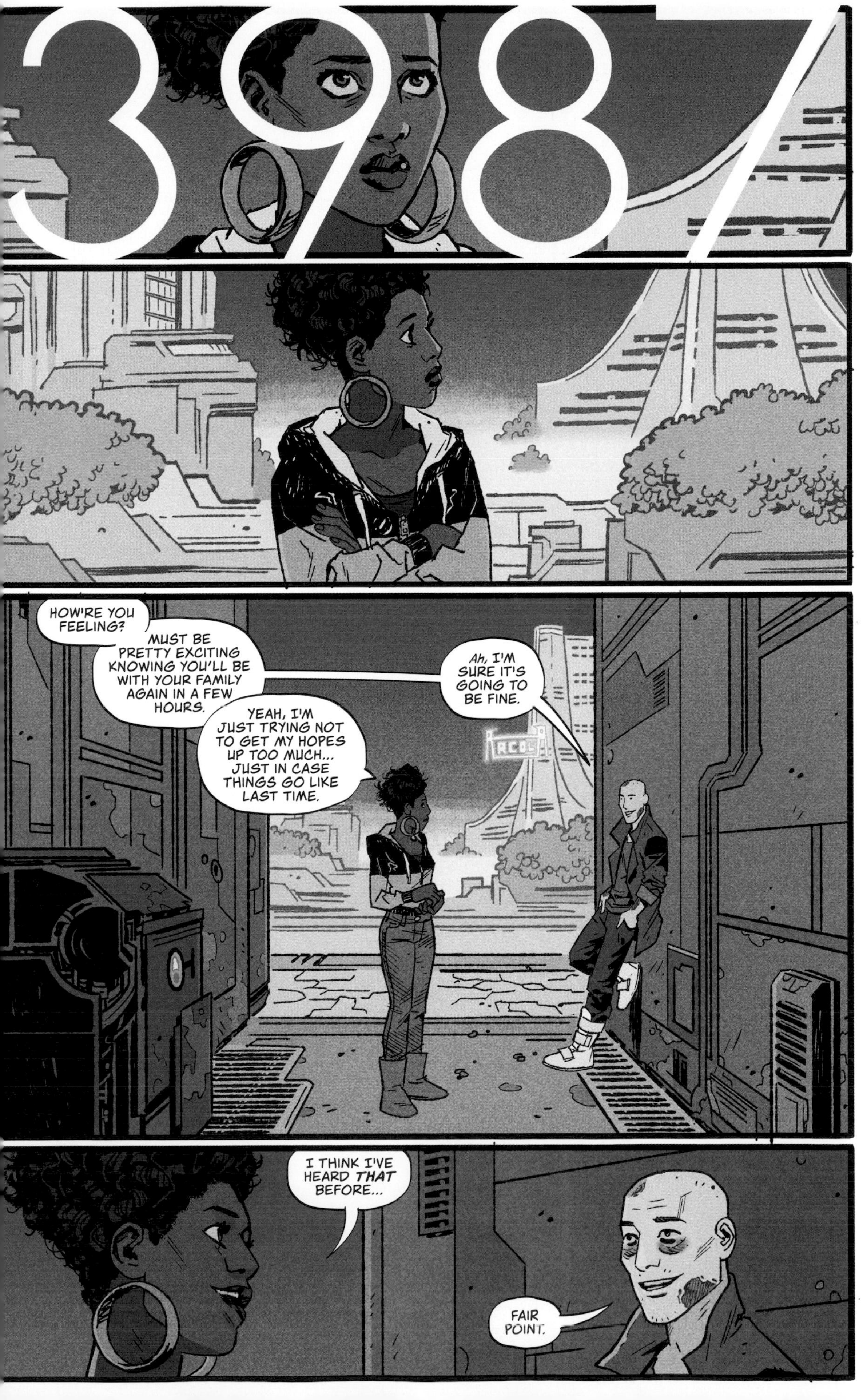
3987
HOW'RE YOU FEELING?
MUST BE PRETTY EXCITING KNOWING YOU'LL BE WITH YOUR FAMILY AGAIN IN A FEW HOURS.
YEAH, I'M JUST TRYING NOT TO GET MY HOPES UP TOO MUCH... JUST IN CASE THINGS GO LIKE LAST TIME.
Ah, I'M SURE IT'S GOING TO BE FINE.
ARCOL
I THINK I'VE HEARD THAT BEFORE...
FAIR POINT.

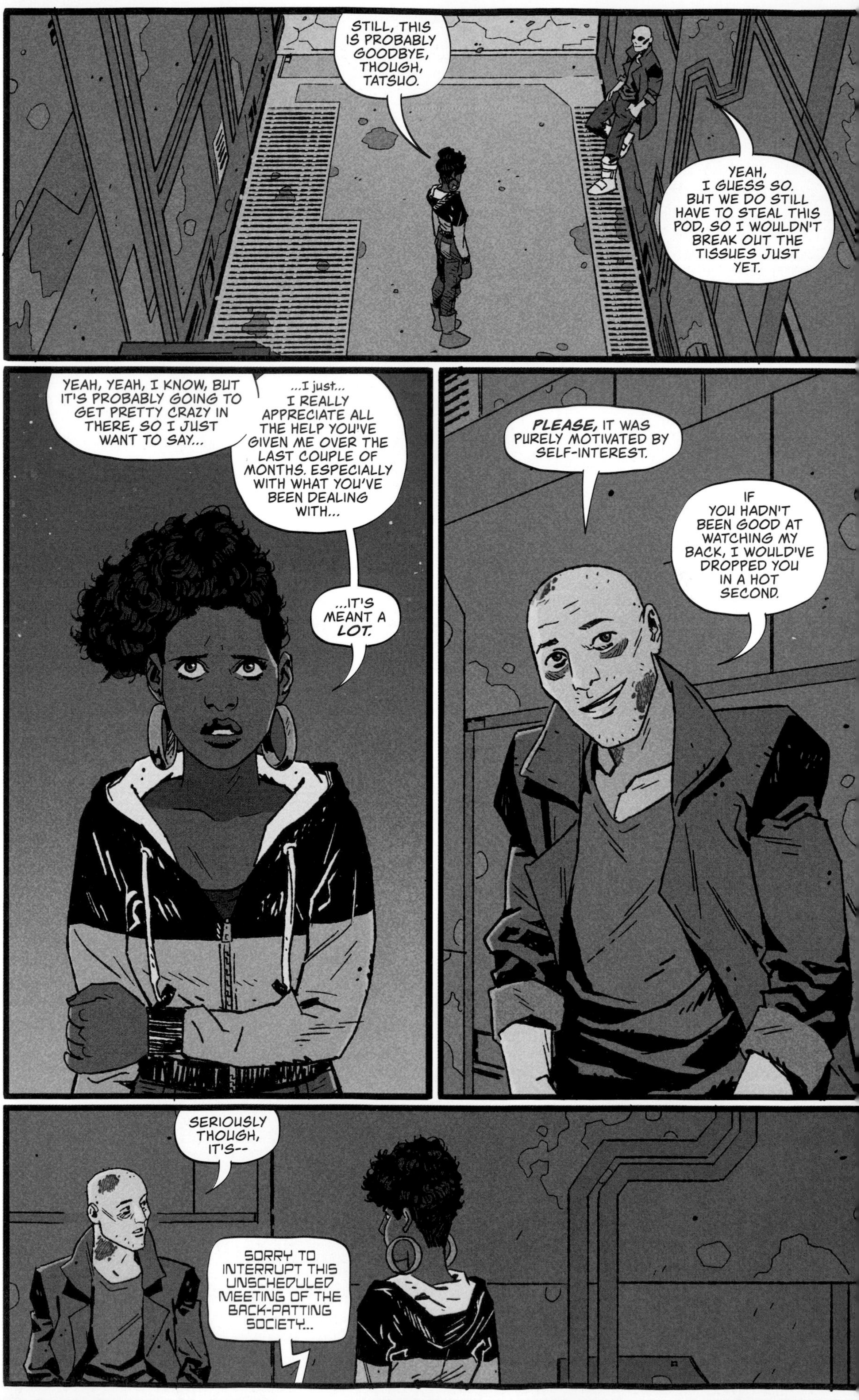
STILL, THIS IS PROBABLY GOODBYE, THOUGH, TATSUO.
YEAH, I GUESS SO. BUT WE DO STILL HAVE TO STEAL THIS POD, SO I WOULDN'T BREAK OUT THE TISSUES JUST YET.
YEAH, YEAH, I KNOW, BUT IT'S PROBABLY GOING TO GET PRETTY CRAZY IN THERE, SO I JUST WANT TO SAY...
...I just... I REALLY APPRECIATE ALL THE HELP YOU'VE GIVEN ME OVER THE LAST COUPLE OF MONTHS. ESPECIALLY WITH WHAT YOU'VE BEEN DEALING WITH...
...IT'S MEANT A LOT.
PLEASE, IT WAS PURELY MOTIVATED BY SELF-INTEREST.
IF YOU HADN'T BEEN GOOD AT WATCHING MY BACK, I WOULD'VE DROPPED YOU IN A HOT SECOND.
SERIOUSLY THOUGH, IT'S--
SORRY TO INTERRUPT THIS UNSCHEDULED MEETING OF THE BACK-PATTING SOCIETY...

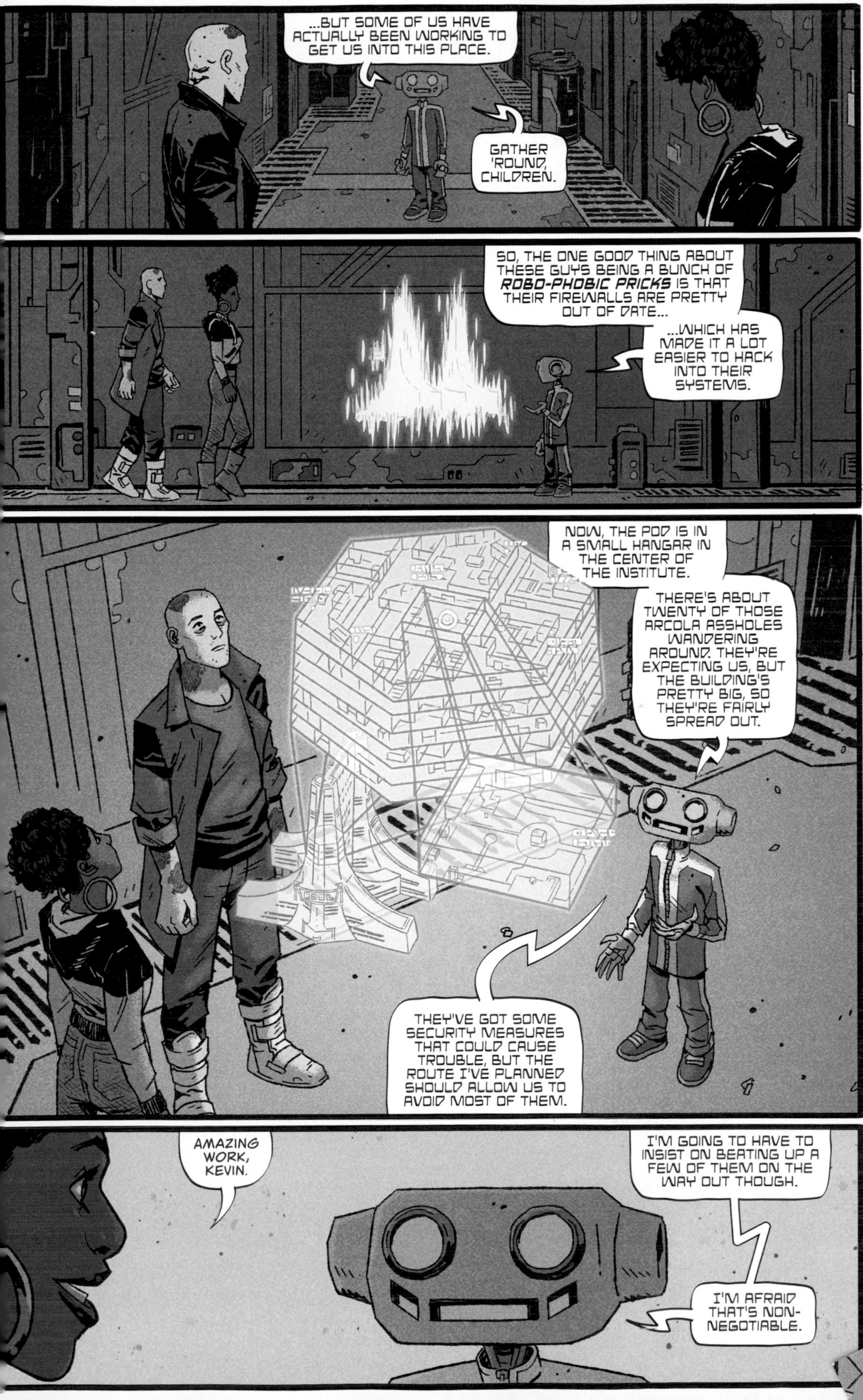
...BUT SOME OF US HAVE ACTUALLY BEEN WORKING TO GET US INTO THIS PLACE.
GATHER 'ROUND, CHILDREN.
SO, THE ONE GOOD THING ABOUT THESE GUYS BEING A BUNCH OF *ROBO-PHOBIC PRICKS* IS THAT THEIR FIREWALLS ARE PRETTY OUT OF DATE...
...WHICH HAS MADE IT A LOT EASIER TO HACK INTO THEIR SYSTEMS.
NOW, THE POD IS IN A SMALL HANGAR IN THE CENTER OF THE INSTITUTE.
THERE'S ABOUT TWENTY OF THOSE ARCOLA ASSHOLES WANDERING AROUND. THEY'RE EXPECTING US, BUT THE BUILDING'S PRETTY BIG, SO THEY'RE FAIRLY SPREAD OUT.
THEY'VE GOT SOME SECURITY MEASURES THAT COULD CAUSE TROUBLE, BUT THE ROUTE I'VE PLANNED SHOULD ALLOW US TO AVOID MOST OF THEM.
AMAZING WORK, KEVIN.
I'M GOING TO HAVE TO INSIST ON BEATING UP A FEW OF THEM ON THE WAY OUT THOUGH.
I'M AFRAID THAT'S NON-NEGOTIABLE.

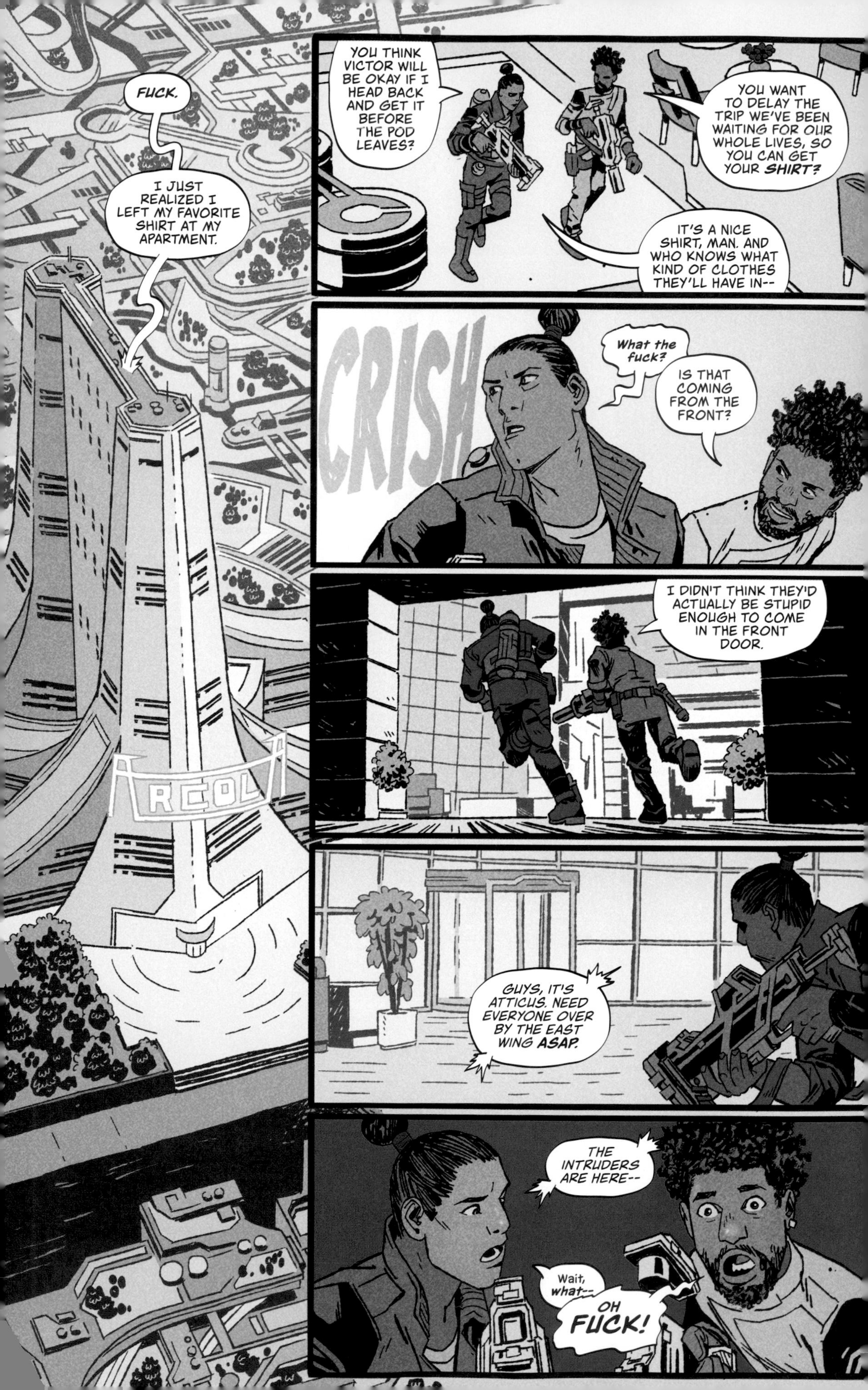
FUCK.
I JUST REALIZED I LEFT MY FAVORITE SHIRT AT MY APARTMENT.
ARCOL
YOU THINK VICTOR WILL BE OKAY IF I HEAD BACK AND GET IT BEFORE THE POD LEAVES?
YOU WANT TO DELAY THE TRIP WE'VE BEEN WAITING FOR OUR WHOLE LIVES, SO YOU CAN GET YOUR SHIRT?
IT'S A NICE SHIRT, MAN. AND WHO KNOWS WHAT KIND OF CLOTHES THEY'LL HAVE IN--
CRISH
What the fuck?
IS THAT COMING FROM THE FRONT?
I DIDN'T THINK THEY'D ACTUALLY BE STUPID ENOUGH TO COME IN THE FRONT DOOR.
GUYS, IT'S ATTICUS. NEED EVERYONE OVER BY THE EAST WING ASAP.
THE INTRUDERS ARE HERE--
Wait, what--
OH FUCK!

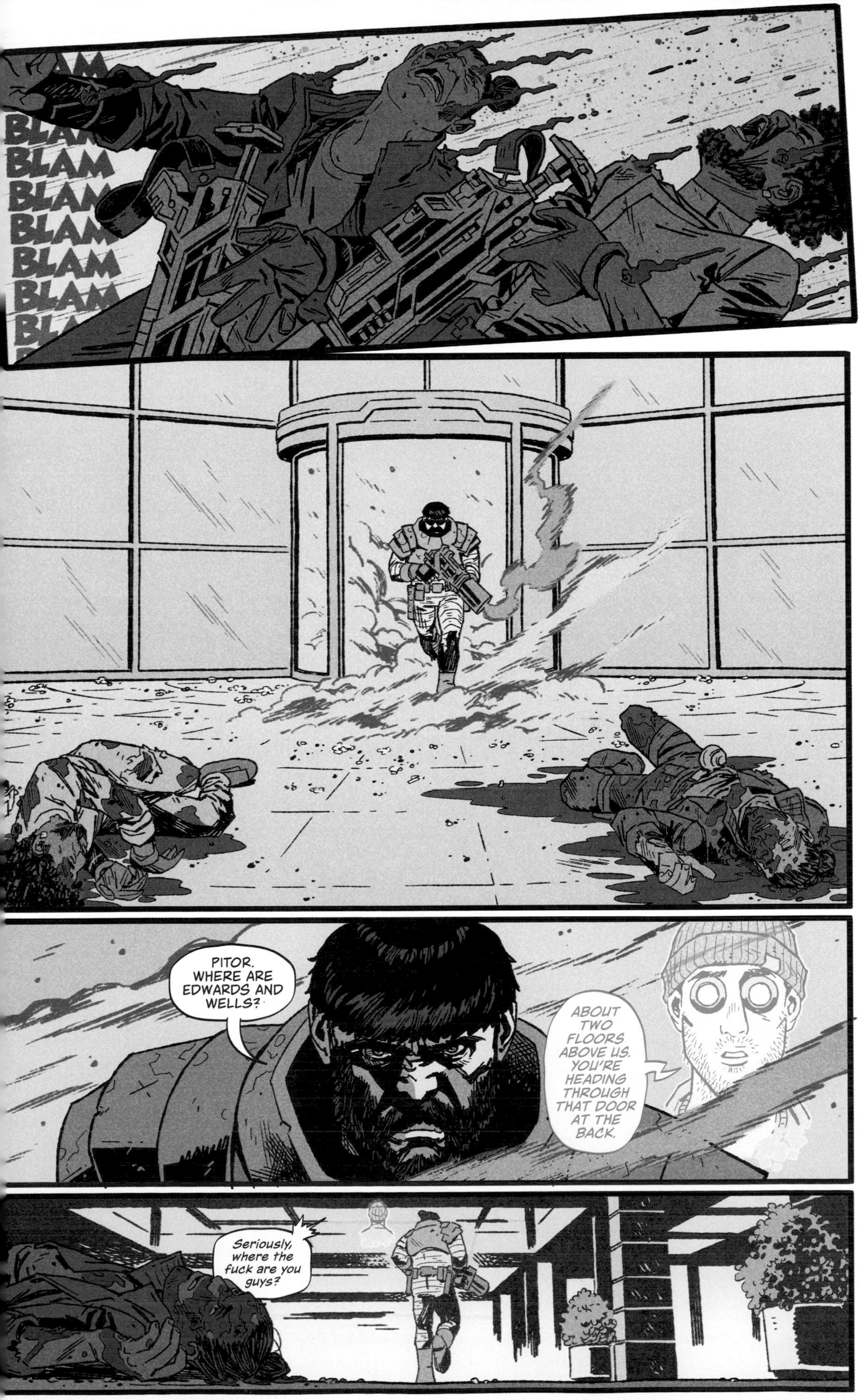

BLAM BLAM BLAM BLAM BLAM BLAM BLAM BLAM
PITOR. WHERE ARE EDWARDS AND WELLS?
ABOUT TWO FLOORS ABOVE US. YOU'RE HEADING THROUGH THAT DOOR AT THE BACK.
Seriously, where the fuck are you guys?

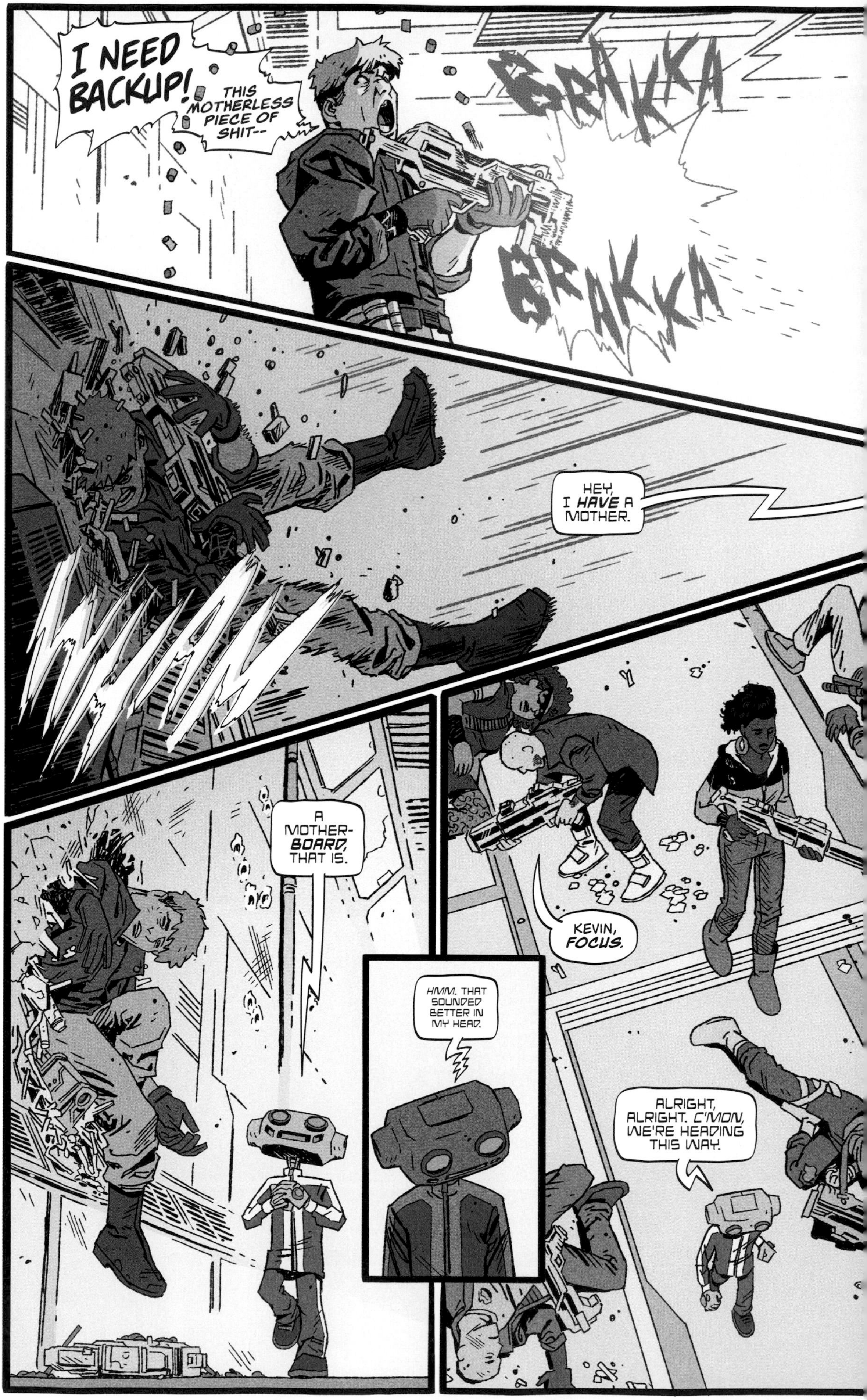
I NEED BACKUP!
THIS MOTHERLESS PIECE OF SHIT--
BRAKKA
BRAKKA
HEY, I HAVE A MOTHER.
WHAM
A MOTHER-BOARD, THAT IS.
KEVIN, FOCUS.
HMM. THAT SOUNDED BETTER IN MY HEAD.
ALRIGHT, ALRIGHT. C'MON, WE'RE HEADING THIS WAY.

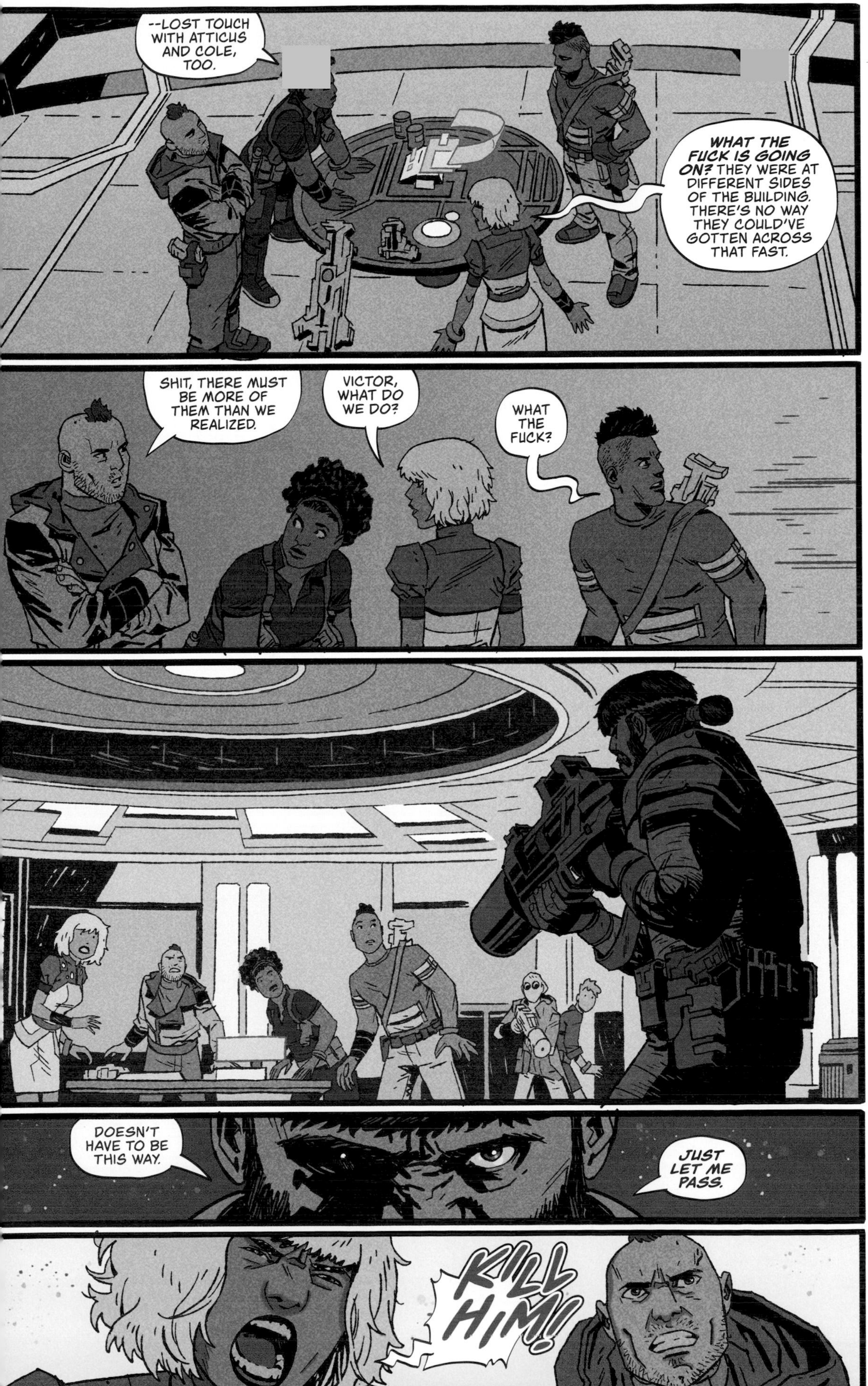
--LOST TOUCH WITH ATTICUS AND COLE, TOO.
WHAT THE FUCK IS GOING ON? THEY WERE AT DIFFERENT SIDES OF THE BUILDING. THERE'S NO WAY THEY COULD'VE GOTTEN ACROSS THAT FAST.
SHIT, THERE MUST BE MORE OF THEM THAN WE REALIZED.
VICTOR, WHAT DO WE DO?
WHAT THE FUCK?
DOESN'T HAVE TO BE THIS WAY.
JUST LET ME PASS.
KILL HIM!

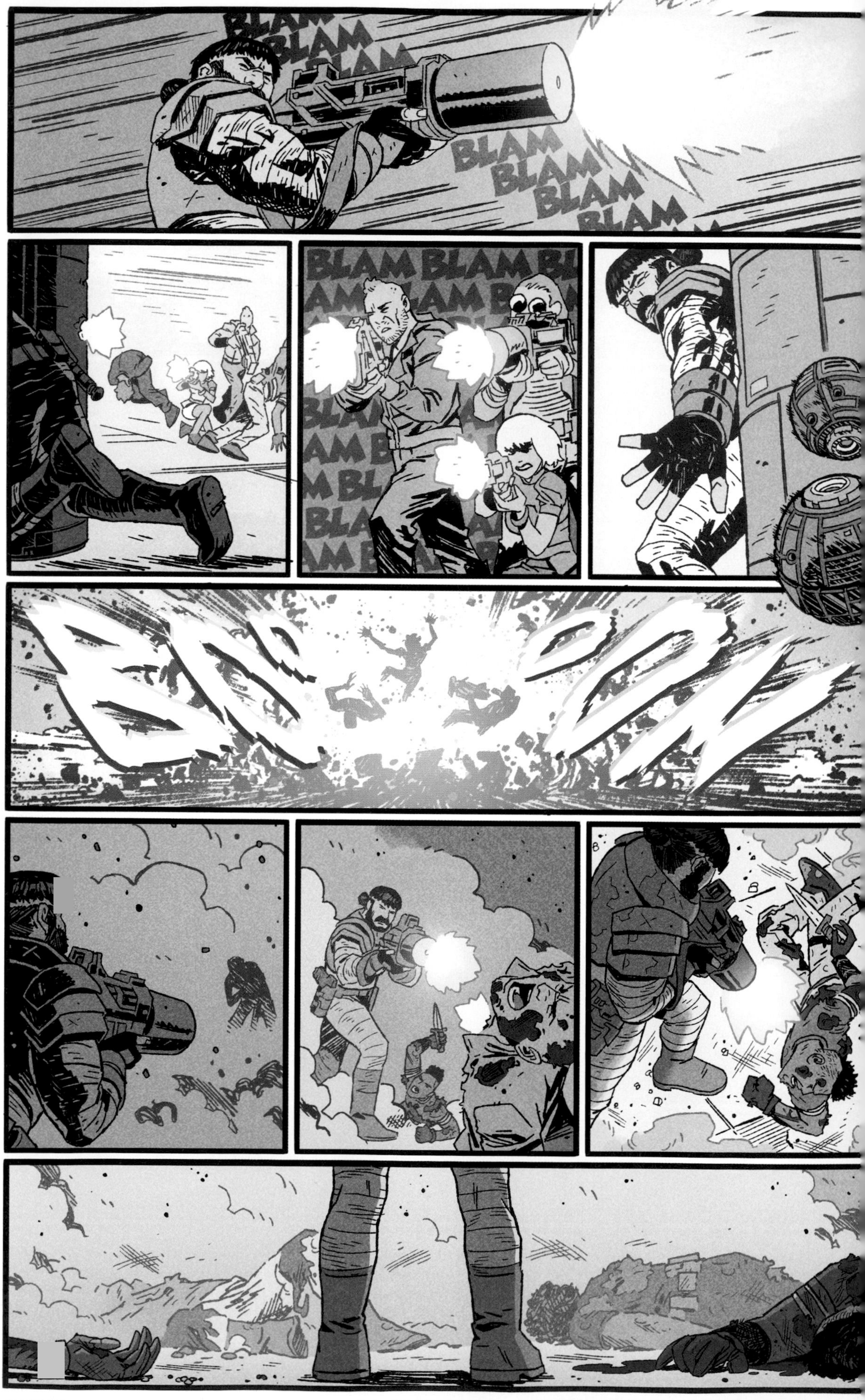
BLAM
BLAM
BLAM
BLAM
BLAM
BLAM
BLAM
BLAM BLAM

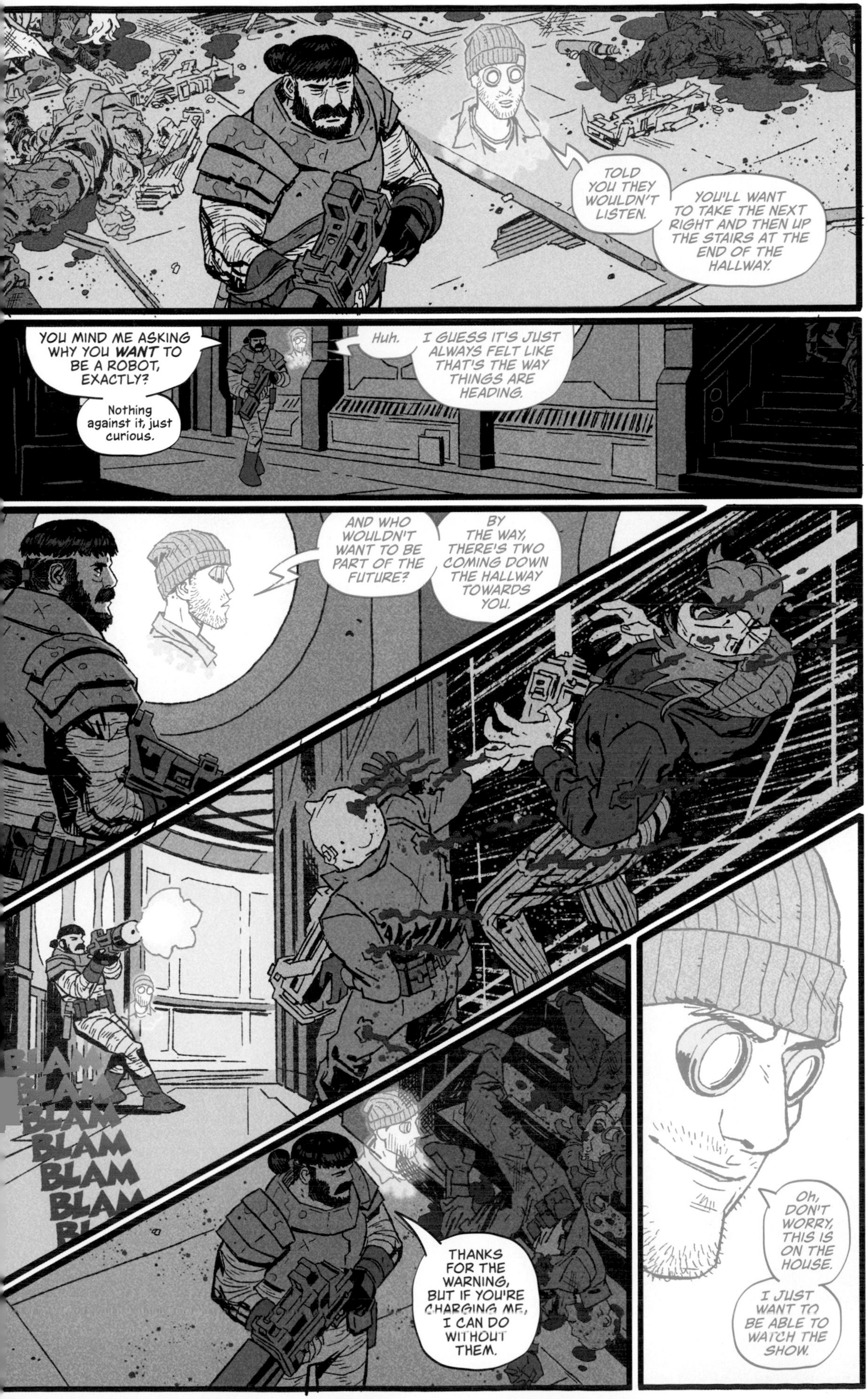
TOLD YOU THEY WOULDN'T LISTEN.
YOU'LL WANT TO TAKE THE NEXT RIGHT AND THEN UP THE STAIRS AT THE END OF THE HALLWAY.
YOU MIND ME ASKING WHY YOU WANT TO BE A ROBOT, EXACTLY?
Nothing against it, just curious.
Huh.
I GUESS IT'S JUST ALWAYS FELT LIKE THAT'S THE WAY THINGS ARE HEADING.
AND WHO WOULDN'T WANT TO BE PART OF THE FUTURE?
BY THE WAY, THERE'S TWO COMING DOWN THE HALLWAY TOWARDS YOU.
BLAM BLAM BLAM BLAM BLAM BLAM
THANKS FOR THE WARNING, BUT IF YOU'RE CHARGING ME, I CAN DO WITHOUT THEM.
Oh, DON'T WORRY, THIS IS ON THE HOUSE.
I JUST WANT TO BE ABLE TO WATCH THE SHOW.

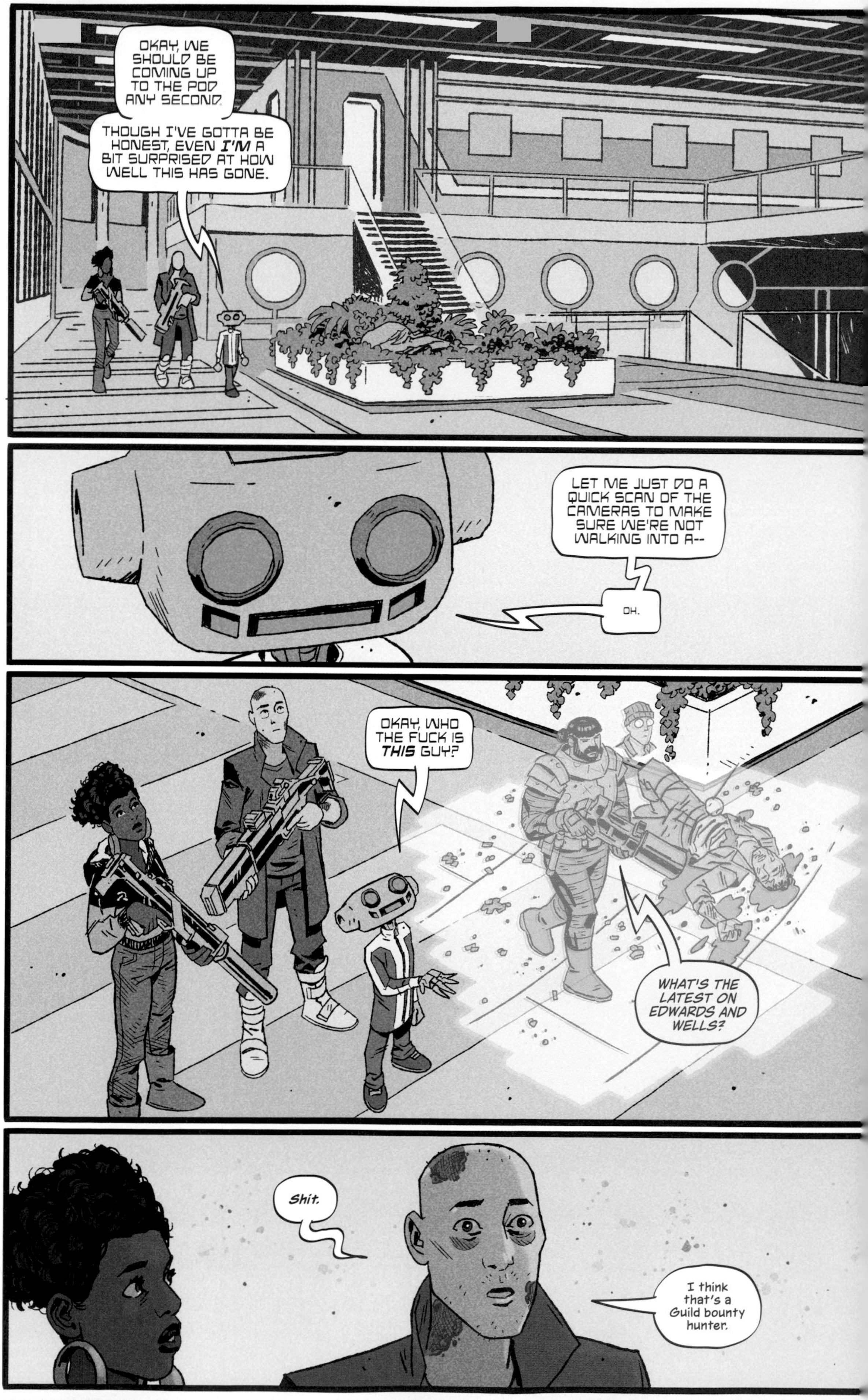

OKAY, WE SHOULD BE COMING UP TO THE POD ANY SECOND.
THOUGH I'VE GOTTA BE HONEST, EVEN I'M A BIT SURPRISED AT HOW WELL THIS HAS GONE.
LET ME JUST DO A QUICK SCAN OF THE CAMERAS TO MAKE SURE WE'RE NOT WALKING INTO A--
OH.
OKAY, WHO THE FUCK IS THIS GUY?
WHAT'S THE LATEST ON EDWARDS AND WELLS?
Shit.
I think that's a Guild bounty hunter.

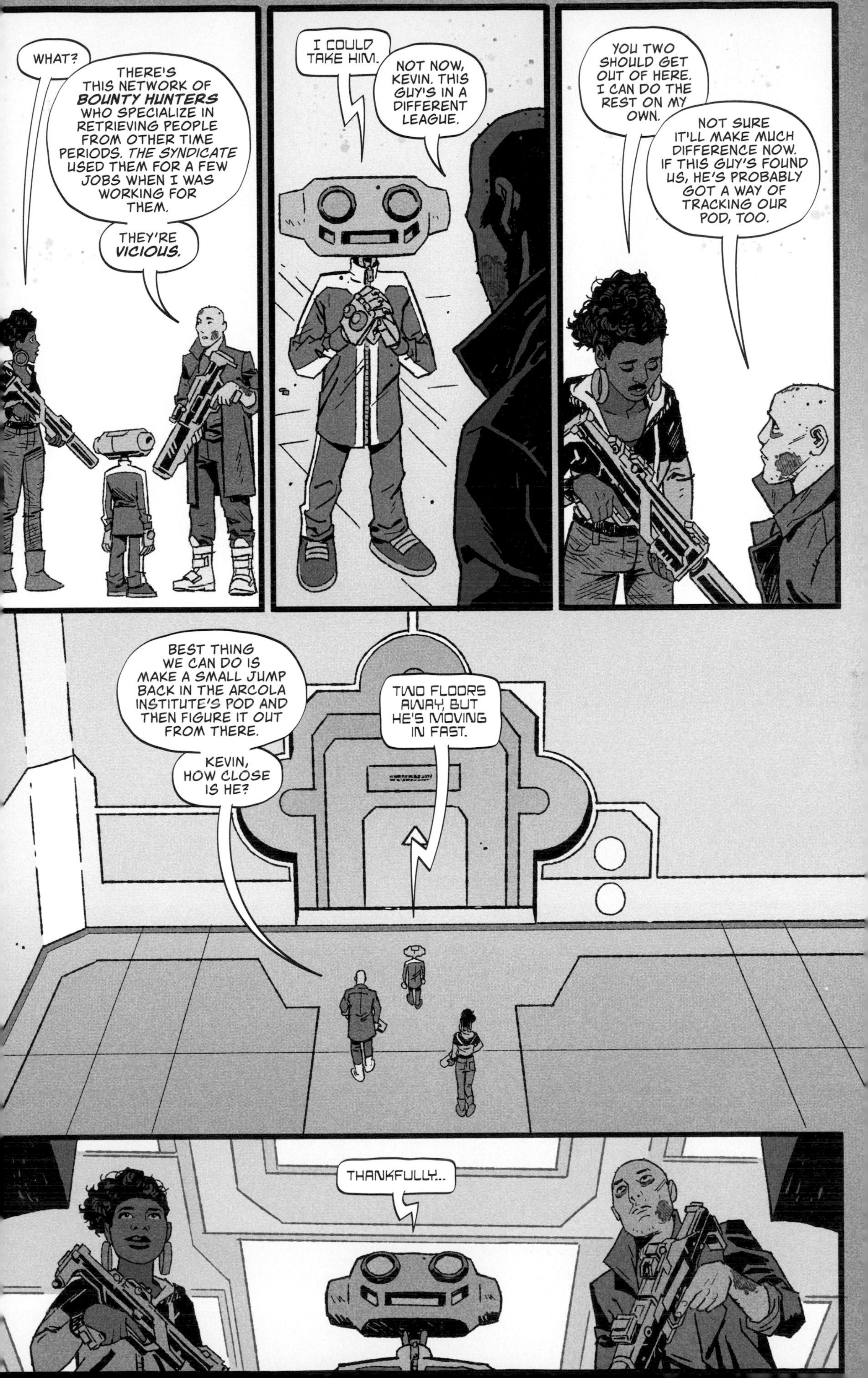
WHAT?
THERE'S THIS NETWORK OF *BOUNTY HUNTERS* WHO SPECIALIZE IN RETRIEVING PEOPLE FROM OTHER TIME PERIODS. *THE SYNDICATE* USED THEM FOR A FEW JOBS WHEN I WAS WORKING FOR THEM.
THEY'RE *VICIOUS.*
I COULD TAKE HIM.
NOT NOW, KEVIN. THIS GUY'S IN A DIFFERENT LEAGUE.
YOU TWO SHOULD GET OUT OF HERE. I CAN DO THE REST ON MY OWN.
NOT SURE IT'LL MAKE MUCH DIFFERENCE NOW. IF THIS GUY'S FOUND US, HE'S PROBABLY GOT A WAY OF TRACKING OUR POD, TOO.
BEST THING WE CAN DO IS MAKE A SMALL JUMP BACK IN THE ARCOLA INSTITUTE'S POD AND THEN FIGURE IT OUT FROM THERE.
KEVIN, HOW CLOSE IS HE?
TWO FLOORS AWAY, BUT HE'S MOVING IN FAST.
THANKFULLY...

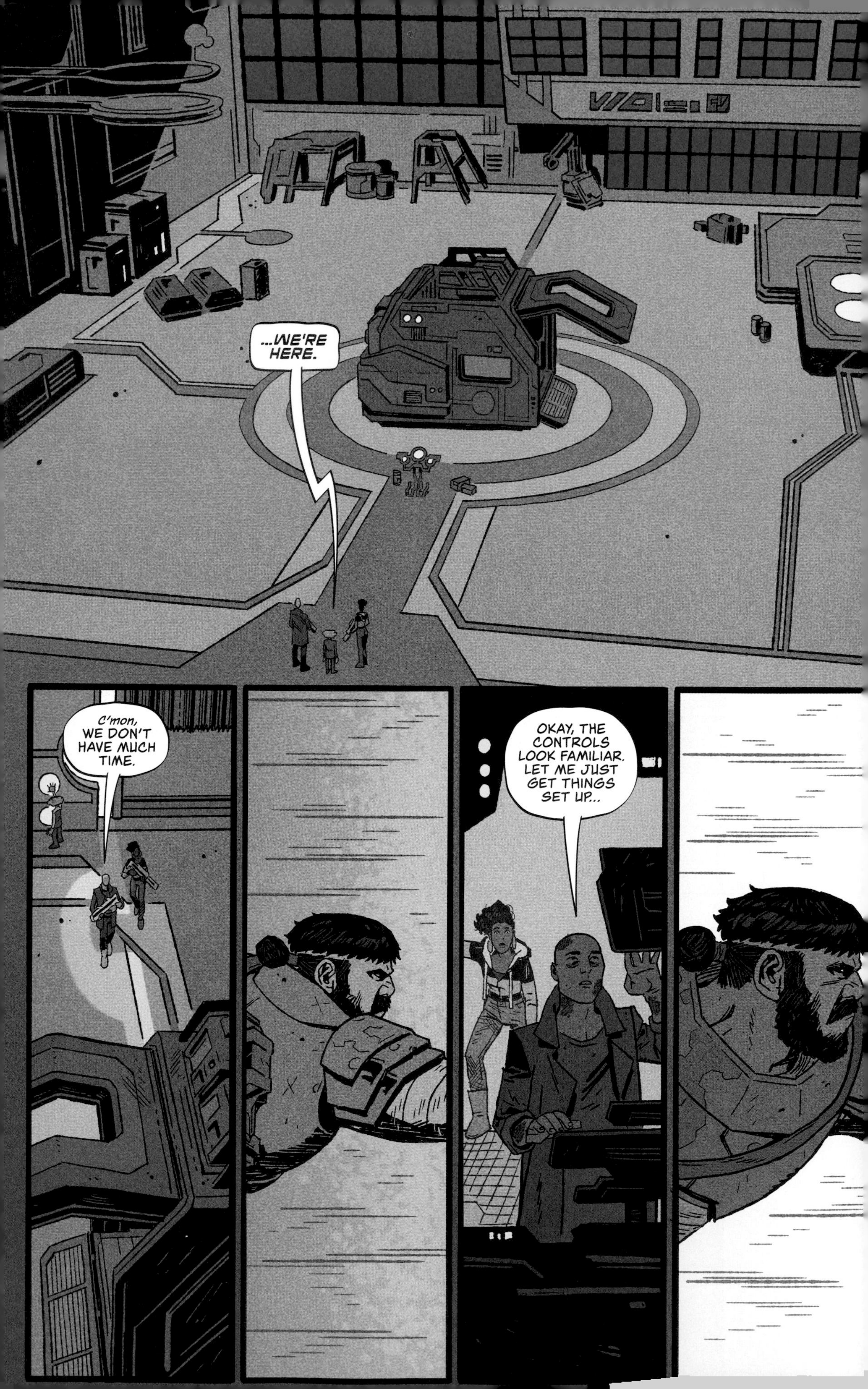
...WE'RE HERE.
C'mon, WE DON'T HAVE MUCH TIME.
OKAY, THE CONTROLS LOOK FAMILIAR. LET ME JUST GET THINGS SET UP...

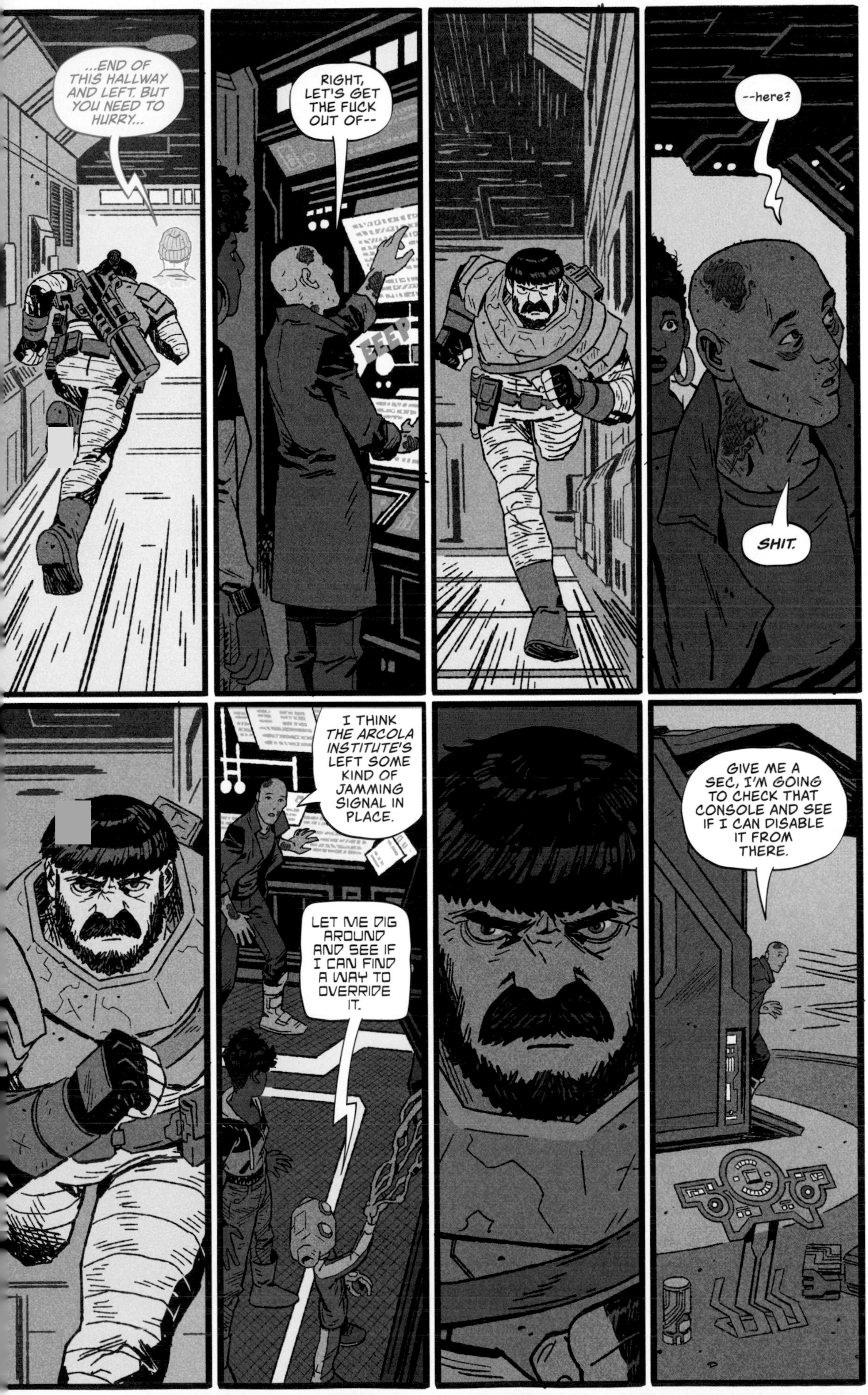
...END OF THIS HALLWAY AND LEFT. BUT YOU NEED TO HURRY...
RIGHT, LET'S GET THE FUCK OUT OF--
EEEP
--here?
SHIT.
I THINK THE ARCOLA INSTITUTE'S LEFT SOME KIND OF JAMMING SIGNAL IN PLACE.
LET ME DIG AROUND AND SEE IF I CAN FIND A WAY TO OVERRIDE IT.
GIVE ME A SEC, I'M GOING TO CHECK THAT CONSOLE AND SEE IF I CAN DISABLE IT FROM THERE.

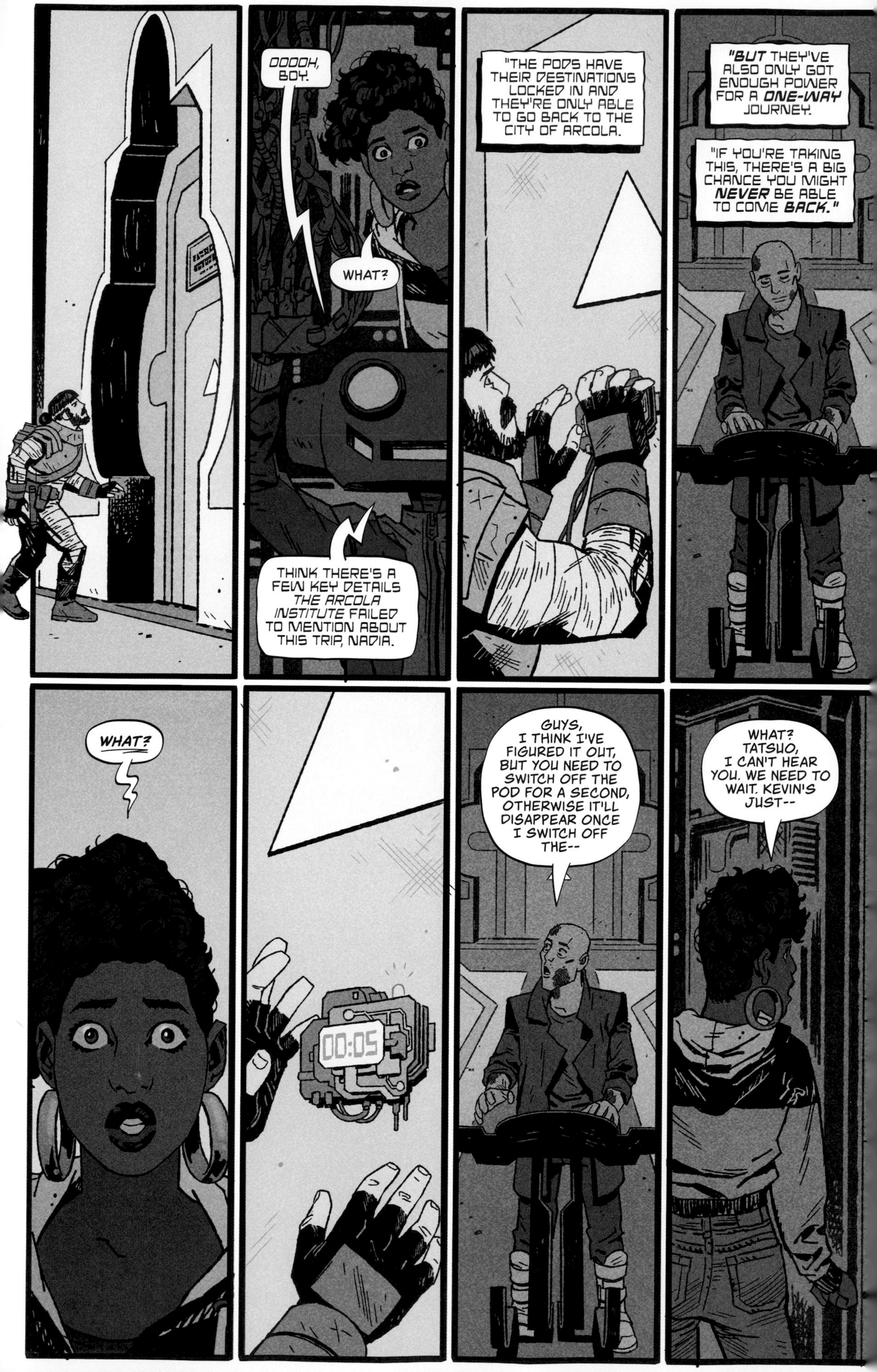
OOOOH, BOY.
WHAT?
THINK THERE'S A FEW KEY DETAILS *THE ARCOLA INSTITUTE* FAILED TO MENTION ABOUT THIS TRIP, NADIA.
"THE PODS HAVE THEIR DESTINATIONS LOCKED IN AND THEY'RE ONLY ABLE TO GO BACK TO THE CITY OF ARCOLA.
"BUT THEY'VE ALSO ONLY GOT ENOUGH POWER FOR A ***ONE-WAY*** JOURNEY.
"IF YOU'RE TAKING THIS, THERE'S A BIG CHANCE YOU MIGHT ***NEVER*** BE ABLE TO COME ***BACK.***"
WHAT?
00:05
GUYS, I THINK I'VE FIGURED IT OUT, BUT YOU NEED TO SWITCH OFF THE POD FOR A SECOND, OTHERWISE IT'LL DISAPPEAR ONCE I SWITCH OFF THE--
WHAT? TATSUO, I CAN'T HEAR YOU. WE NEED TO WAIT. KEVIN'S JUST--

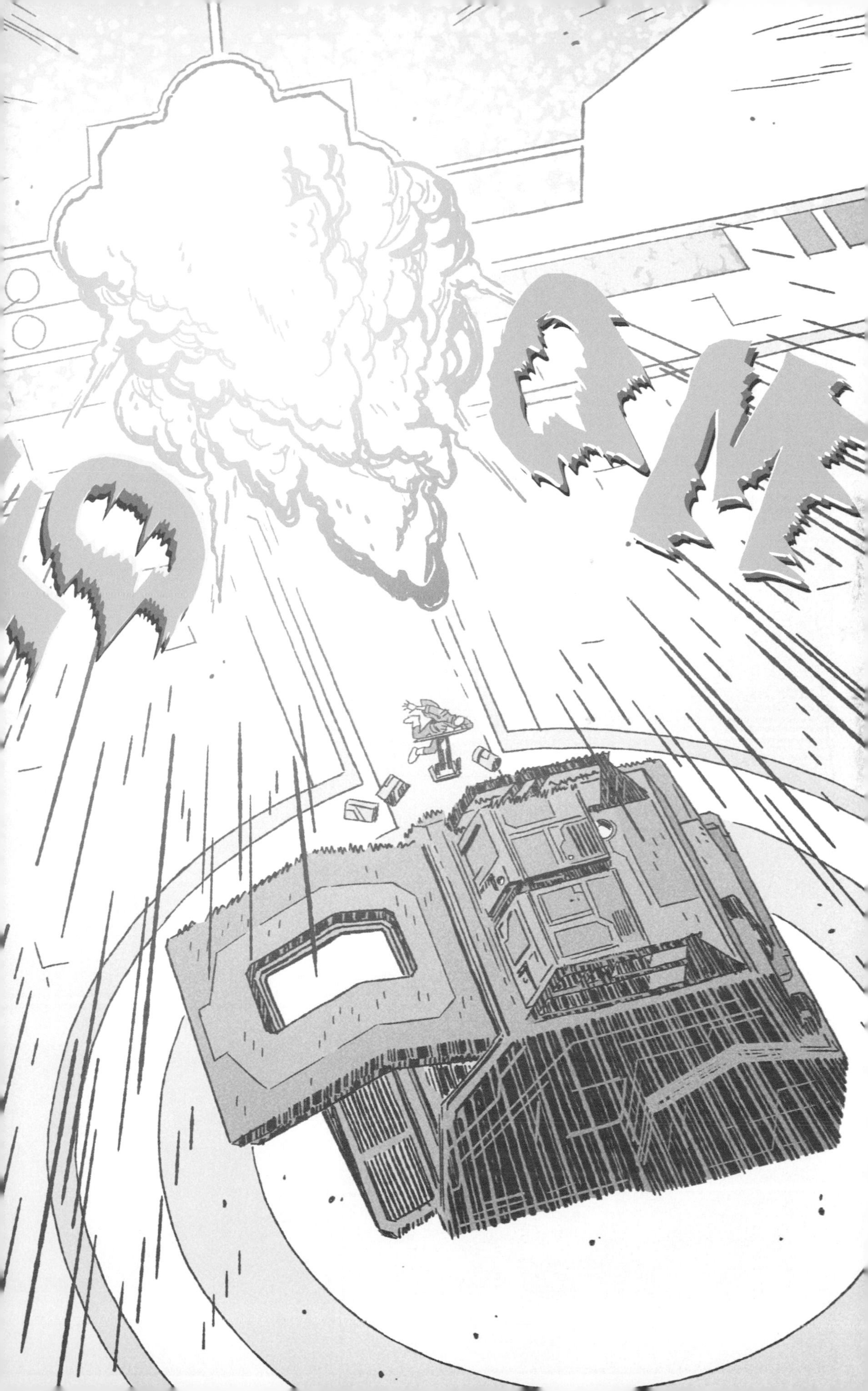
OOM

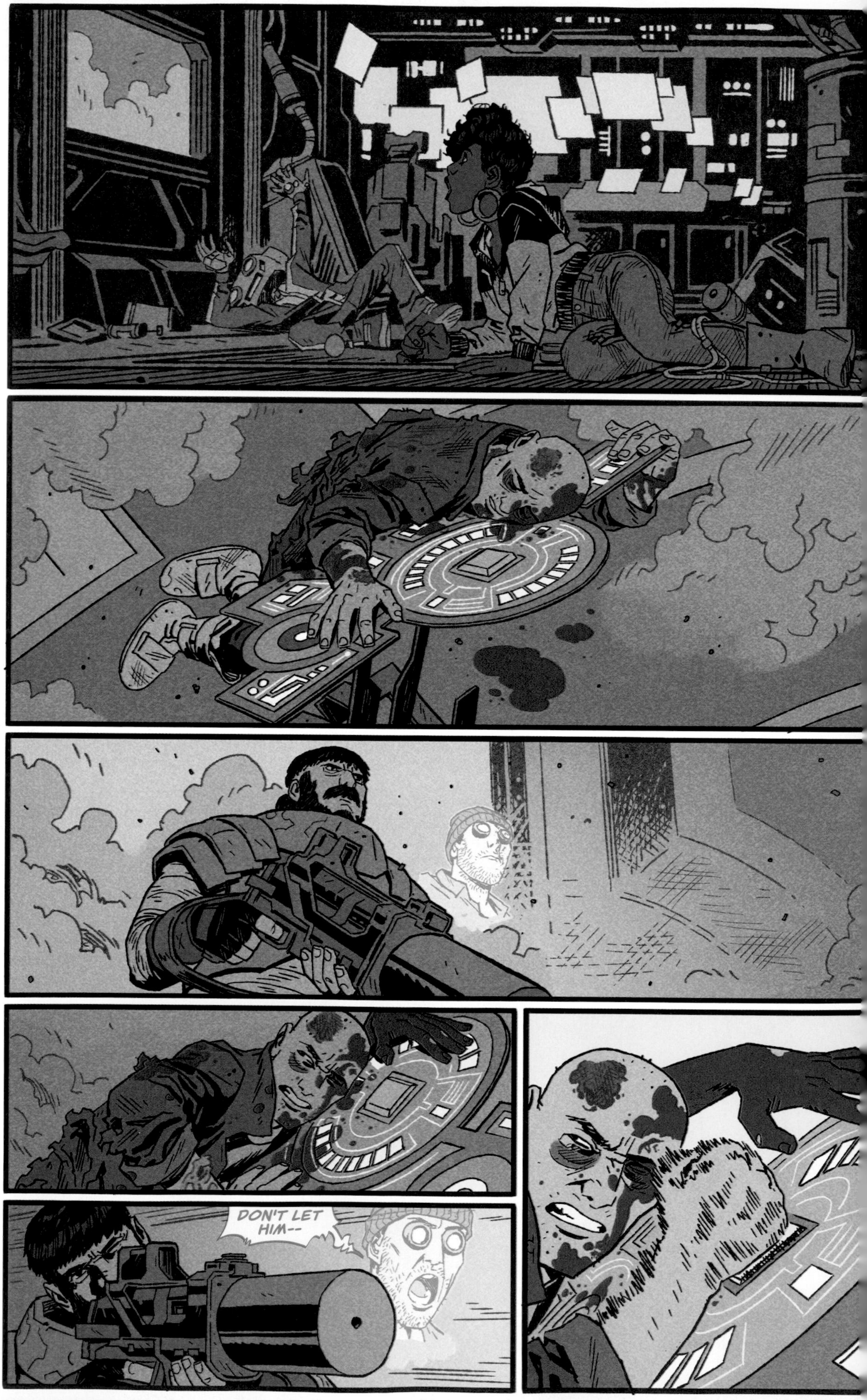
DON'T LET HIM--

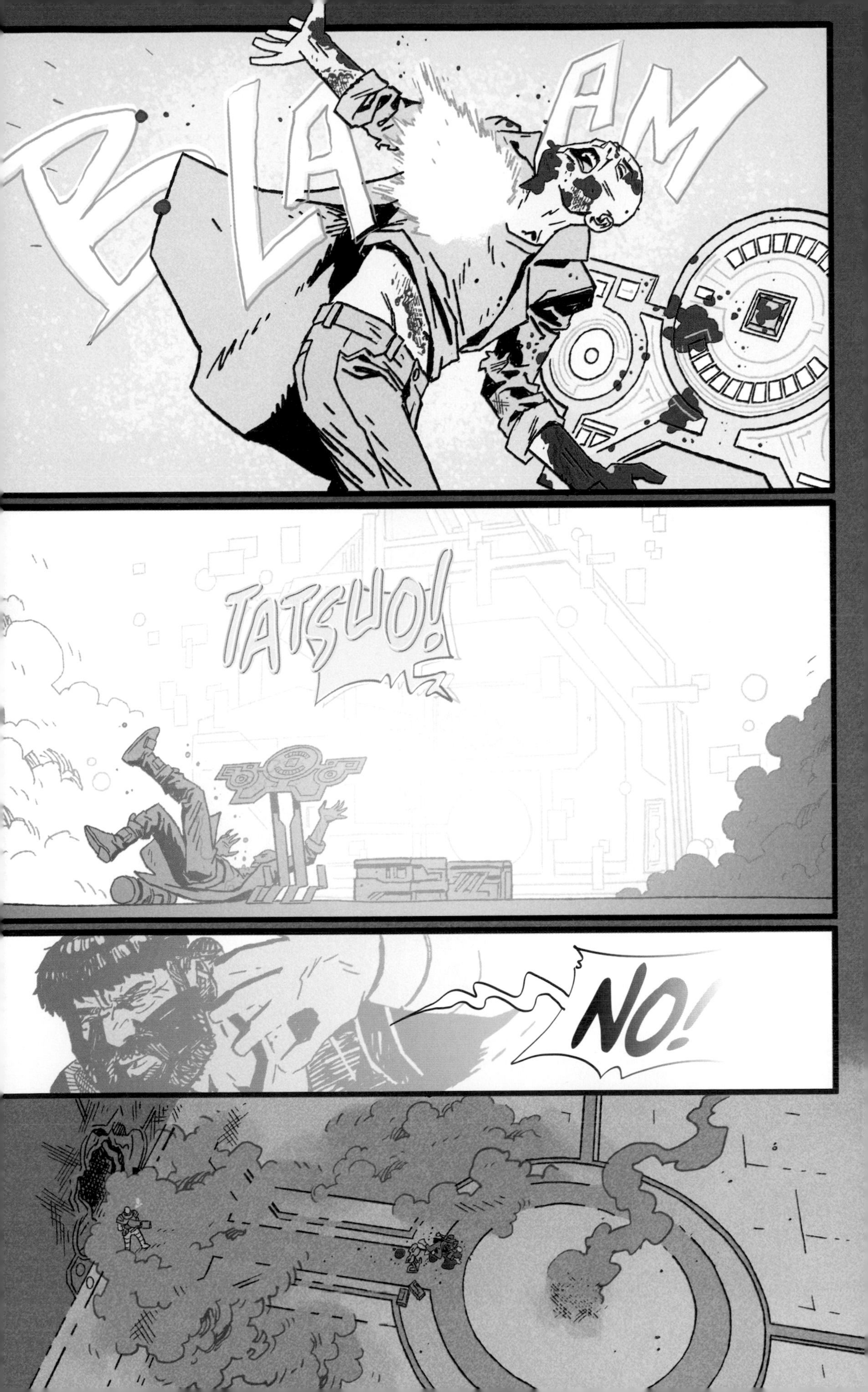
BLAM
TATSUO!
NO!

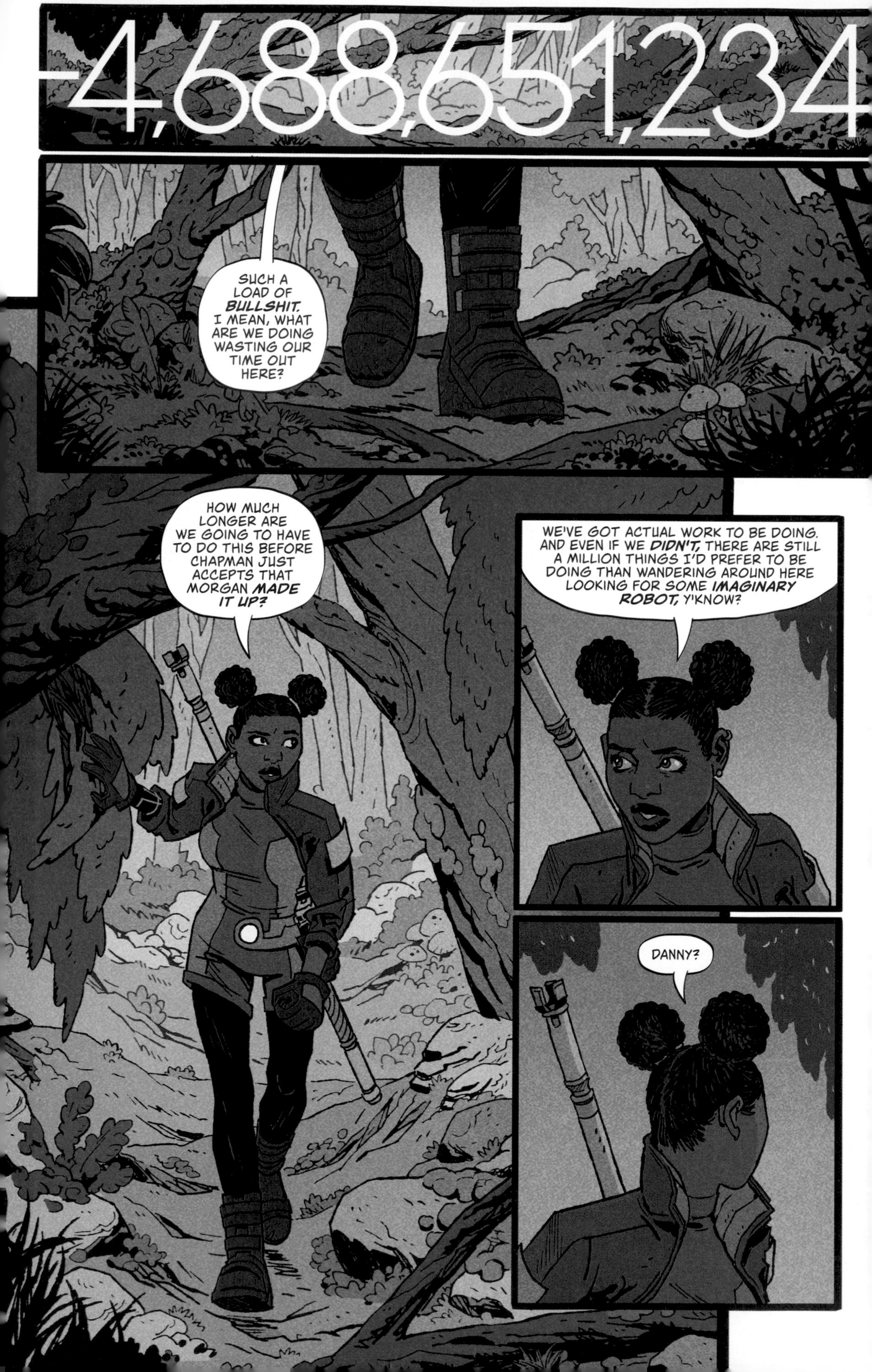

-4,688,651,234
SUCH A LOAD OF BULLSHIT. I MEAN, WHAT ARE WE DOING WASTING OUR TIME OUT HERE?
HOW MUCH LONGER ARE WE GOING TO HAVE TO DO THIS BEFORE CHAPMAN JUST ACCEPTS THAT MORGAN MADE IT UP?
WE'VE GOT ACTUAL WORK TO BE DOING. AND EVEN IF WE DIDN'T, THERE ARE STILL A MILLION THINGS I'D PREFER TO BE DOING THAN WANDERING AROUND HERE LOOKING FOR SOME IMAGINARY ROBOT, Y'KNOW?
DANNY?

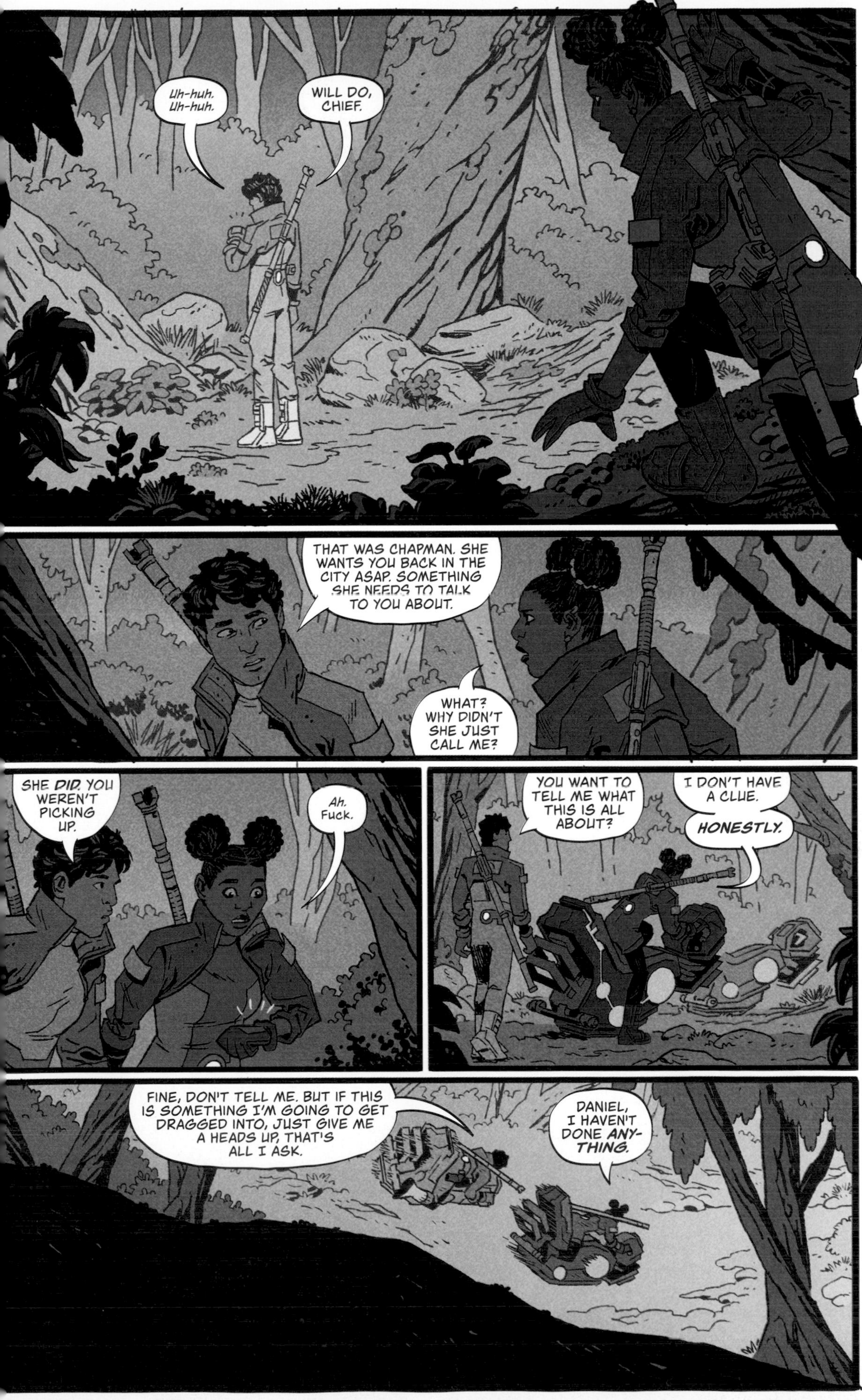
Uh-huh. Uh-huh.
WILL DO, CHIEF.
THAT WAS CHAPMAN. SHE WANTS YOU BACK IN THE CITY ASAP. SOMETHING SHE NEEDS TO TALK TO YOU ABOUT.
WHAT? WHY DIDN'T SHE JUST CALL ME?
SHE *DID*. YOU WEREN'T PICKING UP.
Ah. Fuck.
YOU WANT TO TELL ME WHAT THIS IS ALL ABOUT?
I DON'T HAVE A CLUE.
HONESTLY.
FINE, DON'T TELL ME. BUT IF THIS IS SOMETHING I'M GOING TO GET DRAGGED INTO, JUST GIVE ME A HEADS UP, THAT'S ALL I ASK.
DANIEL, I HAVEN'T DONE *ANYTHING.*

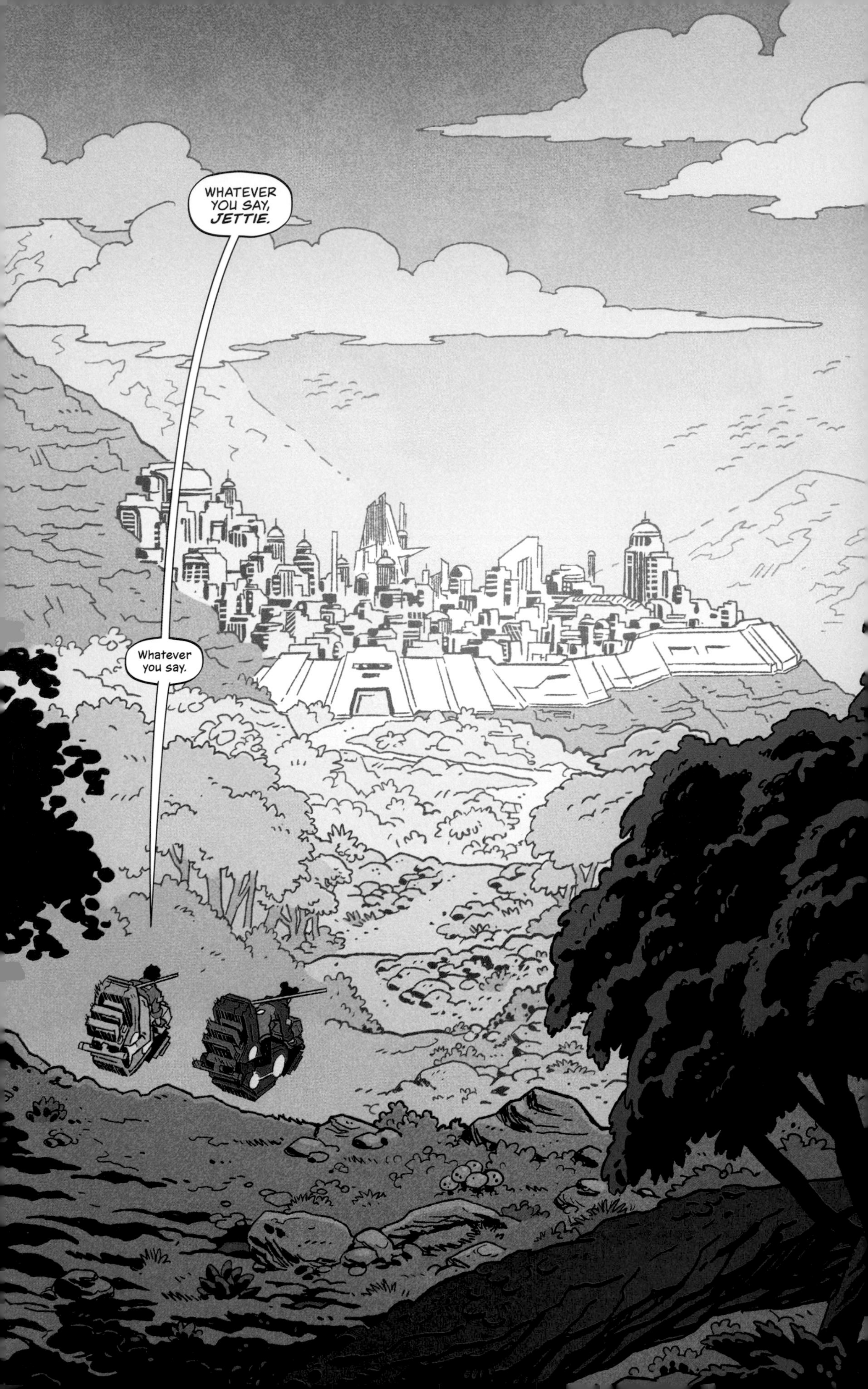
WHATEVER YOU SAY, *JETTIE.*
Whatever you say.

久

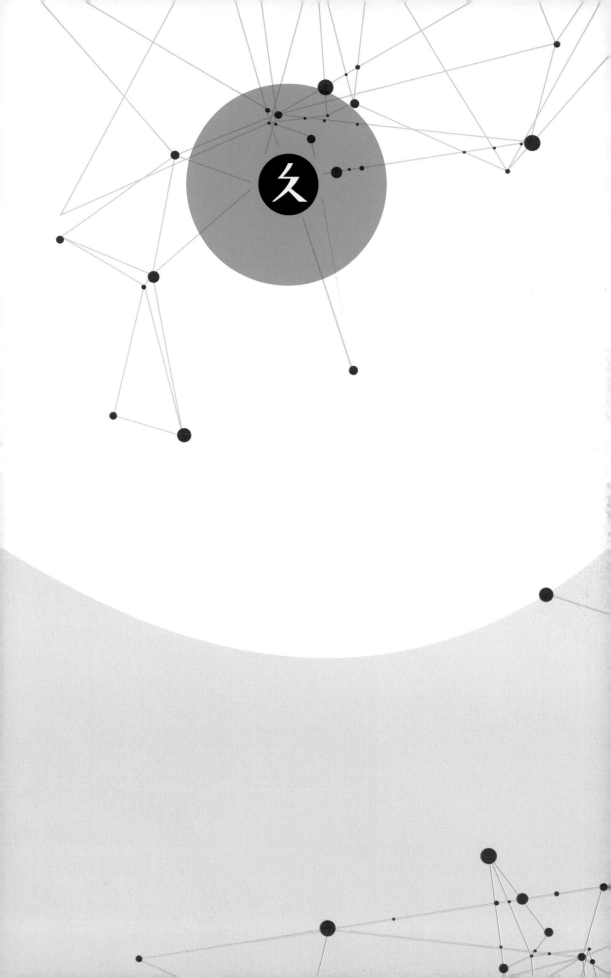

right: *issue 13 and issue 14 connected variants by Vlad Legostaev*

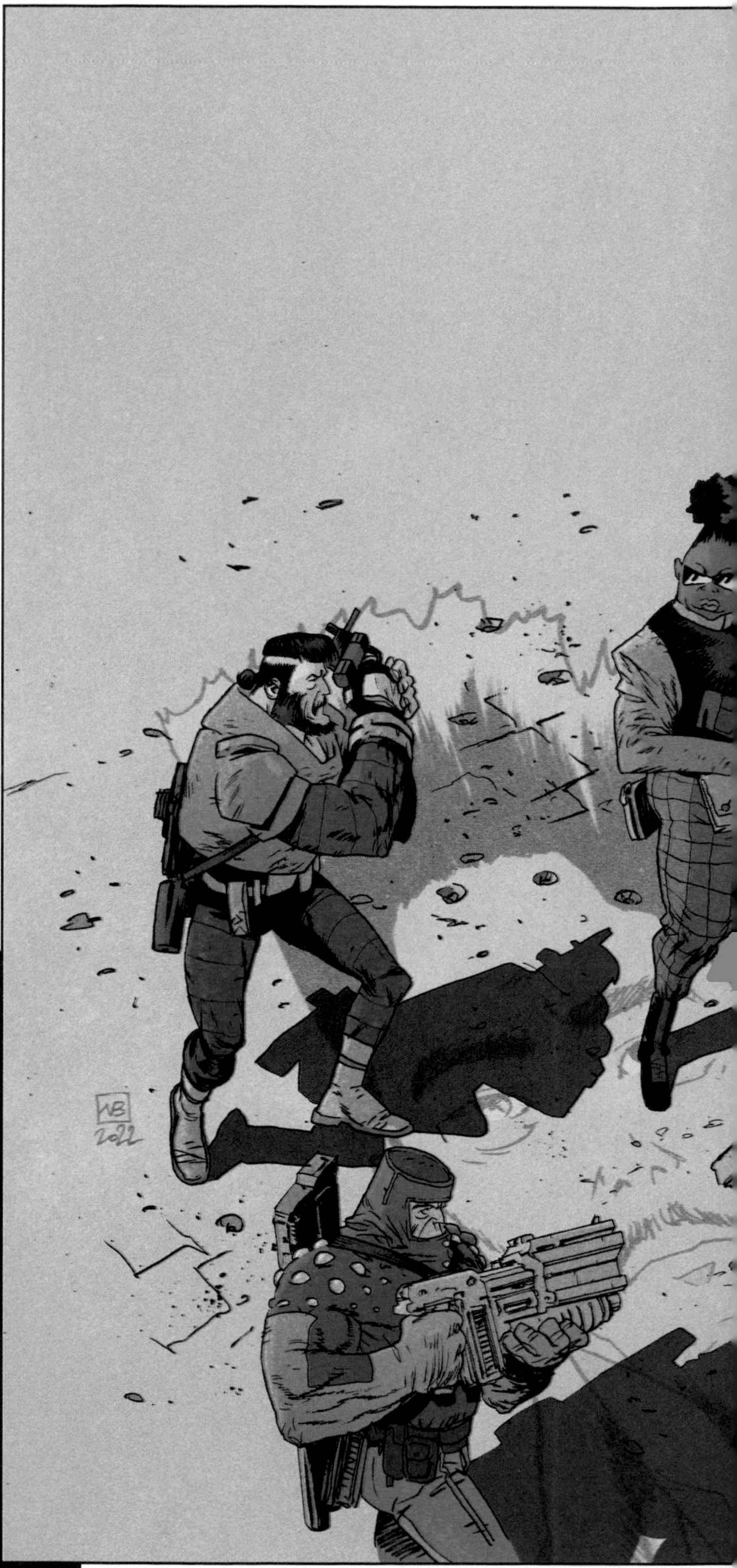
WB
2022

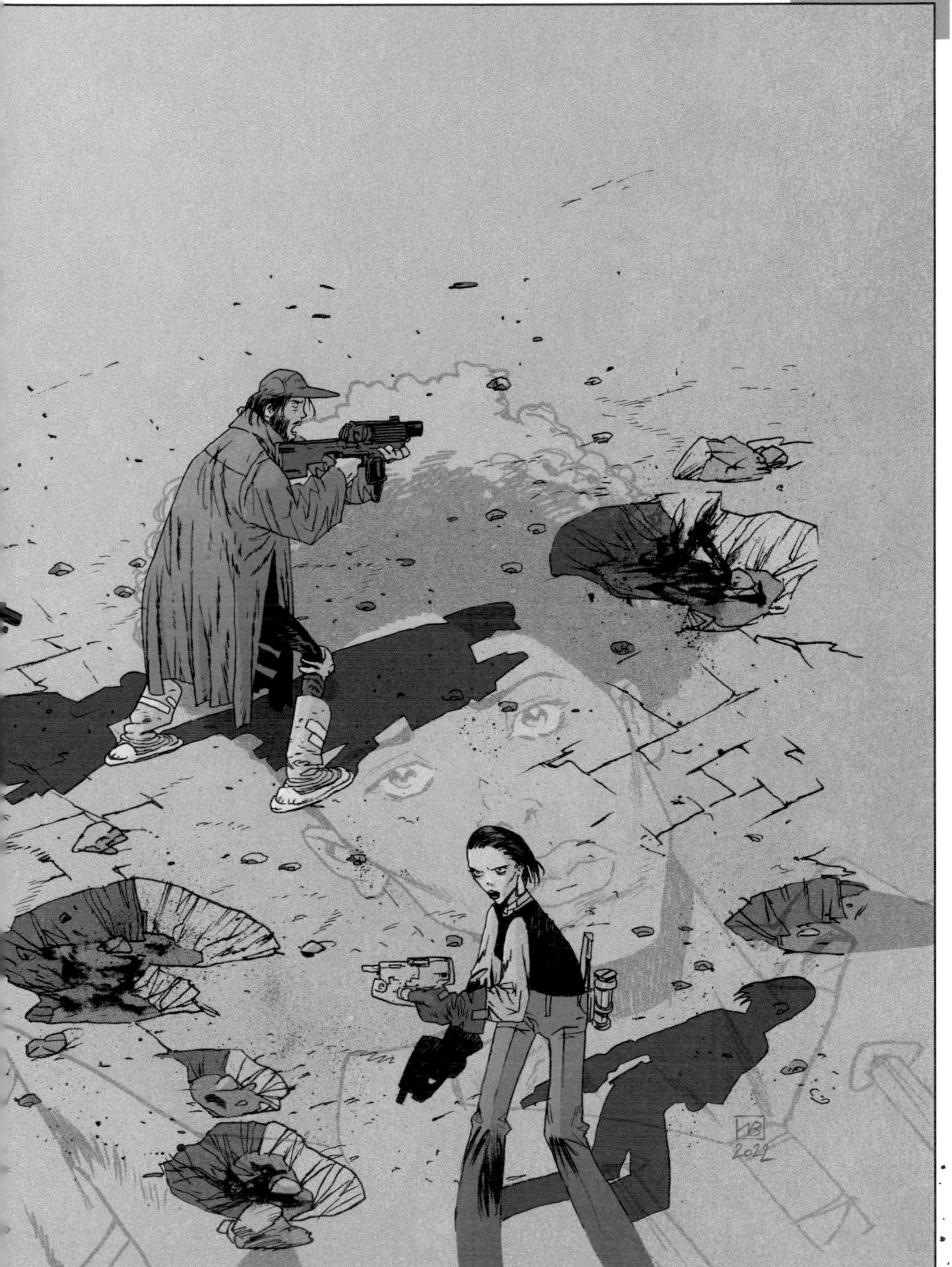
2022

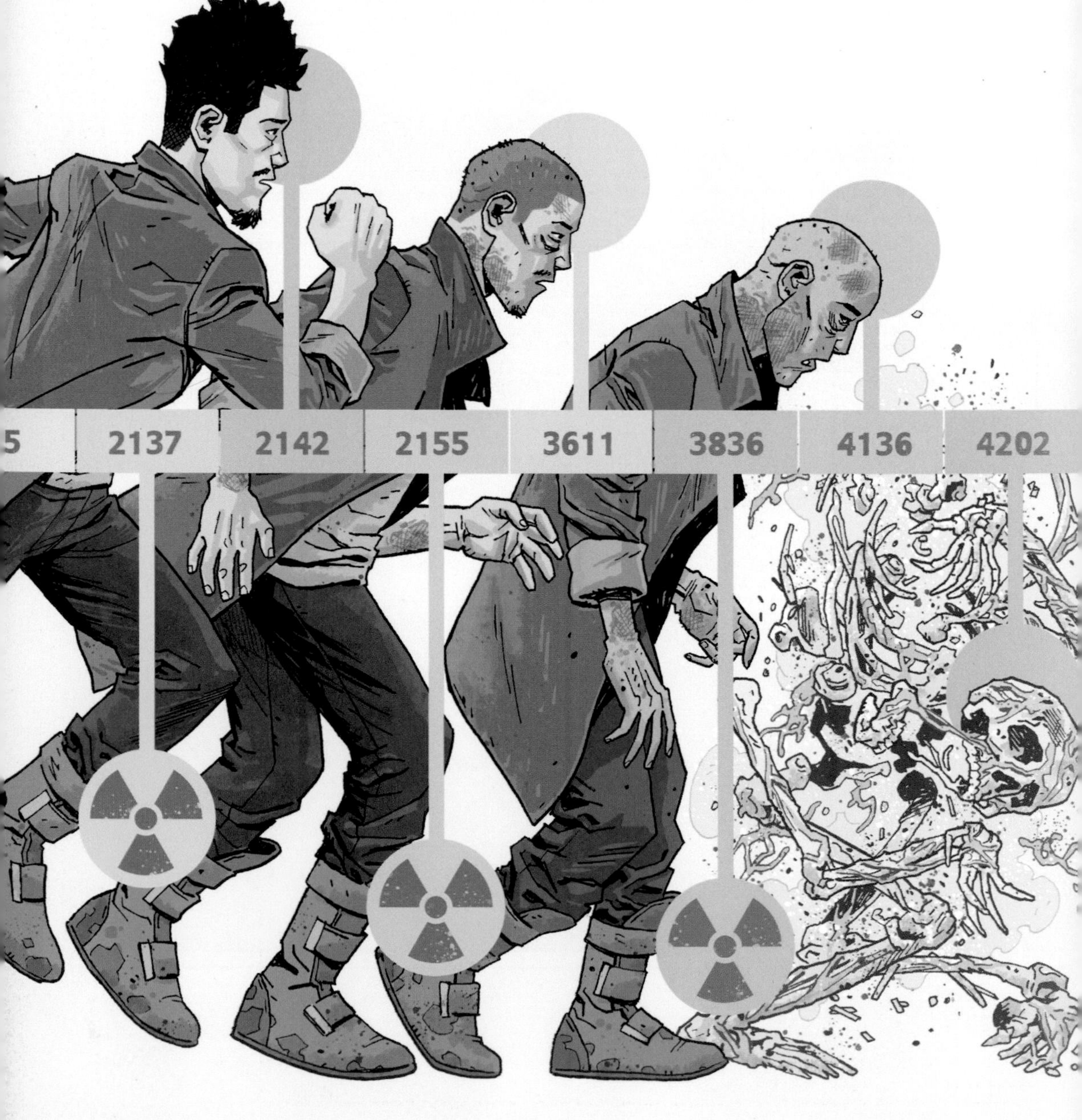
5
2137
2142
2155
3611
3836
4136
4202

left: *issue 15 variant*
by Eric Zawadzki

right: *issue 16 variant*
by Sumeyye Kesgin

below: *issue 17 variant*
by Igor Monti

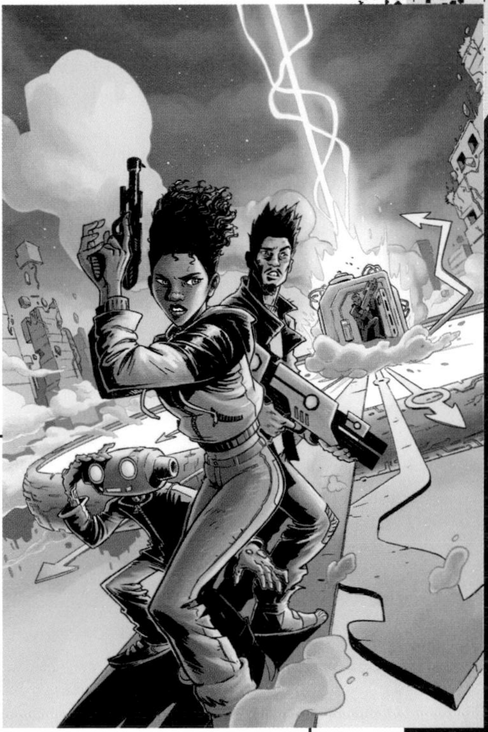

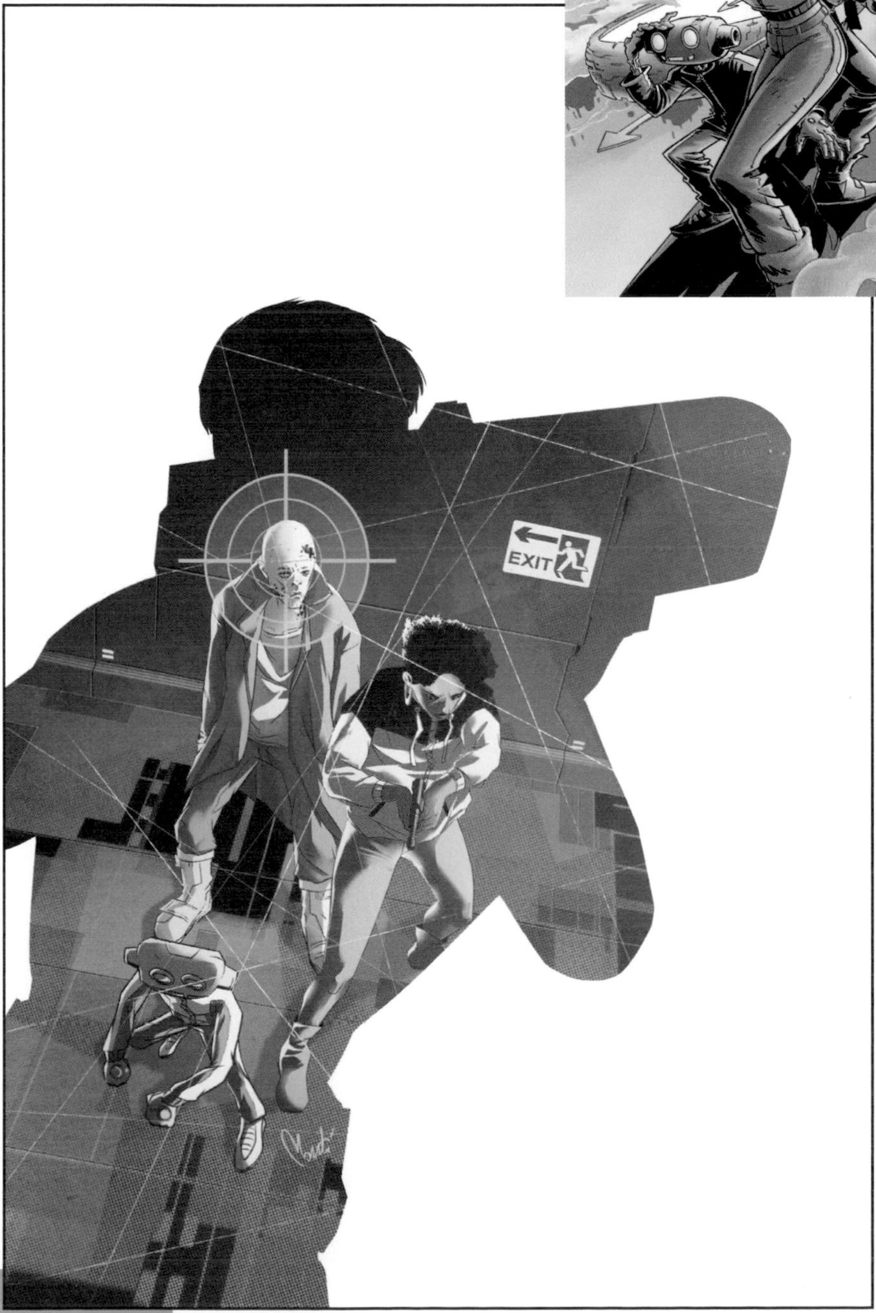
EXIT

DECLAN SHALVEY is an award-winning artist/writer from Ireland. He is best known for his acclaimed run on *MOON KNIGHT* for Marvel Comics (inspiring the Disney+ TV series of the same name) along with hit titles such as *X-MEN UNLIMITED*, *ALL STAR BATMAN*, *INJECTION*, *BOG BODIES* and *OLD DOG* from Image Comics.

RORY McCONVILLE is an Irish writer living in London. His work includes *SPAWN* and *WRITE IT IN BLOOD* for Image Comics, as well as several series for 2000 AD, including *JUDGE DREDD* and *DEPARTMENT K*.

RON SALAS is a Philippine-born illustrator and comic book artist. Based in Glen Allen, VA he has worked as a designer with work for Disney, Universal, Hard Rock Cafe and *Playboy*. His comic work includes *28 DAYS LATER*, *PRINCE VALIANT*, *SIX MILLION DOLLAR MAN*, as well as the creator-owned *EXISTENCE 2.0/3.0*.

ERIC ZAWADZKI is a Canadian comic book artist who is most well known for his work on *THE DREGS* and *ETERNAL* from Black Mask Studios. He recently completed the *HOUSE OF EL* trilogy of graphic novels for DC Comics and *HEART ATTACK* for Skybound / Image comics. Zawadzki lives in Calgary with his wife and two hairless cats.

CHRIS O'HALLORAN is an Irish comic book colorist living in Cork. He's worked on books for Marvel, DC, Image, and others including *ICE CREAM MAN*, *SCARENTHOOD*, *IMMORTAL HULK,* and *WRITE IT IN BLOOD*.

HASSAN OTSMANE-ELHAOU is a British-Algerian letterer who has worked on comics like *WRITE IT IN BLOOD*, *WHAT'S THE FURTHEST PLACE FROM HERE*, and *ROGUES*. He's also the editor of the Eisner-winning *PANELxPANEL* magazine and voice behind the *STRIP PANEL NAKED* series.

HEATHER ANTOS is an award-winning comic book editor and writer most known for her work on Marvel's *STAR WARS* and *DEADPOOL* lines, as well as one of the co-creators of *GWENPOOL*. Now, you can find her editing various titles at Image, IDW, and Humanoids.

SASHA E HEAD is a branding and editorial graphic designer who works in comics and video games. She is best known for her art direction and design work on Image Comics' monthly publication *IMAGE+* as well as her work on Jonathan Hickman & Mike Huddleston's series *DECORUM*.

IMAGE COMICS, INC.

ROBERT KIRKMAN: CHIEF OPERATING OFFICER | **ERIK LARSEN**: CHIEF FINANCIAL OFFICER | **TODD MCFARLANE**: PRESIDENT | **MARC SILVESTRI**: CHIEF EXECUTIVE OFFICER | **JIM VALENTINO**: VICE PRESIDENT | **ERIC STEPHENSON**: PUBLISHER / CHIEF CREATIVE OFFICER | **NICOLE LAPALME**: VICE PRESIDENT OF FINANCE | **LEANNA CAUNTER**: ACCOUNTING ANALYST | **SUE KORPELA**: ACCOUNTING & HR MANAGER | **MATT PARKINSON**: VICE PRESIDENT OF SALES & PUBLISHING PLANNING | **LORELEI BUNJES**: VICE PRESIDENT OF DIGITAL STRATEGY | **DIRK WOOD**: VICE PRESIDENT OF INTERNATIONAL SALES & LICENSING | **RYAN BREWER**: INTERNATIONAL SALES & LICENSING MANAGER | **ALEX COX**: DIRECTOR OF DIRECT MARKET SALES | **CHLOE RAMOS**: BOOK MARKET & LIBRARY SALES MANAGER | **EMILIO BAUTISTA**: DIGITAL SALES COORDINATOR | **JON SCHLAFFMAN**: SPECIALTY SALES COORDINATOR | **KAT SALAZAR**: VICE PRESIDENT OF PR & MARKETING | **DEANNA PHELPS**: MARKETING DESIGN MANAGER | **DREW FITZGERALD**: MARKETING CONTENT ASSOCIATE | **HEATHER DOORNINK**: VICE PRESIDENT OF PRODUCTION | **DREW GILL**: ART DIRECTOR | **HILARY DILORETO**: PRINT MANAGER | **TRICIA RAMOS**: TRAFFIC MANAGER | **MELISSA GIFFORD**: CONTENT MANAGER | **ERIKA SCHNATZ**: SENIOR PRODUCTION ARTIST | **WESLEY GRIFFITH**: PRODUCTION ARTIST | **RICH FOWLKS**: PRODUCTION ARTIST

IMAGECOMICS.COM

DATE DUE